Acclaim for Elin Hilderbrand's *The Five-Star Weekend*

"Elin Hilderbrand's latest is dripping with her signature Nantucket details—the food descriptions alone are enough to get readers to book the next ferry. Readers will be transported both by the setting and by the emotional drama as Hilderbrand sets up seemingly impossible odds, then manages a convincing happy ending...She delivers exactly what her readers want: female friendship, family drama, and gorgeous descriptions of Nantucket."

—Susan Maguire, *Booklist*

"*Hungry with Hollis* is one of the internet's hottest sites, but when Hollis's husband dies in a car crash, her peppy posting flags. To cheer herself up, she curates the perfect house party with five close friends. Well, four close friends—and one follower she's made a special connection with. Wait till she finds out just how special their connection is. If you aren't already addicted to Hilderbrand's Nantucket novels, there's no time like the present." —*Oprah Daily*

"A dreamy Nantucket house party given by a meticulous hostess goes off the rails...The people in Hilderbrand's books may screw up, but she always gets it right...Amazing."

—*Kirkus Reviews* (starred review)

"*The Five-Star Weekend* is a five-star read. (*I know, I know, it was too easy!*) Hilderbrand is a bestselling author and a writing phenom for a reason. She knows how to deliver a satisfying, absorbing read—and not just for the beach. The story packs a punch, with interesting characters and an engaging, unpredictable plot, all set on beautiful Nantucket. There has been talk of Hilderbrand retiring from writing beach reads. I, for one, hope she pushes that off for a long time. Throw this into your beach bag, your weekend bag, or your carry-on, and get ready for a five-star weekend yourself."

—Bronwyn Miller, Bookreporter.com

"A stunning, sun-drenched mix of romance and women's fiction… This should become a beach-bag staple."

—*Publishers Weekly* (starred review)

"An exciting and fun-filled summer read, *The Five-Star Weekend* offers a look into the lives of the well-to-do. Expect the unexpected and prepare for the emotional, personal, joyous, and heartbreaking escapades these women face."

—Nancy Carty Lepri, *New York Journal of Books*

The Five-Star Weekend

ALSO BY ELIN HILDERBRAND

The Beach Club
Nantucket Nights
Summer People
The Blue Bistro
The Love Season
Barefoot
A Summer Affair
The Castaways
The Island
Silver Girl
Summerland
Beautiful Day
The Matchmaker
Winter Street
The Rumor
Winter Stroll
Here's to Us
Winter Storms
The Identicals
Winter Solstice
The Perfect Couple
Winter in Paradise
Summer of '69
What Happens in Paradise
28 Summers
Troubles in Paradise
Golden Girl
The Hotel Nantucket
Endless Summer

The Five-Star Weekend

Elin Hilderbrand

BACK BAY BOOKS
Little, Brown and Company
New York Boston London

The characters and events in this book are fictitious. Any similarity to real persons, living or dead, is coincidental and not intended by the author.

Back Bay Books / Little, Brown and Company
Hachette Book Group
1290 Avenue of the Americas, New York, NY 10104
littlebrown.com

Originally published in hardcover by Little, Brown and Company, June 2023
First Back Bay paperback edition, February 2024

Back Bay Books is an imprint of Little, Brown and Company, a division of Hachette Book Group, Inc. The Back Bay Books name and logo are trademarks of Hachette Book Group, Inc.

ISBN 9780316258777 (hardcover) / 9780316565974 (large print) / 9780316567190 (Canadian) / 9780316571142 (Barnes & Noble exclusive) / 9780316569286 (Barnes & Noble signed) / 9780316569293 (signed) / 9780316259187 (pb)

LCCN 2022952166

10 9 8 7 6 5 4 3 2 1

CW

Printed in the United States of America

To Michael Carlisle and David Forrer,
with love and eternal gratitude

Five stars aren't enough.

The Five-Star Weekend

Prologue: Nantucket

Another summer on the island is upon us and, as usual, we have a lot to talk about. Chef Mario Subiaco proposed to Lizbet Keaton on the widow's walk of the Hotel Nantucket; there's a camera crew filming out in Monomoy (Blond Sharon has it "on good authority" that it's a limited series for Netflix); police chief Ed Kapenash has been admitted to the Nantucket Cottage Hospital after complaining of chest pain—and there's a steamy debate about whether or not Nantucket should allow topless beaches. (We think of ourselves as progressive and sophisticated, but let's face it—we're not France.)

Then we hear a rumor that Hollis Shaw is hosting something she's calling the "Five-Star Weekend" at her house in Squam.

This, of course, captures our full attention.

Hollis Shaw is something of a unicorn.

She started out life as one of us. She was the daughter of Tom Shaw, Nantucket's busiest plumbing contractor, and Charlotte Shaw, a kindergarten teacher. When Hollis was a toddler, not quite two years old, Charlotte Shaw died of an aneurysm in the shower, and Tom Shaw was left to raise his daughter alone. But on this island, we pitch in—it takes a village!—and we all offered moral support as Hollis grew up. We watched her dance in ballet recitals, shoot free throws at the Boys and Girls Club, and cheer for her boyfriend Jack Finigan in the stands at the Nantucket Whalers football games.

Hollis was a good student, an outstanding softball pitcher (the team won the state championship Hollis's junior year and came in second her senior year), and a hard worker. The cottage out in Squam where she lived with her father was modest (though the land it sat on was worth a fortune), and as soon as Hollis was old enough, she kept house and cooked every night. She got a job opening scallops on Old North Wharf after school, and in the summers, she and her best friend, Tatum, waited tables at the Rope Walk.

In her senior year of high school, Hollis wrote what her English teacher Ms. Fox called "the best college essay I've read in thirty-one years." It took the form of a letter to Hollis's deceased mother, Charlotte. *Dear Mom,* it started, *I think you would be proud of the way I turned out. Here are some of the reasons why.*

It was bittersweet when Hollis decided to go to the University of North Carolina at Chapel Hill. We were proud of our girl—she received a full academic scholarship—but once she left, we missed her.

After graduating from college, Hollis moved to Boston, where she worked as the assistant food editor at *Boston* magazine and got to eat, on the magazine's expense account, at all of the city's "Best New Restaurants." Eventually she met Harvard Medical School surgery resident Matthew Madden. They were married in Wellesley, bought a house in Wellesley, and raised their daughter, Caroline, in Wellesley.

When Hollis's father, Tom, died in 2007, Hollis inherited the Squam property. Over the winter, we watched as the tiny cottage where Hollis had grown up was moved to the edge of the lot, and a gracious post-and-beam home was built in its place.

It's official, we thought. *Hollis Shaw has become a summer person.* (But at least she was *our* summer person. After all, she could have immigrated to Martha's Vineyard.) She joined the Field and Oar Club, where she played tennis; she volunteered at the Nantucket

Book Festival; and on Sunday afternoons, we saw her at the Deck, sitting at one of the best tables along the railing above the Monomoy creeks, drinking rosé, and laughing with people we didn't recognize.

Were we bothered that Hollis no longer acted or seemed like a local or that she came to the island only during the summer months and Stroll, with the occasional Thanksgiving and Daffodil weekend thrown in? The honest answer to that question was this: Some of us were bothered, while others were just happy that she was happy.

We were all, however, quick to claim Hollis as our own when she became internet-famous!

During the darkest days of the pandemic—when businesses closed and the stock market crashed and restaurants pivoted to take-out only and the death toll was rising, rising, rising—Hollis posted well-edited content on her then-modest food blog, *Hungry with Hollis* (at the time, it was a "food community" of 274 subscribers). Hollis filmed herself in her Wellesley kitchen making a meat-loaf sandwich with homemade refrigerator pickles on freshly baked Japanese milk bread. The video went viral. Just like the video of the Italian gentleman playing the violin for his neighbors on his balcony in Bologna, Hollis's video struck a chord. The sandwich was elevated: the meat loaf was flecked with onions and herbs and topped with a rosy "special sauce"; the pickles were crisp, bright, and tangy; the Japanese milk bread—that Instagram darling—was pillowy but sturdy enough to maintain the integrity of the sandwich.

Was the sandwich time-intensive? Yes—but suddenly the world had nothing but time.

Was the sandwich cheap? Yes—four sandwiches could be made from merely seventeen dollars' worth of groceries. And an "impossible" version could be made for vegans.

It was what everyone needed: comfort food that was aspirational.

Hollis's modest food blog suddenly became immodest, flashy, even.

In a week's time, the blog's newsletter had over half a million subscribers. Hollis added her recipe for creamy yellow tomato gazpacho and a shatteringly crispy fried chicken. The blog's fans responded not only to the recipes but to Hollis herself. She became the best friend they all wished they had; she served up "everything is going to be okay" vibes. They loved that in her cooking videos, Hollis presented an unvarnished version of herself—wrinkles, freckles, a slight double chin. (The middle-aged women among them thought, *Better her than me; I would never allow a camera to zoom in that close;* the Millennials and Gen Zers thought, *If she doesn't want makeup, fine, but how about a polish-and-glow filter?*) Hollis's blond hair showed a touch of gray, and she styled it in a non-style: straight, parted down the middle, tucked behind her ears. Her neck always looked good. (*What does she use on it,* they wondered, *and will she link the products somewhere?*) She always wore a crisp cotton blouse (she had the same one in a rainbow of colors, though everyone agreed Hollis looked prettiest in the sky blue) with the starched collar flipped up and a pair of gold hoops the diameter of a quarter. Someone asked about the earrings, and she confided that they were a present from her father when she graduated from high school in 1987. Hollis's fans lauded her for "keeping it real," though they couldn't help noticing her enormous diamond engagement ring (it must have been three carats!) and her diamond-and-sapphire wedding band.

After Hollis posted a video for a potato-and-white-cheddar tart with a crispy bacon crust, her blog's newsletter broke the one-million-subscriber milestone. (Leave it to bacon!) With the help of her daughter, Caroline, who was a film student at NYU and extremely tech-savvy, Hollis started a website for the blog and added two features. The first, called Kitchen Lights, was an interactive map of the world. When someone was engaging with the website, a pinprick of light appeared on the map so that visitors to the site could imagine another cook in, say, Spokane, Washington, or Grand Island,

Nebraska, standing in her or his kitchen mincing chives and parsley for Hollis's tortellini salad.

The second feature, called the Corkboard, allowed Hollis's faithful followers to leave messages, post recipes, review restaurants, critique cookbooks, and ask questions such as *Why does Planters still include Brazil nuts in its mixed-nuts can when no one eats them?* Hollis posted on the Corkboard herself once or twice a week, updating the community on her latest triumphs: She had been approached to design her own cookware, she had a book deal looming, there was talk of her own show, which would include not only cooking but lifestyle tips.

Yes, yes, yes! Hollis's millions of fans wanted it all. They couldn't get enough of our Hollis Shaw (and we were thrilled she'd kept her maiden name). Her life was so neat, so tidy, so blessed, and their lives improved simply by being Hollis-adjacent. Hollis had 1,670 newsletter subscribers from Nantucket (including her former English teacher Ms. Fox, who "always knew she would do big things"). In the summer of 2022, Hungry with Hollis was as popular as Wordle and the Wicked Island Bakery's morning buns; we couldn't go to the RJ Miller Salon or for drinks at the Ships Inn without hearing about Hollis Shaw.

She had become a bona fide Nantucket celebrity.

On Thursday, December 15, Ms. Fox is on the website looking for the easy holiday hors d'oeuvre recipes that Hollis promised to post—Ms. Fox has a Yankee swap to attend—when a new Corkboard message from Hollis pops up on her screen.

> To the Hungry with Hollis community:
>
> My husband, Matthew, passed away this morning unexpectedly. I need to ask for privacy as I grapple with this devastating tragedy. I'll be stepping away from the website for a while,

as I'm sure you'll all understand. I hope to return at some point, though right now, I can't imagine when.

Hold your loved ones close.

With gratitude, Hollis

Ms. Fox gasps. *Oh no! What happened?* She searches Matthew, husband of Hollis Shaw. She knows Hollis is married—those rings!—though Hollis never mentions her husband. (Ms. Fox and some of the others wish he were more present, like Ina Garten's Jeffrey.) Whenever Ms. Fox thinks of Hollis with someone, she pictures the high-school boyfriend, Jack Finigan, with his cute dimples.

The next morning in the *Nantucket Standard,* we all see the obituary: "Summer Resident Dr. Matthew Madden Killed in Car Accident." There are also notices in the *Boston Globe* ("Renowned MGH Surgeon and Harvard Med Professor Killed in One-Car Accident in Wellesley") and the *New York Times* ("Dr. Matthew Madden, Leading Cardiac Surgeon and International Lecturer, Dead at 55").

Ms. Fox wants to reach out, and she's not alone—within a matter of hours, there are 17,262 Corkboard messages offering thoughts and prayers, some posted by people who had themselves lost husbands, wives, parents, siblings, children. Hollis's followers find her note so raw and relatable that they can picture her trembling fingers as she typed; they can hear her ragged sobs. They all want to offer solace... but their motives aren't completely selfless. When will Hollis be back on the website? Valentine's Day? (No, too soon.) Easter, maybe?

Here on Nantucket, we think how unfair life can be: Hollis's mother died too young, and now her husband has as well. We wonder if Hollis will return to the island for the summer. Will she feel like playing tennis at the Field and Oar Club or drinking rosé at the Deck? Fast Eddie Pancik, our perennially thirsty real estate agent, asks his sister, Barbie, if it would be in bad taste to see if Hollis is planning on selling the house in Squam.

Yes, you idiot, Barbie says.

On June 21, the first day of summer, Romeo at the Steamship Authority reports that Hollis Shaw has just driven off the ferry in her trusty Volvo, which is packed with boxes, bags, and what looks through the window like a portable pizza oven; Hollis's Serbian sheepdog, Henrietta, is asleep in the back seat. *Good for Hollis!* we think. *She came home.*

For a few weeks, sightings of Hollis around the island are rare. She doesn't attend the Nantucket Book Festival or the annual Squam Road Homeowners Association meeting. Johnny Baylor, who drives for DoorDash, reports delivering sushi from Bar Yoshi to Hollis's house one night and a lobster roll from the Sea Grille another. Hollis's longtime neighbor Kerri Gasperson sees Hollis walking Henrietta at dusk, but Hollis has AirPods in, and Kerri doesn't want to bother her.

We understand that it takes time to process a sudden, unexpected loss. We assume Hollis will spend her summer alone, practicing self-care and privately mourning the man she was married to for twenty-four years.

But when we hear about the Five-Star Weekend—so creative! so unusual!—we all agree: This could be just the thing she needs.

1. Accident Report I

It's early morning on December 15; Hollis Shaw is in the kitchen of her Wellesley home prepping the dough for cheddar tartlets.

Her husband, Dr. Matthew Madden, has a ten o'clock flight to Germany—he's presenting a paper at a cardiology conference in Leipzig and will be gone for five days.

This opening scene, should Hollis show a video of it, would seem to be one of domestic bliss. Hollis wears a pair of tailored red-plaid pajamas; her hair is held back in a clip. She has a footed bowl of café au lait steaming next to the slab of cool, gray-veined marble where she's rolling out her pastry dough. Carols play over the sound system; "The Holly and the Ivy" is Hollis's favorite and she sings along in a faux-operatic voice. Hollis's kitchen is all decked out for the holidays: spruce garlands encircle the weathered wooden beams, and her collection of copper pots gleam like new pennies on her open shelves. She's trimmed a "kitchen tree" with culinary ornaments: a tiny metal whisk, a wooden rolling pin, a bone-china box of doughnuts. Hollis has also hung miniature wreaths on all her glass-fronted cabinets. (Her daughter, Caroline, would probably declare the wreaths—as well as the apothecary jars filled with ribbon candy and gumdrops—"too much.") The picture window above the sink where Hollis does dishes looks over the mature oaks and evergreens of her side yard. The view offers a pleasant distraction, especially this morning as snowflakes as big and fluffy as cotton balls float to the ground. Hollis loves nothing more than snow during the holidays.

Her timer chimes, and Hollis pulls a tray of crispy bacon from the oven. Like magic, her Serbian sheepdog, Henrietta, jingles into the kitchen (Hollis has put bells on her collar) and raises her furry face.

"Fine," Hollis says, and she gives the old girl a piece. She drains the rest on a paper towel next to the red-pepper-and-smoked-Gouda quiche she made earlier that morning. She cuts a wedge of quiche and arranges it on a plate with a few slices of bacon and sections of a Cara Cara orange, which are a delightful and surprising pink.

When she hears Matthew's footsteps on the stairs, she closes her eyes and takes a sustaining breath.

Don't bring it up, she tells herself. *Let him go graciously.*

But the truth is, this trip to Leipzig bothers Hollis; she was up half the night fretting about it. Matthew will present his paper tomorrow morning, so he could easily leave Germany tomorrow afternoon and make it home in time for their annual holiday party on Saturday. Hollis and Matthew have hosted a holiday gathering every year since they moved to Wellesley, and it's always the third Saturday in December. Matthew claimed he "thought it was later," so he made plans to stay at the conference until the end and then travel to Berlin to visit his mentor Dr. Emanuel Schrader, who was just diagnosed with Parkinson's and can no longer practice surgery.

"But you can't miss our party!" Hollis said when he told her.

Matthew had chuckled. "We can both agree this is *your* party, sweet-love. With all the Swellesley glitterati in attendance, you won't even notice I'm not there."

His tone had been light, playful even—but Hollis was still hurt. She *did* throw the party pretty much single-handedly every year. She made all the food—the cheddar tartlets, the tenderloin sandwiches, the tiny potatoes topped with caviar—she buffed the champagne flutes, lined the luminaires along the driveway, stuffed gift bags with her homemade toffee for guests to take home. She sent the invitations, and her list *was* longer every December (except for the year when Hollis broke up with Electra Undergrove and her crew).

Despite this, Hollis can't imagine standing in the doorway to greet everyone without Matthew at her side. It's *literally* unthinkable.

But apparently not for him.

Now Matthew walks into the kitchen. He always wears a suit when he flies, and today he has on the red Vineyard Vines tie printed with

Santas in speedboats—the very tie Hollis purchased for him to *wear to the party!* He hums along to the carol currently playing—"Once in Royal David's City"—and holds his right wrist out so that Hollis can help him with his cuff link, which is a silver reindeer. He's certainly in the holiday spirit.

Hollis inhales the scent of his Kiehl's shaving lotion. She loves the smell; it reminds her of date night and of the (increasingly rare) mornings when she wakes up in his arms.

She can't believe he's leaving.

She wills herself to say, *Here's breakfast,* or *Let me get your coffee*—Matthew takes his coffee black and scalding hot, and she doesn't pour it until he's standing right in front of her. But instead what comes out of her mouth is "I *really* wish you'd change your plans."

After Matthew leaves for the airport—far later than he wanted to—Hollis gathers the pastry dough into a ball, wraps it in plastic, and sets it in the fridge. She no longer feels like cooking. Matthew's breakfast is untouched, but instead of covering the plate with foil and saving it for later—she deplores waste, one product of being Tom Shaw's daughter—she scrapes the food into Henny's dog bowl. Then she rips a paper towel from the roll and wipes at her eyes. She can't believe how quickly their conversation escalated into a fight.

"Lately, you've been making anything but me a priority," she said. "Work, travel, and now Dr. Schrader."

"The man was my mentor, Hollis. Berlin is a two-hour drive from Leipzig. It would be egregious not to visit him, considering the circumstances."

Instead of conceding this point, Hollis launched into her graver concerns. She had felt them drifting apart ever since Caroline left for college. Hollis had always dreamed of a marriage just like Matthew's parents had—they were romantic and devoted to each other to the very end.

But when, Hollis wondered, was the last time their marriage had felt romantic? It would be romantic if Matthew canceled this trip, but that wasn't going to happen. She could tell simply by the set of his shoulders, his jaw; he was eager to get out the door.

"Sometimes it feels like we're nothing more than roommates," Hollis said. She was tempted to mention how long it had been since they'd had sex, but that was as much her fault as his. During the day, she was busy, busy, busy and she fell into bed exhausted every night.

Matthew did his doctor's trick of appearing to listen but not, which was how Hollis knew he wasn't engaged; he was just waiting for her to be done, which was equal parts infuriating and disheartening. Matthew cleared his throat and checked his watch. Hollis wiped away her gathering tears as he pulled on his trench coat and his leather driving gloves. Matthew crouched down to rub Henny's face, then gave Hollis a fierce squeeze—she felt something, at least, in his touch.

Just before he left, he turned around. "You've changed," he said, then sighed. "And we've changed." He stepped out into the snow, closing the door behind him.

Now the words ring in Hollis's ears. *You've changed. And we've changed.* She would like to say she has no idea what he means—but she fears she does. Since Hollis's website took off and the opportunities to exploit her new popularity arose, she's become a different person, one who has a hard time experiencing a moment without wanting to document it for her newsletter subscribers. She is always, now, on a screen—her phone, her laptop, or both. She *has* changed, and by extension, she supposes, they've changed. But surely Matthew understands that, after twenty years of being a wife and mother, Hollis is excited about building something of her own?

She picks up the phone and calls him, ready to apologize for being a bull in an emotional china shop, but she's shuttled to Matthew's voice mail. She calls right back—again, voice mail. She waits for the beep, then says, "My love for you hasn't changed."

In case Matthew doesn't listen to his voice mail (does anyone listen to voice mail anymore?), she sends a text: I love you, Dr. M. You're important to me. We are important to me.

She waits a few moments, but there's no response. It seems suddenly urgent that she convey this message to him, that he hear her say the words *I love you. You are important.* She tries calling again, and again, she gets voice mail.

Fine, she thinks. *He needs time to simmer down.* She'll try him again once she's sure he's settled in the Lufthansa lounge. But the phrase *And we've changed* concerns her. What was he trying to say?

She feels herself growing melodramatic, which is very unlike her. Everything will be fine. Matthew will miss their party, yes, but he'll be home in plenty of time for their family Christmas. Dr. Schrader has Parkinson's. Of course Matthew should visit him.

Hollis sits down at her laptop and decides to make a dinner reservation for two at Mistral on New Year's Eve. She and Matthew will Uber into the city so they can drink as much champagne as they want; Hollis will buy a new dress, something black and flirty. Next, Hollis intends to check her website—her followers are waiting for the cheddar-tartlet recipe—but instead, she logs onto Facebook. After a few pointless seconds of trying to resist her worst impulses, she ends up at the profile page of Jack Finigan, her high-school boyfriend. There are no new posts; Jack posts only two or three times a year. The last time was in the fall: a photo of Jack standing at the edge of a lake somewhere in Western Massachusetts, holding up a trout. He hasn't posted any pictures of Mindy, his longtime girlfriend, since the summer before last. Hollis has done the predictable thing and tried to look at Mindy's profile, but Mindy has privacy settings in place so all Hollis can see is her background photo, which is a quilt, presumably one she made herself. Hollis knows she's stalking, but it's innocent; she would never reach out to him. She wonders if Jack—or Mindy—has heard about the *Hungry with Hollis* blog.

The knock at the front door startles Hollis; she feels caught. She clicks out of Facebook and hurries down the hall. Blue and red lights reflect off the snow in her front yard.

"Mrs. Madden?" the police officer says. He's young, maybe only a few years older than Caroline, and Hollis can't imagine what he's doing there. It's so early; she's still in her pajamas. She nearly corrects him: Her last name is Shaw, not Madden. But in that instant, she realizes he must be here because of Matthew—something about Matthew?

"Yes?" she says.

The precise words are lost but somehow Hollis understands that there was an accident, something involving deer, a mama and baby, the officer says. Matthew's car spun out of control and flipped over on Dover Street.

Dover Street? Hollis thinks. They drive it all the time, every day; they've been doing that for years, decades. And yes, there are always deer running across Dover, especially during hunting season.

"Is he hurt?" Hollis says, her voice still sort of normal-sounding despite the panic that enfolds her. She peeks around the officer's shoulder to his cruiser. Is Matthew in the back? Was he...taken to the hospital? Then she meets the officer's eyes. "Is he okay?"

"He's dead, ma'am," the officer says.

Suddenly Hollis is on the floor, screaming, wailing; she doesn't care that a stranger is watching. Henny comes jingling in and starts licking Hollis's face. Hollis hears the strains of a song playing in the kitchen—"Ding Dong, Merrily on High"—and she covers her ears. The officer asks if there's anyone she would like him to call.

"My husband! Call my husband!" she screams. In that moment, this still seems like a possibility. Matthew is a doctor, a fixer; he'll make this better. He's the only one who can.

Instead of a holiday party, there's a funeral. They bury Matthew next to his parents in the cemetery at St. Andrew's. Afterward, Hollis faces a house filled with people—their Wellesley neighbors, doctors and nurses from the hospital, the women from Hollis's barre class, and her longtime mom-friends, including Brooke Kirtley, who ordered platters of sandwiches from the Linden Store and who stays late to clean up. The only person Hollis cares about is her daughter, Caroline, but things with her are strained. Caroline is poised—at the service she reads "Nothing Gold Can Stay" without faltering—and polite to Hollis in public, but in private, Caroline pushes her mother away. She steps on Hollis's words to correct her memories; she questions Hollis's decision to hold a reception at their house afterward. "Dad is dead and you're throwing a party."

"It's a reception, not a party," Hollis says. "It's what people do." She knows this is, heartbreakingly, Caroline's first funeral.

"It's what *you* do," Caroline says bitterly. "I heard you asking Brooke to get ten pounds of ice. My father is dead and all you care about is ice!"

Hollis is sure things will get better as soon as everyone leaves, once she and Caroline are alone and they can really talk. She envisions the two of them spending entire days hunkered down in the family room, Henny stretched out at their feet, looking through photo albums, crying together, maybe even laughing.

But things only get worse. Caroline barricades herself in her room; she goes out at night with her friend Cygnet and comes home loudly, sloppily drunk, staggering past Hollis, who sits at the kitchen table, listlessly paging through old issues of *Bon Appétit* and *Food and Wine* as a distraction. She can't possibly go to bed until Caroline is home safe, and she wouldn't sleep anyway.

"Did you have fun, darling?" Hollis asks on one such night.

"Fun?" Caroline sneers. "No, I did not have *fun,* Mother." And she stomps upstairs with Henrietta following faithfully behind.

On one of the first days of the new year—after Hollis has cleared the half-eaten casseroles out of the fridge, after she has taken down the Christmas decorations and packed them away in boxes—Hollis sorts through Matthew's things: his bespoke suits, his eyeglasses, his pile of pristine concert T-shirts (Hootie and the Blowfish, Social Distortion, Dave Matthews).

She's interrupted in this task by Caroline, who demands to know why Hollis feels the need to purge her father's belongings.

Hollis stares at her daughter. "I just want to—"

"Be rid of him? Yes, that much is obvious. You must need more room in the closet for your *signature blouses.* And—what, you were just going to do this *without* me?"

"I thought it might be too difficult for you," Hollis says. "I was trying to protect you."

Caroline picks up the Hootie T-shirt. "You're giving this away? Dad loved this T-shirt."

Hollis opens her mouth to defend herself but before she can speak, Caroline goes on a rampage, accusing Hollis of not loving Matthew enough, not grieving him correctly: "You weren't even related to him! You'll find another husband but I will never, ever have another father."

"I know you're hurting, darling," Hollis says, but according to Caroline, Hollis does *not* know. She doesn't know anything. Caroline paces the master bedroom like a wild animal in a cage, saying hideous things—everything short of *I wish it had been you instead*—but underneath the livid facade, Hollis can see glimpses of a little girl whose world has been broken. Hollis sits on the bed, thinking, *I will wait her rage out. I am the adult, the mother, it's my job to take this punishment.* Matthew and Caroline were close; they had a special bond. Matthew was Caroline's favorite parent.

Hollis says, "I'm sorry, darling. It's difficult for me to sleep in a room full of Dad's things... to look at this shirt and know he's never going to wear it again." She holds Caroline's gaze. "I'm doing the best I can not to fall completely to pieces."

She expects these words will make Caroline collapse in her arms and apologize—but Hollis is so very wrong. Caroline storms from the room with the parting shot "It's always *all about you!*" She books herself on the Acela back to New York City three days earlier than planned, leaving Hollis stunned and alone.

The Wellesley police send Hollis an e-mail with the official accident report attached, but Hollis can't bear to read it. She doesn't want the details of how fast Matthew was driving or where on Dover Street he lost control or how many times the car spun before it flipped over. (The car did flip over, she knows; the young officer told her this. That's the only detail she has retained other than the deer, mama and baby, that Matthew swerved to avoid and yet ended up killing anyway.) Hollis yearns to delete the e-mail, then delete it permanently from the deleted-files folder—Matthew is gone, the details don't matter—but instead, she moves it to a folder labeled MM, where she's keeping all of the correspondence related to Matthew's death.

She no longer cooks; she barely eats. Her doctor, Karen Lindstrom, offers to prescribe some Ativan for daytime anxiety, Ambien for sleep. But Hollis doesn't relish the idea of pills; every once in a while, she'll pour herself a glass of Sancerre, but this leads her right to places she wants to avoid: the smell of Matthew's shaving lotion; *You've changed. And we've changed;* the knock on the door.

Friends and neighbors check in. What can they do? "Nothing" is the answer—but they offer her advice anyway: yoga, self-guided meditation, grief counseling, essential oils, travel, an ashram, a psychic, knitting.

Knitting? Hollis thinks.

Hollis puts her new cookware line on hold, ditto her plans for a cookbook, her show. What does any of it matter now?

She wonders how her father coped when her mother died so suddenly. She supposes he focused on taking care of Hollis, going to work; in all the years Hollis knew him, he was stoic and steadfast. He didn't have the luxury of falling apart.

Hollis reaches out to Caroline every few days, but her calls are summarily declined and her texts always garner the same response: OK. Or worse: K. It's just enough to let Hollis know Caroline's alive and breathing. Hollis consults Grown and Flown, her favorite website for parenting older children, as she tries to figure out what to do. Should she take the train down to New York and confront Caroline? Should she stop calling and texting? (This feels so cruel—the girl just lost her father.) Should she stop paying Caroline's credit card? (That would get her attention.) Hollis knows that children are narcissistic, and she understands that the prefrontal cortex doesn't fully develop until age twenty-five. Caroline can't be blamed; she's still growing. But Hollis wants to cry out: *You're hurting me. This will be easier to get through if we bond together!*

Hollis has been trained not to Like or comment on any of Caroline's Instagram posts, though Hollis checks her daughter's account several times a day. There's been only one new post since Matthew died—Caroline wishing her best friend, Cygnet, a happy birthday in Stories. Hollis clicks through it several times, because Caroline has posted pictures of herself and Cygnet as little girls growing up in Wellesley: the two of them in a tent in the backyard, their young faces illuminated by flashlights; the two of them holding the pancake pops that Caroline requested for her tenth birthday. Hollis presses her finger to her phone screen so the picture stays put. *I want to go back,* she thinks. Back to the days of sleepovers and fancy birthday breakfasts.

Hollis feels like she's lost not only her husband, but her daughter as well.

The only time Hollis finds even a modicum of relief from her mourning is when she's texting with a woman who'd reached out to her on her website several months ago—someone Hollis has never met but did not exactly pick out at random either. The direct message from *Gigi Ling, Atlanta, Georgia,* caught Hollis's eye. Gigi was the one who told Hollis about the hidden spots along the Buford Highway that serve the best dim sum, bulgogi, and tacos in the entire South. She also recommended Laurie Colwin's books *Home Cooking* and *More Home Cooking,* which Hollis just adores. (How had she not known about them? Hollis immediately reviewed them on the website and provided a link to buy through Bookshop.org.)

Yes, Gigi Ling is Hollis's favorite person in the Hungry with Hollis community, though she supposes she shouldn't have favorites. (A ridiculous notion—everyone has favorites; it's part of being human.)

A week after Matthew died, Gigi sent her a DM with one simple sentence: I'm here to listen. Hollis had grabbed those words like a life preserver; she realized she'd been waiting to hear from Gigi since she'd posted the news.

From that moment on, they have texted several times a week;

Hollis would be happy to text her every day but she doesn't want to be a burden. Gigi normally checks in on Tuesdays, Fridays, the occasional Sunday evening: Tell me about your day. How goes it? I'm here, I'm here, I'm here. Initially it feels odd texting with a complete stranger, but, Hollis reasons, people do it all the time on dating apps—Tinder, Bumble, Hinge. Soon it feels more liberating than odd. The stakes are low. It's almost easier to confide in a stranger.

Hollis starts sharing details that are very personal. Things between Matthew and me were...unsettled when he died.

Unsettled how? Gigi texts back.

Hollis describes the ways that she and Matthew had grown distant. Part of it was the usual empty-nest stuff, she says. Caroline wasn't home to keep them united as a family. Part of it was the world discovering Hollis's website.

Gigi texts, He must have been threatened by your sudden success.

Had Matthew been threatened? Hollis wonders. *Threatened* isn't the right word—they were, after all, talking about the revered Dr. Madden—but for some reason, Matthew hadn't fully embraced or supported Hollis's good fortune. He had been...*bemused* by it. And, at times, annoyed. He and Caroline made fun of the unbridled adoration of her blog's fans. Had Matthew ever said he was proud of what she'd done with the website? He had not.

Over the next few months, Hollis and Gigi's intimacy deepens to the point where, one day in mid-June, Hollis feels safe telling Gigi about the morning Matthew died—the conference in Leipzig, Dr. Schrader's Parkinson's, the holiday party.

I confronted him about my unhappiness as he was walking out the door, Hollis writes. I made his missing our holiday party into a bigger deal than it needed to be. He responded by saying that I'd changed, that we'd changed. I didn't think this at the time, but I do now, and it haunts me: He was going to leave me. I called him to apologize but he didn't answer. I left a message and then sent a text saying I loved him. I have no idea if he listened to the message or read the text. I want to believe that he did, but how can I be sure? What I do know is that I made him late. He was speeding on Dover Street because he had a flight to catch. I feel guilty. I feel...responsible.

When she hits Send, she immediately feels unburdened. But she also feels implicated. She has set the thought loose in the universe: She contributed in some small way—or maybe a big way—to Matthew's death. She's grateful—oh so grateful—that she didn't tell Gigi that, only moments before the police knocked on her door, she'd been creeping around Jack Finigan's Facebook page. She will never tell Gigi this. She will never tell anyone this.

She waits for Gigi to respond to her text with something like *Don't be silly, Hollis, it isn't your fault. It was an accident. The road was slick; it was snowing; the deer appeared out of nowhere.* But Gigi doesn't say this, nor does she send the predictable reassurances: *I'm sure he listened to your voice mail, played your text over the car's sound system.* For one day, then two, there's no response, not even three dots in a bubble indicating that Gigi is carefully selecting her words.

Hollis is stung. She crafts half a dozen texts asking what's wrong, is Gigi okay, has this admission horrified Gigi, does Gigi feel like she's in too deep? But in the end, Hollis sends nothing. Probably Gigi is just busy. She has a life, after all—though what, really, does Hollis know about her? She's ten years younger than Hollis, forty-three; she's single with no children; she has a cat named Mabel; she lives in the Buckhead section of Atlanta; she's a pilot with Delta Air Lines; she's not on social media; she heard about Hungry with Hollis from some of her flight attendants, who said it would be worth her time—and it has been, Gigi said. Those are the things Gigi has told Hollis. The things Hollis has gathered are that Gigi reads a lot; she cooks at home and also appreciates fine restaurants; she's educated, cultured, discerning. But all of their text conversations have been focused on Hollis. No wonder Gigi is ghosting her; she's probably weary of the one-way friendship.

A week passes without any word from Gigi. Hollis actually goes onto the Hungry with Hollis website to see if there are any Kitchen Lights on in Atlanta. Yes, there are many, but it's impossible to tell if any of the lights belong to Gigi. Next Hollis checks to see if Gigi has unsubscribed from the blog's newsletter—but her e-mail is still there, thank God. She probably just has a busy flight schedule or she dropped her phone in the pool or she's in a new relationship or her cat Mabel died or her father, who lives in Singapore, fell ill. (Gigi mentioned that her mother died when she was young, something else they have in common.)

Hollis tells herself it doesn't matter, that if it's meant to be, she'll come back, or whatever that saying is.

But with Gigi's absence, Hollis's mental state deteriorates—and it doesn't help when she gets a text from Caroline saying: By the way, I'm NOT coming to Nantucket for the summer. I got the internship with Isaac Opoku so I'll be staying in New York. I'm subletting on East 82nd, it's $1,800 a month. Thx.

Hollis immediately calls Caroline but is flung right to her voice mail. She leaves a babbling message that she knows Caroline will never listen to: "*So* proud of you, darling, all your hard work on that essay, your grades—your father would be over the moon! Brava!" Caroline has been scheming to get this particular internship since the fall, and over a thousand aspiring filmmakers applied for this opportunity with Isaac Opoku. But it's unpaid, so the subtext on the sublet is that Hollis will be paying the rent.

Selfishly, Hollis wants to have Caroline around for the summer so they can heal things between them, but Hollis reminds herself the internship is a big deal and is probably what Caroline needs after losing her dad.

* * *

On June 21, the first day of summer, Hollis leaves for Nantucket, her actual home-home. Wellesley is Matthew's place, and although Hollis has adopted it, she's certain that once she's back at the house on Squam Road, things will get better. The change of scenery, the change of season, and the ocean out her back door will help. She won't mind that Gigi has vanished, that she and Caroline are dangerously close to becoming estranged.

But being back on Nantucket doesn't help, because, on Nantucket, there's another version of Matthew to mourn, a more relaxed, summertime Matthew.

* * *

It's their second summer in the house, which is so thoughtfully designed, so soundly built, that Hollis can't believe it's hers. This is the kind of house she used to dream of having when she and her father were living in their tiny five-room cottage, one Hollis feared would be lifted right off the ground during a nor'easter, like something from *The Wizard of Oz.* That cottage was heated by a woodstove. Hollis and her father ate meals at the round kitchen table from which they could see the TV in the living room. They shared a bathroom and had one phone. All winter, Hollis hunkered beneath the covers of her bed wearing an Irish fisherman's sweater and a pair of wool socks. It took the shower a full five minutes to heat up, during which time Tom Shaw could be counted on to clear his throat from outside the door, meaning Hollis should jump in, like it or not.

Hollis used to babysit for the Gasperson family down the road. Their house had nineteen rooms, some of them with individual decks and balconies that overlooked the ocean; there was a room lined with matching bunks in the basement and a screened-in sleeping porch on the third floor. The Gaspersons didn't have a television. When the Gasperson parents and grandparents went out for dinner at the Chanticleer in Sconset, the Gasperson children played cards or board games or curated their collections of shells and sea glass, and they liked Hollis to tell them ghost stories by candlelight. Hollis would have worked for the Gaspersons for free. She wanted to blend into their big family. Her dream was to live on Squam Road only in the summer.

This dream has now come true.

Hollis and Matthew turn onto Squam Road, which is thick with Spanish olives and rugosa roses; on the fences are posted hand-painted signs: SLOW DOWN! PEDESTRIANS! When Hollis was growing up, this road was so rutted and potholed that it was impossible to drive faster than ten miles an hour, but now, every Mother's Day weekend, the neighborhood association grades the road as smooth as a yellow ribbon. Hollis and Matthew pass a gentleman wearing Nantucket Reds and Jack Kennedy sunglasses and walking a chocolate Lab, then a woman in a straw hat cutting the wild cosmos and black-eyed Susans along the side of the road—perfect, Hollis thinks, for a kitchen-sink bouquet. They pull down their new white-shell driveway that's lined on both sides with evenly spaced young hydrangea bushes that their landscaper, Anastasia, assures them will "fill out." Their six-year-old daughter, Caroline, has just fallen asleep in the back seat along with their Irish setter, Seamus.

When Matthew parks in front of the house—they need to come up with a name for the house and the cottage; all proper summer homes have names—he says, "Let's leave them be for a minute. I have something to show you."

"But—" The car windows are down, Caroline and Seamus are snoring in harmony, but Hollis is itching to get the bags and boxes inside, to unpack, to settle.

"Trust me, sweet-love," Matthew says. "It'll be worth it."

He leads Hollis around the side of the house and unlatches the pool gate (yes, they built a pool; it seems nearly shameful when they're only a hundred yards from the ocean, Hollis knows her father must be rolling over in his grave, but she had wanted a pool badly) so they can access the backyard—the pond, the path to the beach.

Hollis gasps. The pond—which was an eyesore when she was growing up, mucky and mosquito-ridden—has been…reimagined. The surface looks like green glass, and it's dotted with water lilies, many of them in full flower. But the most remarkable thing is the arched footbridge with handsome crosshatched sides that now spans the pond.

"Did you do this?" Hollis asks, then she laughs—obviously he did; the pond didn't clean itself, the bridge wasn't built by magic elves.

"Because of how much you loved Giverny," Matthew says.

Claude Monet's garden in Giverny—yes, on a trip to France while Hollis was pregnant with Caroline, she'd been captivated by the bridge. She'd bought a print of one of the Giverny paintings in the gift shop. She can't believe Matthew remembered; she can't believe he'd been paying attention.

"Can we…walk across it?" Hollis asks.

Matthew offers her his hand.

* * *

Hollis is a hostage to her grief; she's not eating, not sleeping. She breaks down, calls Dr. Lindstrom, and asks for a prescription for Ambien. The pills help her *fall* asleep, but by one in the morning, Hollis is wide awake, at which point she pads out to the kitchen and flips open her laptop. With her face bathed in blue light, down the rabbit hole she goes. She types in *What to do when your husband dies,* and the results pop up: "How to Deal with the Death of a Loved One," "A Guide to Grief Journaling," "Sex and the Widow."

"Sex and the Widow"? she thinks. As if.

She takes a bite of one article, a nibble of the next; nothing helps, nothing helps, nothing *helps!* She brings up Jack Finigan's Facebook page. There are still no new pictures of Mindy, but even that doesn't make Hollis feel better.

She texts Caroline asking how she likes her internship.

OK.

And what about the sublet? (*That I'm paying for,* Hollis thinks but does not say.)

OK.

Would you please answer my calls, Caroline?

No response.

Then, on July 15, the seven-month anniversary of Matthew's death (she experiences every day in relation to Matthew's death), Hollis finds something unexpected.

On a site called Motherlode (Hollis has never heard of it), she reads about Moira Sullivan, age fifty-nine, whose husband of thirty years dropped dead at the hardware store while he was buying bird-seed for Moira's feeders.

I was devastated, Moira wrote. *I fell apart.*

Yes, Hollis thinks.

But then I came up with an idea, Moira wrote. She organized a girls' trip for her best friends, one friend from each phase of her life. The photo accompanying the article shows a knot of smiling middle-aged women at a beachfront rental home in Destin, Florida. Moira, who is wearing a floppy-brimmed straw hat, is in the center with the friends orbiting her like planets around the sun.

I wanted to be surrounded by the people who knew me best, Moira wrote, *even though a couple of the women I hadn't seen or talked to in years. Even though our common ground had shrunk. Even though these women didn't know one another well—or at all. I wanted to celebrate the friendships that had made me who I was.*

Moira invited her best friend from her teens (Cate), her best friend from her twenties (Paige), her best friend from her "prime of life"

(Phoebe), and her best friend from "midlife" (Liz). The five of them lounged on the beach reading *Where the Crawdads Sing;* they rented a floating tiki hut and booze-cruised over Destin's emerald-green water; they cooked a lasagna dinner at home on the first night with *lots of wine and a special playlist that Moira made, which got us all dancing on the deck* (wrote Cate), and the second night they went *bonkers* (Phoebe's word) at Lucky's Rotten Apple. The ladies took lots of pictures on their iPhones and shared them in a closed Facebook group, and Moira had a commemorative album made on Shutterfly. The title of the album—and of the article—was "The Five-Star Weekend."

Hollis can't believe she hasn't heard about this idea before. She's struck not only by the poignancy of the idea (it's your life story in friends) but also by the bravery—a weekend with four women whose only connection to one another is *you.*

Hollis imagines hosting such a weekend.

Best friend from her teens: Tatum McKenzie.

Best friend from her twenties: Dru-Ann Jones.

Best friend from her "prime of life": Well, there was Electra Undergrove—but she and Hollis no longer speak. Runner-up is probably Brooke Kirtley, who was such a help when Matthew died.

What about the fourth friend? Hollis wonders. The friend from "midlife" (which, Hollis realizes, means *now*). She doesn't have any friends specifically from midlife. Why is this? It's difficult to meet new people once your kids are grown, especially when you work from home. There's cute Zoe Kern from Hollis's barre class—but Zoe is twenty-nine years old and seven months pregnant.

But then Hollis realizes she does have one new friend. She has Gigi Ling.

Hollis leaves the "Five-Star Weekend" article up on her browser. She paces her Nantucket kitchen, weirdly energized, *revved up,* even, thinking about the possibility of hosting her own Five-Star

Weekend. She loves the double entendre—five women for the weekend, and a weekend filled with elevated experiences worthy of five stars (if anyone can pull this part off, it's Hollis). But what appeals to Hollis most is what Moira Sullivan said about honoring the friendships that had formed her.

Hollis isn't naive enough to imagine this will be a Hallmark-movie experience where her guilt, her melancholy, and her loneliness will all magically disappear once she's surrounded by her friends.

But yes, that is sort of what she imagines.

Nothing else has worked.

It couldn't hurt. (Could it?)

She'll do it, she decides. She'll host a Five-Star Weekend here, on Nantucket, in two weeks.

She goes back inside, snaps her laptop shut, pads down the hall, and climbs into bed. For the first time since Matthew died, sleep comes easily.

2. The Invitation

The next morning, Hollis sends each of her four "stars" the same text (separately): Would you be up for a girls' weekend at my Nantucket house, July 28 to July 31? All you have to do is show up. I'll take care of everything else.

Brooke Kirtley is the first to respond (no surprise there): Girls' weekend? Oh, Hollis, good for you. Are you sure you're ready? If you're ready, DEFINITELY count me in!!!

Hollis's heart aches a little; Brooke loves nothing more than to be included.

Dru-Ann is next: How flexible are your dates? My life is... a blender.

Also no surprise. Hollis's college roommate Dru-Ann Jones is the country's premier agent for female athletes, *and* she's the cohost of an ESPN show called *Throw Like a Girl* that airs on Tuesday afternoons, *and* she writes for *New York* magazine about race and gender politics in sports.

When Matthew died, Dru-Ann was in Fremantle, Australia, signing an Olympic-bound swimmer. She'd asked Hollis what she could do to help and offered to drop everything and fly halfway around the world to Boston, but Hollis told her to wait. "I'll need you later," she said. "After all these people have gone."

"I trust you're telling the truth and not just being a martyr," Dru-Ann said. "When you need me, I will show up."

When Matthew died, you asked what you could do for me, Hollis texts now. You can do this.

There's no response, and Hollis experiences a moment of desperation. If any of them can't make it, she'll cancel the whole thing, but she knows Brooke will want to come anyway, and can Hollis do a weekend with only Brooke? (Frankly, no.) She texts Dru-Ann again: I have a Peloton. And I'll get your tequila. And organic limes.

Tequila, yes, but don't worry about another thing, Dru-Ann texts. I'll be there.

Two down, Hollis thinks. She tries to imagine a weekend with just herself, Brooke, and Dru-Ann, and a different panic envelops her. Dru-Ann and Brooke met a few years earlier at Hollis and Matthew's Marathon Monday brunch—Dru-Ann was in town because she represented one of the elite runners from Kenya—and afterward, Dru-Ann described Brooke as the "human equivalent of something stuck in your teeth. Just. So. Annoying." Meanwhile, Brooke developed an obsession with Dru-Ann. She watches *Throw Like a Girl* every week and she thinks it's *so cool* that Hollis went to college with someone who's *on television* and who, last year, appeared at number 74 on *Forbes*'s Most Powerful Women list.

A little while later, Hollis's phone lights up with a text from her best friend from when she was growing up, Tatum McKenzie, who still lives on Nantucket year-round: Does "girls' weekend" mean I would spend the night at your house in Squam?

Hollis writes back: Yes, won't that be fun?

Okay, Tatum says, which isn't really an answer to the question. But it sounds like she's a yes, and Hollis feels cool relief pass through her. Every summer since Hollis and Matthew built the new house on her father's property, Hollis has invited Tatum and her husband, Kyle, over for dinner, and every summer, Tatum comes up with an excuse for why they can't make it, so Tatum has never been inside Hollis's house. Once, a few years earlier, Hollis got a text from Tatum out of the blue: Kyle and I went for a Sunday drive and ended up at your place in Squam. We peeked in the windows, danced on your pool cover, and had sex in your outdoor shower. (Just kidding!) You have officially become a Summer Person, Holly. Just like you always wanted. This was followed by the one-tear crying emoji.

Hollis wrote back, trying to be funny: You did have sex in the outdoor shower. I know you did.

Tatum responded with the middle-finger emoji.

Hollis has bumped into Tatum a few times since then—once at Dan's Pharmacy, once at the post office, once at St. Mary's (where Hollis and Tatum used to be altar servers together)—but if she's honest, Hollis would admit that things haven't been good or right between them since she left for college.

Forget the Hallmark movie, Hollis thinks. Her Five-Star Weekend might be more like *Real Housewives*.

But three of the four are definitely coming. There's no turning back now.

* * *

When the hottest part of the afternoon has passed, Hollis takes Henrietta for a walk, leaving her phone behind. The hydrangea bushes that line Hollis's driveway have filled in, just as Anastasia promised, though Hollis can't appreciate their pink and periwinkle beauty the way she should.

By the time I get back, she thinks, *Gigi will have texted.*

But she hasn't; the only text is from Brooke: I'm so excited!!! I booked my ferry, I get in at 4:05 on Friday!!! Now, tell me, what can I bring??!!?

Hollis nearly texts back *Nothing, just yourself!* But texting with Brooke is like one of those woven finger traps: the more you engage, the harder it is to extricate yourself. Brooke will react with the heart or double exclamation point to Hollis's text (what kind of sadist dreamed *that* feature up?), then she'll text a question, like *How about Fells steak tips?,* which Hollis will feel compelled to respond to, and Brooke will like or emphasize *that* text...and this will go on until, in exasperation, Hollis stops replying (hint, hint), at which point Brooke will send a string of emoji hearts and kissing faces.

Hollis leaves Brooke's text to bleed out. She clicks on Gigi's name just to double-check that her invitation text went through; the service in Squam can be spotty.

Yes, it was delivered at 9:38 that morning.

Clearly, Gigi is done with her. Hollis isn't sure why this bothers her so much. It isn't as if Gigi is a soul mate; you don't meet soul mates on the internet. (Well, some people might, but not Hollis.)

But when Hollis wakes up the next day, a text is there, sent at three fifteen in the morning: I feel so honored to be included. Are you sure about this?

Hollis stares at the words, blinking, rereading, double-checking that this text is really from Gigi Ling. The text sounds like Gigi:

lovely and gracious. It's all Hollis can do not to respond with *Where have you been? Why have you been ghosting me?*

Instead, she types: Very sure. Can't wait to meet you IRL!!!! Then she deletes that (all the exclamation points make her sound like Brooke) and types: Very sure. Looking forward to getting together.

She hits Send.

3. Chink in the Armor

Caroline Shaw-Madden receives a text from her mother requesting her presence on Nantucket for the weekend.

No, Caroline says to herself. But then she reconsiders.

For the past seventeen sweltering, feverish days, Caroline has been romantically involved with her boss, the Academy Award–winning documentarian Isaac Opoku.

Caroline never dreamed things with Isaac would take this kind of turn, not only because of the age difference (fourteen years) or the power differential (Caroline is a rising senior at NYU who has yet to make even a short film of her own) but also because Isaac is in a committed relationship. His girlfriend, Sofia Desmione, is a bona fide supermodel (*Vogue,* Italian *Vogue,* Valentino, Dolce e Gabbana), and Sofia lives with Isaac in the Chelsea loft that also serves as Isaac's studio.

But...Sofia is rarely around. She's either out on a shoot or partying until dawn at Zero Bond. Isaac, though, suffers from social anxiety; he asks Caroline to go through his e-mails and decline all invitations. From the beginning, Caroline wondered why Isaac and Sofia were together. She'd seen Sofia only once in her first month of work: Sofia breezed in, smelling like a mixture of Jo Malone and tequila and wearing a dress that looked like a Hefty garbage bag, kissed Isaac on the forehead, and told him she'd gotten an assignment with Acne Studios and would be shooting in Stockholm for three weeks. She added, "I'm having lunch with Mauricio at Cluny, then I'm off to JFK. Gemma will come in a little while to pack my bags. Love you."

And Isaac had said in his darling Senegalese accent, "Love you too, *ma chérie*."

Only then had Sofia noticed Caroline. "New assistant? Cute! I'm Sofia." She offered Caroline a cool hand. "Please, no trouble."

Please, no trouble. Caroline was so startled by the statement that at first she was unable to respond. Did that mean what she thought it meant? Had there been "trouble" with other assistants, or did Sofia find Caroline particularly threatening (the thought was laughable)? By the time Caroline had recovered enough to say, "No, of course not," Sofia was gone.

Caroline is, technically, helping Isaac edit his documentary *L'Étoile Verte;* it's about Amira Delacroix, a chef who left her wildly popular restaurant kingdom in Paris to open an elegant French bistro in the Moroccan desert town of Ouarzazate. However, what *helping* means is that Caroline goes to the corner bodega to fetch Isaac's bacon, egg, and cheese sandwiches, she opens his mail, and she sits on a stool to his left as he teaches her how to edit. From the beginning, Caroline found Isaac gentle, lovely, and kind. He hired Caroline to complete the mundane tasks of his day but also because he likes the company. Plus he wants to impart his knowledge to someone, and Caroline is a sponge. But one afternoon shortly after Sofia left for Sweden, Caroline handed him the script with the pages out of order, and Isaac lost his temper. He said, "A kindergarten *bébé* could do this, Caroline, and yet you manage to make it a mess!"

Caroline couldn't help herself—she started to cry, and once she started, she couldn't stop. It wasn't Isaac's reprimand, it was everything, and by *everything,* Caroline meant that her father was dead. She hadn't told Isaac about her father because she didn't want special treatment. Certainly the nine hundred and ninety-nine other students who'd applied for this job had problems too, but those problems didn't belong in the studio.

She said, "I'm sorry. My father died unexpectedly in December, and I'm still fragile."

She wouldn't have been surprised if Isaac had fired her on the spot, but instead he backed away from his computer and took her by the hand, and led her over to the vintage sofa in the loft's living area. He made her a cup of Yellow Gold tea and brought out an assortment of cashews, Turkish figs, and dried apricots from Kalustyan's on Lexington. He told Caroline that he'd lost his mother when he was nine years old, and not a day went by that he didn't mourn her.

He was so sweet in that moment and his loneliness so obvious (his relationship with Sofia was a sham, Caroline decided then; they were together only because they were good for each other's brands) that she forgot herself. She dismissed Sofia's request—*Please, no trouble*—and kissed him. To his credit, he pulled away and said, "This isn't what you want." What he meant was *This will not replace your father's love.* What he meant was *I am in a position of power and you are not and therefore this won't be fair to you. We have seen stories like this play out before and they always end badly.*

Caroline said, breathing into his mouth, "It is what I want. It is." And she kissed him again.

* * *

Caroline receives her mother's text as she's leaving Isaac's loft and beginning the long walk to her sublet on the Upper East Side (it's too hot for the subway and she doesn't have money for a cab). Sofia is returning to New York the following day, and as agonizing as it will be for both Caroline and Isaac, the affair has to end.

Caroline and her mother haven't spoken in months. This, Caroline has to admit, is her fault. Caroline got an A in both Intro to Psych and Social Psych so she understands that she's punishing Hollis because Hollis is the surviving parent. Everyone at the funeral kept commenting on how "strong" Hollis was, which made Caroline *livid.* Hollis used to be a devoted wife and mother, but when her website went stratospheric, she shoved both Caroline and her father into a corner. Well, maybe it wasn't that bad, but there was a marked difference in their family dynamic. Hollis's social media presence became her new baby; it was top of mind for Hollis every second of every day. Caroline and her father used to jokingly call Hollis "the Cooking Kardashian," but now that her father is dead, it isn't funny. Caroline is furious with her mother for reasons she can't articulate, and the stark truth is that Caroline is still in so much emotional pain that holding a grudge feels good.

But Hollis has always been intuitive. Caroline wouldn't be surprised if her mother had somehow sensed that Caroline just experienced the first breakup of her adult life.

Would you consider coming to Nantucket this weekend? Please, Caroline. I've done something.

Caroline hates that Hollis has reached out now, when she is at her most vulnerable. She takes a deep breath—the city air is redolent of exhaust, sweat, and trash—and calls her mother.

Hollis answers on the first ring. If she hadn't, Caroline might have hung up.

"Darling?" Hollis says.

"Yes," Caroline says.

Neither of them speaks for a moment. Caroline breaks first, mostly out of impatience. "You said you've done something. What have you done?" She braces herself for the worst.

"Well," Hollis says, "I've decided to host something called a Five-Star Weekend, and I was hoping you could help."

All Caroline hears is *host* and *five-star,* and she thinks, *Of course she's hosting something fancy.* Can Caroline end the call? She sort of wants to, but she's surprised by how much she's missed her mother's voice.

Hollis goes on to explain: four friends, one from each phase of Hollis's life, coming to stay at the house on Nantucket.

To Caroline, the Five-Star Weekend sounds like some kind of internet challenge for boomers. "What sort of help do you want from *me?*"

"I'd like you to come to Nantucket and film it," Hollis says. "The original woman who did it, Moira, took pictures and made a Shutterfly album. But I thought, since you're a filmmaker"—*I'm a college student,* Caroline thinks, *who, until today, was sleeping with a filmmaker*—"you could document our adventures."

Adventures? Caroline thinks. Like a trip to the needlepoint store? Or ordering a kombucha at Lemon Press instead of a latte? Caroline pictures a glass of chardonnay on a porch railing with beach dunes in the background as Bonnie Tyler sings "Holding Out for a Hero."

Absolutely not, Caroline thinks. But before she can decline, Hollis says, "I'll pay you twenty-five hundred dollars. How does that sound?"

It sounds as good as a hot stone massage, a chilled raspberry White Claw, and a sneaky link with Jacob Elordi. Caroline's pockets are hurting, but she saw the hypocrisy in asking her mother for spending money when she had basically slammed the door in her face.

"Fine, I'll do it," she says. Caroline needs funds, but also, thanks to Sofia's imminent return, she wants to get out of the city. "When do you want me there?"

"Friday morning," Hollis says. "I'm sorry, I know it means missing work—"

"That won't be a problem," Caroline says.

The next day, Caroline shows up at Isaac's loft wearing black to mark the death of their romance. Caroline can tell by the serene energy in the loft that Sofia isn't back yet.

"She lands at five," Isaac says. They gaze at each other with longing and Caroline thinks, *One more time?* But Isaac slices the air between them with his hand. "We must get back to business."

Caroline nods. "I'll be taking tomorrow and Monday off." She knows she can ask for whatever she wants now.

Isaac frowns, then grasps Caroline's chin in his fingers so that she has no choice but to look into his brown eyes. *Sofia Desmione is not worthy of those eyes,* Caroline thinks. "You need time away?" he says. "Where will you go?"

"To Nantucket to see my mother," Caroline says. "She's hosting a weekend for her...friends." After Caroline hung up with Hollis yesterday, she realized she'd forgotten to ask the most important question. She'd texted Hollis: Wait—who did you invite to this thing?

Three dots rose on Caroline's phone, then disappeared, then rose again, then disappeared again.

Finally, a text came in: Tatum.

Okay... Caroline thought. She hadn't realized her mother and Tatum were friends anymore.

Dru-Ann.

Of course, Caroline thought.

Brooke.

Eye-roll emoji, Caroline thought.

There was a pause and Caroline thought, *That's it? I thought there were supposed to be four friends,* but then another text arrived.

Gigi Ling.

Who is that? Caroline had never heard of Gigi Ling. She texted: ?????

Her mother responded: I met her through the website.

Caroline groaned. The Hungry with Hollis community worshipped her mother, and one of Caroline's major beefs was how much Hollis seemed to relish their adoration.

It was *very* alarming that Hollis had invited one of these people to the Five-Star Weekend.

Please tell me you've met this woman in person, Caroline texted.

Three dots rose, then disappeared.

This, Caroline thought, *means no.*

Caroline mentally composed a response to her mother: *I can't believe you're inviting someone you've never met IRL to the Five-Star Weekend. It's probably some scary dude living in his mother's basement who's going to murder you all. Or she's a scam artist, a predator, or, at the very least, someone so needy and friendless that she's going to a girls' weekend with complete strangers. Really, Mom, what are you thinking?*

Now Caroline tells Isaac, "She wants me to film it."

"Mon Dieu," he says. His expression is dubious.

"One of the women my mother invited is someone she's never met," Caroline says. "It's someone from her, you know, foodie website."

Isaac's beautiful eyes widen. "So bizarre. This will be a funny little project for you. And maybe not a complete waste? You can practice shooting landscape."

There was one afternoon in Isaac's bed when Caroline described Nantucket to him: the stretches of pristine golden beach, the moors dotted with green ponds, the peppermint stick of the Sankaty lighthouse.

"May I please borrow a camera?" Caroline asks. "Either the Red or the Alexa? And one of your Sachtler tripods?"

She watches doubt flicker across Isaac's face—he never lends his equipment.

"Of course, *mon petit chou.* And you should take my drone."

His *drone?* Whoa. Maybe he thinks Caroline can get some good footage of the island, or maybe he's patronizing her. Probably a bit of both. It will be a "funny little project," and Caroline will return to New York twenty-five hundred dollars richer.

On Caroline's first day at the loft, Isaac had told her that the most challenging part of documentary filmmaking was finding a worthy subject. *Look for a chink in the armor,* he said, *where you can penetrate the surface and discover a hidden truth.*

As Caroline packs up Isaac's precious equipment, she laughs to herself. There won't be any hidden truths behind a bunch of olds eating lobster rolls, wearing capri pants, and quoting *Sixteen Candles.* That much is for sure.

4. First Light I

Because it faces northeast, Squam is the best place on the island to watch the sunrise. Hollis carries her coffee out to the deck with Henrietta at her heels, and together they feast on the view—the pond, the footbridge, the sandy path that leads through the dunes to the navy-blue stripe of the Atlantic Ocean.

She and Matthew named the house First Light.

What are Hollis's favorite things about the house? The slender windows flanking the front door are inlaid with pieces of actual sea glass in every shade of blue and green. The cathedral-ceilinged great room is white and bright with blond wood beams and trim, but there are surprises too—the blue-moon couch, a comfy semicircle of deep cerulean suede, between shamrock-green lounging chairs that face the glass doors. Leather stools surround the kitchen island—there's plenty of room for Hollis to cook while entertaining—and over the island hangs a chandelier made from vintage Coca-Cola bottles. A chaise upholstered in the palest blue silk is positioned in front of the white brick fireplace. *Mom's throne,* Caroline calls it, because that's where Hollis would spend every waking moment if she could—on the chaise with a book (though recently, *book* has meant "laptop"). In the summer, she keeps the front and back doors open so the breeze can blow through the house, and in the fall and winter, the fire is always lit. Coffee on the side table in the mornings; a glass of cold, crisp sauvignon blanc in the evenings.

Hollis and Matthew turned the original cottage into a charming guesthouse decked out with curvy, colorful midcentury furnishings. They named the cottage the Twist. (The observant guests figure out why.)

Next to the Twist is a two-car garage that shelters Hollis's Volvo and Matthew's "baby," a strawberry-red 1971 convertible Bronco that's perennially filled with sand no matter how often Hollis vacuums it.

Hollis decides to put Tatum in the Fifty Shades of White suite across the hall from her room and next to Caroline's. She'll put Brooke in the Board Room and Gigi in her favorite space in the house, Hibiscus Heaven—both of these suites are on the far side of the living area. Dru-Ann can have the Twist to herself.

"This is happening, girlfriend," Hollis says to Henrietta. "Everyone arrives tomorrow."

Henrietta vibrates with excitement as though she understands. Henny will be happy; as the saying goes, she has never met a stranger.

"Caroline is coming," Hollis says. There was a moment when Hollis questioned whether it was wise to include Caroline—Hollis was afraid of rejection; she was worried that once she offered the money, it would sound like she had to *bribe* her own daughter to visit; and she isn't at all sure that any of what happens this weekend should be filmed—but now that Caroline has agreed to come, Hollis is optimistic. She and Caroline will be together and there will be other people around to make things less awkward.

Hollis flips open her laptop, goes to the Hungry with Hollis website, and clicks on the Corkboard. *To the Hungry with Hollis community: The past seven months have been harrowing...*

Hollis deletes *harrowing* and writes *dismal,* then she deletes that as well. Both words are accurate, as are *lonely, bleak,* and plain old *sad,* but she doesn't want to be a Debbie Downer, nor does she want to make a big deal about her return; she just wants to move forward.

Hollis takes a breath, then types: *I want to thank you all for your thoughts, prayers, and condolences and for the stories you've been kind enough to share with me. Knowing that your Kitchen Lights were still on here at Hungry with Hollis pulled me through some very dark days. Today I write to you with some more hopeful news. I'm hosting something called a Five-Star Weekend at my home on Nantucket. Let me tell you all about it.*

5. Errands

It's eight thirty on Thursday morning when Tatum McKenzie spots her oldest friend, Hollis Shaw, by the deli counter at the mid-island Stop and Shop. Hollis has a pair of sunglasses perched on her blond-gray head, and she's wearing a pair of Lululemon running shorts and a Cisco Brewers T-shirt. She's checking things off a list. Tatum smiles. Hollis has always loved a good list.

Without breaking stride, Tatum swings her cart around and heads in the opposite direction, her heart flip-flopping like a freshly caught fish. *Quick, quick, quick!* She races to the line closest to the exit and loads her bleach and paper towels onto the conveyor belt. Kathy Culbert, who was a year ahead of Tatum and Hollis in school, is behind the register, and as always, Kathy wants to chat. "How's the little guy?" she asks. Kathy's sister, Melanie, runs the day care that Tatum's grandson, Orion, attends.

"Good, good," Tatum says, cursing her lost opportunity to grab a rotisserie chicken. She wants Kyle to have something to eat while she spends the weekend in Squam with the very woman she's running away from.

"I don't understand why you agreed to go," Kyle said to Tatum that morning. "You avoid Hollis every summer like she's poison ivy, and now you're spending the weekend at her house?" Kyle kissed Tatum's nose and goosed her. "After all these years, I still can't figure you out. It's sexy." They ended up having a quickie standing in front of the mirror, Kyle carefully avoiding the spot on Tatum's right breast where she'd been stabbed by the biopsy needle.

The sex put Tatum behind for the morning. Dylan was still asleep—he hadn't gotten home from work until two or three—so Tatum had to drop Orion off at Melanie's before she came here for cleaning supplies, and now she has to go to Holdgate's to pick up Mr. Albright's shirts and still somehow get to the Albrights' house by nine. Tatum is jonesing for a cigarette. Since discovering the lump, she's been smoking twice as many as usual, which she understands is bad, but how is she supposed to handle the stress of possibly having *breast cancer* without smoking? Some women might be able to do it, but not Tatum.

When Tatum leaves the store, it's a quarter to nine; she knows she has to seriously hustle and prays to the Virgin Mary that there isn't a line at the dry cleaner. But even so, she can't help messing with Hollis. She scans the parking lot until she sees the strawberry-red Bronco. Tatum quickly glances behind her, then hurries over. The driver's-side window is open and there are the keys sitting in the console, just as Tatum knew they would be. Hollis leaves them right out in the open like a local, even though Hollis is a summer person now in every other way. Tatum grabs the keys and hides them under the driver's seat.

Five people are waiting in line at Holdgate's Island Laundry, and Amy, the manager, is nowhere to be found. Tatum checks her phone, sees it's 8:51. Tatum's boss, Irina, is a stickler; she fired a girl the week before last for showing up hungover. Tatum texts Irina: I'm at Holdgate's, there's a line, do you want me to come now or get the shirts?

Irina texts back: Get shirts. Then she writes: Cleaner opens at 8:30. You should have gone earlier.

Tatum's fingers hover over the screen. What she wants to say is *I quit.* What she does say is Sorry! Irina is young enough to be Tatum's child; she's only a year older than Dylan. She arrived on Nantucket from Lithuania in 2015 and went from cleaning houses herself to owning a cleaning-and-concierge company, the best on the island, called simply Irina Services. The company does more than just clean; staffers run errands like picking up dry cleaning, taking packages to UPS, provisioning (their clients don't deign to eat anything from the Stop and Shop—for them, it's Bartlett's or Nantucket Meat and Fish), filling the house with bouquets from Flowers on Chestnut, and even taking the family dogs to be groomed at Geronimo's. Irina has filled a niche; she has thirty-seven clients and a staff of sixteen, among whom Tatum is (a) the oldest by twenty years and (b) the only local. Irina gives Tatum the cushier jobs, like picking up the dry cleaning and buying supplies; the younger girls, Tatum knows, will be elbow-deep in the Albrights' toilets by the time she arrives. This is one reason Tatum doesn't quit; the other is the salary. After splitting gratuities with the other girls, Tatum is making something like fifty bucks an hour. It's a lot of money for a daytime job, though it's peanuts compared to what she made waiting tables. Tatum worked at the Lobster Trap for over twenty years, but she quit when Orion was born. She'd missed too many baths, stories, and bedtimes when Dylan was young—she didn't want to miss them with her grandson.

Amy appears from the back and the line moves faster. It's 8:54. The racks *clickety-clack* as they spin, Amy runs the credit card of a woman who must have sixty items hanging on the hook, bright party dresses from the looks of it, lots of Lilly Pulitzer. Normally, this would make Tatum roll her eyes—she wants to declare wearing Lilly Pulitzer to any Nantucket social function an official cliché—but today, Tatum's mind wanders to the weekend ahead. Hollis sent an itinerary (with a note that she would be paying for everything, thank God), and there was some dress-up stuff on the list—Saturday-night dinner at Nautilus, Sunday lunch at the Galley—along with "suggested colors" for each event. Saturday night: black or white. Sunday: orange or hot pink. Tatum would have rebelled against wearing the "suggested colors," but she has both black and white outfits as well as a cute orange Lilly Pulitzer shift dress hanging in her closet (she bought it on sale when Dylan was a baby, over twenty years ago, but it will still fit). Should Tatum wear it? It would be perfect for the lunch.

Should she be a cliché?

When Kyle asked why Tatum wanted to go to the girls' weekend, Tatum said, "I feel like I should. She lost her *husband,* Ky. Can you *imagine?*" Kyle's face darkened. Since the discovery of the lump, the bad mammogram, and the biopsy, both of them could only too easily imagine.

A more frivolous reason why Tatum is going to Hollis's little weekend is that she wants to live like a summer person for a couple of days. Tatum enjoys her summers. She loves the cottage roses and the hydrangeas; she swings by Sandbar to grab an ice cream cone at the end of her shift, then goes for a swim on the strip of public way between Cliffside and the Galley; she spends weekend afternoons with Kyle out at their secret beach, and once a week they get a sitter for Orion and go out for a nice dinner (this normally means Cru because Dylan works there and gets them 30 percent off the check). But Tatum knows there's a whole sparkling social life going on that she has no access to—benefits with pricey tickets, cocktail parties held in private gardens, dinners on the decks of yachts—and, although it's slightly embarrassing to admit this, she wants to be a part of it.

Standing in the line at Holdgate's, she feels a tap on her shoulder and hears, "Hey, sis."

Tatum turns around. It's Hollis.

Tatum blinks. What is Hollis doing *here?* Did she follow Tatum? Does she know that Tatum hid her keys? Tatum imagines Hollis searching frantically through the Bronco and nearly grins, but the

Hey, sis stops her. Hollis is using the old nickname as though no time has passed, as though they're still meeting up in the school hallway, Hollis straight from honors English, Tatum from phys ed.

But that's not fair. Every interaction of the past fifteen years—since Hollis moved back and built the huge house in Squam—has been awkward. Hollis is always overly dramatic, using a fake, high-pitched, singsongy voice—*Tatum McKenzie, you never age a day, how are things, how's Kyle, how's Dylan, show me pictures*—and Tatum stonewalls her, answering in monosyllables and ending the interaction as soon as she can. Because it feels lousy, bumping into a person who used to be as close as a sister, *closer* than a sister! (The girls Tatum and Hollis knew growing up all hated their sisters.) *Best friends* didn't begin to describe their relationship. They were each other's everything. Despite all the pains of growing up, Tatum never felt alone. She always, *always* had Hollis.

And then, one day, she didn't.

Tatum can't bring herself to echo *Hey, sis,* though she does say, "I'm sorry about Matthew." She shoves her phone in her back pocket and gives Hollis a real hug, squeezing her with both arms. Tatum had read Matthew's obituary in the *Nantucket Standard,* but she and Kyle opted not to attend the funeral in Wellesley. Now, of course, Tatum feels bad about that. She's been meaning to send a card but she isn't good with words like Hollis is, and she told herself that anything she sent would just get lost in the outpouring of love from Hollis's crazed social media followers.

This now seems like a terrible misjudgment. If Kyle died (Tatum shudders even thinking about it, she loves the man so much) and Hollis didn't acknowledge the loss in any way, Tatum would never forgive her. "And I'm sorry I didn't call or write or come to the service. I did absolutely nothing."

"But you're coming this weekend," Hollis says.

Tatum wipes at her eyes. She can run away from Hollis all she wants, but the fact remains that Hollis is the first person, other than her family, that Tatum ever loved.

"I'll be there." It's now Tatum's turn at the counter; she gives Amy the ticket, and a moment later, Amy hangs the pastel array of Mr. Albright's shirts on the hook.

"Are those *Kyle's?*" Hollis says. "I can't imagine him wearing pink...or peach."

Tatum checks her phone: 8:58. "These are for a client."

"Client?"

"I clean and run errands for..." She doesn't have time to catch Hollis up. "I have to go. I'll see you tomorrow."

"Everyone's getting in around four," Hollis says.

Four works, Tatum thinks. She finishes work at three, then she'll pick up Orion from day care and go home to pack. Or maybe she'll pack tonight, and tomorrow afternoon she'll treat herself to a blow-out at RJ Miller. "See you then." She leaves with a wave. She has approximately sixty seconds to make it to the Albrights' house.

She opens the back door of her elderly Honda Pilot, sweeps Cheez-It crumbs off Orion's booster seat, and carefully lays down Mr. Albright's shirts. She has to *go*—but she can't stop herself from heading back inside.

"Holly?" she says. "Who else is coming to this thing?"

Hollis smiles. "I didn't tell you?"

"No," Tatum says. She didn't ask because she didn't really care. Hollis's friends are all interchangeable—all wealthy, watching their weight, debating plastic surgery, trying to get their children into Ivy League schools.

Hollis folds the list she's still holding and reinforces the creases with her nails. "It's a thing called the Five-Star Weekend," she says. "So I invited one best friend from each phase of my life."

Each phase of her life? Tatum thinks. *What does that even mean?*

"My friend Brooke from Wellesley is coming. Dru-Ann is coming.

And the fourth is Gigi, a woman I met on my website. I've actually... never met her in real life, but she seems cool."

Tatum nods briskly. She realizes the hook is that Hollis has invited someone she's never even met to her house (who does that?), but Tatum's attention is snagged by the second name.

Dru-Ann. Ugh.

Tatum opens her mouth to say, *After your wedding, I hoped never to see Dru-Ann again.*

But at that moment, Hollis steps up to the counter and says to Amy, "I'm here to pick up shirts for Matthew Madden?"

The words are a bucket of cold water on Tatum's indignation. If Hollis can be brave enough to pick up her dead husband's dry cleaning, then Tatum can deal with Dru-Ann Jones for a weekend.

When she gets back in the car, her phone rings. The display says Nantucket Cottage Hospital.

Tatum flounders for a second. Should she answer it or not? *Yes!* she thinks. Then: *No, no*—she isn't prepared, and she doesn't have time. She hits Decline.

When she left the biopsy appointment the day before, the doctor said the results would be in "early next week," which Tatum assumed meant Monday or Tuesday. Today is only Thursday. Why are they calling so soon? Does she definitely have cancer? Or does she definitely not? An alert sounds—voice mail. Her phone is now radioactive; Tatum is afraid to touch it. She lights a cigarette and inhales deeply. She wants to call Kyle but he's got a big AC-install job at a new build out in Sconset where there's no cell service.

When Tatum pulls up in front of the Albrights' house at 9:02, Irina is waiting on the front porch. Irina is six feet tall with dyed yellow hair yanked into a ponytail; her upright posture—shoulders back, breasts thrust forward—reminds Tatum of an Olympic javelinist. Irina likes to go out on the town with a similarly built friend, Veda, who's brunette to Irina's "blond." The two of them wear full makeup and sharp perfumes, and there's nothing subtle about them or their mission—hunting rich men.

Tatum stubs out the cigarette and grabs the bags from the Stop and Shop and Mr. Albright's shirts, which slid off the back seat into the footwell because Tatum was driving like a bat out of hell. Tatum couldn't care less about Mr. Albright's shirts. Tatum has serious beef with Mr. Albright, to be honest.

Do I have cancer?

When Tatum was a senior in high school, her mother, Laura Leigh—one of the coolest, most beautiful women ever to grace the planet, in Tatum's opinion—was diagnosed with aggressive metastatic breast cancer (back then, the doctors didn't say much about stages, but Tatum figured that Laura Leigh had probably been at stage eleven). She underwent the kind of chemo that left her curled around the base of the toilet twenty-three hours a day—Tatum remembers the moaning, the dramatic weight loss, Laura Leigh's long cinnamon-colored hair falling out by the handful, leaving her as bald as a cue ball. She was dead nine weeks after the diagnosis; the line "You have six months to live" ended up being a pipe dream.

Tatum knows all about the BRCA gene, though she's never been tested because she and Kyle pay for their own health insurance, and besides, Tatum has always been the picture of health. Now, of course, she feels like she's run out of luck, that the Grim Reaper is lurking outside the door. Tatum thinks about her dark hair swirling around the shower drain, about nurses inserting IVs, about the chemo they call the Red Devil coursing through her bloodstream. She thinks about sweating, puking, shivering, about lying on the operating table like a roast on a platter, her very existence in the hands of a surgeon who is, like her, a mere mortal. She thinks about no longer having sensation in her breasts; she thinks about tattooed-on nipples; she thinks about being unable to lift a gallon of milk. There are plenty of scenarios where she'll have to quit her job and Kyle will have to take a leave of absence from his business because who else is going to take care of her? How are they going to afford all the trips back and forth to the hospital in Boston? For the past thirty years, she and Kyle have joked about winning ten million dollars in the lottery—they play Powerball every single week—but even without any windfalls, they've nearly paid off their house. Tatum is supposed to work only another two years, then she and Kyle are going to take some real vacations. Now she thinks about not being around to watch Orion grow up or see Dylan get married. She had a horrifying dream where she was dead and Irina came over to their house on Hooper Farm Road to clean out all of Tatum's things—and Irina ended up in bed with Kyle.

"Ridiculous!" Kyle cried when Tatum told him about the dream. "I will never sleep with Irina. I will never sleep with anyone else, baby. My life begins and ends with you. Why are we even having this conversation? You're going to be fine, you have to believe that."

But the dream haunts Tatum, and their client Mr. Albright is to blame. When Irina took on this account two summers ago, the first Mrs. Albright was dying of lymphoma, and Tatum and the other girls had to maneuver around the hospice workers. Meanwhile, Mr. Albright had already taken up with the woman who would become the second Mrs. Albright. He claimed this was with the first Mrs. Albright's blessing. She wanted him to be happy.

Tatum was absolutely verklempt. Mr. Albright didn't bring the girlfriend to the house, but he brought her to Nantucket—they stayed together in a suite at the Wauwinet. Appalling! Could he not just wait until his poor wife passed before he screwed somebody else?

Tatum wipes crumbs from the plastic bags covering the shirts. She's late; she didn't get to finish her cigarette; Irina radiates impatience. If Irina yells at her, Tatum is afraid she'll start to cry.

The best thing about Hollis's girls' weekend is that it's given

Tatum something else to think about. She'll have to dream up a little payback for Dru-Ann. That alone will make it worthwhile.

6. The Phantom

On Thursday morning, Dru-Ann Jones threads her Phantom through traffic on Lake Shore Drive, and, as usual, everyone around her changes lanes as if sensing that if they don't, she'll run them over. Dru-Ann loves this car—she'd debated getting a Ferrari for the wow factor, but the Phantom is so classy, it can't be argued with.

Dru-Ann's phone rings and a silken British voice announces, "Call from Marla Fitzsimmon."

Whaaaaaa? Dru-Ann thinks. Marla, Dru-Ann's cohost on *Throw Like a Girl,* is a Millennial and will talk on the phone only if she's calling 911.

"Accept," Dru-Ann says. Her tone is guarded when she says, "Hey, girl...what's up?"

"Did Zeke get ahold of you?" Marla asks.

Zeke is their producer. (Yes, it does rankle Dru-Ann that the producer of their woman-forward sports show is a man.)

Zeke has *not* gotten ahold of her. Dru-Ann tried calling him multiple times so she could explain what had happened with Posey, but she had been relegated to his voice mail. Is it concerning that, apparently, *Marla* has spoken to Zeke? Marla is the ingenue on the show, the baby talent. She's a former client of Dru-Ann's. She was a basketball star at Tennessee heading for a starting position with the Chicago Sky until she tore her ACL skiing. The injury ended Marla's basketball career, but did Dru-Ann give up on her? No! Zeke and the execs at ESPN had approached Dru-Ann about doing *Throw Like a Girl,* and she'd agreed to do it only as long as Marla could be her cohost.

"Why?" Dru-Ann says. "Is he angry about the Posey thing? Because for the record, that wasn't my fault."

Dru-Ann can hear Marla sucking on her vape. "Don't shoot the messenger," she says.

"He's not *canceling* the show, is he?"

"No," Marla says. "But he's replacing you until this thing blows over. Crabby Gabby is taking your spot."

"You have got to be joking," Dru-Ann says. The cars in front of her have stopped, which Dru-Ann belatedly notices. She slams on the brakes, and her coffee spills all over the console. "Please tell me he's not doing that."

"He is doing that."

"But it isn't that bad!" Dru-Ann says.

"It *is* that bad, though, Dru," Marla says. "I assume you haven't checked Twitter this morning?"

After Dru-Ann pulls into her parking spot in her office building's garage—is it her imagination or did the attendant give her a *look?*—she brings up Twitter on her phone and types her own name into the search bar.

#DruAnnJones

Trending

#cancelDruAnnJones

13.5k tweets in the last hour

#PrioritizeMentalHealth
11.2k tweets in the last hour
#TeamPosey
4.6k tweets in the last hour

Dru-Ann suddenly feels like her ass is fusing with the buttery leather of her car seat. She can't move, and yet apparently her hands are on a different circuit, because they begin to shake. She holds a trembling finger over the screen. Should she read what people are saying? She has dealt with clients who were in this situation, most notably Tania Oaks, an Olympic champion equestrienne who was caught on video—on her way home from the Games, *with the gold medal around her neck*—calling the flight attendant a "basic bitch." That video went viral. Dru-Ann had helped Tania handle the ensuing media frenzy by taking away her phone so she didn't make things worse.

Follow your own counsel, Dru-Ann tells herself. *Don't look.*

But this is different. This is me. And I wasn't wrong. The people who are #TeamPosey don't know the details. If they did, they would be #TeamDruAnn!

Dru-Ann wishes she could explain what actually happened.

It's Friday evening. Dru-Ann, her client Posey Wofford, and Posey's father, Nick Wofford—who is Dru-Ann's boyfriend and maybe the long-awaited love of her life—are at a restaurant called Whine, which isn't far from the country club in Midland, Michigan. The three of them are celebrating the fact that Posey leads by four strokes in the Dow Great Lakes Bay Invitational going into the final round.

They order cocktails—Dru-Ann a Casamigos over ice, Nick a martini, Posey a Pellegrino with a splash of cran. Dru-Ann peruses the menu; the Yelp reviews of this place were decent. Their drinks arrive and they raise their glasses.

Posey says, "I can't stay for dinner. I have a Lyft coming in twenty minutes to take me to Detroit. I'm flying to Edinburgh tonight."

Nick laughs. Dru-Ann is tempted to join in but she senses that Posey might not be kidding. Dru-Ann takes a measured sip of tequila and waits.

"Phineas just found out he made the open," Posey says. "And as you know, they're playing the Old Lady this year. He had a dream he was going to win. I have to be there."

Dru-Ann looks at Nick; his reaction can best be described as *At a loss for words.* But Nick won't tell his daughter no. Nick never tells her no. That job always falls to Dru-Ann. This is how she earns her money: by saving her clients from themselves.

"No," Dru-Ann says.

"Yes," Posey says, flicking her ponytail off her shoulder with defiance. "It's the *British Open.* At *St. Andrews.*"

Dru-Ann takes another sip of tequila and considers her next move. She can't downplay the prestige or mystique of the British Open. The tournament, when it's played at the "R and A," the Royal and Ancient Golf Club of St. Andrews, is Dru-Ann's secret favorite. (It has to be secret because how can she, as a Black woman, revere a club with "ancient" membership rules? They didn't allow women to join until September of 2014 and they still don't let women change inside the main clubhouse.) Phineas is presently ranked number 127 in the world. Dru-Ann can't believe he's playing in the open at all; this is very big news.

Neither can Dru-Ann diminish Posey and Phineas's relationship. They've been together since their first week at IMG. They've withstood the challenges of a long-distance relationship and the pressures of tournament life—qualifying, rankings, a brutal travel schedule. Someday, Dru-Ann knows, they'll get married and Posey will give birth to Dru-Ann's next generation of clients.

Dru-Ann's best strategy is to focus on Posey herself. "You're in the lead by four strokes," she says. "You've been owning the course. Bella is in her head; she won't beat you and she's your only real competition. You're going to win this tournament, Posey."

Posey smiles at Dru-Ann. "I don't care."

"You don't care about winning a tournament on the LPGA tour?" Dru-Ann says. "Isn't this what you've been dreaming about since Q-school?"

Posey shrugs. "It's the Dow. We're in central Michigan. It's not"—she pauses—"the same thing."

Nick stares at the round surface of his martini like he's considering doing a cannonball into it. Dru-Ann kicks him under the table but he pretends not to notice. Can she love a man who has a blind spot the exact size and shape of his youngest child?

"How are you going to explain this to your sponsors?" Dru-Ann asks. "Ping? Lululemon golf? They *invested* in you."

"I'm going to tell them it's a mental-health issue," Posey says. "Obviously."

"A mental-*health* issue?" Dru-Ann knows her voice is loud enough to draw the attention of guests at surrounding tables, but she doesn't care. "Are you *kidding* me right now? You can't just trot out that excuse at will, Posey. It cheapens the suffering of athletes who have legitimate mental-health issues, like Biles and Osaka and the countless women we don't even know about."

"What I'm telling you is that I won't be able to focus tomorrow. If you and Dad insist on making me stay to play the final round, I'll be distracted thinking about Phineas. I'll regret not going. I'll wish I were there."

"Right, sure," Dru-Ann says, reining her emotions in. *Here,* she thinks, *is a teachable moment.* "But being distracted and wishing you were somewhere else isn't a mental-health issue. Mentally healthy people feel this way all the time, Posey. Like when the Drake concert is the same night as a can't-miss client dinner." She searches

Posey's face for a sign of understanding. Did that example land? "You can easily play eighteen holes tomorrow and then go."

Posey checks her phone and stands up. "My Lyft is twelve minutes away. I'm going to the hotel to get my bags." She looks at Nick. "You'll take my clubs back to Chicago?"

"Posey," Nick says in a tone that is part admonishing, part disappointed. But nothing follows. When Posey bends over to kiss her father's forehead, he closes his eyes in defeat. "Wish Phineas good luck from us."

Dru-Ann can't believe this. Nick is as soft as a shoe full of shit.

Posey leaves Whine without so much as another look at Dru-Ann—*Coward!*—which prompts Dru-Ann to call after her, "Quitter!"

This, she assumes, is what motivates some nosy ass-clown at a neighboring table to whip out his phone and start filming. He captures Dru-Ann's unfiltered rage as she rails at Nick. "I can't believe you didn't stand up to her. She's leaving, Nick. She's flying to Scotland. She's going to tell everyone it's a 'mental-health issue'"—Dru-Ann uses air quotes—"when she needs to *suck it up and play through!*"

Now Dru-Ann watches herself shriek these words in a trim sound bite on three different Twitter accounts, including one that belongs to some dude with a million-billion followers whose only job appears to be posting on Twitter.

Dru-Ann clicks out of the app and storms upstairs, where her partners—all of whom are fed up with dealing with the whims of their entitled clients—will be waiting to talk her off the ledge.

But the offices of the J. B. Channing Agency are oddly subdued. Usually at this hour, everyone is gathered in the common area in front of the 105-inch television, watching *SportsCenter*. But today, the television is off. Dru-Ann blinks. Has she ever seen the television off? There's always a sporting event happening somewhere in the world—cricket, soccer, rugby, polo, Australian-rules football—and chances are, a J. B. Channing client is participating. The blank screen is so unusual that Dru-Ann suspects a power outage—but all the lights are on.

Dru-Ann approaches her corner office with a sense of impending doom. All the office doors are *closed.* This never happens. The men Dru-Ann works with love to showboat the very important conversations they're having—with Federer, with Davante Adams, with the PR people at Emirates airlines who want to feature Dwayne Wade in their new ad campaign.

Dru-Ann's assistant, Jayquan, has her espresso waiting as usual, so apparently the apocalypse hasn't arrived. Dru-Ann accepts the cup gratefully and Jayquan winces. "JB is in your office."

Scratch that—the apocalypse *has* arrived.

J. B. Channing is a force in the world of sports. He founded this agency; he's a five-time winner of Chicago's Businessperson of the Year, and he's perennially on the *Ebony* Power 100 list. Last year he appeared in *People* magazine's Most Beautiful People issue; he dates actresses, and for a few months, he was sleeping with the most successful pop star on the planet. He has very famous friends. (Behind his desk is a photograph of him with Jimmy Kimmel, Jason Bateman, and Chris Rock; they were out together at the Green Door.) JB is not only Dru-Ann's boss, he's her champion. Like Dru-Ann, he graduated from North Carolina and then the Kellogg School at Northwestern. He hired Dru-Ann because they share two alma maters and because she has the best nose for talent that he's ever seen. Dru-Ann is a fierce advocate for other women of color; she doesn't tolerate nonsense, and she speaks her mind. She thinks only two things are more important than natural ability in an athlete: hard work and discipline.

JB has made it clear that he loves these things about her.

But not today.

He doesn't even bother with a greeting. "The video is everywhere and, unfortunately for us, it's a slow news day in the sports world." He sighs and runs a hand over his shaved head. "There are very few hard noes in our business, Dru-Ann. But you can't mess with mental health."

"Right, I know. Except—"

"No exceptions. You were at the retreat with the rest of us."

Yes, Dru-Ann was at the mental-fitness retreat at the American Club in Kohler, Wisconsin, which JB organized after a wide receiver from Baylor—a kid who had been drafted by the 49ers—committed suicide.

"I was *defending* mental health," Dru-Ann says. "Posey whipped it out because it was *convenient.*"

"You've lost four clients already this morning," JB says. "Tamika, Winnie, Nyla, and Linzy. More are sure to follow. I'm placing you on a leave of absence until this blows over, and Jim and his team are drafting your apology statement right now. We want to get it out as quickly as possible."

"I'm not issuing an apology," Dru-Ann says, "because I wasn't wrong. Posey Wofford is mentally healthy. She's using it as an *excuse,* JB."

"You'll issue an apology," JB says, "or I'll be forced to take the next steps."

"And do what, fire me?"

"Obviously I'm not going to fire you, Dru-Ann," JB says.

"Then defend me, please." Dru-Ann gazes out the window at the skyline of Chicago, then turns on her stilettos. He wants a leave of absence from her, she'll give him one.

"We'll be in touch about the statement!" JB calls after her.

* * *

Dru-Ann retraces her steps to the womblike comfort of the Phantom and peels out of the garage (the attendant *is* dishing her attitude!). Like an automaton, she pulls onto Lake Shore Drive and heads north, which feels so *wrong,* so *backward.* She owns a beautiful brownstone in Lincoln Park but she doesn't want to hang out there during the day.

Her phone rings and the posh British voice says, "Nicholas Wofford," making it sound like Nick has appeared on the doorstep in a tuxedo with an armful of calla lilies.

"Accept." Dru-Ann doesn't really want to talk to Nick—this whole thing happened because of his terrible handling (and, let's just say it, *parenting*) of Posey—but the sad fact is that Dru-Ann has fallen in love with him, and also, she's low on friends. "Hey," she says. "Are you at the office? Can we grab coffee?"

A silence follows, then Nick clears his throat and Dru-Ann thinks, *Oh, dear God, no. Not you too.*

"I think we should hit the brakes," Nick says. "And not see each other for a little—"

Dru-Ann ends the call and screams into the rarefied air of her car's interior. Is it possible that absolutely everyone in her life has abandoned her? A text comes in and Dru-Ann assumes it's Nick offering some feeble, patronizing words, but when Dru-Ann checks the display, she sees it's from Hollis. Colors for our outings this weekend, it says. Dinner Saturday: black or white. Lunch Sunday: orange or hot pink.

That's right, Dru-Ann thinks. *Nantucket.* She had intended to cancel. She's pretty sure Hollis was *expecting* her to cancel—not for mental-health reasons but because Dru-Ann just plain old-fashioned hates the idea of any kind of girls' weekend, especially one where they're all wearing the same damn colors in public.

But Dru-Ann is so relieved that there's a place she's actually welcome that she calls Jayquan and asks him to book her a first-class ticket to Nantucket for the morning.

"Am I using the corporate card for this?" Jayquan asks.

Dru-Ann is tempted to say yes just to piss off JB, but the last thing she needs is an inquiry from Accounting. "Personal card, please," she says. "And arrange for a car service on the other side to take me to a place called Squam Road. Put my e-mail on OOO until further notice."

When Dru-Ann hangs up, she feels a tiny bit better. She'll pull her hot-pink Stella McCartney bodycon out of the back of her overflowing closet; she will slurp the oysters and dance on Hollis's deck in the moonlight.

She will *slay* the girls' weekend. She will be the MVP.

Nantucket, she thinks, *here I come.*

7. Poet's Corner

It's a Thursday afternoon in the Poet's Corner neighborhood of Wellesley, and Brooke Kirtley is cropping and editing a photo of herself to post on Facebook.

Take that, world! she thinks.

In the picture, she's wearing a white eyelet LoveShackFancy dress and a straw hat, sitting on the wide, white expanse of her pencil-post bed with the Serena and Lily basket chandelier hanging over her head and her impeccably packed suitcase open next to her. She holds her arms over her head in a *V* for *vacation.* She's *beaming.* She posts the photo with the caption Packed and ready for a girls' weekend on Nantucket! Brooke decides against tagging Hollis because she doesn't want to name-drop—she was friends with Hollis long before she became Hungry with Hollis. Brooke studies the picture, zooming in on her face (she used a smoothing, illuminating filter, obviously) and then her arms (do they look stringy?), then checks for any stains on the duvet cover (that would be mortifying). Brooke has long wanted to show her Facebook friends a photo of her and Charlie's bedroom. (She did the decorating herself.) She wonders if she should tag Serena and Lily. They might want to use this photo for promotional purposes—the linens, the scalloped green-linen headboard, and the bone-inlay table lamps in addition to the iconic chandelier. As Brooke is researching how to tag a brand, her phone makes a noise like a raindrop hitting a puddle. She has a comment on her post—already!

It's from Electra Undergrove.

Well, well, Brooke thinks.

Brooke and Electra are still Facebook friends—whenever Brooke considers posting something, she wonders, *Will Electra see this? What will Electra think?*—even though they no longer speak in real life. Brooke suspects that Electra is too busy or has too many other friends (basically all of Wellesley) to realize that she and Brooke are still connected in this way.

The comment says, I'll be on Nantucket too. Let's grab a drink at Slip 14.

Brooke blinks. Is this some kind of prank? She very carefully clicks on Electra's profile picture—Electra, Simon, and the kids in the front row at a Kenny Chesney concert—wondering if the comment really came from Electra or from some bot that goes around terrorizing insecure middle-aged women on Facebook. There are pictures of the whole gang at Electra's house for rock and roll football, then just the moms—Electra, Liesl, Rhonda, and Bets—sitting in the grass at Sprague Fields, then another picture of just the moms in what appears to be Cinque Terre.

They went to Italy *together?* Brooke thinks.

She feels a longing so intense it makes her nauseated. But it's okay, she tells herself. She reads the comment again: I'll be on Nantucket too. Let's grab a drink at Slip 14.

Yes!!!! Brooke types. Def!!! Do you still have my cell? It's . . .

But as Brooke is typing her number, she makes a complete 180 and deletes her comment altogether. Electra hasn't spoken to Brooke since *that* Sunday five years earlier. *Fart off, Electra,* Brooke thinks. But she's feeling a tad smug. After all this time, it's Electra who reached out—and with a specific invitation. She didn't just say, *Let's meet for a drink;* she picked a place, Slip 14. However, even seeing Electra's name is a trigger. Brooke remembers all the times after *that* Sunday that she drove past Electra's house, checking the cars out front to see who had been invited over instead of her and Charlie.

Brooke types: I'm not sure I'll have time. Sorry! But that sounds catty, and Brooke promised herself that she would never sink to Electra's level. Electra ignores Brooke every time she sees her in line at Quebrada, and Electra iced her out at the Wellesley–Needham football game on Thanksgiving morning. Electra, Liesl, Rhonda, and Bets were in the stands, and when Brooke waved, they huddled together, laughed, then knocked back the traditional nips of Fireball.

Brooke decides not to respond to Electra at all. She heard on one of her self-help podcasts that when you're not sure what to say, you should say nothing.

And it's true; Brooke feels powerful withholding a response.

She sits for a few moments, watching the Likes accrue. Brooke's mother, Doris, comments, Ooooh, I'm jealous! Childishly, Brooke wants to delete this. How mortifying that her seventy-seven-year-old mother is her Facebook friend. But then Milly Soper responds to her mother's comment with Me too!, so Brooke has to leave it be.

There's a knock on the front door, which is so unexpected that Brooke jumps to her feet. She throws off the straw hat and wants to change her clothes as well—this is her dress for Saturday night's dinner out—but then there's a second knock, more insistent. Definitely a man, Brooke thinks. Maybe the Mormons or Jehovah's Witnesses? The Terminix guy? Someone running for office? A salesman of some sort? None of these possibilities makes Brooke want to answer the door, but she's propelled forth by curiosity.

She finds a broad, balding man wearing a dun-colored uniform with a shiny badge. Police? Brooke sways on her feet, thinking something has happened to her son, Will (who is interning at Fidelity this summer), or her daughter, Whitney (who's driving one of the Boston duck boats, the perfect job for a theater major). Or maybe something has happened to Charlie (though this does not inspire the same kind of unadulterated panic).

"Yes?" she says. She sees an official vehicle, still running, in the driveway. The door says NORFOLK COUNTY SHERIFF DEPT.

"Is Charlie Kirtley home?" the man asks.

"No," Brooke says. "He's at work."

"Where does he work?" the man asks.

Brooke spies a piece of paper in the man's hand and she realizes what's happening. This man is serving Charlie.

Charlie is being sued. Again.

At a quarter to five, Charlie walks in the door, and by this time, Brooke has consumed three Tito's and sodas and six salted almonds. She's a bit surprised he's home so early. On Thursdays and Fridays after work, Charlie and his toxic male colleagues from Landover (which Charlie obnoxiously refers to as the "Land Rover of CPAs") go for drinks at Abe and Louie's.

The twins, thankfully, have plans this evening: Will is, as usual, going to the gym, and Whitney has a Bumble date at Row 34. Brooke knows this because she'd lobbied for a family dinner tonight before she went away. Whitney accused her of being melodramatic ("It's only three nights and you're not even leaving the state").

"There's my angel," Charlie says when he walks into the kitchen. He pulls Brooke up to her feet and kisses her sloppily on the mouth. (Charlie kisses like a boa constrictor—Brooke always feels like he's trying to swallow her whole.)

"Did the sheriff's department find you?" she asks.

Charlie pulls Brooke even closer. His body shakes, and he emits the high-pitched noise that accompanies his crying. It's a pathetic sound, but Brooke doesn't feel sorry for him. His actions are deplorable. Every bit of the pain he's experienced as an adult he brought on himself.

"Who was it this time?" Brooke had asked the sheriff's deputy to give her the summons, but he refused.

Charlie takes a deep, shuddering breath. "Irish, from the office."

Irish Fahey, Landover's new brand manager. Charlie has talked about her—the flame-red hair, the freckles, the first name that starts conversations. He refers to her as the "new kid" because she's just out of college.

"What did you do?"

"She blew it completely out of proportion—"

"Charlie."

"I grabbed her from behind. I was just kidding around. I thought she was cool."

Brooke pushes Charlie away, although he's so solid, he doesn't move much. She looks down at *Still Life on Kitchen Island*—her glass with an inch of watery vodka and a raggedy lime wedge, the sweating bottle of Tito's that had been so seductively frosted when she pulled it from the freezer, the can of almonds that she meted out so parsimoniously. She thinks of Irish Fahey, violated. *Grabbed her from behind* means Charlie fondled her tits and rubbed his crotch against her ass. Brooke is *glad* Irish filed charges. Irish's lawyer will learn that Charlie has a history of this behavior. He groped a server named Lola at the Oak Room, which was where Charlie and his disgusting buddies *used* to drink. Charlie's attorney had worked out a private settlement with Lola's attorney—a hefty five-figure sum—and Brooke told Charlie that if he ever did it again, she would leave him.

But leaving Charlie right now isn't a realistic option. Brooke's mother lives in a one-bedroom condo in Boca Raton, so Brooke could never go there, and then there's the matter of the kids, who are happy in their jobs and their comfortable home-for-the-summer-from-their-expensive-private-colleges suburban lives.

Even so, Brooke says, "I'm finished, Charlie. I'm done."

Charlie howls. "You can't give up on me!" he says. "I'll have nothing left. I got fired today."

Fired? Brooke thinks. Despite his reprehensible behavior, Charlie has always been a professional success. He's wildly popular with his clients because he's liberal with deductions and has masterful knowledge of every corporate tax loophole. And he's a favorite among his coworkers, all of them former fraternity boys; there's a Pike contingency (which Charlie is part of) and a TKE group. They've created a clubby, locker-room atmosphere in their office. Landover is all fantasy football, Friday Beers, Barstool Sports, and Pornhub, guys' trips to Vegas and the Kentucky Derby, men complaining about wives who don't put out and kids who treat them like ATMs. During high tax season—from February to April—they pull all-nighters with the Bon Me food truck stationed outside, cases of Red Bull, prescriptions for Adderall, and masseuses from the Happy Orchid.

Brooke has a hard time believing that the bros Charlie works with were morally outraged enough to fire him. Irish probably threatened to take the whole company down, and Charlie was sacrificed. Brooke imagines Charlie's coworkers apologizing on his behalf, saying he "definitely crossed a line," then privately whispering that Irish did him dirty.

Brooke resists the urge to swill directly from the bottle of Tito's and dump the almonds over Charlie's head (she would have to clean them up). She marches down the hall, Charlie following behind, to their bedroom, which is always its most delightful at this hour, suffused with the late-afternoon sunlight. Everything looks gilded—but that's just the surface of things.

Brooke points to her suitcase. "I've already packed."

Charlie throws himself facedown on the bed the way Whitney used to when she was an adolescent in the throes of a tantrum. Brooke feels sorry for the kids, and for Whitney especially. She will soon learn that her father groped a female colleague who's only a couple years older than Whitney herself. And what kind of ghastly example is Charlie setting for Will?

As Charlie sobs, his strong back rising and falling, Brooke looks at him and feels...nothing. Even anger eludes her, although she sees clearly now that the reason they no longer have any friends isn't Brooke's social awkwardness (which is what Charlie has led her to believe) but Charlie himself.

Brooke takes her suitcase and her hatbox and decamps to the guest bedroom, where she will remain until she drives to the ferry the next day.

She checks her phone. Her post has fifty Likes and sixteen comments. It's her most popular post ever. Brooke wipes a tear from her cheek.

8. The Third Margarita

There's a domestic dispute in coach that delays the takeoff from Cancun. Kristen, the flight attendant in first class, pokes her head into the cockpit and tells Gigi, "This happens all the time. People always think the third margarita is a good idea, and they're always wrong."

"What's going on?" Gigi asks.

"The marshal is escorting them off."

Gigi twists in her seat and sees a cross-looking (and *very* sunburned) couple being shepherded down the aisle. *This is your captain speaking,* Gigi thinks. *Bye-bye.* She never had anything like this happen on her Atlanta-to-Rome or Atlanta-to-Madrid routes. But after Matthew died, Gigi gave those routes up. It was just too painful to land at FCO or MAD and not find Matthew waiting for her.

So now here she is—wasting away in Margaritaville.

She doesn't get back to her home in Buckhead until nearly nine o'clock. Melba greets her at the door with an angry meow, and Gigi scoops her up and peppers her face with kisses. There's a note on the kitchen table: *We're making paella tonight, come over!*

All Gigi wants to do is have a glass of wine and go to sleep, but Tim and Santi did cat-sit, and paella does sound good. She drops Melba to the floor and heads down the street.

* * *

It turns out, paella comes at a much higher price than the six-pack of Mexican Coca-Cola she brought Tim and Santi as a thank-you gift. They want to talk about tomorrow's trip. Oh, do they.

"I can't believe you're going," Tim says as he scoops a huge serving of fragrant saffron rice with shrimp, mussels, and sausage onto Gigi's plate. "Girl, what are you thinking?"

"Hollis knows about you," Santi says. "I mean, come *on,* Geej. Out of two million followers, she picks you? She definitely knows."

"That's what I thought too," Gigi says. "I figured Matthew left some kind of incriminating evidence behind and Hollis wanted to, you know, *hash it out.* But I think she's inviting me in earnest. She... *likes* me, and I like her too."

"I have a theory," Santi says. "I think texting with Matthew's wife is your way of hanging on to him."

Gigi blinks rapidly. This whole thing is so confusing. "I want to meet her in person," she says. "I want to hear her talk about him, I want to get a sense of what their marriage was like. He told me only certain things, and I'm not sure if any of it was true."

"He lied to you for *how* long about not being married?" Tim says.

"Seven months," Gigi says—which, as it turns out, was long enough to fall in love. When Matthew finally did come clean about being married—and not only married, but married to *Hollis Shaw*—Gigi hadn't been able to break things off. She'd tried and failed. She cared too much about him.

Gigi meets Dr. Matthew Madden in the Delta lounge during a rogue hailstorm at Hartsfield. Gigi is supposed to fly to Buenos Aires for vacation and Matthew is "heading home" to Boston. Gigi asks the bartender to change the channel on the TV; she wants to watch college football.

Matthew turns to her. "I wouldn't have picked you for a football fan," he says. "With your British accent."

"I'm Bulldogs all the way," Gigi says with a wink.

"Ah, lucky you. I root for UNC, which is only satisfying during basketball season," Matthew says.

"Did you go there?" Gigi asks.

"My ex-wife did," Matthew says without so much as a blink. "One of the habits I can't seem to shake now that we're apart is cheering for the Tar Heels. What about you? Did you go to Georgia?"

"For two years," Gigi says. "Then I transferred to Embry-Riddle. I'm a pilot for Delta, though I'm here tonight because I'm supposed to be flying to Buenos Aires for a little Malbec and tango."

From that point on, they're off to the races, asking each other questions, seeing if they have anything in common other than a love of college sports. Why, yes—they both like classical music as well as Dave Matthews, they both travel all the time, they're both addicted to their work. When their flights are canceled, they decide to order a bottle of champagne. That's when the flirting starts, subtle at first, then more overt. Gigi is no stranger to airport romances—it comes with the job—so when Matthew says he's booking a room at the Marriott Gateway there at the airport, Gigi says she'll get a room as well rather than drive home after she's been drinking. When they approach the hotel desk, they're holding hands, and the idea of two rooms is absurd. Matthew doesn't call anyone, doesn't text, doesn't disappear into the bathroom for a suspicious amount of time. He wears no ring, and there's no mark suggesting he's worn a ring recently.

The following May, when Gigi and Matthew are spending a romantic weekend in Santorini, Matthew tells her he won't see her much over the summer because he'll be on Nantucket with his family.

Gigi looks out the white arched window of their hotel room

in Oia at the sparkling blue Mediterranean and thinks, *Something is up.*

"You mean your daughter?" Gigi says. Matthew has told her about his twenty-year-old, Caroline, who goes to school in New York.

"Yes," Matthew says. "And my wife." Matthew, who is the definition of low drama, pauses dramatically. "Gigi, I'm married."

It's cute of him to tell her when they're on a Greek island and Gigi can't leave. Well, scratch that, she *can* leave, and she threatens to, of course—*How could you, you're a liar, from the minute I met you, you lied, what is* wrong *with you?* But in the end, she lets him comfort her with what are certainly more lies or, at best, half-truths: *Hollis and I have separate lives, we lost that loving feeling a couple years ago, I stay in the house because I want to avoid the mess of a divorce, plus Caroline. Please, Gigi, please understand just how happy you make me. You make me so damn happy.*

He doesn't say *I love you* and that is, perhaps, why she stays. She becomes determined in that moment to make him fall in love with her.

Remaining in a relationship with Matthew while he is married isn't a strong moral choice; this she knows. She tries to rationalize it: She's not the one who's cheating, Matthew is. But when Gigi finds out later that night—once she's processed her fury and is able to ask questions like *What is your wife's name?*—that Matthew is married to Hollis Shaw, Gigi thinks, *You have got to be kidding me.* The flight attendants whom Gigi works with chatter about Hollis Shaw nonstop. They love her recipes, they love her blouses, they love her Serbian sheepdog, they love her preppy-boho vibe. She's a greatest hits of American womanhood and they just *love her so much!* Up until this moment, Gigi has had only a polite, passing interest in Hollis Shaw. *I'll have to check her out.* Now that Gigi and Hollis are…*connected,* Gigi frequently visits the website and sets out to make Hollis notice her.

How will Gigi attract Hollis's attention when she's one of millions? Well, she has inside information. Matthew tells her that Hollis lost her mother when she was a baby—and as it happens, Gigi's mother died when she was only twelve. Gigi gets on the Corkboard and messages Hollis that she's grateful for the cooking demos because my own mum passed away before she could teach me her favorite Cantonese dishes. Hollis writes back immediately: I'm self-taught, my mother died when I was very young. Gigi is in! She responds to Hollis's other posts in the most intelligent and interesting way possible. So many of the other comments are fawning, nearly obsequious: You're my queen, Hollis! Or quotidian, like Yum! Looks delicious (sometimes shortened to delish). Or they ask irritating questions about measurements and substitutions. Gigi notices that Hollis is replying to her comments more and more frequently, and soon they're private messaging about restaurants and books and their favorite shows and podcasts. It turns out they have a lot in common.

Gigi digs into her paella. Tim and Santi are the only people she's confided in about her relationship with Matthew. (If Gigi had broken down and told the flight attendants, it would have been all over the company in twenty-four hours.) They comforted her when she found out—from the post on Hollis's website—that Matthew was dead. But there's a situation they don't know about and she isn't about to tell them tonight.

"I know it's crazy that I'm going," Gigi says. Not only has Gigi befriended her dead lover's wife, she has become the wife's confidante, and the wife *has invited her to a girls' weekend*. "But I have to meet her."

"For closure?" Tim asks.

Gigi isn't sure she believes in closure. "For something," she says. "Besides, it's Nantucket."

Santi raises his wineglass. "To Nantucket," he says. "May you make it back in one piece."

9. The Itinerary

Friday

4:00 p.m. to 6:00 p.m.: Arrivals

6:00 p.m. to 7:00 p.m.: Cocktail hour/hors d'oeuvres

7:00 p.m.: Dinner on the deck

Saturday

8:00 a.m.: Yoga by the pool/continental breakfast

10:00 a.m. to noon: Shopping in town

Noon to 5:00 p.m.: Beach, lunch, pool

5:00 p.m. to 7:00 p.m.: Get ready for dinner; cocktails and snacks

7:30 p.m.: Dinner at Nautilus (suggested colors: black and/or white)

10:00 p.m.: Maxxtone at the Chicken Box!

Sunday

Free morning, continental breakfast

Noon: Lunch at Galley Beach (suggested colors: hot pink or orange)

2:00 p.m.: Sail aboard *Endeavor*

7:00 p.m.: Pizza party

8:30 p.m.: Ice cream truck and fireworks on the beach

Monday

Departures

Hollis sends her newsletter subscribers an e-mail that includes the weekend's itinerary—and oh, do they have opinions. A weekend studded with shopping, sailing, dancing to live music, and incredible meals at Hollis's beautiful beach home and elsewhere?

Yes, please!

They yearn for more details. The Corkboard messages flood in: Please post menu for "dinner on the deck"! How did you manage to get a reservation at Nautilus? Which hors d'oeuvres will you serve? What will the continental breakfast include? Will there be vegan options? Is the pizza at the pizza party takeout or homemade (I'm guessing homemade!)? Will you post recipes, recipes, recipes?

The free spirits among them feel the weekend is too scheduled. They picture Hollis shepherding her friends from one event to the next, tapping on bedroom doors, hurrying the other four stars along if they're running late for the cocktail hour. Why not just let the weekend unfold organically without so many places they have to be?

A virtual skirmish breaks out over the "suggested colors." Aileen Blankenship of Dubuque, Iowa, thinks it's juvenile and silly. Why do grown women have to match?

But Molly Beardsley of Twain Harte, California, says: What's wrong with a little fun? Besides, the pictures will look so much better.

It's a grab for attention, Aileen says. Hollis will inadvertently turn her friends into a circus sideshow.

Circus sideshow seems a bit mean-spirited, some of Hollis's followers think, but then Bailey Ruckert of Baton Rouge, Louisiana, chimes in with a deeper concern. This is a pretty jolly itinerary for a woman who just lost her husband. It feels like dancing on his grave.

Womp-womp-womp. The comments grind to a halt as Hollis's fans consider this point. Hollis lost her husband in December, seven months ago. There are some people who question the curated aspects of the weekend, including but not limited to the frivolity of matching colors. Others can't imagine Hollis hosting a weekend that *isn't* curated; delicious food and gracious surroundings define Hollis Shaw's brand. But hasn't the death of her husband changed her? Hasn't she stopped being so concerned about appearances?

Bailey Ruckert presses her point. I just think there should be time built in for introspection, she says. For honoring the deceased.

Molly Beardsley disagrees. Hollis is circling her wagons. She's gathering the best friends she's ever had as a way of celebrating life. If we criticize her for making delicious food and treating her friends to meals at fancy restaurants, aren't we the ones too focused on appearances? I'm sure there will be a lot of meaningful moments that we'll never know about, nor should we. I'm prepared to die on this hill; Hollis has been through a tragedy and she should be free to throw exactly the kind of weekend she wants without being judged by us.

Bailey writes: She should wait a year. Let some time pass.

Molly comments: Are you kidding me right now? Who made you the grief police?

Bailey doesn't respond.

A woman from Tallahassee, Paige Sweezey, posts this: My best friend from my Florida State days, Moira Sullivan, invented the Five-Star Weekend!!! She invited us all to Destin six months after her husband died, and it lifted her right out of her funk. It was life-affirming not only for Moira but for all of us. Paige adds the link to the Motherlode article about Moira Sullivan's weekend in Destin.

It does seem that Moira Sullivan originated the idea of the Five-Star Weekend. Hollis must have read the article and adapted it for her own purposes. Some of her followers think Hollis should come clean about this and give credit where credit is due. (Paige muses that Moira ought to have copyrighted the idea, but how would that work, exactly?)

The wonderful thing about the Hungry with Hollis website, they all agree, is that every thoughtful, carefully considered opinion is valid.

Hollis leaves a message on the Corkboard a short while later. It's pretty clear she hasn't read any of the comments, or if she has, she's chosen not to engage.

It says: Because I want to give Tatum, Dru-Ann, Brooke, and Gigi my undivided attention, I won't be posting until the weekend is over. I'll provide a full recap next week—and yes, I'll post recipes.

A collective gasp rises from the ether. *Gigi?* Did Hollis invite Gigi Ling, a frequent visitor on the website, to her Five-Star Weekend? Gigi Ling is *always* commenting on Hollis's posts, and (they can't help noticing) Hollis responds as though she finds Gigi the most fascinating creature on earth. They can only presume that Hollis *did* invite Gigi.

Now they're all a little jealous.

Still, it seems risky, doesn't it, inviting someone you met through a website to a weekend like this. How will that go?

They can't wait to find out.

10. Night Changes I

Caroline paces in front of Nantucket Memorial Airport. Her mother is late.

What the actual F? Caroline rose with the pigeons and got her ass to JFK with all of Isaac's bulky filming equipment, and now she's rotting on the curb while everyone else on her flight gets a Lyft or a taxi. Caroline texts her mother: I'm here. Where r u?

There's no response.

One cab—Roger's—idles unclaimed. Caroline *could* hop in and be in Squam in ten minutes, but she refuses to do that on principle. Her mother was so set on having Caroline come, she should be here. She should have been here *early.* Hollis is probably too busy peeling cucumbers for the spa water or folding the ends of the toilet paper into nifty points to come pick up her own child.

The next thought comes to her unbidden: Her *father* would have been here on time. He would have been in the Bronco with the top down, wearing his Hootie and the Blowfish T-shirt, and he'd have a latte and a morning bun from Wicked Island Bakery for her, and Henrietta would be lounging across the back seat. He'd jump out of the car, give Caroline a bear hug, and help her with her bags. Then they'd drive to Nobadeer Beach, where Caroline could enjoy her coffee and pull apart the flaky layers of the cinnamon roll as they watched the surfers.

Caroline's eyes sting with tears. She hadn't anticipated how coming to Nantucket would make her experience the loss of her father all over again.

Because Caroline's mother has a long, complex history with the island, which she seems to want to both embrace and deny, Caroline and Matthew had to create their own Nantucket traditions. Matthew liked to spend the Fourth of July on Coatue, where they would grill clams on the hibachi and watch the fireworks set off across the harbor at Jetties Beach. On weekend mornings, he and Caroline would strap their paddleboards to the top of the Bronco and drive to Sesachacha Pond. They'd dip their oars into the still water while the rising sun turned the surface of the pond into a pink mirror. On Caroline's twenty-first birthday, Matthew took her on a surprise daytime trip to the Chicken Box. They stopped to pick up a pepperoni pizza from Sophie T's and arrived at the Chicken Box at noon, and Caroline ordered her first legal beer. Matthew had arranged for the lead singer of the band that night (Caroline would be going back later with her friends) to come out and sing "Happy Birthday." The bartender and the locals applauded; the lead singer gave Caroline a hug and took a selfie with her.

Now tears fall as Caroline checks her phone. Still nothing from her mother.

She hears the boarding announcement for the JetBlue flight back to JFK. Should she just get on the plane and return to the city? It would serve Hollis right. *And I'll never speak to her again,* Caroline thinks. *I'll orphan myself.*

Back at the Chelsea loft, Isaac and Sofia will now be reunited. They might even be making love on the soft, Egyptian-cottoned acreage that Caroline has so recently occupied. Caroline asked Isaac about his and Sofia's sex life: Was it real? When did they find time? Isaac admitted that they made love in the late night/early morning when Sofia got home from the clubs. She poured herself into bed like syrup, he said, making her sound exotic and luscious in a way Caroline knows she will never be.

Why me? Caroline had asked Isaac another time, and he said, *When you cried, you showed yourself to me. You're pure, unspoiled, you still feel things. I found that irresistible.*

Caroline does nothing *but* feel things—an echoing angst, longing, jealousy. And, at the moment, exhaustion and irritation. Where is her mother?

She types a text to Isaac: I miss you. Will he find *this* irresistible, she wonders, or simply pathetic? Pathetic, she's pretty sure, but she can't help herself; she presses Send.

Then she hears a voice say, "Caroline?"

Caroline turns. A dude holding the hand of a small child is walking out of Crosswinds, the airport restaurant. Caroline blinks. It's Dylan McKenzie.

Because Caroline is a budding filmmaker, she mentally zooms out and watches this scene unfold even as she's living it. (Isaac is always reminding her to *observe* rather than just *see.*) But one thing that a camera can't capture is a person's interior thoughts.

Caroline's at this moment are something along the lines of *Whaaaaaa? Is this happening?* Is Dylan McKenzie really walking up to her?

Dylan McKenzie sounds like a character from *Beverly Hills 90210,* and Dylan looks like one too—thick dark hair that's weekend-mussed, defined cheekbones, and soulful brown eyes. Caroline thinks he might have gotten hotter since she last saw him—and how is that possible?

Caroline first meets Dylan at a bonfire at Clark's Cove when she's sixteen and Dylan is eighteen. She knows who he is, naturally, because he's hot and popular—a lacrosse star at Nantucket High School who'll be going to Syracuse on a full ride. He marches right up to Caroline, beer in hand, and Caroline thinks he's going to tell her she's too young for the party or that summer kids aren't allowed.

But instead he says, "You're Caroline, right? Your mom and my mom were friends growing up."

Caroline nods eagerly, relieved she isn't being asked to leave, though she isn't sure what he's talking about. "Your mom is..."

"Tatum," Dylan says. "Tatum McKenzie."

"Yes!" Caroline says. Hollis has mentioned that someone called Tatum—it's a memorable name—was her best friend, her "partner in crime," though Caroline highly doubts there was any actual crime, her mother is so square. Caroline never paid close attention to the Tatum stories, because what does her mother's ancient history have to do with her own life? Nothing—until this moment. Caroline has never met Tatum; if pressed, Caroline might say she'd assumed the mythical Tatum had moved away or even died.

"They were *best* friends," Caroline says. "Partners in crime."

Dylan grabs two Twisted Teas and leads Caroline to a spot in the sand where they sit down side by side. He asks where she goes to school (Wellesley High), where she lives on the island (Squam), if she plays any sports (soccer, but she sucks; she perseveres only because it looks good on college applications). Dylan enlists a sophomore to fetch them each another drink, then he notices Caroline shivering and asks if she wants to move closer to the fire or wear his Whalers hoodie. Obviously, she takes the hoodie. Caroline's friend Cygnet watches with wide eyes from the other side of the bonfire; Caroline can feel her phone blowing up in her pocket but she doesn't want to text with Cygnet while she's sitting next to Dylan McKenzie wearing his sweatshirt.

At some point, Dylan's leg taps against Caroline's leg and then their bare feet commingle in the cold sand and she thinks, *Dylan McKenzie is into me.* How is this possible? Caroline is nowhere near the prettiest girl in Wellesley; she's not even in the top ten (there are a lot of pretty girls in Wellesley). But that summer, Caroline has undergone something of a metamorphosis. Her hair has lightened to a sandy blond, she's grown a couple of inches and developed a waist, and her skin has finally cleared up. When Dylan puts his arm around her shoulders, she thinks, *This is happening.* It kind of makes sense: Dylan lives on an island, he's probably sick of all the girls he goes to high school with, and Caroline is someone new.

But then there's a disruption. Someone kicks sand in Caroline's face and knocks her drink over. Dylan leaps to his feet and grabs the arm of a girl who looks like a young Kate Moss.

This girl glowers at Caroline and says, "Take that sweatshirt off and get the hell out of here before I cut you, you bitch."

"Aubrey," Dylan says. "Chill."

Caroline is so flustered, so intimidated, and so anxious to shed the sweatshirt that she pulls it off too quickly and takes her T-shirt along for the ride, flashing the entire party her pink Victoria's Secret bra. There are whistles and whoops; Caroline's face burns hotter than the fire. She and Cygnet beat a hasty and ignominious retreat while Aubrey shouts threats at their backs.

In the middle of the night, Caroline plays that scene in her mind the way it *should* have ended: With Caroline casually, carefully doffing the sweatshirt, balling it up, handing it to Aubrey, and saying, *Sorry about that, psycho.*

The next day, when Caroline tells her mother she met Dylan McKenzie (she doesn't get into the details), Hollis sighs. "I should have figured the two of you would meet at some point. You know, for a long time, his mom, Tatum, was my best friend in the world."

"Okay, so, like, what happened?" Caroline asks.

Her mother shakes her head. "I moved away," she says. "And Tatum stayed."

The following summer, Caroline sees Dylan and Aubrey at Cisco Beach. By this point, Caroline has done some digging on Aubrey Collins and learned that Dylan and Aubrey have been together—if social media is to be trusted—for a long time. (There's one Instagram post of five red roses for five years of dating.)

When Dylan notices Caroline, he waves (in her seventeenth summer, Caroline has fully blossomed, boobs, booty, and all), and at the same moment, Aubrey flips Caroline off, which answers the question of whether she should go over to say hello.

For a few years, Caroline doesn't see Dylan either in person or online. His Instagram account vanishes. Caroline goes so far as to follow the Syracuse lacrosse team's account, but she spies him only once, as a freshman on the bench. He doesn't appear to be on Snapchat—or if he is, Aubrey has made him block Caroline, which is amusing to think about. Hold grudges much? It was a *high-school party!*

Caroline next bumps into Dylan as she waits to pick up her family's order from LoLa Burger. Caroline is deep into her phone when she feels a tap on her shoulder, and there stands Dylan in all his super-hot glory. Dylan asks where Caroline is working for the summer and she says that she just finished a six-week film course in Rome and has to be back in the city by mid-August, so there wasn't really time to commit to a job.

"Do you babysit?" he asks.

"Ha-ha-ha!" Caroline says. "No."

"Too bad," he says. "I could use someone. I have a two-and-a-half-year-old named Orion."

"You *do?*" Dylan is a couple years older than Caroline, but even so, she thinks of him as her age, and people her age don't have children of their own. She wonders if Aubrey is the mother, then tries to imagine what Aubrey would look like pregnant (the phrase *swallowed a watermelon* comes to mind).

Before Caroline can ask, her order is called. The bag smells seductively of hot, crispy truffle fries. Caroline smiles at Dylan, thinking, *He got beautiful, bitchy Aubrey pregnant and now he's a father at twenty, what a waste!* "Good seeing you!" she says. "Bye!"

Lights, camera, action! Caroline thinks. There's no more time for backstory; Dylan is upon her.

"Hey there!" she says. She looks at Orion, who, as if scripted, is doing a weird-little-kid thing—sucking on a piece of fatty bacon. "This must be your son. He looks *just* like you." (Caroline is stretching the truth; the kid has a pudgy, mottled face and fair, flyaway hair.)

Dylan is staring at Caroline as intently as he would be if she were directing this scene—*Inhale her with your eyes!*—and Caroline dearly wishes she'd blown her hair out that morning rather than defaulting to messy bun.

"This is the O-Man," Dylan says. "O-Man, say hi to Caroline."

O-Man raises his arms to be picked up, the bacon drooping from his mouth like a cartoon tongue.

"Do you need a ride?" Dylan asks Caroline. He surveys her suitcase and the lumpy bag of equipment. "I take it you're here for the big weekend?"

"I've been hired to film it," Caroline says, then considers how ridiculous this sounds. It isn't Coachella. "My mom wants me to take some footage for her website."

Dylan grins. He's still staring at her, and O-Man is still sucking on the bacon, and Caroline is still missing Isaac, although she has to admit, this is a nice distraction.

"Let me give you a ride home," Dylan says. "I just have to wait for... Orion's mom. She has him this weekend. She's going to meet us here aaaaaaany second."

"Oh, that's okay," Caroline says, checking her phone. Still nothing from her mother. "My mom is picking me up." Caroline sees a blue Jeep coming in hot. Behind the wheel is a woman with long straight hair wearing a baseball cap backward (a cute look, one Caroline can't quite pull off), and surprise, surprise—it's Aubrey!

The only thing better than Caroline recognizing Aubrey is Aubrey recognizing Caroline. She gets an incredulous expression on her face—really, it's meme-worthy. She screeches to a halt, flings open her door, and storms around the front of the car. She snatches Orion up off the ground while at the same time ripping the bacon from his mouth, which she then whips into the street.

Orion starts to cry. "My bacon!" His voice is sweet and clear, and in that moment Caroline both loves him and feels sorry for him.

"I cannot *believe* this!" Aubrey says. She gives Caroline the most withering of looks—Caroline suddenly feels like she needs a shower—then turns to Dylan. "How long has *this* been going on?"

Dylan seems pretty relaxed, maybe even a little amused. "About five minutes. We just bumped into Caroline on our way out of the diner. Orion was showing her his bacon."

Aubrey buckles Orion into a car seat that seems a little janky in its positioning in the front seat of the Jeep (there is no back seat), and Caroline is tempted to speak up. Maybe she is maternal after all?

Aubrey looks at Dylan. "Have your mother come at five on Sunday. I have plans."

"Plans with..." Dylan says.

"Plans with none of your business!" Aubrey says.

Caroline can't believe she's stuck in the middle of their domestic spat.

Dylan pauses. "My mother is busy all weekend," he says. "I'll come get him."

Aubrey slams the car door shut so hard, the entire Jeep shudders. Orion cries louder, craning his neck around to see the fate of his bacon, which has just been snatched up by a seagull. "Whatever, have fun with your little girlfriend, you pathetic piece of—" She starts the car and drives away, flipping them both off as she goes.

"Wow," Caroline says.

"Looks like someone made her jealous!" Dylan says, clearly delighted. He grabs Caroline's suitcase and hoists up her equipment bag. "Come on, I'm parked over here."

Caroline follows Dylan to a truck so big it qualifies as "monster." He opens the passenger door and offers Caroline a hand as she climbs up into the seat (this requires her standing on the running board). The truck is so high off the ground that Caroline feels like she's viewing the parking lot from the second story of a building. She revels in the novelty of a *man with a truck.* Isaac doesn't even have a driver's license.

Dylan climbs in, aims the air-conditioning vents toward her, and changes the radio station from Kidz Bop to the Coffee House, which is playing an acoustic version of "Night Changes."

Whoa.

"To Squam?" Dylan says.

It takes Caroline a second to equilibrate. She's in a truck next to Dylan McKenzie listening to One Direction. For a second, she's sixteen again.

"Yes," she says. Then: "I can't believe you remember where I live."

"It's all my mother has been talking about for days," Dylan says. "Staying at your mother's house in Squam. She's been trying to downplay it but I think she's really excited about this weekend."

Caroline finds she's happy to hear this, for Hollis's sake. Dylan turns the song up, and spontaneously, they both sing along, *Everything that you've ever dreamed of disappearin' when you wake up*... It's such a meet-cute, Caroline can hardly stand it!

She sends her mother a text: Nvm. I found a ride.

11. Provisions

Molly Beardsley, devoted fan of the Hungry with Hollis website, is so invested in Hollis's Five-Star Weekend going well that she wakes up at six a.m. in Twain Harte, California, and checks the weather 3,107 miles away on Nantucket Island. Friday is going to be clear and sunny with a high of seventy-six degrees. Molly is overjoyed for Hollis! All her fans wish they could somehow watch Hollis prepare for the weekend. How is she handling the details? Does she have one master list or several sublists?

Long before Molly Beardsley is awake in California, Hollis is driving past a field of lilies, zinnias, cosmos, and snapdragons in rainbow-hued rows at Bartlett's Farm. It's a vista worthy of Monet, of Renoir, and Hollis considers stopping to take a picture, but she's on a mission. She pulls into the parking lot of the farm market at 7:55.

She did end up reading some of the debate on her website. Is it too soon for Hollis to be hosting a girls' weekend?

Oh, probably, she thinks. But it has lifted her spirits and given her something to look forward to. And since she's throwing it, she'll do it her way. End of discussion.

At eight o'clock sharp, market manager Lily Callahan (who happens to be a frequent visitor to the Hungry with Hollis website; she knows what Hollis is doing here!) flips the sign to OPEN.

Just inside the front door, Hollis stops at the display of fresh flowers. There are galvanized-metal buckets of lilies in white, yellow, peach, and something called "double pink." Hollis selects five stems, then chooses four mixed bouquets that were picked earlier that morning, their petals still damp from the sprinklers. Then it's on to the corn. The ears are snugged into the crib side by side and end to end like a neat puzzle. (Lily Callahan loves to look at the corncrib first thing in the morning. By late afternoon, the corn will be ravaged by people stopping by after the beach, ears flung willy-nilly and half stripped despite the sign that says PLEASE DO NOT SHUCK THE CORN!) Next, Hollis selects hothouse tomatoes, organic butter lettuce, cucumbers, zucchini, and summer squash. She moves on to the herbs: fresh dill, fresh basil, a bunch of chives, and what Lily and the rest of the staff refer to as "porn-star mint" (it's very well endowed). Hollis glides her cart over to the cheese case, where she chooses Taleggio and a clothbound cheddar (five-star cheese; Lily approves!), fancy crackers, a couple sticks of Italian salami, Marcona almonds, a can of salt-and-pepper Virginia peanuts (they're ridiculously addictive), and Alfonso olives.

She holds the olives out to Lily (who has been trying to keep her distance but who is obviously stalking Hollis) and says, "No one ever eats olives, but I love this purple color."

"Oh!" Lily says, feeling caught. "Me too!"

A short hop from Bartlett's is Hollis's favorite fish market, 167 Raw. Maria, who manages the counter at 167, *worships* Hollis Shaw, but she won't do the obvious thing and ask for a picture. She fills Hollis's order—four pounds of harpooned swordfish—and throws in a container of 167's legendary guacamole "on the house."

"Aren't you sweet?" Hollis says.

Maria nearly suggests that Hollis serve the guacamole as an appetizer on Sunday evening before the pizza party, but she won't be that person. Will she? She opens her mouth to speak but all she ends up saying is "Have fun this weekend!"

Hollis's expression is inscrutable. "I'm going to try!" she says.

Hollis's final and, she would argue, most important stop is Hatch's, the liquor store. There's no way Hollis can host this weekend without wine. Lots of wine.

Store owner Ethan Falcone isn't a follower of the Hungry with Hollis website but he recognizes Hollis the second she walks in because she went to high school with his wife, Terri (Prentiss) Falcone. They were on the same softball team; they won the state championship their junior year, then lost it in their senior year in a game so heartbreaking that Terri still gets upset about it. And hasn't Terri recently brought up Hollis's name for some reason? Ethan could swear the answer is yes but he can't remember why. Terri runs a small haircut place on Old South Road and she tells Ethan so much gossip about so many people that he can't keep track of it all.

Ethan watches Hollis choose midrange bottles of pinot grigio, sauvignon blanc, chardonnay, and rosé. She also picks up two bottles of Casa Dragones tequila (Ethan approves), two bottles of Triple 8 vodka, and a bottle each of Hendrick's gin and Mount Gay rum. She gets in line, then swings her cart around and heads for the champagne aisle. She plucks two bottles of Veuve Clicquot off the shelf and goes back to the register.

When she reaches the counter, Ethan says, "Hey there, Hollis."

"Hey..." Hollis says in a way that reveals she's forgotten his name. That's okay; Ethan doesn't mind. He really only knows Hollis because of Terri's (unnatural?) obsession with her high-school softball team. Still, Ethan likes to chat; it's his favorite part of the job. People come into the liquor store in both good times and bad—job security!—and from the looks of it, Hollis is hosting a big party.

"How's everything?" Ethan asks.

"Oh, just fine, thanks," Hollis says.

"How's the good doctor? I haven't seen him once all summer."

The smile falls off Hollis's face so quickly, it should have a sound effect, and in that instant, Ethan remembers why Terri brought up Hollis's name. *Her husband, the big-shot doc at Mass General, died.*

Hollis regards Ethan and says, frankly, "Matthew died in December."

I'm such a squid, Ethan thinks. But he's always been good with people, so he will salvage the moment. "I'm so sorry to hear that," he says. "He was a very personable guy and I always enjoyed chatting with him. I'm sorry for your loss."

"Thank you," Hollis whispers.

Ethan starts ringing up her purchases, sliding the bottles into the cardboard slots of a large box. He wants to tell Hollis her purchases are on the house but...she's bought a lot of stuff, and he's trying to run a business. "That'll be five hundred and eleven dollars."

While Hollis inserts her card into the machine, Ethan tries to think what else he can do. "Let me help you get this out to the car."

Hollis leads Ethan to her vintage Bronco, and after Ethan loads the box, he opens his arms for a hug. She quickly embraces him and says, "Thank you, Evan."

"It's Ethan," he says and they both laugh. Then Ethan remembers something else. "You know what Terri used to call your husband?"

Hollis blinks.

"Your husband would go to Terri for a haircut every once in a while."

"Oh, yes, of course," Hollis says. "What did she call him?"

"Mr. Wonderful," Ethan says. "She called him Mr. Wonderful." He raps on the tailgate of the Bronco, proud of himself for remembering this. "Enjoy your weekend."

Once Ethan is back inside the store, Hollis presses her forehead to the steering wheel. *Mr. Wonderful,* she thinks—and one of her favorite memories plays in her mind with such clarity she could be watching it on a movie screen.

Hollis and Matthew have moved out of the city to a center-entrance Colonial on a wooded lot on Livingston Road in Wellesley. Hollis has left *Boston* magazine, and now she's a stay-at-home mom to Caroline, age three. However, Hollis needs "something else," so she agrees to chair the gala benefit for the hospital's heart center. The development office has never seen a chair as organized and capable as Hollis Shaw. The tickets sell out immediately; they have corporate sponsors, and they book a musical guest who may or may not be Boston's own Peter Wolf of the J. Geils Band—and rumor has it, Steven Tyler will join him onstage.

The night of the benefit, Hollis gets ready, then sits down at her dressing table to put in her diamond stud earrings. Her hair is in a chignon, and she's wearing a slinky purple dress (it's the first slinky thing she's been able to fit into since she got pregnant, and it required a lot of hours at the gym and three months without dessert).

Matthew walks in wearing his tux and holding two flutes of champagne. He hands one to Hollis and smiles at her reflection in the mirror. "To my beautiful wife," he says. "Everyone at work is talking about what a wonder you are. I'm so proud of you."

They touch glasses and drink. Matthew bends down to kiss the back of Hollis's neck. Down the hall, Hollis hears Caroline chattering with the babysitter about what book she wants to read. Hollis closes her eyes and thinks, *I am so lucky.* She thinks, *This is what I've wanted my entire life. A moment just like this.*

Back at the house, Hollis moves at double speed; her Fitbit can barely keep up.

She wants each bed to be as luscious as a bakery confection. She stuffs the duvet covers with two down inserts for extra fluffiness. She arranges an assortment of pillows—some feather, some firm—at the head of each bed and places a farm bouquet on each nightstand next to a water carafe and a stack of new magazines. Hollis uses a TikTok hack to arrange the flowers: She crosshatches tape across the top of the vase so the flowers stand up straight, and she adds vinegar, sugar, and ice to the water to keep the flowers fresh. She recognizes this absurd attention to detail for what it is: a way to control the few things she can control. She can't believe she had to tell poor Ethan at Hatch's that Matthew was dead. For a second, she'd considered pretending that Matthew was at home working in the garden, tending their tomato plants. He used to prune them back, his surgeon's hands confident and adept in the cutting.

She folds pristine white Turkish cotton towels in every bathroom, then unwraps bars of wildflower soap from Nantucket Looms.

In the kitchen, she marinates the swordfish (she'll post the recipe when the weekend is over), softens the cheeses, and prepares her famous bacon and rosemary pecans (she'll post this recipe as well; she can practically hear her members clamoring for it, then asking if they can substitute almonds for pecans).

She sets the table on the deck—two overlapping tablecloths in a blue toile print, wicker chargers, linen napkins, beeswax candles in Simon Pearce holders, a bouquet of hydrangeas cut from the bushes that line the driveway. She hangs citronella lanterns and stacks cashmere blankets on a nearby ottoman in case anyone gets chilly. (The blankets make her feel as though she's thought of everything. *Has* she thought of everything?)

She ices the wine and champagne in the large hammered-silver bucket, polishes her wineglasses, gently pulls the stamens off the lilies using a damp paper towel. She goes out to the shed and wipes the cobwebs from the beach umbrellas. As she's cleaning the inside of the cooler, two cases of sparkling water at her feet, her phone dings with a text.

It's from Caroline. I'm here. Where r u?

Here? Hollis thinks. What does that mean—here on *Nantucket?* It's only 11:30. Did Caroline take an earlier flight? Hollis could have sworn the flight she booked for Caroline landed at 1:30. Hollis quickly finishes rinsing the cooler with the hose and leaves it in the sun to dry. She strips off her rubber gloves and hurries inside to her laptop. She clicks on the confirmation e-mail she sent Caroline the night before and gasps.

Departing JFK 10:13 a.m.

Arriving ACK 11:27 a.m.

Oh no. No, no, no, no, no! Hollis thinks. She needs to call Caroline, but her phone—where is her phone? Back outside with the cooler? No. She finds it on the shelf in the shed, then hurries back through the house thinking, *I blew it. I seriously blew it.* She climbs into the Bronco and is halfway down the driveway, white shells spraying all over the place she's peeled out so fast, when another text comes in.

Also from Caroline: Nvm. I found a ride.

Hollis hits the brakes and releases a breath. She found a ride. Okay, that's good, right? But Hollis knows it's not good. Hollis should have double-checked the flight time.

She remembered the cashmere blankets but she forgot her own daughter.

It takes all of Hollis's willpower not to lurk in the doorway until Caroline arrives. She goes to the kitchen counter and assembles a BLT on toasted Portuguese bread, Caroline's favorite summer lunch, and arranges it on a plate with a handful of Cape Cod chips and a ripe peach. She hears a car and peeks out to see Caroline climbing down from an enormous black truck. Hollis squints; she can't make out who the driver is, but Caroline waves at him (or her). She's smiling. Maybe things aren't as bad as Hollis thinks.

"Darling," Hollis says when Caroline storms in, the screen door slamming behind her. "Welcome home."

"You're kidding, right?" Caroline says. She gives Hollis a death stare before crouching down to pet and kiss Henny, who is shimmying with excitement and love.

"I'm so sorry, darling. I thought the flight landed at one thirty. That's what I had written on my list."

"On your list," Caroline says and she gives a breathy laugh. "Classic."

"You're obviously more than an item on my list, Caroline," Hollis says. "But I had one thirty in my mind, I was planning on—"

"No thank you to lunch," Caroline says, and she sweeps past Hollis and down the hall to her bedroom. Hollis hears the door slam.

Leave her be, Hollis thinks. The big hurdle has been cleared; she's back under Hollis's roof. Hollis will save her lunch for later. She probably just needs a nap.

She taps on Caroline's door an hour later. No response.

Fine, she thinks. She has forgotten how people Caroline's age can sleep.

At three o'clock, Hollis changes into what she thinks of as her "welcome outfit"—white drawstring pants and her signature blouse in pale pink, both forgiving, because although she has lost some weight since Matthew died, she's nobody's idea of thin. She won't be winning any fashion awards this weekend, but she's comfortable with the way she looks. Her hair is still more blond than gray, her eyes are a clear slate blue, her breasts have yet to sag, and her bottom, although plump and round, is firm. She has a light tan, and earlier this week she braved the salon for a manicure, pedicure, and eyebrow tint and wax. She has always had excellent eyebrows, but as fifty-three years have taught her, good eyebrows don't guarantee one a smooth journey through life.

She knocks on Caroline's door again. "Darling?"

Nothing.

At quarter past four, no one has arrived or even texted about arriving. Not even Brooke. Hollis wonders if everyone has had a change of heart.

She wanders through her house, trying to see it for the first time. It looks good, smells good—but something is missing. It's too quiet; she needs music. Hollis has followed Moira Sullivan's lead and made not one playlist, but four—one for Tatum ('80s music), one for Dru-Ann ('90s music), one for Brooke (songs they played when the kids were growing up), and one for Gigi, though they have never once talked about music. Hollis tried to imagine what Gigi would like based on their text conversations, and she came up with something she thinks of as "smart-woman music"—Alison Krauss, Lauryn Hill, Norah Jones. She added vintage Billie Holiday, Nina Simone, Carole King. She rounded it out with some edge: Fiona Apple, Courtney Love, Alanis Morissette. Gigi's playlist is the best one to welcome people; Hollis presses Shuffle.

The first song that plays is Ingrid Michaelson's "Maybe." Hollis takes a seat at the kitchen island, pulls out her phone, and snaps a portrait-mode picture of the cut-glass bowl of bacon-rosemary pecans.

Caroline's lunch plate remains untouched on the counter. When Hollis checks, she finds the bread is dry, the chips stale, the tomato bleeding its juices onto the plate. Into Henny's dog bowl it goes.

Hollis walks down the hall and knocks on Caroline's door, more firmly this time. "Caroline? I'd like you to get up, please. People will be arriving soon."

There's no answer. Hollis reminds herself that *she's* the mother, that this is her house, that forgetting Caroline was an honest mistake, and that she apologized for it. The old Caroline would have said, *Don't worry about it, Mama, you have a lot on your plate.*

"Caroline, may I enter?" Hollis says. Caroline is fanatical about her privacy. She knows nothing of the days when you had to talk to your boyfriend—in Hollis's case, Jack Finigan—on a landline in the kitchen with your father six feet away on the couch watching *Quincy* but also probably listening to every word.

There is, finally, a muffled "What?"

Hollis eases open the door and sees Caroline huddled under her duvet—never mind that it's seventy-five degrees outside—looking at her phone. Awake after all, wide awake.

"Caroline, I'm very sorry I wasn't at the airport to pick you up. I got the time wrong in my head. I apologize."

Caroline sits up, throwing the comforter to the end of the bed. "You had time to get everything ready, though, I see. The flowers.

The fresh-picked corn. Were you the first person at the farm this morning?"

"Caroline."

"Were you?" Caroline says. "Just tell me."

"I was, yes—"

"I remember when I used to be a priority."

"You're still a priority!" Hollis says. "You're my number-one priority."

"Your website is first. Your brand is first. Ahead of me," Caroline says. She pauses. "And ahead of Dad."

Hollis knows Caroline is looking for a reaction, but she won't engage. "I've missed you so much. I'm so happy you came home. It means a lot to me that you're here, darling."

"Don't flatter yourself," Caroline says. "I only said yes because I need the money."

This is Hollis's cue to leave the room, but instead, she sits on the side of Caroline's bed, careful not to crowd her. (Motherhood, she has come to realize, requires a lot of math: How much space is enough; how much is too much?) "Do you want to talk about Dad?" Hollis asks. "I'm sure it's difficult coming this weekend and...he's not here. It was awful for me too." But Hollis won't make this about herself. She remembers how helpful Gigi's simple words were: *I'm here to listen.*

"Of course I miss Dad," Caroline says. "He wouldn't have abandoned me like an orphan child at the airport."

Her voice contains the slightest amount of teasing, which is encouraging. "You're correct," Hollis says. "Your father would never have made that mistake. He would have been right out front waiting, so excited to see you and hear all about your summer in New York." Hollis reaches out and smooths Caroline's hair away from her face. "How *is* your summer in New York?"

An alert comes in on Caroline's phone and she clicks on it. Hollis remembers when she and Matthew bought Caroline her first iPhone, ten years ago. What had Matthew said? That's right: *We will no longer be the most important thing in her life.*

"Mom?" Caroline says. Her tone has changed. "Are you ready for *this?*" Caroline holds up her phone for her mother to see. "Dru-Ann has been canceled."

"What?" Hollis says. She peers at the screen, wishing for her reading glasses. She pinches the screen to enlarge it and squints. Dru-Ann Jones Disses Mental-Health Issues. Hollis begins to read, but the print is small. The article mentions Posey somebody, a golfer, then Hollis defaults to just clicking on the video. She watches her beloved friend shout at some rich-looking white dude, "She's going to tell everyone it's a 'mental-health issue' "—Dru-Ann makes air quotes—"when she needs to *suck it up and play through!*"

Ten years ago, maybe even five years ago, Hollis wouldn't have understood the problem with this, but now, thanks in no small part to her interactions with people on her website, she has been educated in all things mental-health-related.

"Oh, dear," Hollis says. "That's not good."

"It's worse than 'not good,' " Caroline says. "It's *terrible.* And it's everywhere. That article is on Refinery Twenty-Nine, but they got it from Vulture."

Suddenly a voice calls out from the kitchen. Hollis peers through Caroline's shutters to see a black Lincoln—*How did that thing get down Squam Road?* she wonders—turning around in the driveway.

Only one of her friends would hire such a car to get out here.

"It's Dru-Ann," Hollis says.

"Well, you'd better go, then."

Hollis feels torn. She should greet her guest, of course, but she doesn't want Caroline to think she's not a priority. "Can I make you—"

"Just go, Mother," Caroline says. She returns her attention to her phone. "Dru-Ann needs you more than I do."

12. Blowout

The blowout at the salon costs more than Tatum expected but, oh, is it worth it. The stylist with the charming Irish accent, Lorna, eases Tatum's head back against the lip of the sink and scrubs the hell out of Tatum's scalp. Lorna wraps her hair in a fluffy white towel and hands her a latte and the most recent issue of *People*. Tatum feels the tension roll off her shoulders as Lorna blows her hair out, straight and shiny with a little volume on top and some movement at the bottom.

Tatum knows that Lorna herself battled breast cancer a couple years earlier; there was a fundraiser held for her at the Rose and Crown, and Irina Services donated weekly cleanings of Lorna's cottage. Tatum sneaks a glance at Lorna. Her breasts are small and perky, her cheeks are rosy, and her grip on the brush is strong and sure. You would never know she'd been sick. Should Tatum ask about her "journey"? (Tatum at least knows not to call it a "battle.") Breast cancer survivors are supposed to be part of a sisterhood, which sounds appealing as long as you crush the "survivor" part and don't end up in a casket like Tatum's mother.

The Zen that Tatum has managed to achieve for five minutes is gone, but even so, she smiles at Lorna in the mirror. "I wish it could always look like this."

"You're absolutely gorge," Lorna says with a wink. "Now go enjoy your Five-Star Weekend."

* * *

The evening before, Tatum told Kyle about the voice mail from the hospital. They held hands—Tatum squeezing like hell—and listened to it together.

"Good morning, this is Dr. Constable. I have the results of your biopsy, though hospital policy prevents me from leaving that information in a voice mail. I'll be in the office until five today, then I'm out tomorrow. In the event you miss me, I'll be back in the office first thing Monday morning. Feel free to call me after eight a.m. Thank you."

Tatum released Kyle's hand and replayed the message, trying to decipher Dr. Constable's tone. She didn't sound particularly grim, but neither did she sound upbeat. She sounded utterly neutral.

"Call her back," Kyle said.

"She said she's in the office until five. It's six thirty."

"Doctors sit in their offices after hours and write in their charts," Kyle said.

"On TV," Tatum said. She didn't want to call, so she pushed the phone toward Kyle and he called.

Tatum's mind flipped through a mental scrapbook: Ice cream sundaes on her sixth birthday, a bumpy ride on the Steamship when her queasy-ass twelve-year-old self threw up in the sink, the lavender dress she wore to junior prom (Kyle matched with a lavender bow tie and cummerbund), Dylan's baby walker (he liked to ram right into Tatum's heels), a man she'd waited on at the Lobster Trap who asked for extra drawn butter and then *drank* it. Why these things? Why couldn't she come up with better memories?

Kyle sighed. "Voice mail."

"Don't leave a message," Tatum said. "I'll just call her Monday morning."

Kyle said, "The good thing is you can enjoy your weekend without this hanging over your head."

Tatum nearly snapped out, *It's still hanging over my head, dumbnuts,* but she knew he was every bit as nervous as she was and he was trying to comfort her, so she kissed him instead.

Now Tatum texts Kyle: On my way home, we need to leave at 4! She has reminded him of this so often, he's getting cranky about it, but she has a feeling that when he sees her hair, he's going to want to whisk her into the bedroom, and really, they don't have time.

She finds Kyle drinking beer at the teak outdoor table that Tatum and Dylan gave him for Father's Day. He's sitting with some tall, bald guy with a silver goatee wearing jeans, a white polo shirt, and flip-flops.

The man grins at Tatum and says, "Surprise, surprise!"

Tatum blinks. It's Jack Finigan, apparently still alive and breathing.

"Well, well, isn't this *Big Chill* of you," Tatum says as it all clicks into place. "Appearing out of the blue after ghosting us for a million years *this* weekend of all weekends."

Jack crushes Tatum in a bear hug so tight that she feels her sore breast. He's put on some heft and his face has aged, but he still looks good. Men get better-looking as they get older; it pisses Tatum off.

"Your hair looks hot, babe," Kyle says.

"Thanks." Tatum gives Kyle a raised eyebrow: *Did you know he was coming?* Kyle and Jack and Tatum have been friends since middle school when Jack's father accepted a foreman's job at Toscana Construction. She's happy to see him, but a little warning would have been nice. She lights a cigarette.

"Can I get you some wine, Tay?" Jack asks. "I brought you a bottle as a little hostess gift."

Hostess gift! Tatum thinks. *Shoot.* She should bring something, but what can she get Hollis that Hollis can't buy herself? The answer is nothing, but Tatum knows that's not the point. The point is not to show up empty-handed. Tatum thinks about bringing a can of soup, a roll of paper towels, a neon-yellow T-shirt advertising McKenzie Heating and Cooling. She should have rummaged through her photo albums for a picture of her and Hollis—she has approximately three thousand of them—and bought a silver frame for it at Flowers on Chestnut. That would have been cute, but the frame would have cost her seventy-five bucks, money that she doesn't have to spare, especially not after the blowout. Maybe she should just grab a picture? There's the one of them taken in the back of the bus after they won the state softball championship junior year (both of them grinning, Tatum holding up two fingers to signal victory, Hollis with a dorky sweatband at her hairline). Or she could take the one of the four of them—Tatum and Kyle, Hollis and Jack—up at Altar Rock on New Year's Day of senior year. But how meager, presenting just a snapshot. Besides, she doesn't have time to look through the albums; she's late already.

"I need to be in Squam ten minutes ago," she says.

"Squam?" Jack says. "What's out there?"

They all know what's out in Squam, Tatum thinks. Surely Jack remembers that Hollis moved the cottage and built a big-ass house—but does he know that Matthew died, and did Kyle tell him about what he's affectionately calling the "ten-tit weekend"? Did Kyle invite him *because* of the weekend? Jack lives in the western reaches of the state where he owns a bar and grill and also serves as the county game warden. He'd traded ocean for lake, striped bass for...whatever kind of fish live in lakes. Perch? Trout? Tatum has no idea. They haven't seen Jack since Dylan graduated from high school, which was...five years ago? Jack didn't like the way the island had changed, he said. Too many Chads on their phones in their father's Range Rovers, and the good places were all gone—Thirty Acres, the Mad Hatter, the Atlantic Café. But Tatum was pretty sure Hollis figured into the equation somehow. She was the reason he didn't come back to the island.

But now Hollis is a widow, and Tatum will be spending the weekend with her. There's no *way* Jack's visit is a coincidence. He and Kyle must have dreamed this up like a couple of teenage girls.

Tatum pokes her head into the fridge and sees a bottle of Santa Margherita pinot grigio, her favorite. This, she decides, will be her hostess present.

And she'll bring something for that snob Dru-Ann as well.

She grabs her duffel bag from the bedroom, writes *I love you* on the bathroom mirror in lipstick, pops into Orion's room and rummages through his toy chest until she finds what she's looking for, then pokes her head out the back door.

"Kyle is running me up to Squam," she says to Jack. "Why don't you come along?"

He nearly jumps out of his chair. "Already planning on it," he says.

13. Happy Hour I

Four o'clock on Friday finds Brooke Kirtley strolling down the ramp of the ferry wearing a straw hat, a Lilly Pulitzer skirt printed with turquoise giraffes, and a matching pair of turquoise sandals that pinch between the toes. Before she walked out the door, Charlie said, "You look like something Nantucket spit up." Brooke knew Charlie was just jealous—and let's not forget *guilty*—so she said, "Why, thank you," and left.

Brooke feels a tap on her shoulder and turns to find Electra Undergrove on the ramp behind her.

"Wait," Brooke says. "You were on the ferry too?"

"I was," Electra says. She's looking very chic in a clingy blue patio dress with cutouts at the waist. She has a new asymmetrical haircut and a new hair color, the reddish purple of a cherry cola. And, if Brooke isn't mistaken, something else is different. At first Brooke wonders if Electra has lost weight—this would come as no surprise; a bunch of Wellesley moms joined this weird new "mindfulness spa" on Route 16 where they were encouraged to fast—but then Brooke realizes that Electra has had a boob job. Right? She was always flat as a board, but now Electra's breasts are buoyant spheres alluringly tanned on the tops.

The great dress, the new hair and breasts, and Electra's blinding self-confidence all do the easy work of making Brooke feel less-than. Her skirt is frumpy, her hat is silly, her shoes are painful.

Electra peers at Brooke over the top of her giant Kris Jenner sunglasses and says, "How about we go for that drink?"

Now? Brooke thinks. She told Hollis she was getting in on the four o'clock ferry and that she'd just hop in a taxi because this weekend she's determined *not to be a bother* or *require special attention*. She won't talk too much or apologize for things that aren't her fault, and she won't get on anyone's nerves. She wants, desperately, to be thought of as *cool*. But maybe she can start by not rushing out to Hollis's house right away and instead going for a drink with Electra Undergrove.

Besides, there's no way Brooke can turn Electra down, not after years of obsessing over the reasons she had been banned from Electra's house and kicked out of their friend group. Electra runs Wellesley. To turn her down now would be to commit social suicide.

Commit social suicide again, Brooke thinks.

And so Brooke smiles at Electra—though not too eagerly—and shrugs. "One drink couldn't hurt."

* * *

At Slip 14, a kid wearing a Gunna T-shirt ogles Electra's new breasts like they're a couple of bread rolls fresh from the oven. Over the sound system, Kenny Chesney sings about saving it for a rainy day and Brooke thinks, *Amen!* A row of cute guys at the bar are drinking draft beers and slurping oysters. Brooke follows Electra to a table for two on the patio, dragging her suitcase behind her.

Electra orders a bottle of rosé and Brooke says, "I can stay for only one glass."

Electra laughs. "Is there such a thing as only one glass of rosé?"

Yes, Brooke thinks. She will drink only one glass; she won't let Electra *influence* her. She won't let Electra *bully* her.

"Where's Simon?" Brooke asks.

"He's bringing the Rover on the slow boat," Electra says, lifting her glass of wine. "It gets in at five. He'll scoop me up then. Cheers, friend."

"Cheers," Brooke says, though she can't bring herself to echo *friend*. Because the stark truth is, Electra Undergrove is not Brooke's friend. She *was* Brooke's friend fifteen, ten, even five years ago, when the kids were growing up and they were all hanging out together. But those days had come to an abrupt end. Electra might not realize that using the word *friend* is a trigger for Brooke. But Brooke won't get in her feelings about it. *Save it for a rainy day!* she thinks. It's a dazzling summer Friday; they have glasses of chilled rosé and a host of admiring eyeballs on them (or on Electra, anyway). Brooke is going to act natural.

And she does, although she has to navigate the conversation like a sapper in a minefield. She can't say a word about what happened with Charlie, so she sticks to the safe topic of her kids (Will, Fidelity; Whitney, the duck boats) and asks after Electra's son, Carter, and her daughter, Layla. Electra confides that Carter is doing a stint in rehab and Layla is following Imagine Dragons around the country with her boyfriend, then says, "They'll find their way eventually. They were never the achievers that your kids were."

Wow, Brooke thinks. An actual compliment from Electra! She swells with pride. The wine has gone to her head, and she hasn't eaten yet today; she's saving all her calories for the dinner Hollis is serving that night. She asks Electra where she's staying.

"We're renting on the Cliff," Electra says. She tilts her head and Brooke senses a sudden intense curiosity from behind the dark glasses. "Have you been to the 'Tuck before?"

The 'Tuck? Brooke thinks. *Do people call it that?* "Once, as a kid," Brooke says. "All I remember is my brother getting stung by a jellyfish."

"But this is your first time as an adult? So you've never been to Hollis's house."

Brooke shakes her head. *Save it for a rainy day,* she thinks.

"How is that possible?" Electra says. "You two are *so close.* I was invited a couple of times back in the day. She and Matthew had us over for lobsters..."

(Later, when Brooke looks back on this moment, she'll wish she'd changed the subject. But the rosé has loosened her tongue and impaired her judgment.) She leans in. "Hollis is hosting something called the Five-Star Weekend. She's invited one best friend from each stage of her life."

Electra stares for a second, then reaches for her wine. "And you're her...what? Her *Wellesley* best friend?"

Brooke isn't quite sure how to respond, which means it's probably time to make a graceful exit. But instead, Brooke slides her phone across the table. "Here's the itinerary for our weekend. Hollis has thought of everything."

Electra snatches the phone and scrolls up, then down. "You're all wearing the same colors to dinner and to lunch? Isn't that cute."

"It's for the pictures," Brooke says defensively. "They'll look better."

Electra moves her sunglasses to the top of her head and peers at the screen more closely. Brooke feels like Electra is committing the itinerary to memory so she can make fun of it later with people like Liesl, Rhonda, and Bets.

"It's good for Hollis to have something to focus on," Brooke says. "Losing Matthew was such a shock. Those two were hashtag-couple-goals."

Electra is still scrolling. "Do you think so?"

"I mean...yes?" Brooke says. Hollis and Matthew had it all—the beautiful home, an accomplished daughter, the respect of all of Wellesley. Matthew was tops in his field, and Hollis became a nationally renowned domestic goddess. They were mature, thoughtful, generous. They were a cut above Brooke and Charlie—but also above Electra and Simon and everyone else they knew. "They were perfect together," Brooke says. "An inspiration."

Electra finally glances up and holds Brooke's gaze in what feels like a meaningful way. "Simon and I bumped into Matthew last fall when he was guest-lecturing at Emory Medical School. We were visiting Carter and we walked into the Optimist as Matthew was walking out." Electra pauses, her fingers still gripping Brooke's phone. "Did Hollis mention that to you?"

"She didn't. She..." Brooke nearly adds *never talks about you* but trails off instead.

"I think we caught him by surprise," Electra says. "In fact, I know we did. I won't say anything else because I don't like to gossip and especially not about Matthew. Not now."

Brooke drinks what's left of her rosé (an almost-full second glass) and thinks, *I have to get away from this woman.* "May I have my phone back, please?"

"Of course." Electra slides the phone across the table, pours herself another glass of wine, and leans back in her chair so that her face catches the sun. Even with her new hair and perky breasts, Electra Undergrove isn't the most attractive woman in Wellesley, Brooke thinks. Nor is she the wealthiest, and she doesn't have a big career. But somehow, Electra had been deemed the queen bee. She was fun; she threw the parties; she dictated the social calendar; she made the guest lists; she was the leader. Why? Brooke has been wondering this for years.

"I have to go," Brooke says. She pulls two twenties out of her purse for the wine. Is that enough? She adds a third twenty—though she probably shouldn't be throwing money around, now that Charlie has lost his job—and Electra, instead of refusing it (which is what she *should* have done since *she* was the one who invited Brooke to drinks), folds the bills and holds them between her pointer and middle fingers like a cigarette.

"Simon and I were just talking about how much we miss you and Charlie," Electra says. "You'll have to come to the house as soon as football starts up."

Brooke wishes she were strong enough to say *Thanks but no thanks* or even *Screw you, Electra.* But instead, Brooke beams. "That would be great. We'd really love it."

And just like a woman who has been influenced, bullied, manipulated, and *owned,* Brooke brings up the calendar on her phone to confirm the date: Sunday, September 10. Brooke types in the notes: Rock and roll football at Electra's!

"So who else is invited to this little weekend?" Electra asks.

"Hollis's best friend from growing up here on the island and her best friend from UNC," Brooke says. "I don't know the fourth person. It's someone she met through her website, I think."

"Do you know Hollis *blocked* me from subscribing to her blog?" Electra says. "I'm not sure why she's holding such a grudge. After all, you've forgiven me. We're here having drinks! You and Charlie will come back to the house this fall!"

The sun suddenly feels like an interrogation light. *I haven't forgiven you!* Brooke thinks. She's having drinks with Electra because... well, what is the answer to that? Because she needs some kind of sick validation that Electra believes she's worth spending time with. But it's a mistake.

"I have to go," Brooke says. "Hollis is expecting me. I'm already late."

Electra waves a dismissive hand, then grabs the bottle of wine and saunters over to the bar where the cute guys are sitting. "Have fun this weekend," she says. "And congrats on being chosen as a star."

"Thanks," Brooke says. She wants to add that it's no big deal, it's not like she made the Hot List in *Boston Common*—but she suspects Electra is being sarcastic.

Of course she's being sarcastic, Brooke thinks as crushed shells get caught in the wheels of her roller bag. She has new hair and new boobs, but her insides are still rotten.

Brooke wanders in a half-drunk daze toward the taxi stand. She knows she has messed things up. She just isn't sure how badly.

14. On-Time Arrivals

Dru-Ann's driver, Al, is a talker. What does she do for a living, where is she from, is this her first time on the island? Dru-Ann gives perfunctory one-word answers before saying, "I'm sorry I'm such a lousy conversationalist but I have some business matters to tend to on my phone."

No problem, Al gets it; he's driven for all kinds of busy and important people, not to name names but one former vice presidential candidate from Virginia ("We didn't share the same political views, but I still thought he was a great guy!"), one very well-known "piano man," and...Dru-Ann can't believe he's still talking, but she doesn't even really hear him because her social media accounts are a five-alarm fire. Twitter is calling her a "ghoul" and "a shocking disappointment," but sticks and stones, et cetera. The point Dru-Ann would like to get across is that *everyone on the internet has it backward!* Dru-Ann is the person *standing up* for mental health!

As Hollis's house comes into view—Dru-Ann hasn't been here in years, but she remembers the narrow frosted beach-glass windows flanking the front door—she dashes off a tweet. For the record, Posey Wofford is not suffering from a mental health crisis. She quit the #DowGreatLakesBayInvitational for reasons that had nothing to do with mental health! Dru-Ann debates mentioning Phineas's appearance in the British Open, but the details are too complicated to tackle on Twitter, so she types in #TeamDruAnn (hoping this will take hold and start to trend), and she posts.

"Is this the place?" Al asks.

Dru-Ann releases a clear breath. *Screw the apology,* she thinks. She's going to stand up for herself.

"Yes," she says. "This is it."

Al carries her bags to the front porch and asks if she needs anything else. No? Well, in that case, would she mind rating his service on the black-car app? Dru-Ann agrees, anything to be rid of the dude, plus her phone is ringing. She knocks once, then steps inside, calling out, "Hello, hello?" She anticipates walking into a gaggle of women already hip-deep in a chardonnay river. But the kitchen, which is beautifully appointed (those pink lilies are stunning), is empty except for Hollis's bear/wolf of a dog who trots over to sniff her. The only sounds are an acoustic version of Adele singing "When We Were Young" (so appropriate) and the insistent buzzing of Dru-Ann's phone.

"Hello?" Dru-Ann calls out again. "Holly?" She wonders if she read the itinerary wrong. This thing starts today, right? She pulls her phone out. It's JB calling; she has no desire to talk to him, so she dismisses his call and then does the unthinkable. Dru-Ann Jones, who prides herself on being accessible twenty-four/seven, whose phone is essentially an extension of her right hand, hits DO NOT DISTURB. (She can't quite bring herself to turn it off.)

"Coming!" Hollis strides down the hall and into the kitchen, where she finds Dru-Ann sniffing the lilies.

Hollis feels tears rise. *This,* she thinks, *is what the Five-Star Weekend is about.* Hollis Shaw and Dru-Ann Jones were just kids when they were paired together in Old East at UNC. Now, thirty-five years later, they're middle-aged women standing in the kitchen, one of them mourning her husband, one of them "canceled." But for Hollis, Dru-Ann will never be canceled.

When you need me, I will show up.

And here she is.

Anyone who watches *Throw Like a Girl* would have to admit that Dru-Ann Jones is even more glamorous in person than she is on television. Her skin is flawless; she's wearing plum lipstick; her hair is gathered in its usual ponytail (*Allure* once ran a piece on ponytails and featured a picture of Dru-Ann). Dru-Ann's signature wardrobe piece is a tailored blazer. Each season, she buys the entire line from Veronica Beard, and today she's wearing a navy scuba jacket paired with a white T-shirt and jeans. Hollis checks out Dru-Ann's shoes (Dru-Ann is famous for her shoes) and finds cherry-red suede stilettos. Fabulous and impractical.

"Dru," Hollis says. She feels a happiness so powerful, it might lift her off the ground. "Thank you for coming." Hollis stops herself from gushing; she doesn't want to sound like Brooke. "I know you're busy."

"Luck was on your side," Dru-Ann says. "Because it turned out I had some free time this weekend." She sighs. "Do you have any alcohol?"

While Hollis is pouring Casa Dragones tequila over ice for Dru-Ann, a taxi pulls up in front of the house and Brooke steps out. There's a bit of a tango—Brooke reaching into her purse for money, the driver heaving her suitcase out of the back ("What did you pack in here," he asks, "gold bullion?"), Brooke retrieving her straw hat when it falls to the ground, the taxi driver checking out Brooke's backside as she bends over for the hat—but eventually Brooke reaches the front door. She knocks and Dru-Ann opens the door, sees Brooke, and shuts the door right in her face. This is meant to be funny, and it *is* funny, Hollis has to suppress a smile, but on the other side of the door, Brooke is wondering if she's going to be the butt of every joke this weekend.

"Dru-Ann," Hollis says. "Stop."

Dru-Ann swings open the door—this weekend is already more fun than she thought it would be—and says, "You're here for the orgy, right?"

Brooke nods. She can play along. "Right," she says. "I brought the chocolate syrup and the blindfolds."

This makes Dru-Ann laugh, and Hollis relaxes. "Brooke!" Hollis says. "Welcome!" Hollis isn't quite as happy to see Brooke as she was to see Dru-Ann, but she won't make this weekend a competition. She spends time with Brooke at home in Wellesley; they went to Juniper for dinner a couple of nights before Hollis left for Nantucket. When Matthew died, Brooke swooped in like Superwoman.

She drove Hollis to the funeral home, helped her pick a coffin; she drove her to St. Andrew's to speak to the pastor. Brooke had been her person.

Hollis hands Dru-Ann her drink and points across the driveway to the guesthouse. "You're in the Twist. It's all made up for you."

Dru-Ann raises an eyebrow. "You're putting me in the outhouse?"

Brooke gasps. "I'll... I'm... you can have my room, Dru-Ann. I'm happy to stay in the outhouse."

"You *should* be sent to the outhouse," Dru-Ann says, "for wearing that hat." A smile breaks across her face. "Just kidding. Holly knows I prefer my own space."

"The Twist is not an *outhouse,*" Hollis says. "The cottage has a Peloton, an espresso machine, and a bottle of tequila on the kitchen table just for you."

"All righty, then," Dru-Ann says. "I'll see you Monday." She grabs her luggage, steps outside, and closes the door behind her.

"Can I get *you* a drink?" Hollis asks Brooke. She takes a good look at Brooke's outfit. The hat *is* overkill; she looks like she belongs in a Mary Cassatt painting. "A glass of rosé?"

"Just water, please," she says. "I've already had two glasses of rosé and I'm feeling it."

"Did you drink on the boat?" Hollis asks.

Brooke opens her mouth, but no sound comes out.

"There's no reason to be ashamed if you did," Hollis says. "This weekend is about kicking back."

"The past couple of days have been awful for me," Brooke says. "But I'll tell you about it another time. It's not an appropriate topic for the Five-Star Weekend."

Hollis takes a beat. It's true—she isn't prepared to take on any Brooke-drama right now.

Hollis hasn't heard from Gigi Ling about when or how she'll be arriving. She texted Gigi the itinerary and the address and received a thumbs-up emoji. If she wasn't coming, she would have let Hollis know. Right?

"Let me show you to your room," Hollis says.

But before Hollis takes Brooke to her room, she gives her a tour of First Light. The interior design is so good, it's like a *drug.* The deep blue half-moon sofa and the kelly-green club chairs in the living room are the perfect pops of color against all the white. Through the glass doors opposite the sofa, Brooke can see a pond with a footbridge and, beyond that, a stretch of golden sand and the ocean.

They head down the hallway. "This wing has two guest suites," Hollis says, and Brooke thinks: *Wing? Suites?* "I have you in the Board Room."

It's like stepping right into Instagram. The wallpaper reminds Brooke of a man's tailored shirt with classic navy, light blue, and subdued gray pinstripes. (Pin-striped wallpaper, who thinks of that? And is this why Hollis calls it the Board Room?) There's a walnut pencil-post bed dressed up in crisp white sheets and a navy plaid quilt with an arrangement of pillows in blue stripes and florals. At the end of the bed is a rattan bench upholstered in blue ikat; the rattan is echoed in the curvy chandelier and the woven shades on the windows opposite the bed. Over the bed is a line of small-scale surf landscapes, and on the antique writing desk that serves as a nightstand are a blue glass vase bursting with cosmos (Brooke's favorite flower) and the new issues of *Martha Stewart Living* and *O* magazine. (These will find their way into Brooke's duffel; she's known at her dentist's and gynecologist's offices for stealing magazines.)

Brooke removes her straw hat and immediately cools down. This room is the most gorgeous one she has ever set foot in; it makes her bedroom back in Wellesley—which she was feeling so proud of only yesterday—seem like a child's art project.

It's going to take all weekend for Brooke to process this room—the textures and layering of patterns—and figure out how and why it works. She keeps noticing things: the water carafe next to a navy-blue ceramic jug lamp on the side table, an area rug in wide navy- and light-blue stripes, the navy gingham cushion on the desk chair.

"You have your own bathroom," Hollis says. "But between you and me, the outdoor shower is the best in the house."

Brooke pokes her head into the bathroom. It's an explosion of fun color, starting with orange and turquoise wallpaper printed with surfboards—*that's* why they call it the Board Room—and an oval mirror bordered with white coral; on either side of the mirror is a little tiki lamp.

Brooke turns to Hollis. "I feel very honored to be staying here and... *humbled* to be chosen for this weekend." She blinks rapidly. "I want you to know how much I value our friendship and everything you've done for me—"

Hollis can see Brooke getting emo, but at that moment, Hollis's phone starts buzzing in her pocket. *This must be Gigi,* she thinks. *She's here. She came.*

To Brooke, Hollis says, "Get settled, then come join us in the kitchen."

Brooke opens her mouth to speak but Hollis doesn't have time for any more Lifetime-movie moments so she leaves the room and shuts the door with a definitive click. She checks her phone.

It's not Gigi. It's Tatum. I'm here, the text says. Come out to the driveway. I have a surprise.

Caroline hears voices in the kitchen—Dru-Ann and Brooke. This is the five-star "arrival" that Caroline should be filming, not only because her mother is paying her to do that but also because Hollis's subscribers will want to see it.

The whole thing is one giant eye-roll emoji.

But . . . some complications are developing. Her mother's relationship with Tatum is intriguing because of the whole local/summer person dynamic. Dru-Ann is apparently being canceled. Brooke will be socially awkward, as always. And at some point, the mystery woman will show up: Gigi Ling. Her name holds promise; it rolls musically off the tongue. *Bring it, Gigi Ling!* Caroline thinks. *Please don't be a dud.*

Caroline carries Isaac's camera—he asked her to hold it like a literal baby—outside, where a Honda Pilot has pulled into the driveway. Caroline sees a man and woman in the front and a shadowy third figure in the back seat.

Caroline hears Isaac's voice: *Observe.*

Something is happening right in front of her.

Caroline focuses her camera on the woman emerging from the Pilot's passenger side. Caroline thinks, *Well, that's where Dylan gets his looks.* Tatum is tall and slender and has long, dark, movie-star hair. She's dressed in cutoff jeans and a navy-blue Whalers Lacrosse T-shirt. Tatum and Hollis hug—Caroline can't help noticing that Tatum looks ten years younger than her mother—and then a burly guy with a seventies porn 'stache gets out of the driver's side and Hollis says, "Hey, Kyle." Caroline zooms in on her mother and Kyle McKenzie as they hug and rock back and forth. "It is *so* great to see you," Hollis says. "Thank you for driving our girl all the way out here. I'll take good care of her, I promise."

Kyle says, "Someone wants to say hello."

At that moment, the back door of the Pilot opens and a bald guy with a silver goatee gets out. He's pretty cute for a dad type and, wow, is he laser-focused on Hollis. Caroline turns the camera on her mother just in time to catch the shock on her face. This is an ambush of some kind, Caroline can see that, but who is this dude?

He steps forward, saying, "Hey, Halle Berry." (Caroline will only realize when she views the footage later that he says "Holly berry," not "Halle Berry.") And Hollis whispers, "Jack?" like she's a character in a period drama whose lover, reportedly killed in battle, has returned. They walk toward each other—but stop when they're about a foot apart.

Caroline holds her breath. What is her mother *doing* right now?

Jack extends his arms. "Come here."

And Hollis goes to him.

Caroline lowers the camera. She doesn't want to be the daughter who becomes indignant and jealous when her mother has a "moment" with somebody she used to know—but too bad, she is that daughter. Her face flushes, and she kind of wants to scream.

But she knows what Isaac would say: She should have stayed and gotten the shot. Conflict equals content. That dude, whoever he is, is a chink in the armor.

Jack Finigan, Hollis thinks once she's in his arms. She sees ghosts of him whenever she passes Nantucket High School or drives out to Great Point; she sees him every time she's at the Boat Basin because he and Kyle spent their summers working as first mates on fishing charters while Hollis and Tatum waited tables at the Rope Walk. They would all meet up after work, the boys with a couple of striped bass collars and the girls with the night's leftover lobsters and a six-pack of Pabst, and they would head out to Fortieth Pole in Kyle's beater CJ-7 and cook everything over a fire as they listened to Billy Joel on the Jeep's tape deck. *My sweet romantic teenage nights!*

Hollis and Jack had been each other's first everything; they had grown up together. Jack Finigan taught Hollis how to love.

She'd seen him once from afar on Main Street a bunch of years ago. It was around then that she began stalking the poor man on Facebook.

"I'm sorry about your husband," he murmurs into her hair.

She takes a breath and pulls away. She's aware they have an audience, one of whom is her daughter with a video camera. Jack's arrival is very off brand for the Five-Star Weekend, which is supposed to be about her relationships with *women.*

Jack is a star of another kind.

"There's too much..." she says. "Can we talk later?"

"Of course," he says. "It was probably unfair of me to show up like this, but wild horses, you know."

"We'll ride them someday," she says. It's a song that's so much *their* song she hasn't been able to listen to it in thirty-five years; whenever it comes on the car radio, she changes the station.

Hollis turns to see Tatum and Kyle kissing goodbye, and she feels seventeen again.

Jack gets in the car. "Come on, Mom and Dad!" he calls out the window.

At that moment, Dru-Ann steps out of the guest cottage and thinks, *What fresh hell is this?*

Jack waves. "Hey there, Dru-Ann, it's Jack Finigan."

There's a name from the past, Dru-Ann thinks. She squints at the bald dude and, wow, she gets sucked right back in time.

Jack Finigan shows up halfway through their first semester at UNC in his father's pickup (which, it turns out, he's driven seven hundred and fifty miles without permission). He knocks on the door of Hollis and Dru-Ann's dorm room in Old East holding a bouquet of red roses that he must have grabbed out of a plastic bucket at the Kroger on Shannon Drive because the stems are still dripping. Hollis is at her American lit seminar and will be gone for two hours. The kid's face crumples at this news. Honestly, he looks like he's going to cry, and Dru-Ann can't stand to see anyone cry. She's happy for a distraction from her macroeconomics reading, so she takes Jack on a tour of the campus; she shows him Old West, Wilson Library, the Dean Dome (of course), the bell tower, and the Old Well.

"This used to be an actual well that students back in olden days would dip a ladle in and *drink from,*" Dru-Ann tells him. Now it's a water fountain, and during freshman orientation there was a line a mile long. Supposedly, drinking from the fountain as a freshman meant you would have a 4.0 GPA, and most people, including Hollis, just could not help themselves.

Jack gives the Old Well one second of his attention. He couldn't care less, and can Dru-Ann blame him? He's there only to see Hollis. Hollis has a collage of photos on the wall over her bed, and Jack appears in nearly all of them, but Hollis told Dru-Ann that they broke up right before she left.

Broke up, Dru-Ann thinks—and yet this poor kid drove thirteen hours, stopping only to relieve himself and buy those sad-ass flowers.

When Hollis gets back from class and sees Jack, she gasps and hugs him and seems overcome...but not entirely happy. The two of them go for dinner at Hector's, and as they're walking back to the dorm, Hollis breaks Jack's heart (again). But Hollis is the one who stays up all night crying, and she keeps the roses on her desk until they wither, then presses the damn things in her copy of *Bartlett's Familiar Quotations.*

After winter break, the collage comes down and is replaced by Monet's water lilies. But for the next three and a half years, every time Hollis gets drunk, who pops up in the conversation? Jack Finigan. He's not exactly the one who got away, but he's something. Dru-Ann will tolerate five minutes, sometimes ten, of Jack-talk, but that's her limit. The best thing about Hollis falling in love with the cute surgery resident in Boston, Matthew Madden, is that Dru-Ann no longer has to hear about Jack.

Except now, here he is.

Dru-Ann strides over to Hollis, Tatum, and her husband (they're the kind of couple who share an e-mail account, Dru-Ann can tell) and says, "The boys have to go. Now."

"You're not in charge this time, Dru-Ann," Tatum says.

It's nice to see you again too, Dru-Ann thinks. "Hello, Tatum," she says, though she knows enough not to try to hug the woman. Dru-Ann hasn't seen Tatum since Hollis's wedding. Back then, Tatum low-key-hated Dru-Ann, and from the sound of things, maybe she still does. She and the rest of the world now have that in common.

Tatum responds with a side-eye, but the good news is that the hubby gets in the car and backs out of the driveway, and at the same time, Brooke pokes her head out the front door and says, "What did I miss?"

"Nothing," Dru-Ann says. "Let's get this party started."

15. Airport Drinking

Gigi always feels liberated strolling through airports in her civilian clothes, and for this trip she's traded her work luggage—tight, stacked black bags—for her personal luggage.

This trip is personal.

She flies first class from Hartsfield to Logan, cruising altitude of thirty-five thousand feet, not a single bump. The left chair, Bruce, and the right chair, Craig, are known to be the smoothest fliers in the company; rumor has it that Bruce grows very annoyed when his coffee spills. They arrive eighteen minutes early. When this happens, it can be challenging to find a gate, but A7 is magically free and Gigi is the first one off the plane. It's almost too easy.

She makes her way to Terminal C, where she checks in for her Cape Air flight aboard a nine-seater Cessna (it's essentially, she thinks, a toy plane). She's booked on the 3:25, which lands at 4:15. She still has an hour to kill so she goes to Legal Sea Foods, orders a lobster roll and a bloody mary, and asks herself for the three thousandth time what she's doing.

She's going to meet her dead lover's wife.

With the first sip of her bloody, Gigi is transported back to the horrible evening of December 15.

Against Gigi's better judgment, she goes to the Hungry with Hollis website. After her conversation with Matthew that morning, she vowed never to visit the website again, but with the weekend in front of her now unexpectedly free, she stares at the Kitchen Lights map. There are bright spots across the U.S. and Canada—and even in Australia, Brazil, Guam. Gigi imagines people standing in front of their cutting boards with half a stick of butter, an onion, a pile of button mushrooms, their kitchens bright and warm.

Gigi zooms in on the Boston area looking for Hollis's house. Hollis is, no doubt, preparing for the annual Shaw–Madden holiday party. Gigi has heard all about it.

There's a dense concentration of lights on in and around Boston, and as Gigi is zooming in, trying to figure out which light, if any, belongs to Hollis, a message appears on the Corkboard. It's from Hollis herself.

To the Hungry with Hollis community:

My husband, Matthew, passed away this morning unexpectedly. I need to ask for privacy as I grapple with this devastating tragedy. I'll be stepping away from the website for a while, as I'm sure you'll all understand. I hope to return at some point, though right now, I can't imagine when.

Hold your loved ones close.

With gratitude, Hollis

Gigi's mouth drops open. She screams. She snatches up her phone, calls Matthew, and is shuttled straight to voice mail. *This is wrong,* she thinks. Matthew has *not* "passed away"; Gigi spoke to him that very morning. She calls his cell phone again. Again, voice mail—but this makes sense. After their conversation, he must have blocked her. But he's not *dead*—how can he be dead? Gigi rereads the post on Hollis's website, thinking there must be a mistake, Hungry with Hollis has been hacked. Passed away this morning unexpectedly...grapple with this devastating...The condolences are starting to roll in. Is this real, then? Gigi scoops up Mabel and squeezes her too tight; Mabel shrieks and leaps to the ground. Gigi googles Matthew's name but all that comes up is the link for Mass General, for Harvard Medical School, for the paper he delivered in San Francisco that past November. Gigi had met him there; they'd gone to the symphony together, then ordered room service at their suite at the Four Seasons. The next day they rented a convertible and drove to Napa. The autumn colors were breathtaking, the lunch at Bouchon sublime.

Gigi paces her house, thinking, *What do I do? Who do I call?* The only people in the world who know about Gigi's affair are Tim and Santi. Should she run down the street and tell them? No, not yet, she'll wait until she knows for sure. When will that be? Nobody in Matthew's life is going to call her. No one knows she exists. And also, who is she kidding—Hollis wouldn't lie to two million people about her husband passing away. Matthew is dead. But how? What happened?

She lies on her sofa and drifts in and out of sleep until the sun comes up. For a moment, Gigi isn't sure why she's not in her bed. Then it lands with a sickening thud: Hollis's message. In the morning light, the idea of Matthew passing away unexpectedly is newly heinous and also newly inconceivable. Gigi doesn't believe it. But when she goes to her computer, she sees the obituaries. Killed in a one-car crash on the morning of December 15.

No, Gigi thinks.

Then she recalls the start of their conversation: Matthew had told her it was snowing.

He crashed. He's dead.

After listing all Dr. Madden's honors and accolades, the papers report that he is survived by a wife and daughter.

A text comes in from Hollis: Hi, just checking in. What's your ETA?

Gigi promptly orders a second bloody mary. She has always been fascinated by airport drinkers. It's as though the rules of polite society fly out the window when people see an airport bar. Six o'clock in the morning? Great time for a beer and a shot. The woman sitting next to Gigi has ordered a plate of French fries and an entire bottle of champagne just for herself. *Not all superheroes wear capes,* Gigi thinks. She finishes her drink and pays the check. By the time she gets back to the Cape Air gate, there's a second text from Hollis with the address of the house. Call me if the cabdriver can't find it! Hollis adds.

In the days following Matthew's death, Gigi waited for an e-mail or a phone call. She pictured Hollis going through Matthew's desk drawers and finding something that gave her pause—the strip of pictures from the photo booth at the wedding Gigi and Matthew crashed in Baltimore when Matthew was lecturing at Johns Hopkins or the handwritten menu they saved from lunch at Bouchon. Matthew had assured Gigi he was careful; as a surgeon, he knew how to keep things sterile.

A week after Matthew's passing, when Gigi's sadness was festering like something infected, she had an epiphany: The only person who understood how she was feeling was Hollis. There were thousands upon thousands of condolences posted on the Hungry with Hollis Corkboard, so Gigi went straight to Hollis's DMs. I'm here to listen, she wrote, and she added her cell phone number. That very night, there was a text: Hi, Gigi, it's Hollis. I'm sorry to bother you.

Gigi responds immediately: Not a bother. I'm here. How are you doing?

In this way, a friendship was born.

But, Gigi thinks now as they call the 3:25 flight, *it's a friendship built on a massive deception.* Gigi stays in her seat as the other eight passengers line up to board, then as her name is called over the loudspeaker. She whips out her phone and checks flights back to Atlanta—there's a direct at eight o'clock. She thinks about just staying in Boston; she loves the hotel Fifteen Beacon. Or she could hop over to Martha's Vineyard.

A third text comes in from Hollis. Is everything okay?

Gigi's fingers hover over her screen. She types, but doesn't send, Sorry, something came up. *My conscience, as it turns out,* she thinks. She should never have agreed to come in the first place; it was positively psychotic.

Except, Gigi thinks, she *wants* to go. She wants to meet Hollis in real life; she wants to see the house; she wants to hear the stories (*does* she want to hear the stories?). If it gets weird or uncomfortable, she can leave.

She approaches the desk. So sorry, she missed the 3:25, is it possible to get the next flight, the 4:40?

The 4:40 is sold out, the gate agent, Bonnie, tells her in a tone that's on the corner of unfriendly and impatient (but Gigi has sympathy; a gate agent's job is frustrating). Ditto the 5:15, Bonnie adds, and ditto the 6:05. "I'm sorry," Bonnie says. "It's a Friday in July."

Gigi's heart sinks. Back to Atlanta, then?

"I do have one seat left on the six-fifty flight, arriving Nantucket at seven forty," Bonnie says.

"Yes," Gigi says. "I'll take it."

"Are you sure you're not going to 'miss' it again?" Bonnie says, using air quotes. "I saw you sit through our announcement, you know."

Oops, Gigi thinks. *Busted.* "If I told you why I didn't get on the three-twenty-five, you wouldn't believe it. But yes, I'm sure."

Bonnie lets a fraction of a smile slip. "That's all I need to know."

16. Happy Hour II

Hollis opens the wine that Tatum brought as a hostess gift and pours two glasses, one for herself and one for Tatum. Dru-Ann picks up the bottle and scrapes the price tag off with her fingernail.

"Twelve ninety-five," she murmurs. "Classy."

"Dru-Ann, shh!" Hollis hisses. Back when Hollis and Matthew got engaged and then married, there was all kinds of friction between Tatum and Dru-Ann. That's ancient history, but—as Hollis knows only too well—no one holds a grudge like Tatum McKenzie. "Tatum brought me this wine because it's one of my favorites."

"If you say so," Dru-Ann says.

"Sorry it's not a Montrachet," Tatum says. "I finished that bottle this afternoon."

Touché, Dru-Ann thinks.

Brooke reaches for the bottle of Whispering Angel rosé resting in the ice bucket. Her hostess gift is an ocean-breeze-scented candle, but now that Brooke has seen the relaxed elegance of Hollis's home, she worries the candle is down-market, maybe even cheesy (what does an "ocean breeze" smell like, anyway?), and because Brooke bought it on sale at the Christmas Tree Shop, it cost even less than twelve ninety-five.

Hollis wants to raise her glass for a toast—she wants to thank everyone for putting their lives on hold and coming to spend the weekend with her—but they should really wait for Gigi.

It's six o'clock and there's been no word from her.

Will this end up being a four-star weekend? she wonders.

She needs to change the energy in the room. The music is, maybe, a touch too angry? Hollis presses Shuffle on Tatum's playlist. REO Speedwagon's "Keep On Lovin' You" floats down from the speakers. It's suddenly the 1980s.

When Hollis sets out the cheese and charcuterie board, Brooke whips out her phone and starts taking pictures. She wants to post this on Facebook as soon as she can; she wants Electra to see what she's missing: melty baked Brie in a golden pastry crust, thinly cut salami fashioned into flowers, tiny bowls of Marcona almonds, purple olives, and cheese straws. There are dishes of mustard and chutney, a winding river of seeded crackers, clusters of frosted grapes, plump strawberries, dried apricots—and in the center of the board, a pile of Hollis's famously addictive bacon and rosemary pecans.

"I hope this is dinner," Dru-Ann says. The tequila is doing its job; she feels her joints loosen. She'll ignore the tension between herself and Tatum the same way she's ignoring her real-life problems. She has left her phone in her bag, and her bag is on the blue silk chaise at least ten feet away.

"Send me those pictures," Dru-Ann says to Brooke. She types her number into Brooke's phone, then chooses the only decent photo of the food and texts it to herself. "Now you have my number, but it's to be used only in case of emergency."

Brooke beams like a Girl Scout who has just won the award for selling the most Thin Mints, and Dru-Ann feels herself softening. The woman can talk the face off a clock, but she's actually kind of sweet, and would it be so bad for Dru-Ann to have an ally this weekend? "For example, if you're at the Wellesley Country Club and you see some twelve-year-old on the tennis court serve her way to victory, you can text me. Because that could be my next client."

"Yes!" Brooke says, raising her arms over her head in a *V* for victory. "I'll text you!"

Caroline returns to the kitchen cradling Isaac's camera. She raises it and pans around the room, focusing on one image (the champagne bottles with their bright orange labels), then another (Dru-Ann's Balenciaga hobo bag slouching like an actual hobo on the blue silk chaise). Brooke is attached to Dru-Ann like Velcro—until Dru-Ann turns to Tatum.

"Sorry I made that crack about the price tag," Dru-Ann says.

Tatum locks her arms across her chest and gives Dru-Ann a cool look. Caroline edges the camera closer. *What have we here?*

"I don't care anymore what you think of me," Tatum says. "If you don't like my wine, don't drink it."

Don't worry, I won't, Dru-Ann thinks. But as she studies Tatum—the woman has barely aged, and she has great hair, though it's maybe a little *Charlie's Angels*—she remembers something that happened at Hollis's wedding. Dru-Ann made a joke and Tatum took it the wrong way. Big-time. Dru-Ann would apologize now, but it's probably better not to bring it up.

She rattles the ice in her glass. "I drink tequila."

Then Dru-Ann notices the camera trained on her. She gives it the middle finger.

Despite herself, Caroline smiles. What would her mother's fans think of *that?*

Tatum's playlist segues from "I Don't Like Mondays" by the Boomtown Rats to "Vienna" by Billy Joel.

Caroline films the four stars crowded around the cheese board as they construct perfect bites. There's a lot of eating, a little bit of singing along: *But then if you're so smart, tell me why are you still so afraid?* (This is Hollis, terribly off-key.) The only person talking is Brooke: *Oh, my goodness, Hollis, you must have been pulling this together for days, these pecans are addictive, the Five-Star Weekend is such a clever idea although I couldn't do it, I haven't talked to anyone from high school since my mother sold our house and moved to Boca.*

Caroline considers shutting off the camera; even Hollis's most devoted fans would be bored to tears. But instead, she zooms in on the other women's faces. All of them seem to be in their own worlds—even her mother.

Hollis is thinking about how Jack's arms felt when they were wrapped around her. She's probably making too much of it. This isn't going to be like a romance novel where the lonely widow is reunited with someone from her past and things are even better than when they were young because not only are they both more mature, they have no agenda but to enjoy each other's company and revel in the glow of their second chance at love. Things like that don't happen in real life.

Tatum is pissed at herself for not checking the wine she brought for a price tag. Tatum knows that Hollis doesn't care about hostess presents or how much they cost; she could have shown up empty-handed and it would have been fine. Dru-Ann is just intent on making it known that she has money and Tatum doesn't. Which has been the problem from the beginning (the bachelorette party at the Ritz in Boston; the searing comment about the pearls).

Tatum should have just gone through the albums at home and brought snapshots. She realizes now that it wouldn't have mattered if she was late. The fourth chick hasn't even shown up yet.

Dru-Ann wonders if she should take Tatum aside to explain the stress she's under. *I'm in the middle of a public relations crisis! Twitter wants my head on a platter!* Would Tatum *get* it? Why, oh, why did she not keep her mouth shut about the price tag? Maybe Dru-Ann will tell Tatum that the man she's involved with has just put things on hold. *I finally found a man I care about and then this mess happens!* Dru-Ann might even confess to Tatum that she's fallen in love with Nick. *That* Tatum will understand; she seems obnoxiously happy with her own husband.

She watches Tatum pick up an olive, sniff it, then set it on her cocktail napkin. Dru-Ann pops an olive into her mouth. "They're good," Dru-Ann says in the tone of a mother trying to persuade a child.

"I guess my palate isn't as *sophisticated* as yours," Tatum says.

Dru-Ann closes her eyes.

Brooke realizes she's the only one talking. The others are nodding along, murmuring, *Mmm-hmm,* but Brooke doesn't feel like they're really *listening.* It's hard to concentrate on anything other than the magnificent grazing board in front of them. Brooke wants to exercise restraint but the bacon-rosemary pecans are so delicious they should be illegal, and the cheese straws are made from scratch with some combination of aged cheddar, grated Parmesan, and herbs picked from Hollis's garden. Brooke washes one down with more rosé, then looks around the table.

"When is Gigi getting here?" she asks.

* * *

When *is* Gigi getting here? Hollis wonders. Hollis has texted her three times: asking for her ETA, giving her the address of the house, then finally asking if everything is okay. Gigi hasn't responded to any of the texts, and at seven o'clock, when Hollis finally calls, she's sent straight to voice mail. She's tempted to say, *You're still coming, right?* But instead she leaves a bright, cheerful message: "Just checking in, no hurry, take your time, we'll see you when we see you!"

Then, for the seven thousandth time, she thinks: *What kind of idiot invites someone she has never met to her house for the weekend?* If this is truly Hollis's "life story in friendship form," then what does it say about her that her best friend from midlife is someone she met online? Is it a sign of the times or a sign that Hollis's standards are at an all-time low?

She should have invited cute Zoe Kern from her barre class back home.

But Hollis wanted Gigi. She still wants Gigi. Where is Gigi?

"Tatum?" Hollis says. "Will you come outside and help me with the grill?"

Tatum knows Hollis doesn't need help with the grill. Hollis was raised by Tom Shaw; she can start a fire with a pile of dry leaves and a dirty look. Hollis probably wants to give Tatum a talking-to about being nice to Dru-Ann. She can say whatever she wants, but Tatum has a score to settle.

Then she remembers something.

"Okay," Tatum says. "Just let me run to the ladies' room real quick." She heads down the hall to her Fifty Shades of White guest suite, which is like something straight out of *Selling Sunset.* Right after Hollis left Tatum in the room to "get settled," Tatum whipped out her phone, took a video, and sent it to Kyle. There's a white "soufflé" bed (this was what Hollis called it) with a fluffy ivory duvet and a trillion pillows in shades from French vanilla to pure driven snow. A clear egg-shaped swing chair hangs from the ceiling. Hollis showed her the "fireworks chandelier": hundreds of tiny LED lights attached to fibers that explode out in all directions so it looks like a fireworks display over the bed. (Tatum has to admit this is very extra.) Tatum understands that the white is "understated luxury," but all she can think is how quickly this room would be decimated if Orion were let loose in here with his Cheez-Its, his Oreos, and his markers.

Tatum rummages through her bag until she finds Orion's rubber snake. She knows that Dru-Ann is staying in the guest cottage by herself. (This tracks; Dru-Ann is *such* a diva.) Tatum slips out the side door and crunches across the white-shell driveway to the Twist. The real "twist," Tatum thinks, is that this cottage is where Hollis and her father used to live. Tatum spent countless hours sitting on the shag rug in Hollis's Pepto-Bismol-pink bedroom, mooning over Rick Springfield's picture on the cover of *Working Class Dog.* Tatum sees the house has been renovated—it has that whole groovy-retro midcentury vibe going on, lots of curves and pops of color, red leatherette chairs in the kitchen, an art deco bar cart so when Frank Sinatra comes over, he can make himself a martini. Tatum heads to the bedroom and slips the snake between the sheets of Dru-Ann's bed.

Instantly, she feels better.

She makes it back to the main house, grabs her glass of wine, and gets to the deck just in time to watch Hollis light the grill with the press of a button, no assistance needed. Hollis looks up and says, "You don't have a cigarette, do you?"

Hallelujah, Tatum thinks. She has been wondering when she could sneak in a smoke. She pulls her Newports out of her shorts pocket and offers one to Hollis. "I didn't think you smoked anymore," Tatum says.

"I don't." Hollis inhales deeply. Her lungs burn and she experiences an instant head rush. *Hello, nicotine, my old friend.* "Except in case of emergency."

Tatum takes a drag of her cigarette and tips what's left of her wine into her mouth. "I was as surprised as you to see Jack. He and Kyle must have cooked it up."

"How did he find out about Matthew?"

"Kyle texted him when it happened," Tatum says.

"Is he still with Mindy?" Hollis asks. She doesn't say that she's been stalking Jack's Facebook page and that the last picture of Mindy appeared on August 25, 2020.

"She got tired of waiting for a ring and left him," Tatum says. "She married some retired tech guy and they bought an inn in Lenox. So, if you're asking—yes, Jack is currently single."

He's single, Hollis thinks. But he's so damn good-looking that he could probably sleep with any woman in Western Massachusetts. "He looks exactly the same," she says. "Don't you think?"

"He's bald and has a silver goatee," Tatum says. "If you remember correctly, in high school he had a full head of hair and was so skinny he couldn't keep his pants up."

"You're right," Hollis says. "I guess what I mean is that he *seems* exactly the same."

"Like he's still madly in love with you?" Tatum says. "Yes, I noticed that as well."

Brooke offers to clean up the appetizers—the few remaining dried apricots, pecan dust, and smears of cheese—and Dru-Ann leaves her to it. "I'm going to have a chat with my goddaughter," she says.

Dru-Ann wanders down the hallway to the right, guided by faint strains of "Practice" by DaBaby, until she comes to a door with a stripe of light at the bottom. She knocks; the music stops.

"What's up?" Caroline says through the closed door. "Is Gigi here?"

Dru-Ann cracks open the door. "Sorry, it's just me."

Caroline is at her desk uploading the footage she's shot so far to her laptop. The scene between her mother and the surprise visitor from the car is *seriously* unsettling. Caroline has watched it half a dozen times with the predictable emotions. She has never seen her mother look at anyone that way, not even her father.

"Hey," Caroline says. "My mom said I didn't have to come back out until Gigi got here."

"Who *is* Gigi?" Dru-Ann asks.

Caroline shrugs. "Someone from my mom's website. Nobody's met her in real life. Not even Mom."

"Wow," Dru-Ann says. "That sounds sketchy."

"I mean, no offense, but this whole *weekend* is sketchy." Caroline finally grants Dru-Ann some eye contact. "My father just died, and my mother is flexing with this whole five-star festival. She's having me film it for her website so people can . . . what? See that she's moving on? See her and her friends dancing at the Chicken Box?"

"Hey," Dru-Ann says. "Take it easy on your mom. It's giving her something positive to focus on."

"It's too soon."

"I don't think that's for either of us to say. She was lonely, she wanted people around. She wanted you around."

"It's a gimmick for her website," Caroline says. "She wants clicks."

"Caroline, I'm your godmother, and I know that means I'm supposed to take your side, but in this case, I would ask that you grant your mother some grace. She's been through a lot."

"*I've* been through a lot." Caroline stares at her computer screen. "My mother's just going to get married again and move on."

Dru-Ann is searching for some words of wisdom—but who is she kidding? She has proved useless at communicating with twenty-somethings—when an alert lights up Caroline's phone next to her on the desk. Dru-Ann sees her own name.

"I guess you heard what happened with Posey Wofford?"

"I did."

"Well, then, I'm glad I'm here to explain it to you in person. Posey doesn't have mental-health issues. She was using that as an excuse."

Caroline doesn't want to do that Gen Z thing of explaining to Gen X why some of their comments are no longer acceptable, but what choice does she have? "You shouldn't have commented on Posey's mental health. Only Posey can do that."

Dru-Ann sighs. "There are two sides to this."

"I'm sure there are, but the internet sees only one side: You make money off Posey's money, so of *course* you wanted her to stay in the tournament."

"It wasn't about money, Caroline," Dru-Ann says. "I have plenty of money without Posey Wofford."

"Have you considered 'breaking your silence'?" Caroline uses air quotes, and she can't help but smile. "And issuing an apology?" An apology alone might not cut it, Caroline thinks. Dru-Ann should probably make a generous donation to the Jed Foundation as well.

"I need to write a statement explaining what happened," Dru-Ann says. "Posey was using mental health as an excuse—"

Caroline says, "You're her representation. It's your job to create a safe space for her."

There's no term Dru-Ann loathes more than *safe space.* First of all, it's a complete fantasy; no space in life is safe unless you live in bubble wrap. People will disagree with you; people will attack you; people will lie right to your face! In Dru-Ann's line of work, every single day is a competition—someone wins, a lot of people lose. There is no safety.

"I wanted her to honor her commitment," Dru-Ann says. "Show some good old-fashioned grit. Do you know why she dropped out of the tournament?"

"She didn't feel up to it," Caroline says.

"She felt fine!" Dru-Ann says. "Her boyfriend, Phineas Pine—"

"I'm not sure Twitter cares about the details," Caroline says. "You should probably just issue an apology."

"That's not happening."

There's a tense moment as Dru-Ann and Caroline stare at each other.

Dru-Ann thinks, *Your generation is both fragile and entitled, and no one is allowed to call you on it because you have been given the power to ruin a person's career by pushing a few buttons.*

She also thinks, *I used to change your diapers, and now you're my fixer?*

Caroline thinks, *If you don't issue an apology, you will be sunk. The longer you wait, the worse it will be.*

Caroline changes the subject. "What's up between you and Tatum?"

"You'll have to ask Tatum that," Dru-Ann says. She blows Caroline a kiss and closes the door. Caroline hears the *clickety-click* of her heels heading back down the hallway.

It's only seven o'clock on the first night, but one thing has become apparent: This weekend will be about more than just the landscape.

Brooke has been left to clean the kitchen like Cinderella. Hollis and Tatum are outside on the deck; Brooke can see them through the glass doors smoking cigarettes. Since when, Brooke wonders, does Hollis *smoke?* Brooke wipes off the oak serving board with increasingly aggressive strokes. Of course she's the one who's left out. She has no idea where Dru-Ann went, and she can't interrupt Hollis and Tatum when they're clearly *having a moment.*

Brooke reminds herself that Hollis is entitled to have a moment with whoever she wants to. She's endured a tragedy. But who was there for her when Matthew died? Who made all the calls, who organized the meal drop-offs, who checked in night after night for over a month? Not Tatum. Not Dru-Ann. (Neither of them had even come to the service!) The person who had *been* there was Brooke.

Brooke is pouring herself another glass of rosé, thinking she might as well finish off the bottle, when the front door opens and a woman pokes her head in.

"Hi," she says. "This is Hollis Shaw's house, right? I'm Gigi Ling."

Gigi Ling! Brooke thinks. Here's the fifth star, the one no one has met, not even Hollis herself. *Make a good impression,* Brooke thinks. *But act natural!*

"Yes, hello, welcome." Brooke hurries to the front door. "I'm Brooke Kirtley, Hollis's friend from Wellesley, we raised our kids together, I have boy-girl twins who are the same age as Hollis's daughter, Caroline—" Brooke takes a breath because she feels herself gushing. She extends a hand. Gigi Ling shakes it and gives Brooke a warm smile.

"It's lovely to meet you, Brooke." Gigi Ling has a British accent, which is a surprise, right? Brooke *loves* British accents! Gigi wheels in her luggage—there's a soft pink leather roller bag (so chic!) and, secured to the top, a fawn-colored suede tote that looks like it was purchased from a charming shop on a side street in Florence. "I'm sorry I'm so late." She waves a hand. "I won't bore you with the dreary details. I made it, that's all that matters."

"Can I get you a drink?" Brooke asks. "The others should be back in a minute. We haven't had dinner yet."

"A glass of cold water would be just gorgeous, thank you," Gigi says.

Just gorgeous, Brooke thinks. She gets down one of Hollis's cobalt-rimmed glasses and pours from the pitcher of chilled cucumber water in the fridge. Brooke hands the glass to Gigi, thinking that Gigi Ling is *just gorgeous* herself. And so stylish! Gigi removes her straw fedora, which is cuter and simpler than the fussy straw hat

Brooke chose, and Brooke admires her pixie cut. (Brooke longs to shave off her curly mop of hair, but she fears she'd look like Oliver Twist.)

Gigi's outfit is perfect simplicity: a ribbed olive tank and slim distressed white jeans with frayed hems. How do other people find good jeans? Brooke wonders. Hers are always too high-waisted and show too much ankle. For jewelry, Gigi has layered delicate gold necklaces, and on her wrist she wears one gold bangle and a leather-banded watch. There's a ring with some kind of cool greenish stone on her index finger. On her feet she wears white Veja sneakers. Gigi has deep brown eyes and luminous skin, and she emanates the kind of rarefied grace associated with women like Princess Diana and Jackie Kennedy.

Suddenly, the glass doors open and Hollis steps inside. Brooke can't help but feel a bit crushed; she and Gigi have barely met, and now she'll have to share Gigi with everyone else. Tatum trails behind Hollis, both of them smelling distinctly of cigarettes, and Dru-Ann materializes from down the hall.

"Gigi!" Hollis says. "Is that you?"

The others watch as Hollis strides over to Gigi, offering a hand, but Gigi opens her arms, and Hollis laughs, and the two women embrace.

Henrietta starts barking. She sniffs Gigi's leg, raises her nose to the ceiling, and howls.

"Henny!" Hollis cries. "Stop!"

Henny's barking becomes a low, sustained growl.

Gigi laughs. "She probably smells my cat, Mabel." She reaches out to pet Henrietta and the dog snaps at her.

"Henny!" Hollis yanks her back by her collar. "I'm so sorry, she never acts like this." To Henny, she says, "I'm banishing you to the dungeon." She walks Henrietta down the hall. Gigi smiles brightly (and oh so falsely) at the other women, thinking, *The dog knows.*

When Hollis returns, she says, "Don't worry, the dungeon is my bedroom, she'll be fine. Please forgive her—that's highly unusual."

"It's okay," Gigi insists. "I've been growled at by worse."

Hollis holds out her arm like a game-show hostess. "Let me introduce you to everyone. This is Tatum, my best friend from high school; Dru-Ann, my best friend from college; and Brooke, my friend from when the kids were growing up."

Brooke notices that Hollis doesn't call her a *best* friend. But she won't let it bother her; she won't get *offended;* it's fine—she doesn't have to be Hollis's best friend, she's here, that's the important thing. But Brooke assumes that everyone in the kitchen noticed that Hollis didn't say *best friend,* and they're probably thinking that Brooke is inferior.

The rosé has taken Brooke's good sense hostage. She blurts out, "And Gigi is your best friend from the internet."

There's a beat of silence and Brooke chastises herself. She needs to *edit* her words before she speaks.

Gigi laughs. "That makes me sound rather suspect."

Hollis says, "Let me show you to your room. Dinner is just about ready." She holds out a hand and Gigi grasps it, and the two of them head down the hall. From behind, it looks as though they've known each other all their lives.

Brooke whispers to Tatum and Dru-Ann, "She seems nice!"

"Sure," Dru-Ann says. "But who *is* she?" She turns to Tatum. "Did Hollis tell you anything about her?"

Tatum blinks at her.

Dru-Ann says, "Are you really going to be like that?"

Brooke looks at the two women. "I guess I didn't realize you two knew each other before," Brooke says. "When did you meet?"

"Hollis's wedding," Tatum and Dru-Ann say together.

"Oh," Brooke says. She didn't know Hollis back then. She met

Hollis when they were both pregnant. "What was the wedding like?" Brooke asks.

Neither Tatum nor Dru-Ann responds; the question just hangs there like a fart. It's a relief when Hollis and Gigi reappear and Hollis shepherds everyone out to the deck for dinner.

17. Fake It to Make It

Caroline pans around the dinner table. For Hollis's fans, this is the money shot.

Hollis is serving her cilantro-and-lime-marinated swordfish with avocado sauce, a summer squash tart with goat cheese and mint, a large green salad, and homemade baguettes with black pepper butter that, yes, her mother churned herself like a pioneer woman. This will be followed by peach cobbler with a hot sugar crust topped with fresh whipped cream, and tiny squares of Japanese chocolate.

Tatum smears a hunk of baguette with the peppery butter. The swordfish is so perfectly cooked and seasoned that it doesn't even need the avocado sauce. She thinks, *If I don't have cancer, I'm going to learn to cook like this. I'm going to take classes at the culinary center, I'm going to buy a freaking butter churn.* She isn't going to worry about the money; she's just going to do it. *Do I have cancer?* She watches Brooke pile salad on her plate and thinks, *If I can count to five without Brooke speaking to fill the silence, that means the tumor is benign.* She gets to four, then Brooke takes a breath... but Brooke stops herself and stuffs her piehole with salad. Tatum exhales. She should have called the doctor back right away; this is making her crazy.

Brooke was about to ask how everyone could eat and drink so much without worrying about gaining a hundred pounds. She starts out with only salad and a small piece of fish (no sauce). But the tart is a work of art—the discs of bright yellow squash have been snugged into the tart crust, dolloped with goat cheese, and sprinkled with fresh mint. She'll have a small piece; it would be rude not to. But she won't have bread. But then Gigi, who is sitting next to Brooke, hands her the ramekin of butter and says, "This is witchcraft. Let me get you the bread."

Brooke accepts the butter, thinking, *A piece of bread will help soak up the alcohol.* Brooke has had a lot to drink. There were the two glasses of rosé with Electra (although Brooke would like to discount these, since she's trying to pretend she never went for drinks with Electra) and almost an entire bottle of rosé tonight. Gigi is watching her with a kind smile, waiting for her to butter her bread, and what can Brooke do? Does anyone even count calories anymore? There are more fashionable ways to lose weight, like intermittent fasting or going keto, where you eat only steak, eggs, and broccoli rabe. Younger people have stopped caring about weight altogether because to care about being thin is to threaten body positivity. Does Brooke want to threaten body positivity? Well, no, but neither does she love her muffin top. She weighs the decision for a moment, then butters the baguette and pops it in her mouth. It's so delicious that she doesn't care if they have to roll her off the island in a wheelbarrow.

Hollis can't stop staring at Gigi Ling. She's every bit as lovely as Hollis imagined. *I chose well,* Hollis thinks. Gigi Ling is better than normal—she's exceptional. Her accent is like music; Hollis would be happy listening to her read the phone book.

"Tell us about yourself!" Hollis says. She's had so much to drink that she nearly adds, *I know next to nothing about you!*

"I'm an Aquarius and I like long walks on the beach," Gigi says.

Gigi is funny! Hollis thinks.

"I know you're from Atlanta," Hollis says. "But where did you get the accent?"

"I was born and raised in Singapore," Gigi says. "My father is Chinese, my mother was a country girl from Pine Mountain, Georgia. They met because my mother was a flight attendant on the Concorde and my father used to travel back and forth between New York and Paris for business."

This is a cooler answer than Hollis could have imagined, but something is off…

"I thought your mother was Chinese? Didn't you say something about her Cantonese recipes?"

Gigi's mind stalls for a second. Shoot, yes. On the Corkboard, she'd written, My own mum passed away before she could teach me her favorite Cantonese dishes. That was back when Gigi was trying to get Hollis's attention. She never dreamed she'd someday be sitting in Hollis's kitchen relaying her origin story.

"I did!" Gigi says. How does she explain her mother's "Cantonese dishes" when her mother grew up "a country girl" in western Georgia? It's not impossible that her mother was Chinese American and learned the Cantonese dishes from her own mother or grandmother. Would that be believable? "My mother learned to cook once she moved to Singapore. My father used to say she made the best zongzi in the nation, even better than the private chefs, and there were a lot of those." Gigi laughs, mostly at the absurdity of this answer. Gigi's mother not only didn't cook, she didn't eat; she subsisted on Tab and cigarettes and was dead of emphysema at forty. But Hollis laughs along, and is anyone else even paying attention? Gigi moves to more solid ground: She attended the Singapore American School, then her parents split; her mother died, and, to honor her, Gigi attended her alma mater, the University of Georgia, for two years. Gigi then got it in her mind that she wanted to fly planes for a living, so she transferred to Embry-Riddle. She's forty-three years old and has been a pilot with Delta for eighteen years. She most often flies internationally; she keeps her mouth shut about Rome and Madrid, but she mentions that, thanks to her travels, she's become fluent in Italian and Spanish.

"That's"—Hollis has a hard time coming up with the right word—"so *interesting!*" She looks around the table at her other friends' faces, which are glowing in the candlelight. "Isn't it?"

Tatum discreetly rubs under her arms. Is it her imagination or does that area feel tender and swollen? *Lymph nodes,* she thinks.

Dru-Ann is gazing at her bag on the blue silk chaise. What is happening on her phone? Has Nick called? By now he must be regretting what he said about hitting the brakes. He probably stopped by Dru-Ann's house, and when he realized she wasn't home, he might have gone to look for her at the Aviary. When she wasn't *there,* would he have started to worry?

Brooke thinks, *Hollis seems pretty obsessed—and for good reason. Gigi is fabulous!*

It doesn't take long before someone—the woman with the curly hair; Brooke?—asks the question Gigi is dreading.

"So, is there a Mr. Ling?"

"Only my father," Gigi says.

"Do you have a boyfriend?" Brooke asks. "Or...a partner?" She pauses. "I'm sorry, is that too personal?"

Yes, it's too personal, Gigi thinks. "I was in a relationship," Gigi says. "But it ended."

Hollis is glad that Brooke asked. Hollis wanted to know if Gigi was with someone, but she'd never been brave enough to bring the topic up via text.

Gigi laughs. "So now I'm doing that hot-girl thing of 'decentralizing men' from my life."

Is that a hot-girl thing? Dru-Ann wonders. If so, Posey Wofford doesn't know it.

Tatum has been married to Kyle for thirty-one years. She has always had the goal of making it to sixty years, and she's only halfway. She knows it's not a "hot-girl thing" to be so in love with her husband, but she is. *Please God,* she thinks. *Give me more time with Kyle.*

"I'd like to decentralize Charlie from my life," Brooke says.

"Is there something you want to share with the group?" Dru-Ann says. She's kidding—the last thing any of them wants is to hear some deep, dark confession about the state of Brooke's marriage. Right? Dru-Ann looks around. Gigi, Tatum, and Hollis are all gazing at Brooke with interest.

"No," Brooke says. "Maybe later this weekend, but not right now."

Gigi relaxes a bit; this kind of chat is unusual for her. She has never had close girlfriends. At SAS, Gigi occasionally befriended a girl whose parents had been relocated by a bank or corporation, but the stint in Singapore was always temporary—the parents got transferred or the family couldn't adjust to the oppressive heat or the strict laws and they left after a year or two. Gigi's classmates at Embry-Riddle were nearly all men, and this carried through to her life as a pilot. On the rare occasions that the female flight attendants Gigi works with invite her out for drinks, she says yes—and after a few cosmos or negronis, the talk always turns to sex. Always.

Gigi takes a sip of wine. "Let's change the subject," she says. "How do you all feel about faking your orgasms?"

The table sits in stunned silence.

Oops, Gigi thinks.

Caroline is so glad she has the camera rolling. This woman is awesome.

Tatum takes a swallow of pinot grigio, which goes down like water—headache tomorrow for sure—and says, "I've never faked an orgasm in my life."

"Liar," Dru-Ann says. "Everyone fakes. It's the reason men are so insecure. They can never be sure if it's real or if we're pulling a Meg Ryan."

Who is Meg Ryan? Caroline wonders.

"I. Have. Never. Faked. An. Orgasm," Tatum says. "Kyle knows how to make me *scream.* He stands behind me..." She stops. "Do you want to hear this?"

"Uh, *no,*" Dru-Ann says. "We're eating."

"I want to hear," Brooke says.

"I have to admit, *I'm* intrigued," Gigi says.

"He lifts me off the ground with one arm and rubs me with two fingers of his other hand." Tatum shrugs. "Sometimes we do that in front of a mirror. Very hot. That always works, but he has other tricks. I taught him what I liked back when we were both young, and he knows I haven't been with anyone else, so there's no one he needs to compare himself to. But I never fake. Why would I?"

"Damn," Dru-Ann says. "I fake to, you know, move things along."

"Because you have a chicken in the oven," Hollis says. "Or you just want to go to sleep."

Ew, Caroline thinks. She'd hoped Hollis would recuse herself from this part of the conversation.

"I've never had an orgasm with Charlie," Brooke says.

Again, the table goes silent. From outside, they can hear the waves breaking, then the suck of water back to the sea.

This, Caroline thinks, *is what's known as a mic drop.*

Finally Dru-Ann clears her throat. "Now I understand why you want to decentralize him from your life." She pauses. "Never?"

"Never with Charlie or any other guy, actually," Brooke says. "Only with myself."

"Does *Charlie* know this?" Hollis asks. She can hear her voice becoming high-pitched and she's probably one sip of wine away from slurring. She should switch to water, but she doesn't want to. This is the kind of frank, intimate talk that *should* be happening this weekend. Gigi Ling understood the assignment.

"He has no idea," Brooke says. "He thinks he's a porn star."

"You poor child," Dru-Ann says. She's developing an actual fondness for Brooke. The woman is *such* a basket case, it's endearing. "We need shots. Now." She goes to the kitchen for shot glasses—Hollis has two dozen on display; she must use them to serve gazpacho or some nonsense—and grabs the bottle of Casa Dragones and the bowl of cut limes. Back at the table, she pours five shots and passes four around: Brooke, Tatum, Hollis, and Gigi.

Dru-Ann hoists her shot glass. "To satisfaction." She winks at Brooke. "We're gonna get you some, girlfriend."

They all throw back the shots. Hollis winces, Brooke winces, Tatum winces; Gigi squeezes a lime into her tequila, and her gold bangle chimes against her watch as she throws the shot back with undeniable elegance.

Where did Hollis find this woman? Caroline wonders. She's a queen.

Hollis is a little unsteady as she stands to get dessert, the peach cobbler with a hot sugar crust, which has been warming in the oven. She brings the cobbler out and sets it on a trivet, then scoots back to the kitchen to whip the cream. For a few moments she stares into the bowl as the whisk beats around and around. She hears laughter in the other room over the strains of Bon Jovi and she thinks, *This is working.* Just as surely as the cream turns from liquid to solid, her friends are coming together. This metaphor might not apply, but there is no denying that things on the deck are going much better than they were earlier. Gigi's appearance has done wonders. Everyone is on her best behavior.

Hollis suspects that Gigi is fibbing about her mother's Cantonese cooking, but she thinks it's endearing. Hollis has lied about her own mother in the past—oh, has she. She and Gigi are so... *simpatico.*

For an instant, Hollis feels pleased with herself. *She* brought these amazing women together, and she has curated the *perfect Nantucket weekend.*

But as she's walking toward the open slider, she overhears the conversation on the deck.

Brooke says, "That cobbler could be on the cover of a magazine!"

And Caroline says, "My mother's life always looks good from the outside. It's the only thing that matters to her."

The table goes quiet. Hollis wants to reverse her steps, go back to the kitchen, go even farther back, to two weeks ago before she sent the invitations, before she thought this weekend would save her.

But then Tatum catches her eye. "Hey, sis," she says.

Hollis holds the frosted bowl aloft. "Whipped cream," she says feebly.

Tatum leaves the table, and after a beat, Dru-Ann stands up and follows her down the hall. Tatum disappears into the powder room. Dru-Ann hears the hum of the fan, the roll of the toilet paper, then the toilet flushing and water running in the sink.

The door opens. When Tatum sees Dru-Ann, she rears back. Then she sets her mouth in a grim line and tries to breeze right past her but Dru-Ann grabs her arm. "Do we have a problem?"

"Let go of me, please," Tatum says. "Everything's fine." *As long as you stay out of my face,* she thinks.

"I can't believe you're still bent about a joke I made a million years ago," Dru-Ann says.

"The thing is," Tatum says, "it wasn't a joke." She sees Gigi coming down the hall toward them and clamps her mouth shut.

"Are you two all right?" Gigi asks.

No, Tatum thinks.

No, Dru-Ann thinks. But she's not dragging a stranger into this. She cocks an eyebrow at Gigi. "I notice you didn't answer your own question. Do you fake your orgasms?"

"Well," Gigi says. She pauses dramatically. "I'd rather be a Tatum than a Brooke."

Both Tatum and Dru-Ann laugh. Tatum forgets she's angry for a second; Dru-Ann thinks, *All right, score one for Gigi.* (Though Dru-Ann notices she didn't actually answer the question.)

Caroline is a few yards away, filming. *That's a moment,* she thinks. Hollis's fans are in for way more than they can imagine.

Hollis is, somehow, left at the table with only Brooke. Where did everyone else go? Hollis is tempted to start clearing. Would that be rude? Would Brooke feel slighted, feel as though her company wasn't enough? (Yes.)

Brooke realizes she has Hollis all to herself. Now is the time to tell her that she had drinks with Electra. Because what if Hollis finds out another way? Hollis *won't* find out, how would she—and isn't it a free country? Can't Brooke have drinks with whoever she wants?

Brooke won't mention it. Uttering Electra's name at all would be dropping a stink bomb on an otherwise flawless evening.

But she can't just sit in silence. It's too awkward.

She says, "I'm sure wherever Matthew is, he misses your cooking. He was so proud of you." Immediately, Brooke chastises herself: What a moronic thing to say. *Wherever Matthew is,* what does *that* mean? Heaven? Hell? The ether? Buried in the dirt with the worms?

Hollis offers a faint smile of acknowledgment. "This peach cobbler was his favorite." She stares into the candlelight as her mind wanders. Matthew loved any kind of fruit dessert and always ordered halibut if it was on the menu. He couldn't abide Joe Buck calling a football game, though he loved Cris Collinsworth. His favorite color was green; his car was a color he called "hunter green." (Hollis can't think about his car; she yanks herself back from the topic like she's pulling her hand from a hot stove.) Matthew preferred blondes over brunettes, or so he always claimed, though all of his old girlfriends were brunettes. He wore Ferragamo loafers to work, driving moccasins on the weekends, Chuck Taylors if he was going to a rock concert. He hated gambling and wouldn't even throw five bucks into the football pool; he'd had an uncle who had lost everything on a craps table in Vegas. He read Michael Connelly, David McCullough. Did he have any regrets? He used to say he wished he'd coached Caroline's soccer team when she was little, but who was he kidding, he barely made it to Sprague Fields as a spectator. He had better friends from college than from high school, and he had no friends from medical school unless you counted his professors—like Dr. Schrader, his mentor. Hollis had e-mailed Dr. Schrader only hours after Matthew died to tell him the news right away because Dr. Schrader would have been expecting Matthew's visit. Dr. Schrader's wife, Elsa, had written back with her condolences. Our hearts go out to you and Caroline. We had no idea Matthew was planning a visit; how sweet for him to want to surprise us. He was such a good egg on top of being the most brilliant student Manny ever had.

This struck Hollis as odd because Matthew loathed surprises, for himself or anyone else. He was a planner.

Matthew's favorite city was San Francisco; he and Hollis always stayed at the original Fairmont on Nob Hill and ate, their first night, at Swan Oyster Depot—it was the one place Matthew didn't mind waiting in line. He preferred an aisle seat to a window seat on an airplane; his guilty pleasure was a root beer float; he loved movie theaters, especially historic ones, and he always got popcorn with lots of butter. He donated a mind-blowing sum every year to the Pine Street Inn in Boston—homelessness was his cause, though he also talked about joining Doctors Without Borders once he retired. Hollis had privately suspected that he would never retire.

"Hollis?" Brooke says. Both Tatum and Dru-Ann call her Holly, but Brooke can't imagine doing that. "Are you okay?"

"Yes, yes," Hollis says. "I'm sorry, I was just remembering things about Matthew."

"Do you think he's...*watching* us?" Brooke asks.

This makes Hollis laugh. If Matthew were alive and she'd told him she was hosting a weekend for Tatum, Dru-Ann, Brooke, and someone she'd met on the internet named Gigi Ling, he would have run for the hills. Nothing would have interested Matthew less than what's transpiring here at Hollis's Five-Star Weekend.

"No," she says.

Caroline checks her phone. There's a text from Dylan: Meet me at Cru later if you can?

OMG, she thinks. Does Dylan actually want to link?

K, she responds. Depends what time the fun ends here. She adds the laugh-crying emoji.

Hearing from Dylan is a boost, but there's nothing from Isaac. The *I miss you* text is just dangling there, a bad judgment call. He probably deleted it as soon as it came in. She's aching to send another text, something about what she's filmed so far. She is, after all, using his equipment. And the material is so much better than she expected.

Tatum returns to the table, followed by Dru-Ann, Gigi, and finally Caroline. Hollis gets a second wind. The evening can't end yet—the food was impeccable, and the conversation was spicier than she expected, but what about fun? Can she make this fun? When "American Girl" by Tom Petty starts playing through the speakers, Hollis turns up the volume.

Brooke shrieks, "I love this song!"

In so many ways, this song was Hollis's anthem growing up. She sings out, *"She couldn't help thinking that there was a little more to life somewhere else!"*

In another second, everyone starts dancing on the deck. Caroline can't pretend to be surprised; she knew this was coming. The follow-up song is the Romantics' "What I Like About You," and Brooke bops her head from one shoulder to the other in a way that must hurt her neck.

Dru-Ann pours another round of shots for everyone. *Really, is this necessary?* Caroline wonders. It's nearly eleven o'clock now. How much gas is left in the tank here? She wants to go into town to meet Dylan.

The song changes to "I'm Still Standing," by Elton John. Brooke raises her arms over her head and shimmies her hips and the rest of the stars form a circle around her, their unlikely hero. Caroline wonders if she can quietly slip out. Would anyone notice (well, her mother would notice) and would she miss anything important?

The next song in the queue is "Take My Breath Away" by Berlin, which brings a totally different vibe.

"Everyone backward-skate!" Dru-Ann shouts.

What does that even mean? Caroline wonders.

Hollis reaches for Tatum's hand, and the two of them spin, twirl, and dip. Dru-Ann grabs Brooke, who is so smashed she simply clutches Dru-Ann around the middle and rests her head against her chest.

What have I done? Dru-Ann thinks. Dru-Ann and Brooke shuffle in a tight circle and an unwelcome memory pops into Dru-Ann's mind: a seventh-grade dance with a boy named Philip Price. The song then was "Stairway to Heaven," eight minutes of torture—or of ecstasy, if you were Philip Price pressing your thirteen-year-old erection into Dru-Ann's leg.

Caroline focuses the camera on Gigi as she sits at the table watching the other women dance. Gigi's expression is neutral; she doesn't seem hurt or offended that she's a fifth wheel, and she doesn't fidget or check her phone or pick at the remaining cobbler, which is right in front of her. Instead, she remains so present and serene she might be a painting. Her gold necklaces glint in the candlelight; the breeze off the beach lifts her bangs off her forehead. *What could she be thinking?* Caroline wonders.

Gigi feels like a villain of literary proportions. She's Lady Macbeth. She's the narrator from "The Tell-Tale Heart." Her guilt pounds in her ears, stains her skin. How can the others not see it, hear it?

She longs to come clean. She fantasizes about interrupting the music, making an announcement—*I was Matthew's mistress!*—then dramatically exiting through the glass sliders while the others stare after her in shock and confusion. It would be hideous, yes, but also cleansing, cathartic. The yoke of guilt biting into her shoulder would be lifted.

She imagines visiting the Hungry with Hollis website before she goes to bed. A Kitchen Light will appear here, at Hollis's Nantucket house. Gigi will write on the Corkboard:

> To the Hungry with Hollis Community:
>
> My name is Gigi Ling, and I've been interacting with all of you under false pretenses. I led you to believe I was enthusiastic about banana bread and bouillabaisse, but really, I came here because I was conducting a love affair with Hollis Shaw's husband, Dr. Matthew Madden, and I was curious

about the woman whom I saw as my rival. After Matthew died, Hollis and I became so close that she invited me to her home for her Five-Star Weekend.

I realize some of you might not care about the interpersonal drama, and to those of you, I say: Hollis served grilled swordfish with avocado sauce, fresh baguettes with butter she churned herself, and a peach cobbler with a hot sugar crust. Hollis Shaw is the genuine article.

I, however, am not.

What would Molly Beardsley of Twain Harte, California, think of that? How about Bailey Ruckert from Baton Rouge? Gigi wonders which of Hollis's subscribers would cast stones. Nearly all of them, she assumes, though she's curious if there are any out there who might offer mercy, empathy, understanding.

It hardly matters. Gigi is too much of a coward to reveal herself.

18. First Light II

Caroline gets to Cru at midnight. Dylan meets her at the podium, looking smoking hot in a navy button-down, a navy blazer, and jeans. He leads her to a seat at the front bar and asks if champagne is okay.

"Obviously," she says.

A coupe glass of Pol Roger appears, and as Caroline sips it, she wishes Isaac could see her. She considers taking a selfie and texting it to him, but that feels childish and predictable. She considers taking a selfie and posting it to her Instagram stories—Isaac pretends not to have time for social media, though Caroline knows he creeps on her account occasionally—but does she want to be *that* girl, taking selfies and posting them? She does not. She tries to channel Gigi Ling. She will be present: Sip her champagne, admire the deft handiwork of the oyster shucker on the other side of the bar, listen to the music ("Kids" by MGMT). She assumes Sofia is back at the clubs and Isaac is in the loft alone, maybe waiting for his DoorDash from Momoya, maybe working, maybe watching *My Octopus Teacher* for the umpteenth time (he says he finds something new to admire about the film with every viewing). Should Caroline step outside and call him?

She should not. Dylan appears; he's ready to go. He asks the barback for "wine on wheels," and the barback hands him a fresh bottle of Pol Roger and two plastic cups. He and Caroline head down Straight Wharf to the parking lot. "Your chariot awaits," Dylan says, and he opens the passenger door of his monster truck.

They drive to Monomoy Beach, which is dark, quiet, and empty. Dylan pulls a blanket out of the back seat (he came prepared, Caroline thinks at first, but then he shakes it free of Cheez-Its crumbs and she realizes it must be Orion's playground blanket). They sit in the sand and Dylan pours them champagne. It's the most romantic setting Caroline can imagine; the crescent moon shows off like a diva in the spotlight. She tries not to think of Isaac. She tries not to think about not-thinking about Isaac.

Dylan says, "So how were things at the house?"

"They did shots of tequila, talked about orgasms, and slow-danced together."

Dylan chokes on his champagne. "That sounds like cinematic gold."

"It was a start," Caroline says. The night went pretty much as Caroline had expected, though she realizes there's stuff going on below the surface. How does she mine it? Maybe she should divide and conquer. Talk to the women individually.

"It seems like your parents are still really in love," Caroline says. "You're lucky."

"They are," he says. "It's disgusting." He laughs, then says, "Were your parents happy before your father died?"

"They were happy enough that I never had any reason to wonder if they were happy," Caroline says. "I'm not sure they were as happy as your parents." Caroline shivers—the off-the-shoulder blouse and flirty skirt she's wearing aren't enough for the breeze coming off the water. Dylan gallantly removes his blazer and drapes it over her. "Do you remember the night we met?" she asks. She reminds him of the Whalers sweatshirt and then Aubrey appearing out of nowhere. "This is a sweet reprisal. Minus Aubrey."

"She's like Voldemort," Dylan says. "One should never speak her name."

Caroline has questions about Aubrey: What is their deal? Was Aubrey getting pregnant the reason Dylan left Syracuse? How did that feel? Why did they break up? Dylan seemed pretty tickled by how jealous Aubrey was when she saw Caroline. Does he still have feelings for her?

But Caroline can take a hint. She tosses the topic away like a pebble into the water.

The champagne is gone, and Caroline has to pee. Caroline asks Dylan if he minds driving her back to the parking lot so she can get her Jeep, and he says, "Do you want to go to my house? You can use the bathroom and we can have one more drink."

She considers saying no. She woke up at four o'clock that morning in New York, a moment that feels like it happened three days earlier, and she's supposed to start filming the next morning at eight because her mother has arranged for a yoga instructor to come lead a practice at the house. Caroline will capture shots of the five stars in child's pose or warrior three.

Besides this, she misses Isaac. But Isaac is with Sofia. *Please, no trouble,* Sofia said. Why hadn't Caroline listened? Sofia might have been predicting what would happen: Caroline obsessed with someone who isn't hers. Caroline in agony.

"Sure," she says.

When they get to Dylan's house on Hooper Farm Road, he opens a couple of beers and they settle on the sofa.

"What was it like when your father died?" he says.

"What was it *like?*" Caroline asks.

"We don't have to talk about it if you don't want to," Dylan says. He spins his beer in his hands, then sets it down without drinking. "It just seems like a big deal."

Is Dylan McKenzie interested in her as a *person?* she wonders. Is she interested in *him* as a person?

"He was in a car crash." Caroline takes a breath. "It was a week or two before Christmas, my father was driving to Logan in a snowstorm. He was flying to Germany to speak at a conference; he was running late; the place he spun out was a road near our house—a couple of deer ran in front of his car." Caroline pauses. She wonders about the seconds right before the crash, after Matthew lost control of the car. Was he scared? Did he know he would die? Did he have time to cry out? Did he think about Hollis and Caroline? "I was at college in my World Cultures final; my mother texted me saying there was an urgent situation and please call. My mother is really prone to hyperbole. I thought *urgent* meant that she needed more gift ideas for me or my dad. I finished my test and went to Sweetgreen for lunch, and then my mother called again, and honestly, I almost sent her to voice mail. But at the last minute I answered and she told me."

Dylan sucks in his breath and Caroline hears her mother's voice. *Caroline, are you in a safe place to talk?* This had been such a strange question, and Caroline thought, *Where is safer than Sweetgreen?* But she heard something unusual in her mother's voice—this call was *not* about Christmas presents—so Caroline fit the plastic top over her crispy rice bowl and stepped out onto the Bowery. She said, *Okay, Mom, tell me. What is it? What's wrong?* And her mother said, *There was an accident. Your father...*

Caroline's crispy rice bowl had hit the sidewalk, splattering everywhere. Caroline ran, blinded with tears, back to her apartment. She called her best friend from high school, Cygnet, who went to Columbia. Cygnet rode the subway downtown and somehow got Caroline to JFK and then onto a plane to Boston, though Caroline doesn't remember much of this.

What was it like? Caroline thinks. It was like being suspended over a deep, dark endless hole knowing you were going to fall in and never get out. She would never see her father again.

Suddenly, Caroline is crying and shaking. Dylan is holding his head in his hands and saying, "Shit, I'm so sorry. I shouldn't have brought it up." Caroline nearly tells him it's fine, he was sweet to ask—but does she really need to make Dylan McKenzie feel better about himself right now?

After a minute or two, Caroline regroups. "That's how it is these days," she says. "Most of the time I'm fine, and then...I just lose it." She wipes under her eyes. "I should probably get home."

Dylan scoots closer to her on the couch and kisses her. The kiss is nice; he lingers and kisses her again and slips his tongue between Caroline's lips, and just as Caroline is asking herself if she wants to do this (she *should* want to do it; this is super-hot Dylan McKenzie, her teenage crush, and Isaac is probably making love to Sofia at that very moment, and Caroline desperately needs a rebound), Dylan pulls away.

He shakes his head. "I don't ever bring girls home," he says. "Because of Orion. It just feels...wrong."

"I get it," Caroline says. She doesn't get it, she's not a mother, but she finds she's relieved that things aren't going any further.

"Why don't you just sleep here on the couch?" Dylan says. "We've both been drinking and after that story..."

Caroline sinks into the sofa cushions. Going to town, then having to drive all the way back to Squam seems impossible. Dylan drapes a blanket over her shoulders, then kisses her forehead like she's four years old. But it feels nice, and Caroline closes her eyes.

When she wakes up, she has no idea where she is at first. She's on a couch that smells vaguely of cigarettes; she's fully clothed and covered by a green chenille blanket. On the coffee table is a glass of water and two cans of Bud Light.

Dylan's house, she thinks. *Shit.* Her neck is stiff, so she moves her eyes only—there's a kitchen to the right and a staircase over by the front door. There's no sign of Dylan or anyone else. She takes note of the huge train set dominating the living room—Thomas the Tank Engine—and the play workshop against one wall. The toys make her uncomfortable. She has to get out of here, but how? Dylan is most likely upstairs in his bedroom asleep. Should Caroline text him? He works so hard, he deserves to rest; she can order a Lyft. She puts on her sandals, folds the chenille blanket, carefully steps around the train tracks, and opens the front door.

Outside, the air is cool and heavy with mist. When Caroline goes to order a Lyft, it says, No cars available. It's a quarter to seven in the morning; how can there be no cars available? Don't people have to get to the ferry, the airport? She checks the street in both directions. Hooper Farm is nothing like Squam Road. This is a mid-island neighborhood, where locals live. Across the street is a small ranch house. The paint of the white trim is peeling; there's a surfboard leaning against the front steps and a couple of beater cars in the driveway. It's probably a rental for kids who are here working for the summer. She wonders if anyone works an early shift, if she can bum a ride to town.

She's about to go knock when she hears the screen door closing behind her. She turns around as a man steps out of Dylan's house. It's that guy Jack, the one from the car yesterday, the one her mother was so *entranced* with.

Ugh, she thinks. *Is he staying here?*

"Hey," he says in a hushed voice. He's wearing a T-shirt advertising something called Finigan's Bar and Grill. "You're…Hollis's daughter? I saw you yesterday, but we weren't introduced, I'm sorry." He holds out a hand. "Jack Finigan."

Caroline has no choice but to shake Jack's hand, look him in the eye, and say, "Caroline Shaw-Madden."

The corners of Jack's mouth lift and a dimple appears in one cheek, but Caroline won't let herself be charmed. He nods back at the house. "You trying to make a quick getaway?"

Lyft of Shame, she thinks. Except there are no Lyfts, and in the end, there was just the one kiss, no reason for shame. "Yes, I need to get home to film. My mom and her friends have yoga at eight."

"Is someone coming to get you?"

"I tried ordering a Lyft but they don't have any cars right now." She looks longingly down the street. "My car is in town. I could walk, but it's pretty far."

"I'll take you," Jack says. "I'm sure Kyle left his keys in the van."

"You don't have to," Caroline says. She doesn't want to drive anywhere with Jack Finigan—although he seems perfectly nice, and how else will she get to town? Her mother has proved unreliable in the ride department.

Jack opens the passenger door to a black panel van that says

McKENZIE HEATING AND COOLING on the side and Caroline climbs in. The floor of the van is littered with white paper bags from Henry's Jr. and coffee cups and discarded Powerball tickets. The back is filled with tools and equipment, lengths of PVC pipe, and insulation sleeves that look like big foil snakes. The van smells of gasoline or oil, not unpleasant but not familiar, and Caroline nearly laughs. She can't believe her day is starting by riding in a van with a complete stranger. This is how people end up on *Dateline*.

When Jack turns the key in the ignition, the radio blares, and he reaches to turn it down. "We were listening to Rush last night, sorry."

That's what the olds do, Caroline thinks. *They sing and dance to old music.*

"And I apologize for the mess, though I'll blame that on Kyle. Kid has always been a slob." He notices Caroline checking out a Powerball ticket and says, "He's been trying to win the lottery since we were in high school."

Caroline dreads getting into a whole "those were the good old days" conversation, but how will she avoid it? "You grew up on Nantucket with my mom?" she says.

"I moved here in seventh grade," Jack says. "My father took a foreman's job with a big construction company."

They go around the small rotary and head into town on Pleasant Street. In five minutes, maybe six, she'll be safely in her car.

"The good thing was I played football and we started practicing at the Boys and Girls Club the second week of school, and Kyle was the quarterback of my team. We became friends and he was dating Tatum—"

"They were dating in *seventh grade?*" Caroline thinks about Tatum saying, *I taught him what I liked back when we were both young,* and rolls down her window. She needs air.

"It was innocent stuff; they held hands at the movies and passed notes. Tatum was best friends with Hollis, and Kyle and Tatum decided that Hollis and I should be boyfriend and girlfriend."

Caroline laughs. "They decided?"

"They set us up on a date at the Sweet Shoppe, which was the ice cream parlor downtown back then. Tatum brought your mom, and Kyle brought me. I knew Hollis was too pretty and too popular for me. She had this thick blond ponytail and a smile that lit up her face, she and Tatum were the best girl athletes in our class, plus Hollis was smart—she was in my language arts class and she was always raising her hand. I tried to pay for her ice cream, but she said she had a job opening scallops down on the docks and she would pay for herself. But we called that our first date because by the time we walked out of the Sweet Shoppe, we were somehow 'going out.' "

Caroline should just let it drop but she feels herself getting sucked in. Her mother's memories about growing up on Nantucket were pretty selective, and Caroline has never heard about this "date." She has never heard about Jack Finigan at all. It wasn't as though Caroline thought her mother was a nun when she met Matthew—but yes, she did kind of think that.

"How long did that last?" Caroline asks.

"We dated all through high school, right up until your mom left for North Carolina," Jack says. "So a little more than five years."

Five years! Caroline thinks. Hollis and this dude were together for five years and Caroline is only now hearing about this?

Jack turns onto Summer Street and they wend their way down through the fish lots to Union Street. Caroline has two, maybe three, minutes left. "What was my mom like in high school? I figured she was smart and I know she played sports—"

"Hollis and Tatum were softball stars. They won the state championship junior year and lost in the finals senior year. That game was a heartbreaker." Jack pauses. "Did you ever know your grandfather?"

"He died when I was little," Caroline says.

"Well, that's too bad, but also not surprising because Tom Shaw smoked two packs of Camels a day. Great guy, very well respected, and he raised your mom by himself. He taught her to hunt and to fish, and every Friday night he took her to the Anglers Club. He never once invited me along."

Fishing? Caroline thinks. *Hunting—like, with a gun?* Caroline can't imagine this, and she doesn't even know where the Anglers Club *is*.

"The first day of scalloping season every year, Tom would pull Hollis out of school. She'd put on her waders and grab her rake, and the two of them went to their secret spot up in Pocomo." He laughs. "They never invited me scalloping either."

"Sounds like my grandfather didn't like you very much," Caroline says.

Jack says, "He loved me. I was the son he never had. But..." He shrugs. "Things didn't work out the way I thought they might."

He pulls into the parking lot and Caroline points out her Jeep. "I can't believe my mom knows how to hunt and scallop," she says. "It sounds like she used to be a completely different person."

Jack chuckles. "You can be more than one kind of person in your life," he says. "But I've always been a person who loves Hollis Shaw."

Caroline rears back. "Ohhhh-kay?"

"That just slipped out, sorry," Jack says. "I know you lost your dad recently. You didn't need to hear that."

Caroline reaches for the door handle; she can't get out of the van fast enough. "Thanks for the ride," she says.

19. Child's Pose

Newly minted yoga instructor Avalon Boone cuts her morning meditation short so she'll be at Hollis Shaw's on time—but when she pulls into the driveway on Squam Road, the front door is shut tight and all the shades are drawn. Avalon gets the distinct feeling that the household is still asleep.

Hollis is paying Avalon three hundred dollars to lead this practice, money Avalon desperately needs. She'll wake everyone up with her gong if she has to.

She pulls her basket of yoga mats, blocks, and straps out of the back of her Camry and approaches the front door. *Lightness and nobility,* she thinks. *First impressions matter.* Hollis has never practiced with Avalon before; over the phone, she admitted that she'd seen Avalon's ad in the back of *N* magazine.

Avalon notices the sea-glass windows on either side of the front door and she whips out her phone to take a picture. If she ever saves enough money to buy a house on this island, she wants windows just like these. She knocks, but there's no response—no footsteps, no voices. She knocks again. Nothing. She checks her phone. It's ten minutes to eight. Should she wait in her car until eight o'clock sharp? That seems silly; they have to set up on the pool deck, and Avalon has a vinyasa class to teach on Amelia Drive at nine thirty.

She texts Hollis: Good morning, this is Avalon, the yoga instructor. I'm here!

She waits another minute. There's no answer and no noise from inside.

The door is unlocked; Avalon cracks it open. "Hello?"

The house is as silent as a crypt. Avalon steps in and eases the door closed behind her.

What a house! Past the gracious entryway, there's a white brick fireplace and a sitting area—Avalon loves the pale blue silk chaise—and to the right is a bright, white kitchen with cathedral ceilings, white marble countertops, and high-end stainless-steel appliances, including a floor-to-ceiling wine fridge lit from within. Someone has set out breakfast—a big bowl of granola; two carafes of milk, one labeled SKIM and the other ALMOND; glass pitchers of juice—orange and pineapple—and the most exquisite fruit salad Avalon has ever seen, with raspberries, kiwi, blackberries, sliced peaches and plums, and chunks of pineapple and mango. Avalon can't help herself—she plucks a fat blueberry off the top and pops it in her mouth. The pièce de resistance is a platter of the fragrant cinnamon morning buns from Wicked Island Bakery. These are nearly impossible to get, so *someone* was up bright and early today.

"Hello?" Avalon calls again.

She's met with only the distant cries of gulls and the sound of the ocean; the back sliding door has been left open, and Avalon pokes her head out to see a pond with a footbridge, the beach beyond.

This home is breathtaking, she thinks. *And that breakfast looks sublime. But where* is *everyone?*

Hollis's alarm wakes her at six o'clock. She's still in her clothes, lying on top of her covers. Half a glass of sauvignon blanc mocks her from the nightstand. She grapples for her phone; she has to make the dinging noise *stop,* but she knocks over the wineglass in the process and she thinks, *Oh, for heaven's sake, what is wrong with you?* She saves her phone from the wet and squints at the screen. The alert says MORNING BUNS.

Forget the morning buns, she thinks. She needs sleep.

But she's the hostess, and this is supposed to be a Five-Star Weekend. She propels herself to her feet and staggers out to her car. She ends up being the second person in line at the bakery, and she makes a very lame early-bird-catches-the-morning-bun joke to the poor teenage girl behind the counter. Then she drives back home in a haze, twice nearly pulling over to throw up. Those tequila shots.

At home, she sets out the breakfast things like a robot, thanking God she prepped everything in advance. It's only six forty-five; she can squeeze in an hour of sleep before yoga. Back in her room, she climbs into bed naked without realizing she's left her phone in the car.

While Avalon is in the kitchen sneaking a piece of pineapple and a ball of honeydew from the fruit salad, Hollis is fast asleep.

Tatum wakes up at six thirty as usual, even though today she can sleep in instead of pouring Orion's cereal, setting up his game on the iPad, packing Kyle a lunch, and getting herself ready for work (Saturdays at Irina Services are a special kind of hell). She tries to fall back to sleep but she can't quite get there. Tatum doesn't remember the last time she spent an entire night in bed by herself; it might have been when she was in the hospital after having Dylan. She and Kyle are never apart; when they go off-island, they go together. Tatum stretches out like a starfish. It's nice, but she misses Kyle's warm body, his morning wood poking her backside, his breath in her hair, the way his hand rests on her hip as they sleep. She rolls over to grab her phone and sees she already has a text from him.

I miss you. How was last night?

How *was* last night? It was better than Tatum thought it'd be.

The music was all the good '80s stuff and the food was, of course, incredible. The most satisfying part of the evening was that she succeeded in freezing out Dru-Ann exactly the way she'd dreamed of doing for twenty-five years.

When "Take My Breath Away" played, Hollis reached for Tatum's hand, and they did the dance that they'd choreographed in middle school (and performed any chance they got, including at junior prom, senior banquet, and both of their weddings). They hadn't done those moves in a long time but they both remembered every step.

Tatum can't figure out how Gigi fits in. She seems nice, but why did Hollis invite her?

It's fine, Tatum texts Kyle. She won't get too complimentary yet; there's still plenty of time for things to get weird. It's pretty clear Tatum has far less money than everyone else, though she was pleased to discover that she's having better sex. She'll tell Kyle about the orgasm conversation in person—he'll *love* it.

What did you guys do last night? she asks.

Went to the Tap Room for steaks. Then drinks at Straight Wharf.

Whaaaaa? Tatum thinks. The Straight Wharf bar is filled with gorgeous twenty-somethings. She can't *believe* Kyle went to the Straight Wharf. Did he pay sixteen bucks for a Goombay Smash or eleven bucks for a Bud Light? Did he get hit on? (He's fifty-three but he looks ten years younger, the bastard.) If he and Jack wanted a nightcap, why didn't they just stroll a hundred yards farther down the dock to Cru? Dylan would have given them drinks for free! These petty feelings of jealousy are unfamiliar and *very* unpleasant. Why shouldn't Kyle be allowed to have fun? He *should* be allowed is the correct answer, but Tatum would far prefer it if Kyle had stayed home eating microwave popcorn and watching the Red Sox.

Another text comes in from Kyle. She expects it to be an explanation or an apology but it says: Then we went to see Buckle and Shake play at the Gaslight.

Tatum idly fingers the tender spot on her right breast; she presses harder so she can feel the hard little nugget she now knows is either a cyst or a tumor. She replayed the voice mail on her phone before she went to bed, thinking she might hear something new in the doctor's voice. *Do I have cancer or don't I?*

It sounds like Kyle and Jack had a proper Nantucket night out on the town. They went to the Gaslight, a building Tatum hasn't set foot in since it was the Starlight movie theater and she and Kyle snuck in to see *9½ Weeks.* Tatum has heard good things about the nightclub—Dylan goes on occasion—but it always seemed too young and fabulous for Tatum and Kyle.

She leans back into the pillows. She *isn't* the first Mrs. Albright. She won't be the kind of wife who tells her husband to start dating while she's still around, nor will she reassure Kyle that he should find someone once she's gone. She doesn't want him to find love again, start over, have a second act. If that's a character flaw, she's sorry-not-sorry.

Another text from Kyle comes in: I'm headed out to fix a boiler on Crooked Lane. Jack and I are going for breakfast at Black-Eyed Susan's around ten. Want to meet us?

"Meeting husband for breakfast" seems against the rules when she's on a girls' weekend—but there's no way Tatum is missing it. Sure thing, she texts back. See you then. At ten, the itinerary says *shopping in town,* so Tatum will just slip away for an hour. No one will even notice.

Tatum hears a knock at the front door, and she jumps from bed to peer out the window. There's a young woman with dirty-blond curls piled on top of her head and a mandala tattoo on her shoulder. She's bracing a basket of yoga mats against her hip. Tatum scurries back to bed. She has no desire to do yoga today or any day. While the others do their upside-down dog or whatever, Tatum will smoke on the back deck like the rebel she's always been.

But there's no movement in the house, no response to the knock, thank God. Tatum closes her eyes. She will sleep in until it's time to go to town and then she will meet her husband no matter what Hollis and the others think. The fireworks chandelier is cool, but it's not love.

While Avalon settles onto a stool at Hollis's kitchen island, wondering if it would be egregiously rude to help herself to a morning bun (yes, it would, she decides, and all the sugar and gluten would interfere with her teaching and most likely give her heartburn), Dru-Ann is kicking around under the covers. Something is wrapped around her leg—yes? No? She's having a dream? She lifts the sheet and shrieks. There's a long, thin black thing coiled around her shin. A *snake?* She leaps from bed and the snake falls to the ground and lies there. Dru-Ann squints. It's not moving. It's rubber.

What the hell? she thinks. Do they call this place the Twist because of surprises like this?

Her heart is beating so fast she doesn't need the Peloton, but she powers out a forty-five-minute HIIT and Hills ride with Tunde anyway. When Dru-Ann climbs off the bike, dripping with sweat and smelling *very* strongly of last night's tequila, she feels a tiny bit better. She heads out to the kitchenette and grabs a water out of the vintage icebox. Rubber snake aside, the interior of the Twist is a midcentury dreamscape. There's an angular, tangerine-hued sofa in the living room flanked by two chairs upholstered in wavy olive-and-white stripes. There's a standing lamp that looks like a birdcage on a wooden tripod; the rug is a cool yellow-and-white geometric pattern, and on the walls are groovy abstract prints. In a little niche in the far wall is a Bakelite turntable over which hangs a framed 45 record. Dru-Ann has no idea why they call it the Twist. Is it a cocktail reference—a twist of lemon or lime? Or maybe it's called the Twist because you're expecting more beachy decor but instead you feel like you're walking onto the set of *That Girl.* It makes Dru-Ann want to wear patio dresses and throw fondue parties.

These thoughts serve as a nice little distraction—but suddenly, Dru-Ann can't wait another second. She snatches up her phone.

On Twitter, she checks for #TeamDruAnn. Only one person has retweeted her post—Dru-Ann's assistant, Jayquan. That kid is getting a raise.

There's a text from JB: Tried calling. Is your phone off? Plz listen to voice mail. There's also a text from Nick. *Finally!* Dru-Ann thinks. It has been her rule to keep the upper hand in every romantic relationship, and because of this Dru-Ann Jones can honestly say that at the age of fifty-three, she has never had her heart broken. She'd assumed Nick Wofford cared for her more than she cared for him, but the way she's been feeling since he said he needed to "hit the brakes" tells her she might be wrong about that.

Nick has two older sons by his (dreadful) first wife, Artice, to whom Nick still pays a seven-figure alimony. The boys, Sean and Declan, work for Nick at his hedge fund, and Nick is a hard-ass with both of them. Posey is the only child from Nick's second marriage, to a woman named Catherine; she died of ovarian cancer when Posey was eight. Catherine was the love of Nick's life—she was kind, sweet, and generous. (*Saint Catherine* is how Dru-Ann always thinks of her.) It makes sense that Nick coddles Posey, but can't he see that he should have demanded that she honor her obligation to finish the tournament? It was *one round of golf.* She could have hopped a plane to Edinburgh as soon as the trophy was in her hot little hands.

What a mess! Dru-Ann can't believe how this has played out.

She listens to JB's voice mail first.

"Dru-Ann, the situation is escalating. What possessed you to post that tweet yesterday? Hashtag Team Dru-Ann? Are you serious? It has *blown up* and not in the way you intended. Two more clients are dropping you, Sharese Morris and Kendall Hennaker, though

Kendall says she'll stay if you issue an apology. I've e-mailed you the statement that Legal drafted. You must sign it today. There's no other way to get back to good. I think we can lure Linzy back too; I spoke to her mother, who said she was on your side in all of this." There's a long pause. "But Linzy's mother is very much in the minority, Dru-Ann. Your shame is the company's shame. If you don't issue the apology today, I'll be forced to take next steps. Thank you." There's another pause. "I hope you listen to this."

Dru-Ann deletes the voice mail. She won't be issuing an apology. She has never liked Linzy's mother but she's happy to have at least one ally in the world.

She opens the text from Nick, fully expecting an apology and/or a declaration of love. It says: FYI, Phineas just eagled 14 and broke into the top ten.

Dru-Ann snatches up the remote and flips through the sports channels, though she knows U.S. coverage of the British Open won't start until this afternoon, and even then it'll be minimal until the final round tomorrow. She fires up her laptop and checks the standings, and sure enough, Phineas Pine is in ninth place at four under; he's on the sixteenth hole of the round now. The top of the field is close; McIlroy is the leader at seven under. Phineas is three shots back with twenty-one holes to go.

There are no phones allowed at St. Andrews so real-time developments are hard to come by. Is Posey somehow texting Nick? Or did Nick fly to Scotland? Dru-Ann wonders if Nick feels that Phineas's remarkable showing somehow *justifies* Posey's decision to quit the Dow. *He had a dream he was going to win.* Maybe Nick thinks it's romantic, Posey sacrificing her own nearly certain victory to be at her boyfriend's side.

It's not romantic, Dru-Ann thinks. *It's pitiful!*

While Avalon is making herself an herbal tea in the kitchen and texting Hollis yet again—Hi, I'm here! Should I stay or should

I?—Dru-Ann snaps her laptop shut, clicks off the TV, and powers off her phone. She needs a shower.

Brooke is lying in bed in the Board Room with her fingers between her legs, masturbating. All the talk of the night before has gotten her worked up. She thinks about being in the center of the circle last night, dancing, only in her fantasy, she's naked.

She hears someone in the hallway whispering, "Hello? Hello? Namaste?" It sounds like the person is right outside Brooke's bedroom door, but Brooke double-checked that the door was locked and so this heightens Brooke's excitement. The yoga instructor is only a few yards away from where Brooke is lying, but she has no idea what kind of eye-rolling, toe-curling, back-arching *ecstasy* Brooke is experiencing.

Who needs yoga to find enlightenment? Brooke thinks. She's finding it here all by herself.

The door to Gigi's room is ajar, and Avalon takes this as an invitation. She wants to find *someone* before she leaves. She taps on the door and says, "Hello? Hello?" And then, to identify herself as the goddamn yoga instructor, she adds, "Namaste?"

There's no answer, and Avalon boldly pushes the door open. This room is as swoon-worthy as the rest of the house. There's deep green jungle-print wallpaper, a rattan sleigh bed sheathed in white and hibiscus pink linens, a simple sisal rug, and a trunk at the end of the bed inlaid with mother-of-pearl. The far end of the room is a living garden—there are hanging succulents, two potted palms, a white shelf displaying a row of bonsai trees. Again, Avalon whips out her phone and takes a few quick pictures, despite her mounting frustration. Avalon steps out—really, what is she doing prowling around like this?—then notices a door at the end of the hallway, and through the window she spies a slice of turquoise. The pool!

Avalon hurries down the hall, thinking maybe the joke is on her, maybe everyone is out on the pool deck, waiting for her.

But the pool deck is empty. *What the hell?* Avalon thinks.

Gigi has taken a walk on the beach. She sees seagulls, sandpipers, oystercatchers, and, in the distance, a red-and-white-striped lighthouse on a bluff. She does not see another living soul, which suits her just fine.

She sits in the sand, drops her face into her hands, and cries.

Back at First Light, Avalon packs up her Camry and leaves. That was a yoga fail, she thinks—but at least she has a morning bun, swathed in a napkin, for later.

20. Shotgun I

As they're all climbing into Hollis's Bronco to go to town, Dru-Ann says, "Guess what I found in my bed? A rubber snake."

"What?" Hollis says. "That's impossible. I made up all the beds fresh yesterday."

"It's like that scene from *The Godfather*!" Brooke says. "Remember the horse head?"

Tatum, who is sitting shotgun next to Hollis, says, "It sounds like someone was trying to send you a message."

Well, Dru-Ann thinks, *that mystery is solved.*

21. Stone Alley

Brooke expects they will all stroll through town together, but as soon as they climb out of Hollis's Bronco, Tatum says she has an errand to run and that she'll meet everyone in an hour.

"Okay?" Brooke says. The cleft between her first and second toes was rubbed raw by the sadistic sandals from the day before, so Brooke is wearing a pair of purple Skechers that make her feel like the kind of woman who walks at the mall. "Where shall we meet up?" She surveys the scene on Main Street: There's a line of glowing young people in yoga clothes at Lemon Press; the Bartlett's Farm truck is parked on the corner, its sectioned flatbed bursting with ears of corn, zucchini, carrots, and radishes with the frilly green tops still attached; a balding gentleman in horn-rimmed glasses reads the newspaper on a bench with a golden retriever lying at his feet. "I'd like to go to Murray's Toggery. I want to buy a Nantucket Reds skirt." She looks to Hollis for validation or instruction of some kind, but Hollis is gazing down Centre Street.

"I'll be right back," Hollis says. "I'll text if I can't find you." She moves around a couple pushing a double stroller and darts off after Tatum.

Brooke tries to summon the mellow afterglow that she felt that morning in bed, but it's gone. She'd thought that they would be like five stars in a constellation, doing things together. (Was this silly?) While Brooke tried on her skirt, the others would browse, and when

Brooke popped out of the dressing room, they would give her a thumbs-up or a thumbs-down. That's what girlfriends *did.*

"There's a store I want to check out, but it's on the other side of town," Dru-Ann says. "It's the only place that carries Dries Van Noten."

"Dries Van..." Brooke has no idea what Dru-Ann is talking about; it sounds like she's speaking German.

"I'll meet you later." Dru-Ann waves a hand in the vague direction of Pacific National Bank and takes off down the street.

Brooke turns to Gigi with a forced smile. "Looks like it's just us," she says. She feels like they're the last two kids picked for a team in gym class.

Gigi is wearing her straw fedora, a pair of dark round sunglasses, and the cutest white T-shirt dress with her Vejas. "I wanted a chance to get to know you better anyway," she says. "We barely got to talk last night."

This cheers Brooke up. She will have Gigi and her fabulous accent all to herself. Brooke wants to ask the obvious question: How did you connect with Hollis? Did she just pick you off her website at *random?* But really, what a rude question. It's no wonder people avoid Brooke like she's got some contagious disease; she can always be counted on to say the wrong thing.

When they cross the street, Brooke veers toward Murray's, where her new skirt awaits, but Gigi peels off into Mitchell's Book Corner—and Brooke feels she has no choice but to follow.

"Look at this winsome little place!" Gigi says. "I just love independent bookstores."

Brooke knows it's noble to patronize independent bookstores, but when she buys a book—which isn't often; she read *Fifty Shades of Grey* ten years ago, and more recently she ordered *A Gentleman in Moscow* because everyone else was reading it but she never even cracked it open—she orders from Amazon because it's cheaper and easier.

Gigi heads straight for the fiction section and chooses a book by someone named Maggie O'Farrell. "Have you read this yet?" she asks Brooke.

"Um, no?" Brooke says. "I've never heard of—"

"What? Well, you must try her, she's *so* clever. In fact, I'm buying this for you, no arguments." Next, Gigi takes down a novel called *A Spool of Blue Thread* by Anne Tyler. "Anne Tyler is a *goddess.* I've been reading her since I was at uni and she has only gotten better."

Brooke has heard of Anne Tyler, hasn't she? Wasn't she the one who wrote the vampire books when Brooke was in college?

"Oh!" Gigi says, plucking a novel called *Our Little World* off the shelf. "I just finished this gem—she's a debut author, so I've been recommending her book to everyone, because you know how important it is to champion new writers. I'm buying this for you as well."

"No, you don't have to—" Brooke can't let Gigi spend money on books Brooke will never read.

"The thing I love best about reading fiction is that it gives you a way to connect the experiences of your own life to the larger world," Gigi says. "Don't you find that to be true?"

Brooke isn't sure what to say. The most literary thing about Brooke is that she lives on Thackeray Road in the Poet's Corner section of Wellesley. She has a hard time getting into books, and she has certainly never read anything with a character like herself. Her life is so dull, so artless, that it falls well outside the realm of literature.

But...maybe Brooke *will* give reading another try. Maybe with this push-start from Gigi, Brooke will evolve into someone who champions new writers and recommends them to others. There are, of course, *numerous* book clubs in Wellesley. Once upon a time, Brooke belonged to one, lured in by the reassurance that "no one ever talks about the book, all we do is drink wine!" Except that they *had* talked about the book, which Brooke hadn't even started. The leader of the first discussion, Trinh Nguyen, a professor at Wellesley College (Brooke was in way over her head), had asked Brooke what she thought of the "hero's journey," and Brooke had turned so pink she was purple and said, "I haven't gotten to that part yet." Trinh said (in a voice reminiscent of Brooke's tenth-grade English teacher, Mrs. Dolan), "The whole book is the journey, Brooke."

Is it any wonder Brooke doesn't like to read? Her phone never asks her to think; Netflix doesn't demand in-depth analyses. Reading takes effort, and Brooke has a hard enough time dealing with Charlie, the house, the kids, and her various insecurities.

Brooke stares at the colorful spines of the New Releases and plucks a novel with a sky-blue cover off the shelf. The flap copy says that the book is set on Nantucket; it's a "beach book." Brooke can handle a beach book, can't she? She'll begin it that very afternoon; it'll be so appropriate, reading a Nantucket beach book on a Nantucket beach!

She wanders over to Gigi, holding the book out like an offering. "I'm getting this one."

Gigi takes the book from her and blinks. "Yes, I've heard this author is very popular." Brooke can tell that *popular* is an insult in disguise. Probably the book Brooke has chosen is the literary equivalent of *The Masked Singer.* (Brooke loves *The Masked Singer.*) "But I'm still buying you these two. It'll bring me such joy."

"Okay?" Brooke says. How can Brooke refuse Gigi—with her impeccable taste and her delicious accent—*anything?* Even if the books end up collecting dust on Brooke's nightstand, she'll be able to look at them and remember Gigi's kindness. When Gigi hands her the brown bag, it has a satisfying heft. It feels like self-improvement, and Brooke stands up a little straighter.

Back on the street, Brooke leads the way to Murray's Toggery, explaining the phenomenon of Nantucket Reds pants. "They're made from a canvas material that starts out brick red and then fades with each washing to a distinct shade of pink. Men's pants are the most popular item, but I want to get a skirt."

Gigi links her arm through Brooke's. "Let's make that dream come true."

The first thing Brooke notices about Murray's—other than its delightful smell of leather and starch—is how colorful it is. Inside the door is a stack of men's pants in yellow, cornflower blue, kelly green. There are spinning racks of festive ties—Brooke fingers a pink tie printed with blue crabs—and there are carousels of crisp shirts in ginghams and stripes. There are shorts embroidered with mallard ducks, American flags, shamrocks; there are needlepoint belts; there's a stack of cable-knit sweaters in colors like melon and turquoise. Every article of clothing seems to promise a life spent sailing, golfing, and attending tailgate picnics, fox hunts, and graduation ceremonies at places like Princeton and Duke.

Gigi pulls a violet plaid shirt from the rack and says, "I wish I had someone to buy this for." Her voice sounds wistful, and Brooke wonders if this is an invitation to ask Gigi if she is thinking of dating again now that the relationship she was in has ended. Is she on Hinge or Bumble? She's a pilot, so isn't she surrounded by men every day?

Brooke says, "I have someone to buy for, but he's not getting a thing." This, she realizes, might be construed as an invitation to ask what's happening with Charlie, but Brooke doesn't want to talk about Charlie. She wants to pretend Charlie doesn't exist. She marches with purpose into the women's department.

Brooke admires the cashmere cardigans, the classic white blouses with Peter Pan collars, the grosgrain headbands, and the espadrilles. She fondly recalls her grandmother, who dressed this way when she hosted bridge or went to her garden-club meetings. Then Brooke finds what she's been looking for: a whole wall of Nantucket Reds skirts in different lengths. Brooke spies a youthful miniskirt, and there's one with a thirty-one-inch waist near the back.

Gigi reaches out to touch the material. "Isn't this *unique?*" she says.

Unique for a skirt might be the same as *popular* for a novel, but Brooke doesn't care. She takes the skirt to the dressing room. Only once she has shed her linen shift does she realize she has no top to wear with the skirt. She can't very well model it for Gigi in just her bra—but at that moment, there's a tap on the door and Gigi says, "I picked out the smartest jumper for you to try on with it."

Brooke cracks the door and Gigi's disembodied hand holds out a navy-and-white-striped cotton boatneck sweater, which is, in fact, "smart." Brooke pulls it over her head and fastens the skirt. When she pops out of the dressing room, Gigi beams and claps her hands. "Aren't you a beauty! Oh, Brooke, yes, you were right. It suits you!"

Brooke is so happy, she nearly starts to cry. She's *glad* the others aren't around. *Things always work out like they're supposed to,* she thinks; Brooke and Gigi were meant to have this time to bond.

Brooke decides to buy the sweater as well as the skirt. Maybe she'll wear this outfit tomorrow night for the pizza party, ice cream truck, and fireworks. When the cashier folds the skirt, she says, "The color will fade with a few washings."

"Oh, yes, I know," Brooke says. She hands the cashier her Visa, praying that Charlie in his desperation hasn't done anything rash like run up a huge gambling debt with the Barstool Sports book. But the charge goes through smoothly; the cashier hands Brooke her shopping bag and Brooke floats out of the store.

She's in such high spirits that she doesn't see Electra until it's almost too late. But some instinct makes Brooke turn, or perhaps it's the bumblebee yellow of Electra's dress or the Clydesdale clomping sound of her platform wedges on the crosswalk that catches Brooke's attention. Electra is heading straight for them.

"Where to next?" Gigi asks.

Brooke *cannot* risk a run-in with Electra, but how will she avoid it? She takes Gigi's arm and turns the corner, even though the street is, very clearly, residential.

"This way," Brooke says, pulling Gigi along. She hears Electra call out, "Brooke!" but Brooke pretends not to hear. She speed-walks forward. (Thank God for her Skechers.)

She needs an escape route! It might have been okay to bump into Electra if she were alone, but she can't introduce Gigi because it will get back to Hollis. To the left, Brooke sees what she thinks is a driveway...until she notices one of the tasteful Nantucket street signs; it says STONE ALLEY.

"I want to check this out," Brooke tells Gigi, and she basically races down the steep cobblestone path tucked between the backs of the Main Street businesses and the sides of private homes. Electra won't be able to pursue them in those wedges she's wearing without snapping an ankle.

"This is so whimsical!" Gigi cries. "Like something from a storybook."

Is it whimsical that Brooke is so desperate to avoid Electra that she's bolting down the cobblestones, shopping bags slapping against her legs? She could easily break a bone herself but she doesn't care; she has to get away. If Hollis finds out that Brooke and Electra reconnected, Hollis will never forgive her. Why on earth had Brooke agreed to have drinks with the woman? Why had she not confronted Electra about all the harm she'd caused? Instead, Brooke had genuflected at Electra's altar; she had put the date of rock and roll football in her phone's calendar.

Brooke keeps going all the way down the hill, Gigi following along, until the path becomes a set of stone steps that deposit them on Union Street. Brooke is out of breath and more than a little mortified. Gigi is going to think she's a head case. And isn't she?

But when Gigi catches up with her, she seems exhilarated. "That was a snazzy detour," she says. "As we were descending, I could just picture whaling captains using that path to visit their mistresses. And Quaker girls in their frilled caps meeting their beaux for stolen kisses."

Brooke no longer questions why Hollis invited Gigi to the Five-Star Weekend. The woman is an absolute delight.

Gigi looks at her phone. "It says there's a place on the next block called the Handlebar Café. Shall we go get a coffee?"

"Yes, let's!" Brooke says, now affecting a slight English accent of her own. "That would be just gorgeous."

22. Under the Influence I

Dru-Ann is sorry she isn't a better "gal pal" or whatever is expected of her this weekend, but she likes to shop alone. She knows what looks good on her and what doesn't, and she gets in and out of stores as expediently as possible. She's also a snob, and the prospect of popping into a bunch of shops that sell Nantucket T-shirts, brass porthole mirrors, or watercolors of the harbor makes her itch. Brooke wanted to go to Murray's, which is where the women who hand out programs at the Episcopal church shop. No offense, but Dru-Ann's tastes are a little more urban.

Gypsy does not disappoint. It's in one of the grand old homes on

Federal Street; it has a pleasant outdoor garden where two young women are sitting on a comfy-looking sofa with shopping bags at their feet. One of the women is Black with close-cropped hair, wearing fire-engine-red lipstick and head-to-toe Gucci. The other is a porcelain-skinned blonde in one of those long, floral, puff-sleeved dresses that make Dru-Ann think of *Little House on the Prairie*. The Gucci woman is showing Laura Ingalls something on her phone; Dru-Ann hears her say, "This was from the shoot at Rashad's apartment on Bleecker." They both look up as Dru-Ann approaches, and she smiles if only to prove that, even as a native Chicagoan, she can be nice to people from New York.

When Dru-Ann steps inside Gypsy, she enters her own personal fashion nirvana. She's been looking for a particular Dries Van Noten shirtdress in amethyst that the website says is sold out, and she immediately spies it across the room. A tall, slender, painfully chic salesperson takes in Dru-Ann's look—her Mother jeans, Golden Goose sneakers, Rick Owens tee under a cream linen Veronica Beard blazer—and gives her a nearly imperceptible nod of approval. Dru-Ann isn't a day-tripper who has wandered in looking for "something cute to wear out for lobsters." Dru-Ann belongs here.

"Welcome to Gypsy," the salesperson says. "My name is Joey. May I offer you a glass of champagne?"

Does Dru-Ann want champagne at ten thirty in the morning? Hell yes she does. "I'd love it, thanks. My name is Dru-Ann."

In a tiny but beautifully appointed kitchenette behind the counter, Joey pops a bottle of Moët et Chandon that's sitting in ice. Dru-Ann is pleasantly surprised; she'd been expecting lukewarm prosecco. She accepts the flute from Joey, moves her sunglasses to the top of her head, and whisks the amethyst shirtdress in size small off the hook.

"I'll start you a room," Joey says.

Dru-Ann glides around the store, touching sleeves, holding up sweaters. They have the Nili Lotan pants that are all over the internet. Dru-Ann likes them in the eggshell but are they too trendy now? Would they qualify as "coastal grandma," a look Dru-Ann is desperate to avoid? She sees a Raquel Allegra dress she'll try on just for fun and an ivory camisole top by Chloe. She tries to banish Nick from her mind, though she can't help but replay a Saturday only two weeks earlier—before the Dow Invitational disaster—when she and Nick had mimosas at the Hoxton, shopped the boutiques in the West Loop, had a very late lunch at Beatrix, then went back to Dru-Ann's town house and had the kind of sex you see in movies. It feels *very* weird that Nick doesn't know she's on Nantucket—she mentioned the weekend to him when Hollis first invited her, but she doubts he remembers—and that she has no idea where Nick is today. He owns a lakefront estate in Winnetka, where he lives with Posey; he's waiting for her to "launch" before he sells the big house and buys the penthouse at no. 9 Walton.

Is he home in Winnetka, Dru-Ann wonders, or did he fly to Scotland?

If Nick flew to Scotland, can Dru-Ann ever forgive him? Would her forgiving him even matter since they've "hit the brakes"? Dru-Ann throws back her champagne and picks up a red leather Isabel Marant motorcycle jacket. She's going to... what? Spend money until the pain goes away?

The best thing about the other four stars, even Tatum, is that they have distracted her from thinking about all of this.

The two young women from the garden enter the store. *They must be influencers,* Dru-Ann thinks. They carry themselves as though the world is watching. Dru-Ann considers befriending them and seeing if they want to go to a bar. She can tell them about the

Five-Star Weekend and how one of the other women hid a rubber snake in her sheets to settle a twenty-five-year-old grievance. Joey refills Dru-Ann's champagne and whisks the motorcycle jacket to the dressing room. Dru-Ann follows him before she decides to try on the entire store.

The amethyst dress is a yes (she knew it), the Raquel Allegra is a no (Joey is refreshingly direct: "That's not flattering on you"). The ivory camisole top underneath the red leather jacket is such a big hit that the influencers gravitate over, and the one in Gucci whips out her phone to take a picture.

"Is that Isabel Marant?" she asks.

"It is," Dru-Ann says. She poses with her champagne. "I think I'll treat myself today."

Laura Ingalls billows over to the rack to check the price tag on the jacket. "Twenty-six hundred bucks," she says with a note of awe in her voice.

Dru-Ann winks at Joey. "I'll take the purple dress and the camisole."

"Outstanding," Joey says.

The Gucci influencer is still holding up her phone. Now, it seems, she's filming Dru-Ann. "We know who you are," she says.

"You disrespected our girl Posey," Laura Ingalls says. "As well as the fifty-three million other Americans who suffer from mental illness."

Dru-Ann nearly drops her champagne. Talk about an ambush. She's pretty sure these two wouldn't know a nine-iron from a curling iron—and yet Posey Wofford is their "girl"? Dru-Ann wants to snatch the phone out of Gucci's hands and smash it. Then she wonders if maybe this is her chance. These women are influencers; they might have hundreds of thousands of followers apiece. They can help her get the word out.

"I'm sure you ladies want the inside scoop," Dru-Ann says. "Which is that Posey Wofford was faking 'mental illness'"—here, Dru-Ann uses air quotes—"so that she could duck out of her commitment at the Dow Invitational."

Gucci drops the phone and gives Dru-Ann a withering look. "If you think I'm going to amplify that garbage, think again."

"I know mental-health struggles are real," Dru-Ann says. "I was speaking out on *behalf* of the fifty-three million Americans who suffer. Posey Wofford was using the excuse because it was convenient for her."

"Come on, Bex," Laura Ingalls says. "Let's go."

Gucci follows Laura Ingalls out the door, but before she leaves, she turns around. "You were my hero, you know. I watch *Throw Like a Girl,* I read your pieces in *The Cut,* I found you smart and insightful, a *role model,* until I saw that video. It was such a disappointment. *You* are such a disappointment." Gucci's polished facade cracks open for one instant, and Dru-Ann glimpses her authenticity. This woman, Bex, looked up to Dru-Ann and feels that Dru-Ann has let her down. It is, frankly, sobering.

Maybe Dru-Ann should just issue the apology and be done with it.

But the fact remains that Posey's mental state is just fine.

"I know it seems that things are one way," Dru-Ann says. "But trust me, they're the opposite. You have to believe me"—blood is pulsing in her ears, and she's nauseated from the champagne; she came to Nantucket to lie low, but news of her disgrace is everywhere, even here—"Posey Wofford is the one who's a disappointment."

"Say less," Laura Ingalls snaps.

Gucci's expression hardens back into an impenetrable mask. "Girl, bye," she says, and they walk out, shutting the door firmly behind them.

There's a beat of incredibly awkward silence, then Joey relieves Dru-Ann of her empty champagne flute and whisks the amethyst dress out of the changing room. "I'll just wrap this up," he says.

"What did you decide about the jacket?" Joey already knows what Dru-Ann will say; being uncomfortable makes people spend more money. His commission is going up!

"I'll take it," she says.

23. Rye Toast

Hollis trails Tatum down Centre Street like someone who has read *Espionage for Dummies.* She stays five or six paces behind, and when Tatum turns onto India Street, Hollis turns onto India Street. When Tatum weaves through the crowd of people waiting outside Black-Eyed Susan's, Hollis follows—but people are annoyed only at Hollis. "We've been *waiting!*"

Tatum scans the restaurant—it's bustling as always and smells richly of coffee, butter, vanilla, and bacon—until she sees Kyle and Jack at a four-top with two empty seats next to them. She grabs Kyle by the hair at the back of his head and plants a juicy kiss on his cheek, then slides down next to him.

"I think I was being followed," she says.

"Really?" Kyle says. "By whom?"

A second later, Hollis plops down in the seat across from Tatum. "Surprise!"

"No surprise here," Tatum says. "I saw your reflection in the window of Don Freedman's gallery."

"No surprise here," Jack says with a wink. "I always knew you'd come back to me."

"Oho!" Kyle says. "He went there!"

Hollis laughs. The headache she's had all morning is suddenly gone. "It's just breakfast," she says.

Kyle raises his mug. "The band is back together."

It's good, it's fine, it's innocent, Hollis thinks. This is the perfect time to catch up with Jack. Kyle and Tatum make this seem normal—she's visiting with old friends. But does she feel normal? No, she does not. Jack Finigan is here, and Hollis can't ignore the fizzing inside of her.

Tatum wants to tell Jack to run for the hills. Kyle wants to tell Jack (and possibly did the night before) to get some action and *then* run for the hills.

Hollis flags their server for coffee. She was so hungover at home that all she could manage was ice water, and now she's *starving.* Jack hands her the menu and says, "I know what you're going to order."

"Oh, please," Tatum says. "We all know what Hollis is going to order."

"Two scrambled eggs, crispy bacon, rye toast, and hash browns—as long as they're actual hash browns and not home fries," Kyle says.

"Well, now you stole my thunder," Jack says.

"And mine," Tatum says.

What no one eating or working at Black-Eyed Susan's that morning could know is that, back in high school, these same four people ate breakfast at the Downyflake every Saturday morning after the Friday-night Whalers football game, and whereas Jack, Tatum, and Kyle mixed it up with French toast, omelets, and the Downyflake's famous doughnuts, Hollis always ordered the same thing. She had been the predictable one.

How do they know I haven't grown into other tastes? she wonders. Maybe she'd get the huevos rancheros or the spicy Thai scramble.

But she doesn't want those things.

"That *is* what I'm getting," she says, slapping her menu down.

"These boys went out hard last night," Tatum says. "They went to the Straight Wharf. Then they went to the Gaslight."

Kyle holds his palms up. "I was just trying to be a good wingman. Jack was searching for some nocturnal companionship."

Hollis studies her diamond engagement ring, her wedding band. "Did you have any luck?" she asks lightly.

When Tatum hears the phrase *nocturnal companionship,* the tender spot in her breast starts to throb. "I leave you alone for one night and you go out on the prowl?"

"I'm innocent," Kyle says. "I stood by while Jack worked his magic with your boss and her sidekick."

It takes Tatum a minute to figure out what Kyle is telling her. *Your boss and her sidekick.* Tatum's boss.

"You saw *Irina?*" Tatum says. "With *Veda?*" She grips the sides of the table. She was expecting to hear that Jack chatted up some tourists from Menasha, Wisconsin, named Melissa and Debbie who had ended up at the Gaslight because the line at the Club Car piano bar was too long. It's far, *far* worse that Jack talked to Irina and Veda. Yes, they wear too much makeup and their perfume makes your eyes water, but they have sexual confidence—and doesn't Kyle remember Tatum's hideous nightmare, the one where Irina and Kyle end up in bed together? "Why didn't you tell me this earlier?"

"*I* wasn't talking to them," Kyle says. He looks at Jack across the table. "Back me up here, bud."

"They were the only two ladies in the place who weren't vaping or filming TikToks," Jack says.

"Did Irina see you?" Tatum asks Kyle. "Did she say anything?" To her knowledge, Kyle and Irina have met only in passing. This past winter when the Pilot was at the mechanic, Kyle would drop Tatum off at work and pick her up, so there had been an introduction—Irina was far more charming with Kyle than she'd ever been with Tatum; no surprise there.

A sweetheart, Irina had commented then. *Your sweetheart husband.*

What did Irina think about seeing Kyle out alone while Jack chatted them up?

Tatum isn't sure what to do with her anger. Kyle squeezes her knee and Tatum swats his hand away with so much force that she jostles the table and everyone's coffee splashes over the rims of their mugs.

Hollis tries to change the subject. "Do you still own a bar?" she asks Jack. But her question is lost in the static coming from across the table. Kyle assures Tatum that he was minding his own business, trying to listen to the band, and Jack was the one who talked to Irina, Jack was the one who danced with Irina and her friend. Hollis feels a strange pang at hearing this, which is completely absurd; Hollis and Jack broke up while Ronald Reagan was still president.

Their server, a longtime breakfast veteran named Naz, appears with their plates, but he can't quite make the drop because the dark-haired woman at the table shoves her chair back and stands up and—whoa!—she's crying. (Naz sees more people crying at breakfast than one might expect.) Hollis notices Tatum's crying as well and she tries to catch her eye but Tatum pushes past Naz and heads for the restrooms at the back of the restaurant.

Naz sets their plates down. "Is there anything else I can bring you?"

Kyle is staring after Tatum. Jack says, "Can we have some orange marmalade, please?"

"Sure thing." Naz beats a hasty retreat.

Hollis looks at her golden-brown rye toast, then at Tatum's blueberry pancakes, then at Kyle. "I guess it's nice to know she can still feel jealous."

"She's not jealous," Kyle says. "I mean, she is, but that's not why she's upset." He grinds pepper over his eggs Benedict. "I assume she told you about the biopsy?"

"The biopsy?" Hollis says. "What biopsy?"

"Oh, crap," Kyle says.

Hollis stares at him.

"Lump in her right breast," he says. "She missed the doctor's call with the results on Thursday, and now she has to wait until Monday."

Hollis exhales. How can Kyle—and Jack, for that matter—be so calm? They all lived through Laura Leigh's cancer together. Tatum's mother, Laura Leigh Grover, wore a knit Nantucket Whalers hat over her bald head to their graduation; three weeks later, she was dead. Kyle and Jack had served as pallbearers; they had lowered the woman they all fiercely loved into the ground.

Tatum! Hollis thinks. How had Tatum kept this news to herself? She is so brave but also such a dummy. Hollis is her best friend—or was. It pains Hollis that Tatum apparently doesn't trust her enough to confide in her. Laura Leigh's breast cancer was *very* aggressive; the end was swift and brutal. Tatum must be terrified.

But thirty-five years have passed since Laura Leigh was diagnosed. There has been research; there have been breakthroughs and clinical trials. Tatum will be treated in Boston, maybe even at Mass General, where Matthew worked and where Hollis will be able to get her access to the best doctors *in the world.* And, too, the lump might turn out to be benign.

But this all feels like magical thinking. A possible cancer diagnosis, especially with a family history like Tatum's, is frightening. Hollis thinks back to the night before: Tatum eating, drinking, smoking a cigarette, dancing. Before she retired to the Fifty Shades of White guest suite, she'd hugged Hollis and said, "Thank you for having me, sis."

There was a lot to unpack in that one line, not least of which was

Tatum using their old nickname. Hollis could have reminded Tatum that she'd invited her for dinner every summer since she'd built the new house and Tatum had never come—but this would lead other places that neither of them wanted to go, and it was late and they'd both been drinking, so Hollis said, "Thank you for *coming,* sis." And they'd stumbled off to their respective bedrooms.

"She didn't tell me," Hollis says. "She seemed fine last night. She had fun. We did our dance."

"Oh, the dance," Jack says.

Kyle stands up. "I'm going to check on her."

He leaves the table as Naz drops off a pot of orange marmalade. Jack slides it over to Hollis.

"You got this for me?" she asks.

"You want it, don't you?"

Well, yes, of course. Hollis's buttery rye toast wouldn't be complete without orange marmalade. "I can't believe you remember."

"Oh, Holly," he says and he sighs. "I haven't looked at a piece of rye toast in the past four decades without thinking of you slathering it with the most revolting of all condiments, orange marmalade."

Hollis shakes her head, her eyes misting with tears.

Jack puts his arm around her and gives her a squeeze. "She's going to be fine," he says.

While Kyle and Tatum are having a long kiss goodbye outside Black-Eyed Susan's, Jack insists that Hollis take his cell phone number. "Call me later if you're not busy."

"I'll be busy," Hollis says. She thinks guiltily of Brooke, Dru-Ann, and poor Gigi, all of whom she left to fend for themselves. But... wild horses couldn't keep her away from Jack. When she looks at him, she sees a fifty-three-year-old man but also a seventeen-year-old kid. His smile is like sunshine on her face. "Okay, fine." She takes his number.

"I met your daughter this morning," Jack says. "I probably shouldn't tell on her, but she woke up at the McKenzie household and couldn't find a Lyft, so I gave her a ride to town."

"The McKenzie household?" Hollis says. "She was... what? With Dylan?" *That* must have been who dropped Caroline off yesterday, Hollis thinks. Dylan McKenzie!

Jack holds up his palms. "We didn't discuss it."

"What *did* you discuss?" Hollis says. "Caroline isn't exactly my biggest fan these days."

"Well, she seemed surprised to learn that you used to hunt and scallop with the old man."

"Oh, jeez," Hollis says. "I haven't been scalloping in eons."

"Bet you still remember where your dad's secret spot is, though," Jack says.

"I do," Hollis says. She swats at him. "And no, I'm not telling you."

Finally, Tatum and Kyle separate; they all say goodbye, and Tatum turns around one last time to wave. Hollis had planned to ask Tatum about the biopsy the second they were alone but she decides she should let Tatum be the one to bring it up.

Tatum stops in the middle of the sidewalk to light a cigarette. "Holly?"

Here it comes, Hollis thinks. "Tay?" she says.

Tatum releases a stream of smoke out of the side of her mouth. "Irina better stay away from my husband," she says. "Or I'm putting a snake in *her* bed, and it won't be rubber."

24. Shotgun II

There are multiple sightings of Hollis Shaw and her "stars" in town on Saturday morning. We hear from Naz at Black-Eyed Susan's, from Joey at Gypsy, and from the priest at St. Mary's, Father John, who spies the women on his way to the church to prepare for a wedding. (Father John knows nothing about the Five-Star Weekend but he does recognize parishioner Tatum McKenzie, and it looks like she's in some kind of altercation with a woman who might be the host of *Throw Like a Girl.* Is that possible?)

Blond Sharon is just popping out of Erica Wilson with embroidery thread in a rainbow of colors for her daughter (apparently, friendship bracelets are back) when she sees a scene unfolding by Hollis Shaw's strawberry-red Bronco. Sharon, who has been hoping to catch a glimpse of Hollis and her friends, gets as close to the Bronco as she can without revealing herself as the shameless eavesdropper she is.

Tatum reaches for the door handle of the front passenger side of the Bronco, and Dru-Ann swats her hand away.

"Nope, nuh-uh, you sat in front on the way here, I'm taking shotgun now."

Tatum turns to her. "What are you, nine years old?"

"Me?" Dru-Ann says. "You're the one who put a rubber snake in my bed like we're rivals in a Disney movie."

"I have no idea what you're talking about," Tatum says.

"You're holding this weird grudge against me because of what I said in the bathroom at Hollis's wedding," Dru-Ann says. "It was a *joke.*"

"There were other things that pissed me off as well," Tatum says.

"Things that happened *twenty-five years ago!*" Dru-Ann says. "How can they possibly still matter?"

Dru-Ann's voice is loud enough to draw attention, and Tatum looks around. Main Street is crowded with summer people living their best lives. Out of the corner of her eye, Tatum glimpses Father John from St. Mary's. (Tatum has known Father John for years and she doesn't want him to see her acting in a manner unbecoming.) Tatum knows she's blowing the whole wedding thing out of proportion; probably only 10 percent of her anger is about Dru-Ann—90 percent is about other stuff.

So Tatum huffs and lets Dru-Ann have the front. It doesn't matter, except now she'll be squished in the back bench seat with Gigi and Brooke. Brooke offers to sit in the middle, and Tatum is the last one to climb in, which puts her behind Dru-Ann. She pokes Dru-Ann's shoulder and says, "Slide the seat up, please. I'm chewing on my knees."

Dru-Ann ignores her. Hollis backs out onto the road. Blond Sharon watches the Bronco buck and bounce up Main Street. Evidently the Five-Star Weekend has its share of drama! Sharon, of course, is dying to know more.

"How was everyone's shopping trip?" Hollis asks once they turn left onto the smoother surface of Orange Street. "What did you all get?"

Tatum noticed that Dru-Ann was carrying a large matte-black shopping bag from Gypsy, a store where everything costs four figures—not really, but yes, really. Tatum wouldn't dare set foot in the place but it comes as zero surprise that this is where Dru-Ann shopped.

Brooke leans forward and shouts, "Gigi and I had the *best* time! We went to Mitchell's and Gigi bought me two books, the new Maggie O'Farrell and a novel by a debut author named Karen Winn, and I got one for myself—it's a beach book *set on Nantucket.* What could be cooler than that?" Brooke pulls the beach book out of the brown paper bag at her feet and the pages flap in the breeze like the wings of a distressed bird.

Ha, Tatum thinks. The author of the beach book is a local, a client of McKenzie Heating and Cooling, but Tatum won't mention this because Brooke's enthusiasm is already pretty grating. Tatum wishes she were heading out to Smith's Point with Kyle and Jack. They'd bring a cooler of beer and stay until sunset, and on the way home they'd stop at Millie's for margaritas and lobster tacos. Instead, Tatum will be left to wonder what Kyle and Jack are getting up to. She can't believe they saw Irina and Veda while they were out last night. Jack *danced* with them. Tatum will be damned if she's going to become another sickening story: *They were high-school sweethearts, married thirty-one years, then she died and he married her boss!*

No. Tatum pulls cigarettes out of her purse and turns to Brooke. "Will it bother you if I smoke?"

But Brooke is on a roll and can't be stopped. "Then we went to Murray's!" she says. "And I got this Nantucket Reds skirt!" She pulls the skirt out, and the rushing wind over the car snaps the material like a flag. It doesn't hit Tatum in the face but it comes close, and Brooke's curly hair is also flying all over the place. She probably thinks it's romantic, letting it loose in a convertible. Tatum edges away from Brooke, though she has only inches to spare. "You're going to look like you dressed up as Nantucket for Halloween," she says.

"Tatum," Hollis says. "You and I both wore those skirts. You probably still have yours and it probably still fits."

"That was for work," Tatum says. The summers of 1986 and 1987, when she and Hollis scored jobs serving at the Rope Walk, they had to wear Nantucket Reds skirts and tight white T-shirts. "We didn't wear them *voluntarily.* We didn't spend good money on them."

Brooke folds her skirt and tucks it back into the bag. "And I got a sweater," she says meekly. "Gigi helped me pick it out."

Brooke is a grown woman who needs help picking out her own clothes, Tatum thinks. *That pretty much sums her up.* What is Tatum *doing* here with these people? When they reach the rotary, she nearly asks Hollis to drop her off at home. It would be such a relief. But Tatum doesn't quit things. She doesn't *abandon* people.

Brooke leans into the front seat. "What did *you* get, Dru-Ann?" she asks. "Show us!"

"I don't feel like showing you right now. And can you tone it down, please? You're at an eleven and we need you at a three."

Amen, Tatum thinks. At least they agree on that.

Brooke sinks back into her seat. She opens her mouth to apologize (she shouldn't have had a coffee at the Handlebar Café; she knows too much caffeine makes her unbearable to be around, or so says Charlie), but no, she won't. She will just sit quietly the rest of the ride. Forget enthusiasm, forget sharing.

Gigi squeezes Brooke's forearm and it's this tiny kindness that makes Brooke's eyes burn with tears. Probably Gigi pities her. Brooke digs through her purse, finds an elastic, and ties back her hair.

Tatum can't wait another second; she lights the cigarette. They are, after all, in a convertible. She inhales deeply, then blows smoke out the side and dangles her hand outside the car as well. Nobody complains. Gigi has her eyes closed and her head back. Hollis is watching the road and, Tatum would bet, dreaming about Jack. The two of them reverted right back to their seventeen-year-old selves. It was hilarious to watch.

Tatum takes another drag. She feels her tension ease a bit but then Dru-Ann whips around. "Are you *smoking?* You are—and you just blew smoke right into my *hair!*"

Tatum nearly exhales in Dru-Ann's face, but that's a step too far even for her. She lets the smoke slip out the side of her mouth and taps off her ash. "I most certainly did not."

"Who smokes in a car full of people?" Dru-Ann says. "Talk about trashy."

Tatum leans forward. "What did you say?"

"What you're doing is beyond inconsiderate."

"You called me *trashy,*" Tatum says. "I heard you." Here it is, then, solid proof of what Tatum has suspected all along. "I'm sorry I don't make six figures like you."

Try seven, Dru-Ann thinks, but she doesn't say it and now she wishes she'd kept her mouth shut because she doesn't want Tatum to hate her any more than she already does. "It's not about money," Dru-Ann says. "It's about manners."

"We're in a convertible!" Tatum says. She flicks the cigarette away. "But whatever, I'm sorry." She hates herself for apologizing to Dru-Ann, though, really, she's apologizing to Hollis. "I hope your hair survives."

Hollis is tempted to speak up on Tatum's behalf—the poor woman is awaiting biopsy results—but if she does, Dru-Ann will no doubt say, *Why do you always protect her? You've been doing it your whole life,* and then Tatum will jump in and say, *Because she's known me her whole life.* Hollis is quiet, and everyone else is quiet, and Hollis exhales, hoping that's the end of it. The ride home, she thinks, is a three-star experience, maybe only two stars. When they pull into the driveway, the only person smiling is Gigi.

Thank God for Gigi, Hollis thinks.

25. Maybe: Sofia

When Caroline wakes up for the second time on Saturday, there's a note on the kitchen table from her mother. *Shopping in town. Back at noon,* it says. *Hallelujah,* Caroline thinks. She has the house to herself. Breakfast has, of course, been cleaned up (her mother is so type A, she's triple A), but Caroline finds the morning buns wrapped in an origami of wax paper and she makes herself a bowl of café au lait with almond milk. She repairs to her favorite spot on the property—the footbridge over the pond.

The bowed middle makes a fine perch from which to survey the Shaw–Madden kingdom. Caroline sits cross-legged in the sun, enjoying the breeze across the pond and the view of the beach over the dunes. She sips her coffee, devours the first morning bun in three bites, then tosses pieces of the second bun into the pond. There's a soft plashing sound as the fish break the surface of the water. A dragonfly hovers over Caroline's bare forearm. *Nature,* she thinks. Introspection. Is she having a moment? Maybe, but it's fleeting. She thinks about the night before and how strange it was that Dylan didn't try to sleep with her. Caroline didn't particularly want to have sex with him, though it would have been nice to feel desired. If Caroline told Isaac that she'd slept with her longtime crush, she knows he would be happy for her because Isaac's generous heart would not want Caroline to be alone. After all, *he* isn't alone. He's with Sofia.

Caroline pulls out her phone and googles Isaac Opoku and Sofia

Desmione—and then, like the pathetic weenie she is, she starts to scroll.

There's the article from the *New York Post* on December 5, 2018, speculating that Isaac and Sofia were dating ("It's the crossover we didn't know we needed!"). Next is a picture of Isaac and Sofia on the red carpet at the 2019 Oscars—Isaac looking absolutely fine in a midnight-blue velvet Oscar de la Renta tux, Sofia in Givenchy. There's a link to a *New York* magazine article predicting that documentaries are the only kind of films that will survive into the next decade; Isaac is mentioned. Finally, Caroline lands on Sofia's Instagram page with its 19.3 million followers (a lot of them Italian; Caroline has checked before). There are five pictures of Isaac in Sofia's feed. Four of these are at public events—the Toronto Film Festival, Sundance, Cannes, and the Givenchy show during Paris Fashion Week. (Caroline takes a moment to feel awe that she has slept with Isaac, and Isaac has won awards at Cannes, making Caroline Cannes-adjacent.) But the best and most heartbreaking picture on Sofia's feed was taken this past April, after Caroline submitted her application for the internship but before she'd been chosen. The photograph is of Isaac sitting on the white Kagan sofa in the loft. He's wearing a white T-shirt, jeans, and white Chucks; the *New York Times* crossword puzzle is open against his thigh, and there's a cup of golden tea on the table in front of him. It seems as though Sofia has caught him by surprise, as if she called his name and he looked up. His brown skin is luminous; his eyes are wide and soulful. In the other photos, Isaac's expression is guarded, but in his face here, Caroline can see the nine-year-old boy who lost his mother. Caroline is arrested not only by his beauty but by his vulnerability.

The caption reads, simply, My love.

A text comes in and Caroline assumes it's Hollis with their ETA, but when she looks, she sees it's from a number with a 917 area code, and the caller ID reads Maybe: Sofia.

What? Ever so gingerly, Caroline swipes on the alert. The text says: Hi, Caroline, how is your weekend?

Caroline sets her phone down on the planks of the bridge; even touching it seems dangerous. Sofia has never, ever texted Caroline before. Sofia doesn't have her number. She must have gotten her number from Isaac. Or taken it out of Isaac's contacts.

Hi, Caroline, how is your weekend? It's definitely Sofia; the syntax is what you'd expect from someone who's fluent in English but isn't a native speaker. *How's your weekend going?* is how a person would ask if she really wanted to know, which Caroline assumes Sofia does not.

What is happening here? Caroline has a solid understanding of social media and she knows that you can't tell when someone is looking at your account unless that person Likes or comments while you're watching in real time, and Caroline has done neither. Sofia would be able to see if Caroline was active on Instagram if Caroline followed her, but she doesn't. It's a very spooky coincidence that Sofia texted *while Caroline was stalking her page.*

What can Caroline think but that Sofia has found out about her affair with Isaac? Maybe she checked Isaac's phone and saw Caroline's I miss you text. It was stupid to send that, so stupid! Maybe one of Caroline's blond hairs turned up on the pillow. (Isaac said he was going to wash the sheets, but did he?) The text could be explained away—Caroline sent it to Isaac by mistake. Ditto a stray hair; Caroline worked in the loft, her DNA was everywhere.

Caroline decides to play it cool. Isaac probably told Sofia that Caroline was away for the weekend filming this thing for her mother and that he'd lent her his equipment as a mitzvah. Maybe Sofia found the idea intriguing; maybe when she was in Sweden she'd had a personality transplant and now cared about little people like Caroline. Or maybe—this was most likely—Sofia had an *inkling* something was going on but she wasn't 100 percent sure. Or maybe

Isaac broke things off with Sofia and she wants to cry on Caroline's shoulder. (Not a chance.)

Caroline knows she shouldn't respond, but she's worried that silence implies guilt. Hey, she texts back.

A second later, Caroline's phone starts to ring. It's Maybe: Sofia.

Nooooooo! Caroline thinks. She can't pick up. She might be able to come across as casual and unconcerned via text, but on the phone, her voice will betray her: *I slept with Isaac, I fell in love with him. He ended things before you got home. I am heartbroken.*

Caroline declines the call, then types: Sorry, can't chat, I'm filming rn. I'll call u later.

To which Sofia immediately responds: K.

Caroline's hands are actually shaking. She takes a breath. Should she reach out to Isaac? The answer is obviously no. Sofia might have his phone in her other hand, waiting for that exact thing to happen. Caroline thinks about Sofia saying, *Please, no trouble. Trouble* for Caroline now means losing not only Isaac but her internship, and not only her internship but her reputation. What if Sofia goes to the *Post* and breaks the news of the affair and the *Post* sends a stringer up to Nantucket to take pictures of "Isaac Opoku's other woman," intern Caroline Shaw-Madden, film student at NYU? Caroline will be briefly infamous, like the nannies who break up the marriages of actors and rock stars. Being pursued by the paparazzi might seem glamorous but what would it mean for Caroline's future? Would she be shunned by the documentary community? Or...would she be embraced by it? After all, she caught the eye of the great Isaac Opoku. She replaced (for a matter of weeks, anyway) Sofia Desmione!

Would anyone believe it? It's so preposterous that, for a second, Caroline imagines making a documentary about herself: *Sleeping with Genius: My Brief Affair with Isaac Opoku.*

Caroline hears the crunch of tires over shells—the stars are home. Caroline stands up and shoves her phone in her back pocket.

* * *

The mood in the house is weirdly subdued. The women are quiet when they walk into the kitchen. Dru-Ann is missing; she must have gone straight to the Twist. Gigi and Brooke peel off down the hall. Tatum takes the remaining morning bun off the table and heads to her room.

"Did something happen in town?" Caroline asks her mother.

"No," Hollis says. "Everything's fine."

Of course that's her mother's answer.

"How are you, darling? Did you get breakfast?" Hollis asks.

"Yes," Caroline says. "Thanks."

Hollis smiles. "I heard my friend Jack drove you to town this morning."

"How did you hear that?"

"I had breakfast with him at Black-Eyed Susan's," Hollis says. "He told me you slept at the McKenzies'?"

"I did." Caroline glares at her mother, daring her to pass judgment. "I met up with Dylan last night and I was too tired to get myself home, so I stayed over. Nothing happened."

"Mmm-hmm," Hollis says.

Caroline is suddenly incensed. First of all, she's twenty-one, a full-blown adult, and what she does at night is none of her mother's business. And second of all... "I can't believe you had breakfast with *Jack*. Isn't the whole point of this weekend to spend time with your friends? You are *such* a phony. You send the whole itinerary to your subscribers for them to fawn over, but little do they know, it's a total sham. *Shopping in town* really means 'I'm going on a cute breakfast date with my old boyfriend.' And also, Mother"—here, to Caroline's embarrassment, her voice breaks—"Dad *just* died, and you're already moving on?"

"I'm not moving on," Hollis says. "Jack is an old friend."

Caroline is no idiot. She knows this is what happens—old people reconnect with their high-school sweethearts on Facebook and months later they're getting married in the back garden with their adult children as attendants. "He told me he was still in love with you," Caroline says.

"What?" Hollis says. "That's ridiculous. He has a whole life elsewhere. Please, darling, you don't have to worry about Jack." Hollis holds her daughter's gaze but she feels like Caroline can see right through her. Jack said he was still in love with her?

Caroline shakes her head. "If I posted the unedited footage of this weekend, your fans would have a whole new opinion of you."

What can Hollis say? She has become popular for showing her followers her real life, but Caroline has a point: It's not her real life at all.

26. Book in Hand, Feet in Sand

Back in her bedroom, Caroline feels a twinge of guilt. She considers apologizing to her mother, but breakfast with Jack? Kind of inexcusable.

Caroline's phone dings. It's her mother Venmoing her twenty-five hundred dollars with the memo Filming for HWH.

Caroline won't lie: She's hyped about the money. But it's also a reminder that she isn't here to mend fences with her mother; she's here to do a job. The other ladies are all heading outside for the next item on the itinerary: *Beach, lunch, pool.*

There's a bluebird sky. Caroline is going to fly Isaac's drone.

The day Isaac taught Caroline to fly the drone was the most romantic of their time together. The night before, there had been violent thunderstorms, and when Caroline and Isaac woke up, the city air had that rare scrubbed-clean quality. Isaac declared they should fly the drone in Central Park.

Caroline didn't *pretend* to be shocked—she *was* shocked. "You mean we're taking our relationship outside?"

Central Park was showing off—green and leafy, flowers blooming. Everything seemed refreshed by the rain, even the people with their strollers and dogs and crazy exercise outfits, and none of them gave Isaac and Caroline a second look. While the two of them were wandering down the mall—lined on either side by benches, elms arching overhead to form an emerald canopy—Isaac put his arm around Caroline and kissed the side of her face. Right there in public! For one fleeting moment, they were just a couple of lovers enjoying the summer morning.

Caroline thought they would film at Bethesda Fountain or Sheep Meadow, but Isaac's favorite spot was Conservatory Water, the pond on the east side.

He showed Caroline how to take the cover off the gimbal, the actual camera mechanism, and slide her phone into the controller.

"See, *mon petit chou?*" he said. "So easy!"

Conservatory Water was famous for the toy yachts zipping across its surface. From high above, they looked like so many dropped handkerchiefs, but Isaac showed Caroline how to lower the drone so close to the water's surface that she felt like she was a little person riding along on the bow of the boat.

Now Caroline sets Isaac's drone on the outdoor table by the pool, and, recalling Isaac's instructions, she pushes the buttons that bring the drone to life.

It's like a cute mechanical pet. But whereas most drones sound like a swarm of bees, Isaac's drone is completely silent—and therefore stealthy. Caroline is thrilled when it floats over the table, across the pool, and above the dunes to the beach.

On the screen of her phone, Caroline has a bird's-eye view of Hollis and her friends as they settle into their afternoon.

There are three navy beach umbrellas shading five teak chaises swathed in navy-and-white-striped towels and a long table that, Caroline assumes, will soon be set up with lunch. She lowers the drone in for some close-ups.

Tatum's chaise is out in full sun; she's reclining, her face raised defiantly to the sky.

Brooke's chaise is in the shade; she has covered her legs with a towel and she's wearing a long-sleeved rash guard over her suit. She pulls a book from her bag and cracks it open.

Gigi is the only one of the women wearing a bikini. It's solid turquoise with strings. Gigi's stomach is perfectly flat with gently defined obliques. (*She must do side planks,* Caroline thinks.) She has on a matching batik pareo, which she whips off and ties to her chaise. She's wearing her gold chains, her bracelet and watch, her straw fedora, and sunglasses. Effortlessly chic. The drone approves, and apparently so does Brooke. Her gaze lingers on Gigi for a prolonged second—*Girl crush?* Caroline wonders—then Brooke tightens the blanket around her legs like a cocoon.

Dru-Ann is out in the water swimming, and when she yells, the other women snap to attention. Dru-Ann points to a sleek, dark head twenty or thirty yards away.

Gigi jumps up from her chaise and Hollis follows. They both walk toward the water.

Caroline maneuvers the drone out over the ocean. There's a seal frolicking in the waves. Caroline is tempted to send the drone farther out on an exploratory mission. Would she find other seals or something more sinister? She loves the symbolism: Is something lurking out there, threatening the seemingly idyllic weekend?

Gigi and Hollis gravitate toward each other until they're standing side by side, watching Dru-Ann. Then Gigi points up at the drone, and she and Hollis both smile and wave. Caroline presses the Return to Home button. When viewed from above, her mother's weekend is undeniably flawless.

Hollis's eyes drift down to Gigi's feet in the sand. Her toenails are painted a red so dark, it's nearly black, and she's wearing a gold toe ring. Every aspect of Gigi is beautiful, Hollis thinks. Even her feet.

Hollis and Gigi drift down the beach until they're out of earshot of the others.

"How are you doing?" Gigi asks.

It's ironic that, of all the women, Gigi feels the most like a confidante to Hollis. She's tempted to tell Gigi about Tatum's biopsy, Dru-Ann's public relations disaster, Brooke's rampant insecurities, and the issues between herself and Caroline. But that's just...a lot.

She says, "While you all were shopping, I went to breakfast with my first love."

Gigi gasps. This is *not* what she expected Hollis to say. "You did?"

"I did," Hollis says, and she's relieved that Gigi doesn't seem to be as horrified as Caroline was. "I broke every rule in the Five-Star Weekend handbook."

"I'm not sure there is a handbook for this weekend," Gigi says. "Or, rather, I'm not sure there should be any rules. We're grown women with agency; we can all make the best decisions for ourselves." Waves wash around their ankles. "Tell me about him. Or... her?"

"Him," Hollis says. "Jack Finigan." She sighs. How to begin? When Jack was thirteen years old, before his voice even changed, he rode his dirt bike all the way out to Squam on the weekends, and upon his arrival, Tom Shaw put him to work raking leaves, collecting kindling for the woodstove, fixing the overhead fan in the cottage's only bathroom. In exchange for Jack's help, Tom let Hollis and Jack hang out on the beach unsupervised for an hour. They kissed for the first time in the dunes not far from where Hollis and Gigi are now.

In high school, Hollis and Jack strolled the halls with their hands tucked into each other's back pockets. They were frequently told to stop making out at their lockers (PDA wasn't allowed in school), but eventually the teachers gave up. Jack got his driver's license and bought a used pickup truck with money he saved over the summer, and he and Hollis drove into the moors at night. They found a clearing in a circle of trees that they named the Round Room, and this was where they always parked. (Once they got stuck in soft sand, and once their battery died, and both times, Kyle and Tatum came to their rescue with a tow rope and jumper cables, respectively.) They listened to *Sticky Fingers* on repeat on the tape deck, always rewinding and replaying "Wild Horses" three times.

"That sounds like something out of a movie," Gigi says after hearing all this. "So American."

"Oh, it was," Hollis says. But the summer before their senior year, Tatum and Jack and Kyle started talking about "the plan." Hollis agreed to the plan—but she didn't take it seriously the way the rest of them did.

Hollis and Gigi have walked so far down the beach that Sankaty lighthouse is visible in the distance. "We should probably head back," Hollis says.

They turn around and Hollis says, "Thank you for talking. Not only today but after Matthew died. You were a lifeline for me. I hope you know that."

"I'm glad I could be some comfort," Gigi says. She *is* glad, isn't she? Yes, but she can't pretend she was acting out of altruism. She isn't that delusional.

"Why..." Hollis pauses. "Why did you agree to come this weekend? Didn't you think I was nuts, inviting you when we'd never met?"

"It did feel a little...*risky,*" Gigi says. "But you and I have a connection. When you asked, it felt like the right thing."

"You said at dinner that you were in a relationship but it ended," Hollis says. "Was that around the same time I lost Matthew?"

"It *was* around the same time," Gigi says. She's being reckless now. She's basically asking Hollis to figure it out: *The person I lost is the same person you lost. That is our connection.*

"I thought so," Hollis says. "There was a point in our DMs where you went dark for a while, and I figured something must be going on with you."

Yes, Gigi "went dark" right after Hollis confided in her about what had happened on the morning of Matthew's death—how angry she was that he was missing their holiday party, how they'd quarreled. Hollis had said she was afraid Matthew was going to leave her. She'd left a voice mail for him and sent a text, both saying she loved him, but she had no idea if he'd received them. *This* had thrown Gigi for a loop. Imagine being Hollis and not only losing your husband but having all of that unresolved emotional business.

You have to tell Hollis what happened! Gigi thought at the time. But that would only have made things worse. Why hadn't she just cut Hollis off?

"I should have asked questions about your life," Hollis says. "But I was completely self-absorbed. I do care about you, Gigi, and I'd love to hear more about what you went through."

Gigi shakes her head. "It wasn't quite the same as what you're going through. The man I was with...we weren't married and we didn't have children together. But in a way, that makes it harder.

I don't have much to hold on to now that he's dead except my memories...and I'm not sure if you've experienced this, but memories lose their clarity with time. I find myself wondering, *Did that really happen?*"

The *now that he's dead* stops Hollis in her tracks. "Dead?" she says. "The man you were with died too?" Suddenly, she feels short of breath. Gigi's boyfriend, partner, significant other—he *died?* Right around the same time as Matthew?

Gigi had meant to say *Now that he's gone,* which could be interpreted more than one way. She can't believe she said *dead.* By coming here this weekend, she was choosing to stand at the edge of a cliff, and now...what? She's going to jump? She has approximately two seconds to correct course and say something like *Dead to me, I mean,* but that won't work.

"He died, yes," Gigi says.

"Hold on," Hollis says. "Wait a minute." She shakes her head and Gigi chastises herself for taking this walk. "Why didn't you *tell* me?"

Well, Gigi thinks. She has no words to offer in her defense. Any second now, Hollis is going to figure it out.

Hollis sucks in a breath. She's confused, shocked; she feels weirdly *deceived.* All those other people on the website reached out to her with their stories of sudden, unexpected tragedy, but not Gigi. Gigi just sent the simple words *I'm here to listen.* And later she let Hollis spill her guts about losing Matthew, but she didn't say a word about her own situation. Something isn't right here—and Hollis fears that something is her. Gigi didn't offer the information because Hollis *never gave her a chance.* Hollis assumed Gigi was being altruistic. And, worse, Hollis thought Gigi felt *honored* to be the person Hollis chose to confide in.

Caroline is right, Hollis thinks. She is a phony.

"I am so mortified," Hollis says. "Everything you said to me was so insightful, so spot-on, exactly as if you'd been through the same thing. I should have guessed that you'd experienced a similar loss." Hollis reaches out to touch Gigi's arm and—is this her imagination?—she feels Gigi flinch.

Oh, this is awful. Hollis let her status on the website blind her; it created a power dynamic where Hollis's grief was somehow more important than Gigi's. *You've changed. And we've changed.*

But still, Hollis wonders: In all their conversations, why didn't Gigi *say* something?

"What happened?" Hollis asks. "To your...to...what was his name?"

"Oh," Gigi says. She can't construct an alternative narrative under pressure like this, can she? *His name was Mike, he was a pilot for United. His name was Mark, we met at the gym. His name was Maxwell, he was Mabel's vet.* "I want to tell you all about it. But honestly, Hollis, I'm...just trying to let it go while I'm here." She opens her arms to the sky, a gesture so theatrical that Gigi is embarrassed for herself. "You have given me the greatest gift I could have asked for, which is a complete escape."

Hollis stares at her, though she's wearing sunglasses, so Gigi can't tell if she buys this. Gigi thinks, *I should have just said, "Mark. We met at the gym." The most boring answer is always the most believable. Heart attack on the treadmill. Maybe a history of cocaine use that he was hiding.*

It makes perfect sense now why Gigi agreed to come, Hollis thinks. She needed this weekend every bit as much as Hollis needed it. "I'm so happy you're here. Last night when we were dancing...I hope you didn't feel left out? Or like a fifth wheel?"

Gigi laughs, mostly from relief. "I enjoyed the show."

They walk along a little while without speaking, Hollis thinking how she must have *intuited* that Gigi had been through something similar, Gigi thinking that when she gets back to Buckhead and relates this part of the story to Tim and Santi, they will never, ever believe that Gigi got that close to the fire but managed not to get burned.

Dru-Ann isn't a "There's something healing about the ocean" kind of girl, but—there's something healing about the ocean. It's the chill of the water, the saltiness, the waves that roll over her shoulders and occasionally over her head. *The ocean,* Dru-Ann thinks, *is vast. It's profound. What do a handful of Twitter trolls matter compared to the magnificence of our planet and the mystery of human existence?*

She has to stop thinking this way; she sounds like a poster in the dentist's office.

Dru-Ann sees Hollis and Gigi finishing their walk. Dru-Ann windmills an arm. "Come on in!" she shouts. Hollis waves but heads back toward the house. Gigi smiles, takes off her watch and her sunglasses, sets them inside her hat, and steps into the water. She dives in, and a moment later, she surfaces right next to Dru-Ann. She has the kind of eyelashes that clump together when wet and hold drops of water like little jewels.

"This water is *sublime,*" Gigi says.

"Are you a beach person?" Dru-Ann asks.

"City person," Gigi says. Dru-Ann thinks, *Right—Singapore, Atlanta.* She was actually listening last night. "But it's hard to beat this."

Dru-Ann has to agree. Nick's house on Lake Michigan is lovely, it has its own beach, but the lake is nothing like the Atlantic.

Gigi says, "So, I have to admit, I did the predictable thing and googled you last night."

Dru-Ann groans. "How much did you read?"

Gigi shakes her head. "Just a bit. The tweets were all rubbish."

"Everyone hates me," Dru-Ann says. "My clients are dropping me. My boss wants me to issue an apology."

"And will you?" Gigi asks.

"I don't want to," Dru-Ann says. "But I might not have a choice."

"Of course you have a choice," Gigi says. "The reason you're so popular in the first place is that you speak your mind and stand by your convictions."

Gigi is right, Dru-Ann thinks. That *is* why she's so popular. Not apologizing is actually on brand for Dru-Ann.

Gigi kicks her legs out in front of her. "Frankly, I'm impressed by how you're handling it. If I hadn't looked online, I would never have known there was a single thing wrong. You're so present. So calm."

"It's the ocean," Dru-Ann deadpans. "It makes everything better."

Gigi laughs. "I saw a needlepoint pillow in town that said the exact same thing."

When Dru-Ann gets back to her chaise, she considers checking her phone, but Gigi's words ring in her head. *You're so present. So calm.* Dru-Ann pulls a cucumber-flavored seltzer out of the ice in the cooler. When she looks up, she sees Hollis coming over the dune with one of those antique French market baskets looped over her arm, and the thing is piled with sandwiches.

"Straight from Something Natural," Hollis says when she sets the basket down on the table. She's also made an enormous bowl of Asian noodle salad. There's a platter of cold sliced watermelon sprinkled with lime zest and sea salt as well as Paloma sugar cookies, flavored with grapefruit and tequila. Is it any wonder that Hollis has millions of fans? She's a goddess—and Dru-Ann is starving.

Gigi approaches the table. She has dried off from her swim and knotted her pareo at her chest. "Hollis, this spread..." she says. "Any other woman would have called a caterer or had a nervous breakdown. I hope you're getting photographs for the website."

"Oh!" Hollis says. She looks back toward the house. Where did Caroline go? She had the drone out earlier. Hollis takes a few pictures of the lunch with her own phone, including a swoon-worthy shot in portrait mode of the noodle salad with the blurred ocean in the background. Then Hollis turns her phone toward Tatum, who is striding through the sand, tall and lithe in her black tank suit. Hollis's eyes land on Tatum's breasts, which are still the round, buoyant orbs they were in high school.

Tatum crosses her arms over her chest and says, "Are you taking pictures of me?"

"Tatum Grover, voted Best Body of the Class of '87," Hollis quips.

Tatum snatches the phone from Hollis and stares at the picture. Hollis tenses. What does Tatum think about now when she sees herself in a bathing suit? Does she think her body has betrayed her? Does she worry about losing one—or both—of her five-star breasts?

Tatum's fingers fly over the screen. "I'm sending this to Kyle," she says. "I look hot."

Brooke wants to skip lunch.

At breakfast, she made herself a cup of tea instead of the café au lait that she wanted and she piled a plate high with fruit salad, which felt virtuous. But then she noticed the bowl of granola. It was very clearly homemade, chock-full of almonds, pecans, dried cherries, and slivers of fresh coconut. It seemed a shame that Hollis had gone to all the trouble and everyone was ignoring it. Brooke ate a bowl and decided she wouldn't have a morning bun. But there were five buns on the plate and when Brooke picked one up, it smelled so strongly of cinnamon and butter that she took a nibble, which turned into more than a nibble; she ate the entire thing and licked her fingers. Then she considered eating a second.

Now Brooke feigns sleep under the umbrella. She was alert and watchful while Dru-Ann was swimming (she'd heard stories about the rip currents on Nantucket, people getting swept out so far that they couldn't make it back), and when Gigi entered the water,

Brooke considered joining them—but then she assured herself that just because Dru-Ann and Gigi were swimming together did not mean they were becoming best friends. Or were they? Brooke squinted, trying to read lips and facial expressions. She leaned forward, straining to catch a word or two, but it was impossible with the breeze and the sound of the waves. She was relieved when Gigi swam off and Dru-Ann headed for shore. Then Brooke noticed Hollis approaching the table with the sandwiches and she dropped her book (who was she kidding? She was never going to read it; even a beach book set on Nantucket couldn't hold her attention. She had too many other things to obsess about, and reading was for people with peace of mind and Brooke had none), leaned back in her chaise, and closed her eyes.

But she's a terrible actress. When Dru-Ann returns to her chaise to dry off, she says, "Brooke, lunch is ready," and Brooke's eyes fly open.

"I think I'm just going to nap," Brooke says.

Dru-Ann stares at her a second and Brooke can practically hear her thinking: *What kind of fool gets invited to Hollis Shaw's house for the weekend and doesn't eat?* "Suit yourself."

Suit yourself is right, Brooke thinks. Just because they're on a girls' trip doesn't mean they have to do everything together. If Brooke wants to skip lunch, she'll skip lunch!

But she finds herself rising from her chaise and following Dru-Ann to the table. There are sandwiches: toasted Portuguese bread overflowing with lobster salad and thick BLTs with avocado. Brooke takes half a lobster salad and half a BLT. There's an Asian noodle salad that looks healthy. Brooke puts a modest amount on her plate, then a bit more because it smells like lime and mint. She adds some watermelon (healthy!), and then she's faced with the platter of Paloma sugar cookies.

She can't. She won't.

She sits down next to Gigi, whose plate is heaped with food. Gigi takes a bite of the corner of her lobster salad sandwich and closes her eyes in ecstasy.

"*How* do you stay so thin?" Brooke asks.

Gigi dabs her lips with a napkin. *She's a movie star,* Brooke thinks. A Bond girl. Her pixie cut is a little damp around the ears; her skin glows from the sun; her pareo is knotted between the breasts. "I savor every bite," Gigi says. "And when I'm sated, I stop eating."

Sated. What an elegant word. (Brooke thinks she knows what it means but she's going to look it up later to be 100 percent sure.) Brooke brings the BLT to her mouth, thinking, *I will savor this bite.*

She tries, she really does, but then her thoughts start whirring. Why wouldn't Gigi like Dru-Ann better than Brooke; she's far more interesting; maybe Brooke should try harder with Tatum, but if she does that, will she alienate Dru-Ann? Dru-Ann and Tatum don't get along. The problem with having an odd number of people is that someone is always left out. Hollis and Tatum are a pair and now maybe Gigi and Dru-Ann are, leaving Brooke by herself. As she's thinking this, she crams first the BLT and then the lobster salad into her piehole. She flops down on her chaise, her entire body feeling bloated and leaden, and decides to try again with her beach book—she has now read the first paragraph four times; when is she supposed to get invested? Her eyelids droop. There's no hope; the book falls into the sand.

Caroline is in her bedroom reviewing the drone footage. It's incredible, if she does say so herself. She captured the majesty of their property—you see the house, the pond, the pool, and the ladies on the beach all from overhead, like God is watching—before swooping in for a closer look. The shots of the seal swimming are delightful; you feel like you're right alongside him. The traffic on her mother's website will go through the roof thanks to this; Caroline is sure of it.

She prepares a clip to send to Isaac. It's technically a landscape study, but it's better because of the human element.

She hears someone knocking on the front door. "Mom?" Caroline calls out. There's no answer. Everyone must be out on the beach having lunch. She heads for the front door. The guy with the sandwiches came a little while ago, though this could be some other delivery. For one terrifying second, Caroline wonders if she's going to find Sofia Desmione on her porch.

More knocking, then a male voice calling out something Caroline can't understand. When she opens the door, she recognizes the man standing there, a perspiring, red-faced dude in khaki shorts, a blue oxford unbuttoned over a FREE BRADY T-shirt, a pair of flip-flops, and a green Red Sox hat, the kind Irish people like to wear.

"Caroline!" the man says, opening his arms wide and stumbling forward.

Instinctively, Caroline steps back. "Hey, Mr. Kirtley," she says. There's no chance she's letting Charlie Kirtley hug her. The few times that happened when she was in high school, the hugs were too tight and lasted too long. And anyway, what is he doing here?

"Can you get my wife for me, please?" he says. He is ever so slightly slurring his words, which isn't exactly surprising. Mr. Kirtley is a fun-haver. When Caroline was in middle school, this had seemed cool. He was the parent who would take all the kids sledding on snowy Saturdays. His office had a suite at Boston Garden and he'd brought all of Will's and Whitney's friends to Celtics and Bruins games, and on the way into the city and back, he'd play whatever music they asked for at top volume, even if the lyrics were explicit, *especially* if the lyrics were explicit. But as Caroline got older, she realized Charlie Kirtley was the kind of man who had never really grown up. When he walked into a party at Owen Gaither's house to pick up Will and Whitney, he'd knelt and done a beer funnel. When the kids all cheered, he pumped his fist in the air. Did Caroline need to say more? That moment defines Charlie Kirtley.

"Okay?" Caroline says. She knows the polite thing to do is invite Charlie Kirtley inside and offer him a big glass of ice water, but Caroline gets a troubling vibe. Doesn't Charlie understand this is a *girls'* weekend? What's good with him showing up out of the blue? Charlie turns around, sits on the top step of the porch, and drops his head into his hands. Caroline very quietly closes the front door and hurries to find her mother.

27. Calm and Present

Dru-Ann leaves the beach right after she finishes lunch. Brooke is fast asleep on the chaise next to her, faceup and snoring loudly; Gigi is reading, and Hollis is cleaning up but refuses any assistance, claiming it's her Zen. The only person Dru-Ann could talk to is Tatum, and that's obviously not happening. Dru-Ann puts on her cover-up, grabs her towel and sunscreen, and goes over the dunes, around the pond and then the pool, out a little gate, and down a flagstone path to the guesthouse. The cool, dark air of the cottage feels good. It's quiet; Dru-Ann is alone. She takes one breath, then another. *You're so present. So calm.* Dru-Ann is amused—and a little flattered—by this description. In real life, Dru-Ann is never "present." She rushes from one moment to the next; she likes to get it done, then move on. And calling her *calm* is downright laughable. Dru-Ann is calm only when she's asleep, and sometimes not even then.

Is Dru-Ann calm and present enough to open her laptop and check the standings of the players at the British Open? Probably not, but she does it anyway—and what she sees makes her do a double take.

Phineas has advanced to third place. He's at five under, behind McIlroy and Hovland.

He had a dream he was going to win, Posey said.

Well, he's not going to beat McIlroy, and he probably won't beat Hovland, but third place at the British Open is nothing to sneeze at. He'll take home a tasty share of the purse and he'll be seen in a whole new light where sponsorships are concerned. One tournament does not an elite golfer make, but even so, good for Phineas.

Yes, Dru-Ann actually thinks, *good for Phineas.*

Today's round is over; there's only tomorrow's round to go. Will Phineas be able to tough it out and hold on to third place? As a sport, golf requires as much from a player psychologically as it does physically. If she were Phineas's agent (he's repped by some underwhelming minion named Gannon at ISE), she would advise him to pretend he's playing golf at a bachelor party for bragging rights and free drinks. Smile, relax, enjoy yourself. That's how he'll play his best. But Gannon is probably talking to Phineas about the Eye of the Tiger.

Dru-Ann closes her laptop and stares for a moment at her phone. She hates the thing so much, she fantasizes about setting it on fire. But that would change nothing. It's not her phone's fault she's in this predicament.

Dru-Ann presses the button and the famous bitten-apple icon appears. Maybe, she thinks, there will be a sweet text or a voice mail from Nick. They haven't spoken in two and a half days, and she misses him the way she'd miss hot running water or a second pillow: She'll survive, but it's not at all pleasant. She closes her eyes as her phone comes back to life with buzzes and dings. This goes on for a while. So many people want to talk to her, she figures one of them must be Nick.

Dru-Ann starts to scroll. There are three missed calls and a voice mail from JB; a voice mail from Jim in Legal; a voice mail from Zeke, her producer at *Throw Like a Girl;* a voice mail from Dean Falzarano, her editor at *New York* magazine (this is somewhat troubling because she and Dean have never spoken on the phone; they communicate only by e-mail); and a missed call from Rosemarie Filbert, the president of Dru-Ann's neighborhood association. Rosemarie is the nosiest person in Lincoln Park. She's a Realtor and makes it a point to know everyone's business—divorce, bankruptcy, pregnancy, ailing parents—on the chance it might lead to a purchase or sale.

There are no missed calls from Nick.

Dru-Ann clicks into her texts, thinking, *Come on, baby, you know you miss me.* But there's nothing from him, not even an update on Phineas's miraculous finish on the day. There is, however, a text from Dru-Ann's cohost, Marla Fitzsimmon: Nantucket? I'm jealous! Isabel Marant is getting so much publicity, she should be paying you.

What? Dru-Ann thinks. How does Marla, who is sleeping with half the White Sox bullpen and spends every Saturday at Comiskey Park, know that Dru-Ann is on Nantucket, and what does that comment about Isabel Marant mean?

Oh no, she thinks. That annoying TikTok song plays in her head: *Oh, no, no, no, no, no!*

She clicks into Instagram and searches for her name-as-hashtag. The first hit is an account called SexyBexxx, and—surprise, surprise—the profile picture is the woman in Gucci. She has posted the video of Dru-Ann drinking champagne, modeling the red leather jacket, and saying into the camera, "I think I'll treat myself today."

Here, Dru-Ann thinks, is the final nail in her coffin. She could have issued an apology and kept a low profile, but instead, she drank

Moët et Chandon and made a glib and incredibly tone-deaf comment while modeling luxury goods.

The caption reads: @DruAnnJones disrespects her client's mental-health issues then treats herself by spending her client's royalties on @isabelmarant. #disgusted #DruAnnJones #gypsynantucket

The video was posted at noon and it already has 692,000 views. The first comment, which Dru-Ann can't help reading, says: Cancel this ghoul. And somehow, this person has copied Dru-Ann's avatar—a cute brown-skinned woman with a ponytail wearing a blazer—and placed it inside a red circle with a slash through it.

Dru-Ann comments on SexyBexxx's post: I was standing up for mental health! But then she deletes it. It'll only make things worse.

Dru-Ann powers off her phone. She wants to flush it down the toilet but she can't screw up Hollis's plumbing. She'd like to bury it in the dunes, but she wouldn't want anyone to say that Dru-Ann Jones doesn't care about the environment!

She hears a commotion out in the driveway and for an instant, Dru-Ann worries it's reporters who have discovered she's at Hollis's house and want a statement. This would actually be welcome; maybe Dru-Ann should be proactive and call the press. She has a solid contact at *Sports Illustrated.* She could "break her silence" before her silence breaks her.

Dru-Ann peers out the window. There's some clown standing on Hollis's front porch waving his arms and shouting at Brooke.

Not on my watch! Dru-Ann thinks, and she steps outside.

28. Pardon the Interruption I

Caroline gives her mother, who is relaxing out on the beach, a heads-up. "Mr. Kirtley is here. He's out front. And I think he had a couple pops at the Gazebo."

"You're kidding," Hollis says.

"Not kidding. He asked me to get his wife."

Hollis groans as she stands up from the chaise. She wakes Brooke up and says, "Brooke, honey, I guess Charlie is here."

Brooke gives Hollis a glassy stare. "No."

"He's out front," Caroline says. "Everything is okay, I think he's just looking for you."

"No," Brooke says again and she closes her eyes. "Tell him to go to hell."

Caroline and her mother exchange a look. Should they send Charlie away? Caroline is itching to grab her camera. Conflict is the best content. *Look for the chink in the armor.*

Brooke slides her feet to the ground, then staggers through the sand toward the house, Hollis and Caroline following behind.

When Brooke steps onto the front porch, Charlie says, "There's my angel."

Charlie's angel.

There was a time when Brooke thought this was the sweetest thing she'd ever heard.

* * *

It's a summer night in 1995, and Brooke is at the Tent in Quincy Marina. She's dancing with her friends to "Waterfalls" by TLC—it's the song of the summer—when she feels someone dancing close behind her. When she turns around, she sees a guy who's cute in that frat-boy way she likes, and she's flattered that he singled her out rather than her friends Amy and Megan, who are prettier. He says his name is Charlie and Brooke follows him to the bar, where they do kamikaze shots. *Gah! Awful!* Yet they have the desired effect, at least for Charlie. Brooke goes home with him that night to a town house in Dorchester that he and his brother are meticulously restoring. In the morning when Brooke wakes up, Charlie shows Brooke the crown molding in the dining room, the barn board in the kitchen, and a pew bench in the front hall that they salvaged from a church in Salem. Brooke mistakes Charlie for a person who cares about craft, quality, the integrity of old buildings (in reality, the person who cares is his brother. Charlie is merely parroting him in order to impress Brooke). The next week, Brooke again sees Charlie at the Tent and again they hook up. The morning after, Charlie takes Brooke out to breakfast at a bar down the street called Flanagan's where the old bartender with an Irish accent knows Charlie by name and calls Brooke "luv." They eat fried eggs, sausages, grilled tomatoes. This experience somehow leads to Charlie and Brooke dating, then getting engaged and married, then having boy-girl twins and buying a house in the Poet's Corner section of Wellesley.

Brooke knows her marriage hasn't been perfect—she'd been making excuses for Charlie's dirty jokes and inappropriate behavior even before the first lawsuit—but she liked her life. She was able to stay home; she was deliriously happy being a mom. Will and Whitney were good kids, exceptional, even, and their success in school and on the stage and on the athletic fields made Brooke feel like she was doing something right. But there has always been something off between her and Charlie. Back in 1995, Brooke was afraid no one better would come along—and she's been paying the price ever since.

"This is a girls' weekend, Charlie," Brooke says. "You're not welcome, and frankly, it's embarrassing that you showed up here to grovel."

"I booked us a room at the Wauwinet tonight," Charlie says. "And I made a reservation at Topper's. You can rejoin the ladies tomorrow. Just spend the night with me, please. I need you. I'm not doing well, angel."

Brooke studies her husband. His face is bright red and she can smell the Jameson emanating from his pores. "You've been drinking."

"I had one beer on the boat."

She stares at him.

"And a beer and a shot at the Tavern while I booked the hotel and dinner." He reaches out a hand. "Come on, angel."

"No," Brooke says. She wants to *scream* at him. He's being sued because he groped some poor young girl. He lost his job because even the deplorable men he works with understand he went too far. He and Brooke can't *afford* a night at the Wauwinet or dinner at Topper's! But isn't it exactly like Charlie to make such a wasteful and grandiose gesture? He could have sent apology flowers here—the other women might have been envious—but instead, he'd spent ten or twenty times as much money and to less effect. Brooke holds her tongue, however, because Hollis and Caroline are standing behind her.

As Caroline watches this domestic drama unfold, she thinks about how she could make an entire documentary about the Kirtley family. Here's what has always puzzled her: Brooke and Charlie are both cringey, but they produced two of the coolest humans Caroline has ever known. Will and Whitney Kirtley are brilliant, funny, kind, and magnetic. Will goes to Wesleyan and Whitney is studying theater at Yale. They're literally *amazing* and have not one trait in common with either of their parents. Caroline once asked Hollis if Will and Whitney were adopted. (The answer was no.)

Brooke lowers her voice. "You have to leave, Charlie. Please, *please* don't make a scene." *I'm having a hard enough time fitting in as it is,* she thinks. "Cancel the Wauwinet and take the next ferry home."

Charlie's face twists into a snarl and he starts to rant. "You ungrateful bitch, I've worked my ass to the bone for you and the kids, two college tuitions, the fancy house you had to have in Swellesley, the Escalade you begged for because you thought it would make you look cool in front of Electra."

Brooke closes her eyes. Why did Charlie have to mention Electra?

"Get out of here right now!" Brooke says. Her lunch is roiling in her stomach and for one hot, queasy second, she fears she's going to boot into the flower beds. She breathes in through her nose and tries to think of what Gigi would do. Gigi wouldn't stand for this kind of verbal abuse, that's for sure.

"I'm not leaving here without you!" Charlie screams.

Hollis places a hand on Brooke's shoulder and says, "Why don't you go back to the beach? I'll call Charlie a cab and book him on the four-thirty ferry."

Brooke feels tears of shame burn her eyes. "I'll just go with him," she says. She starts to blubber. "I'm a fifth wheel here anyway."

"What?" Hollis says. "That's not true at all!"

"You have Tatum," Brooke says. "And Dru-Ann has Gigi."

At that instant, they hear a door slam, and they all look across the parking lot to the guest cottage. Dru-Ann is striding over to Charlie. "Is there a problem here?"

Charlie rears back. "Hey...you're the chick from *Throw Like a Girl.*"

Dru-Ann offers her hand. "Dru-Ann Jones," she says with a tight smile. Brooke can see Dru-Ann crushing Charlie's fingers. "Don't ever call me—or any other woman—a 'chick' again, please." Charlie opens his mouth to speak but Dru-Ann stops him. "You're crashing a very exclusive party, my friend. Brooke is staying here with us. You will respect her, and me, and our hostess, Hollis, by leaving promptly. Am I clear?"

Emboldened by Dru-Ann—she's saving the day like Superwoman!—Brooke says, "Yeah! Get out of here, Charlie!"

Charlie flexes and unflexes the fingers that Dru-Ann mangled. "My wife doesn't need to be part of this cougar committee," he says to Hollis. "You're all... Wiccans!"

"We're friends, Charlie," Hollis says. "I've called you a cab. You should wait at the end of the driveway."

Reluctantly, Charlie heads down the hydrangea-lined drive. He turns around and calls out, "Have fun burning your sage and gossiping about Luke and Laura!"

Dru-Ann marches up the porch stairs, puts an arm around Brooke, and says, "Girl, I'm sorry. I had no idea that's what you were dealing with."

Caroline bumps into Tatum as she comes in the side door. "What's going on?" Tatum asks. "Where did everybody go?"

Caroline will let her mother explain later, but right now, she has an idea. "Are you busy?" she asks. "Because I'd love to talk to you alone and ask you some questions about my mom."

"I'm free as a bird," Tatum says. "Lead the way."

* * *

Hollis isn't sure how much more drama she can take. There was the breakfast with Jack, the news about Tatum's biopsy, the revelation that Gigi also lost a man she loved, all the challenges with Caroline—and then Charlie Kirtley shows up out of the blue and calls them Wiccans?

"Are you okay?" Hollis asks Brooke.

"She'll be fine," Dru-Ann says. "We're going back to the beach where the world can't bother us."

Hollis sees Tatum following Caroline down the basement stairs. "What are you two up to?"

"We're going to have a little chat," Caroline says.

Hollis blinks. "A chat? About what?"

Caroline smiles. "I want to talk to Tatum about her friendship with you."

"That's not on the itinerary," Hollis jokes. "Sweetheart, I appreciate your creativity, but I don't think Tatum wants to be grilled about our friendship."

"I don't mind," Tatum says. She gives Hollis a look. "What's wrong, Holly? Are you worried about what I'm going to say?"

"I'm just trying to get some historical context," Caroline says.

"Historical context?" Hollis says. "You make it sound like we're a hundred years old."

"For depth and texture," Caroline says. "Otherwise I'm just making a video scrapbook."

That's what Hollis wants, a video scrapbook. She appreciates that Caroline is taking this seriously, but she doesn't have to go full-on Ken Burns and conduct... *interviews.*

"This kind of chat sounds too personal for the website," Hollis says. "I don't need people hearing details about my most intimate relationships."

"Can you just relax, Mother? These are your *friends.* I just want to dig a little deeper. That's what makes this weekend meaningful. Otherwise it's just duvet covers and pecans."

Henrietta rubs against Hollis's legs, probably sensing her discomfort. "All right," Hollis says. She raises her eyebrows at Tatum. "Be kind?"

"I'll be honest," Tatum says.

29. Pardon the Interruption II

Brooke and Dru-Ann are on the beach; Tatum is with Caroline. Where is Gigi? Hollis assumes she's also on the beach, which gives her time to make the sour cream and roasted onion dip that she's serving during the cocktail hour. But then Hollis hears Henny growling and finds the dog standing by the door to the library. Hollis checks the room, which is possibly her favorite in the house, with its blond-wood built-in shelves lined with books, interesting pieces of driftwood, and a world-class collection of quahog shells and beach glass. There's also a fireplace and oversize armchairs for reading. The television is in here as well; this is where Hollis and Matthew used to watch the Patriots games when they were here on autumn weekends.

Hollis sees Gigi standing in a far corner of the room holding a framed photograph.

"Oh, hey, sorry, I didn't realize anyone was in here," Hollis says. She feels a little . . . unsettled by Gigi's presence in the library, though she isn't sure why. Gigi has revealed herself to be a bookish person—she even persuaded Brooke to buy a novel—and the library is directly across from Gigi's guest suite. Why wouldn't she explore it? Hollis's laptop is open on the antique escritoire, but what is Hollis hiding? Her recipes? Her online stalking of Jack?

Did something about the conversation on the beach change their dynamic? *Maybe a bit,* Hollis thinks. She needs to acknowledge that, despite how well Gigi fits in, she's still a total stranger.

Gigi wonders why there are no photographs of Matthew anywhere in the house—it's almost as though he never lived here. Gigi figures they're hoarded in the master suite, but then she peeks in the library. There she sees a series of photographs lined up in silver frames, each engraved with the year, starting when Caroline was a little girl in 2007 and going all the way up to last summer. Every photo is of Hollis, Matthew, Caroline, and the dog (before Henny, there was a sleek Irish setter) on the beach in front of the house. Each shot was taken around sunset, so their faces are bathed in a rose-gold light.

Matthew, Gigi whispers to herself, picking up the last picture. She only knew the version of him that appears in this final photograph, where, to her eyes, he's the most handsome. Had he been thinking of her then or had he been wholly consumed with this family tradition? Gigi wishes she knew what date the picture was taken so she could go back and check her schedule. Had she been in Sorrento, maybe, or Cap d'Antibes? She hopes she was, but even so, she would have been longing for him—more than he was longing for her, that much is now clear.

Gigi smiles at Hollis. "I hope it's not an intrusion, me looking at these," she says. A vessel in her forehead pulses.

"Not at all," Hollis says. She reaches a hand out and touches the photograph Gigi is holding; Gigi notices Hollis's diamond ring, her wedding band. "This was shot last summer. Laurie Richards took our portrait every year in the last week of August."

Henrietta is now whining like a child. It's Gigi who's agitating her; the dog senses something. Pets are intuitive that way.

"Beautiful family," Gigi murmurs.

Beautiful family, Hollis thinks.

Summers are the best season with Matthew. He arrives every Thursday evening and leaves Sunday evening, which gives them three full days together. They have a lovely routine: Thursday nights, Hollis cooks a meal at home so they can catch up on their weeks; Friday, Matthew goes to Hatch's, gets his hair cut, and putters in the garden before settling by the pool to read his medical journals. Friday evenings, they go to the jazz-band dinner on the patio at the Field and Oar Club. Saturdays, Matthew paddleboards on Sesachacha Pond with Caroline. Sometimes Hollis can talk him into a bike ride (this happens roughly once a summer), and they grab sandwiches from Claudette's. Saturday nights they go out—there are cocktail parties, benefits, places they've been invited to. If they drink too much, it's on Saturday night; if they have sex, it's either Saturday night or first thing Sunday morning. Sunday is sacredly lazy—Hollis makes omelets or blueberry pancakes, they read the paper, and eventually they make their way out to the beach for the afternoon. At four o'clock, Matthew will sigh and heave himself up from his chair and go inside to shower and get dressed. Hollis always packs him a picnic and drops him off to catch the seven o'clock ferry back to the mainland. There's a kiss, a *See you Thursday, have a good week.*

This summer, though.

Something is wrong, but Hollis can't put her finger on what. Matthew misses Memorial Day weekend because he's giving a talk somewhere, Hollis doesn't know where—Rome? Athens? She doesn't care, she's had it, why is he always agreeing to travel at the expense of family time? Hollis is left to unpack the car and open the house by herself. When Matthew finally shows up the first weekend in June, he and Hollis are at odds; Matthew refuses to do the things they've always done. For example, Hollis has made a Thursday dinner of ribs, corn bread, fresh coleslaw, but Matthew announces he wants to get lobsters from 167. Hollis says, "We can get lobsters tomorrow night, but tonight I've made dinner and we're going to eat it." She sounds like his mother and she hates it. Friday night, they get lobsters just like Matthew wants but this means Hollis has to move their dinner at the Field and Oar Club with the Gaspersons to Saturday night, and because the Field and Oar is having a dinner dance Saturday night, the Gaspersons invite them over to their house instead. Matthew declares he doesn't want to go to the Gaspersons' house, Kerri is okay but the husband torches all the food on the grill, Matthew would much rather stay home and have a peanut butter sandwich.

"What is up with you?" Hollis says. She's ready for a fight; she has a lot of frustration she'd like to vent, but Matthew just shakes his head and says, "Fine, I'll go. But under protest."

Sunday, Hollis has been invited to the Deck for lunch by one of the women she plays tennis with at the club. This woman's wife is coming to lunch as well. The wife sits high up on the masthead at *Bon Appétit* and has specifically asked to meet Hollis.

"They might want to do a feature on my website!" Hollis tells Matthew.

In a rare moment of what Hollis can only describe as mocking, Matthew says, "Oh, heavens, you can't miss that. By all means, sacrifice an entire Sunday getting plastered on rosé!"

Hollis has no intention of "getting plastered on rosé," and yet, because she is so angry, that's exactly what she does. She Ubers home, leaving the Bronco in the parking lot at the Deck, and immediately falls asleep in a chaise by the pool. When Matthew wakes her up, the sun is low in the sky. It's time to go to the ferry, and they have to take the Volvo because she left the Bronco at the Deck. There's the predictable quarrel—he told her she was making a bad decision but she did it anyway and now she'll have to figure out how to get the Bronco back home if it hasn't been towed already—and Hollis says, "Do you get tired of being so righteous?" in the nastiest voice she can muster. That ends the conversation. They say nothing else, and there is no kiss, which is frankly no surprise, since they haven't had sex since April.

Things continue in this vein throughout July and August. It's good luck but also bad luck that *Bon Appétit* does want to do a feature—and they want to shoot it in the Nantucket house at the end of August. Matthew is extremely put out and Hollis feels bad—it's the last week before things ramp up at the hospital and Matthew's semester starts for the class he teaches at Harvard. It's Caroline's last week before returning to NYU, and Matthew says, "I'll hang with you, honey, since your mother is busy."

Hollis wants to ask who spent the first two decades of Caroline's life "hanging" with her, but she feels guilty. The shoot is invasive. There are people dressed in black everywhere, cameras and lights, hair, makeup, wardrobe, and food stylists. Frankly, with Matthew and Caroline out of the house, it's easier, though it's not at all the last week of summer that Hollis imagined.

On Sunday afternoon, the camera crew finally leaves. Hollis has scheduled her usual family photo shoot with Laurie Richards at five o'clock, enough time to take an hour's worth of pictures before Matthew has to go to the ferry. Is Hollis cramming this in? Yes, but what choice does she have? The shoot threw a wrench in things—she shouldn't have agreed to it, but it was a big deal; it will take Hollis's website to the next level. Both Matthew and Caroline understand that, don't they?

Maybe they don't. They headed out to paddleboard earlier that morning and haven't returned. Hollis calls their respective cell phones and is blasted straight to voice mail on both. She texts: Where are you? Don't forget we have our family photo at 5! Henny and I are waiting! But there's no response.

At 4:45, Hollis has heard nothing from her family, and she's frantic. She doesn't want to waste Laurie's time but she also doesn't want to miss this photo shoot. It's a tradition, the last weekend of the summer, out on the beach; they've been doing it for fifteen years. Hollis gets the idea in her head that if they don't take the portrait, the family will fall apart. Then she tells herself she's being ridiculous. It's only a picture.

When Laurie arrives, Hollis explains that Matthew and Caroline are running late. Not a problem, Laurie says, she'll go down to the beach to get set up. Tonight is a beauty, maybe the best weather they've ever had. Hollis is wearing her signature blouse, this one in lavender; she has asked Caroline to wear white and Matthew navy. But at this point, she'll take them in anything, she'll take them naked, where are they?

Hollis calls them both again—nothing—but she doesn't text for fear of saying something regrettable. She told them both about the photo shoot this morning before they left the house—but then she groans, wondering if maybe they thought she was still talking about the *Bon Appétit* shoot. *No, no,* she thinks, she definitely said, *Laurie Richards, family photo,* and they both said, *Yes, okay,* or something like that.

At five thirty, as Hollis is apologizing to Laurie—she'll pay Laurie for her time, of course—Matthew and Caroline appear over the dunes. Hollis deserves an Academy Award for her performance as an only mildly annoyed wife and mother. "Where were you guys?" she says. "Laurie was just about to leave."

"We were up at Great Point," Matthew says. "I was surf-casting, Caroline was reading. It was the best day of the summer."

Hollis isn't sure how to read his tone. It was the best day of the summer and Hollis missed it? Or it was the best day of the summer because Hollis wasn't there?

But she notices he's wearing the navy polo and Caroline is in the white eyelet halter just like she wanted, so they cluster together, rein Henny in, and smile for the camera.

As Hollis peers over Gigi's shoulder at the photo, she thinks how Gigi won't be able to see that what binds Hollis to Matthew in that particular photo are waves of anger and resentment. To Gigi's eyes, they must look like the perfect couple.

But they weren't at all.

You've changed. And we've changed.

It feels like Gigi is holding a lie.

30. The Drop I

In the home theater in the basement, Caroline sets up two chairs across from each other and turns on the ring light.

"Is it okay if I film this?" Caroline says. She thinks it's a stroke of genius to have clips of Hollis's friends for the website. She doesn't want this to be like *The Office*—that's the most imitated format in Hollywood these days—but yes, she's thinking exactly that.

Tatum shrugs. "I look like a dirt sandwich, but sure, have at it."

Tatum's hair, which was so sleek and glossy yesterday, is now damp from swimming and pulled back into a ponytail. She's gotten some sun on her face, and freckles pop across her cheeks. She doesn't have a swim cover-up like the other ladies; she wears a gray Nantucket Whalers T-shirt and jeans shorts, and her feet are sandy in flip-flops. (She must have missed the footbath outside the door; Hollis will have a fit, but it's too late now.) Caroline couldn't have styled her any better. Her look is Local Island Girl.

"Great, thank you," Caroline says. She feels a little awkward, to be honest, but maybe only because she hung out with this woman's son the night before and woke up in her house.

Tatum knows that Caroline and Dylan met up because right before Hollis crashed breakfast, Jack was telling Kyle and Tatum that he'd found Caroline in their driveway trying to order a Lyft, and Jack ended up driving her into town.

While Tatum was on the beach she sent Dylan a text that said: Caroline, huh?

Dylan texted back: It was one kiss. She slept on the sofa.

Tatum laughed. Dylan tells her everything, a result, she supposes, of how calmly she handled the news "I got Aubrey pregnant. We're having a baby."

Tatum typed: Do u like her????

She's nice, Dylan wrote back.

There's nothing worse than calling someone "nice," and Tatum is disappointed. She wants Dylan to find someone to take his mind off Aubrey. There's also her crazy idea that if Dylan and Caroline get married and have children, Tatum and Hollis will be sister-grandmothers—Tatum the cool one, Hollis the rich one. Tatum laughs, and Caroline gives her a quizzical look.

"I'm ready," Tatum says. "What do you want to talk about?"

Caroline says, "Let's start at the beginning, I guess. How did you and my mom become friends?"

Tatum says, "I can't remember ever *not* being friends with Hollis. Our mothers taught kindergarten in adjacent classrooms at Nantucket Elementary, so it was a big deal when they both got pregnant at the same time because they both went out on maternity leave, and back then, you took the whole school year. They would get together a few times a week, take us for walks, push us in the baby swings, that kind of thing. And then—we were both far too young to remember this—Hollis's mother, Charlotte, died."

Yes, Caroline thinks. *Aneurysm in the shower.* Hollis was twenty-one months old.

"Tom Shaw was left taking care of this baby girl by himself. My mom, Laura Leigh, helped. Tom would drop Hollis off at our house on his way to work. So in my earliest memories, Hollis is there. She had her own toothbrush at my house, an extra pair of pajamas. My mother made the cupcakes for Hollis's birthday, and whenever Hollis got sick, my mom was the one to come pick her up." Tatum pauses. "In fourth grade, we had this thing called Mother's Day Tea. We had to write poems for our mothers and read them in front of the class, and then there'd be a party with cookies and juice. I remember Hollis raising her hand and asking what she should do since she didn't have a mother. For a second, I thought our teacher was going to cry. But then I whispered in Hollis's ear that we could share my mother. And that's what we did. We were like sisters."

Caroline needs to take a beat. "Um, okay…wow. And you two stayed close friends all through high school?"

"Oh, hell yes," Tatum says. She studies Caroline. How can she make this child understand the way things were between her and Hollis in the 1980s?

* * *

It's their junior year. Tatum and Hollis—and Kyle and Jack—are high-school royalty. Kyle and Jack play football; Tatum and Hollis play softball. The four of them go to bonfires at Gibbs Pond, just like generations of Nantucket High School students before them. They eat their Saturday breakfasts at the Downyflake; they see movies at the Dreamland, then go to Vincent's for pizza. Tatum loses her virginity first, then Hollis.

There's one tense week when Tatum thinks she might be pregnant. She can't buy an EPT because those are sold only at the pharmacy and *Tatum's father* is the pharmacist. Tatum and Hollis plan a shopping trip to Hyannis—two hours over on the ferry, two hours back, a whole Saturday squandered so they can go to Kmart to buy a test. Tatum pees on the stick right there in the store's bathroom with Hollis guarding the door. "What are you going to do if you are?" Hollis asks. Tatum says, "My mom will take care of the baby while I finish senior year."

Hollis is quiet then and Tatum senses her dismay. "What about college?" Hollis says.

But before Tatum can answer that there's no way she's getting rid of or giving away her and Kyle's baby, the three minutes are up and no second line has appeared.

Negative.

They celebrate by getting Orange Juliuses at the food court. Tatum feels a dizzying relief but she also realizes, maybe for the first time, that she and Hollis are becoming two distinct individuals.

The summer before senior year, Tatum and Hollis wait tables at the Rope Walk, where they wear the god-awful Nantucket Reds skirts that are so short the girls can't bend over without flashing the customers; the owner claims this is "good for business." Every night some rich dude passes Tatum a coaster with his number or the name of his yacht and a note, variations on *Come join us for a nightcap!* Tatum never considers saying yes, but Hollis is all for it. She wants to drink Dom Pérignon and dollop the caviar onto the blini with the mother-of-pearl spoon. She, unlike Tatum, is fascinated by wealth and privilege; she wants access to the world beyond Nantucket.

Tatum tells Caroline all this, even the part about her suspected pregnancy, which only Hollis and Kyle know about. "The definition of *best friend* is the person who guards the door of the Kmart bathroom while you're peeing on the stick and never tells a soul." Caroline nods eagerly, and Tatum thinks she's probably gotten all the "historical context" she can handle.

A secret even bigger than the pregnancy scare was what happened during the state championship softball game their senior year.

"Senior year, things were different," Tatum says. "The four of us—your mom, me, Kyle, and Jack—decided we would all go to UMass Amherst together. But then one day, out of the blue, Hollis tells us that our senior English teacher, Ms. Fox, said her college essay was the best she'd read in thirty-one years of teaching." Tatum remembers this like it was yesterday: They were in the school parking lot sharing a cigarette; the leaves on the big oak at the corner of Sparks and Surfside had just started to change color.

"She wants me to expand the list of colleges I'm applying to," Hollis says. "She thinks I should apply to UNC, which is where she went. UNC is the oldest public university in the country, I guess?"

"Ms. Fox wants you to go to her alma mater?" Tatum responds. "Isn't that precious."

"It's in a place called the Research Triangle," Hollis says, shrugging. "She says she can picture me there."

Tatum is flummoxed by this. They all make fun of Ms. Fox. She dresses like a Quaker woman from the 1800s—long black skirts, prim collared blouses. Is that how Hollis wants to end up? "But you're still applying to just UMass?"

"I might apply to UNC too," Hollis says. "But I'll definitely go to UMass." She pauses. "My dad can't really afford anything but UMass."

Tatum relaxes; she's pretty sure this is true. Hollis is just applying to the other school as a game, to see if she gets in.

College letters arrive in the mail on April 15. Tatum, Kyle, Jack, and Hollis all get accepted to UMass, and by lunch the next day, the whole school knows it. But as Tatum and Hollis are hanging in the hallway—Tatum wondering if they should room together, Hollis saying it's too soon to think about that, Tatum saying, "It might make sense if we didn't room together, that way you'd have a roommate and so would I, so we'd meet new people and could build a little empire"—Ms. Fox comes over (wearing a high-collared navy-blue dress that skims the floor) and gives Hollis a hug. "You got into UNC!" she says. "With a full scholarship. I'm so proud of you!"

Hollis is subdued; Tatum is shocked. "Yeah," Hollis says. "Thanks. I still have to talk to my dad about it, obviously."

When Ms. Fox leaves, Tatum turns to Hollis. Now she knows why Hollis thought it was too soon to talk about rooming together. "UNC?" she says. "Why didn't you tell me you got in?"

Hollis takes a breath. "I don't know, Tay. Because it doesn't matter?"

"Because you're not going there, right?"

"Right," Hollis says quietly. "My dad will never let me. It's, like, a twelve-hour drive from Hyannis."

Tatum is equal parts terrified and pissed off. Who cares if UNC is the oldest public university in the country? Why would Hollis want to go to a school twelve hours away where she doesn't know anyone? The only answer Tatum can come up with is that Hollis wants to get away—from the island and everyone who lives here. Including Tatum.

Final decisions about college have to be made by May 1, which is the same day as the state championship softball game.

Tatum decides to bring it up on their way to the game, probably because the game is being played in Amherst. "You sent your deposit in to UMass, right?" she asks Hollis.

Hollis stares out the window at Route 32. "Tay," she says.

"What?" Tatum says, though she knows what. Hollis has decided on UNC. Tatum feels all her dreams of her and Kyle and Jack and Hollis kicking through autumn leaves on the Quad hit the sticky, gross floor of the bus with a splat.

Hollis starts to cry and Tatum says, "Why are *you* crying, Holly? You're the one who's doing this."

"I know," Hollis says. "But..."

But what? Tatum thinks. She feels so *duped,* so *dumped,* that she decides to do the unthinkable.

Tatum bats cleanup; her season batting average is .322, the best not only on the team but in their division, but she strikes out at her first two at-bats and then pops up, all on purpose. In the final inning, Nantucket is up by one run and a girl from the Amherst team named Miranda Coffey goes to bat. She's got a platinum flattop like Brigitte Nielsen and a cold eye; she's going to wallop the ball no matter how unhittable Hollis's slider is. As if scripted, Miranda sends a deep one to left field, and honestly, it's nothing Tatum can't handle. She sees the runner on second shooting for third, and thinks, *Nantucket High girls softball, state champs two years in a row,* that's what she and Hollis have dreamed of since they were little kids hitting a Wiffle Ball off a tee. But then, a lot of things Tatum and Hollis dreamed of aren't coming true. Hollis is going to the University of North Carolina. Hollis turns around on the mound; she's watching Tatum, and for one second, Tatum meets her eyes in a look of sheer fury and thinks, *How could you?* And she catches the ball but lets it drop from her glove. The runners score and Amherst wins.

If Tatum is going to be heartbroken, then Hollis will be as well.

"I threw the game," Tatum tells Caroline. "I've been ashamed about it for thirty-five years. I robbed not only Hollis but our team and our school—hell, our island—of a championship title. I was the ultimate poor sport."

Caroline's expression is more fascinated than horrified, Tatum thinks. She's getting way more than she probably expected.

"So then what happened?" Caroline asks.

"Hollis left for college," Tatum says. "And she never came back. Not really."

Hollis returns to Nantucket for the holidays her freshman year, but the summer after freshman year, when Tatum thinks they will both work at the Rope Walk again, Hollis announces she's staying in Chapel Hill to wait tables at Chili's.

Chili's? Tatum thinks. Why would Hollis want to stay in swampy, sweltering North Carolina slinging fajitas when she could come home and make three times as much money with a view of the water? It makes no sense!

Tatum calls Hollis long-distance and begs her to reconsider. By that point Tatum's mother, Laura Leigh, has been dead a year and Tatum's father is dating Alison, a young woman he recently hired at the pharmacy. Tatum needs Hollis. Hollis is her sister.

"I promise I'll go out on the yachts with you," Tatum says, though she knows she won't because of Kyle. "I'll help you find a rich husband."

"Sorry, Tay," Hollis says. "Dru-Ann and I have decided to stay here."

Dru-Ann, Tatum thinks. *Of course.* Hollis talks nonstop about

Dru-Ann Jones, her roommate, whose father is some bigwig on the Chicago Mercantile Exchange.

"We're working at Chili's and conquering our summer reading list—Nella Larsen, Joan Didion, Angela Carter."

Tatum doesn't know or care who any of those writers are and Hollis *knows* she doesn't know or care. *Hollis is like a snake,* Tatum thinks, *shedding her old life as though it's a skin she's grown out of.*

"So when my mom stopped coming back here over the summers, did you two stop being friends?" Caroline asks.

"No, we were still friends," Tatum says. "But it wasn't the same." She pauses; she needs a cigarette. "Kyle and I got married, and your mom was my maid of honor—she and I did our dance, things were still fine. Then... your mother got engaged."

Hollis calls Tatum to say that Matthew is finishing his surgery residency and they've decided to get married. Tatum wants to know about the ring, the proposal, was it romantic?

"He didn't get down on one knee or anything," Hollis says. "I *cannot* imagine him doing that."

Right; Tatum can't either. She and Kyle met Matthew the one and only time Hollis brought him to Nantucket. They went to the Lobster Trap for dinner and Matthew became absorbed with dismantling his lobster with precision so as not to leave a single shred of meat behind. Every time Tatum or Kyle asked him a question, he startled as though he'd forgotten he was at dinner with other people.

Hollis goes on to say that she and Matthew will be married in Wellesley, where Matthew grew up, in February—because that works best with Matthew's schedule. Matthew's mother, Judith, is planning the wedding. Hollis doesn't have to do a thing.

"Great?" Tatum says. She and Kyle had a small wedding on the beach at Brant Point, followed by a reception at the Admiralty Club in Madaket, but she made every decision herself. Tatum gets down to what she assumes is the reason for this call. "How many bridesmaids are you having?"

"Six," Hollis says. "You, Dru-Ann, Matt's cousin Cora, Gretchen and Ellie from UNC, and Regency from Boston."

Tatum has never met Gretchen and Ellie, though she knows they're a couple, and she has never heard of Regency from Boston nor even realized that Regency could be a first name. But fine, whatever. "Just get me everyone's address, I guess," Tatum says, "so I can organize things."

"Organize things?" Hollis says.

"I *am* the matron of honor," Tatum says. "Right?"

What follows is a beat of silence that Tatum can only describe as loaded. *Loaded* like a gun threatening to murder their friendship once and for all.

"Yes, of course!" Hollis says. "You and Dru-Ann *both!* I'm having one matron of honor, you, and one maid of honor, Dru-Ann."

Tatum's mother, Laura Leigh, was a kindergarten teacher, and because of this, Tatum was raised to share. But no, sorry, not in this instance. Hollis is supposed to choose her best friend as her maid—or matron—of honor. *Best* is a superlative; there can be only one. If there's more than one person, the job becomes watered down, it means only half as much. Hollis is diminishing Tatum, and (Tatum hates herself for this) her response is to cry.

"I have known you your entire life, we're not just friends, we're sisters, my family took you in, my mother treated you as her own!" Tatum feels affronted not only for herself but for her mother, who braided Hollis's hair and got the grass stains out of her softball uniform and helped her shop for a prom dress. Tatum realizes that Hollis and Dru-Ann grew close in college and she felt wildly jealous about this (and in response started hanging out with Terri Falcone more than she might have otherwise), but there's no *way* Dru-Ann and Hollis are as close as Tatum and Hollis. Hollis is just impressed by Dru-Ann, or maybe she's been strong-armed by her.

Hollis goes into damage-control mode. "I definitely want you to be my matron of honor, Tay, it's just that Dru-Ann knows the other girls better and she has all these cool ideas."

"What kind of ideas?"

"She wants to have the bachelorette party at the Ritz-Carlton in Boston with a spa day and then dinner at Sorellina—"

Tatum can't afford the Ritz-Carlton and she doesn't know what Sorellina is. "So what you're saying is that she has more money and fancier taste."

"No!" Hollis says so emphatically that it can only mean yes. She sighs. "Please don't be like this, Tay."

Tatum's tears have dried; now she's just angry. No, not just angry—furious. "Like *what?*" she says, though she knows: She's being possessive and small-minded and jealous when apparently what she should say is *Great, Dru-Ann and I will divvy up the responsibilities and shoot rock-paper-scissors to see who walks in last.*

Instead, Tatum says, "I don't want to do it at all. Have fun getting married without me." And she hangs up.

Hollis calls right back. Tatum lets the answering machine pick up. Hollis leaves a message; now *she's* crying, which Tatum childishly finds satisfying. Hollis says she can't get married without Tatum, she'd rather elope, but please can't Tatum understand that she's working on a compromise here, she's trying to make everyone happy but she feels like King Solomon's baby (whatever that means).

The next day, Tatum decides to be the bigger person and she calls back and says fine, she'll be the co–maid/matron of honor as long as she can be the one to walk in last.

* * *

"But it was a crushing disappointment," Tatum says now to the camera. "I was hurt. Your mother went away and met another person who became her best friend and I stayed on Nantucket and didn't. Hollis has always been my only best friend. Even all the years we weren't really talking, I thought of her as my best friend."

This story is so much...*more* than Caroline anticipated. She thought it would be a stroll down memory lane with sound bites she could share on the website. But Tatum has given her real stuff, heartbreaking stuff. "But it all worked out in the end, right?" Caroline asks. "Because you're here?"

Not really, Tatum thinks. This is backstory, but it's also front story: Things have never been the same between Tatum and Hollis. Tatum hides from Hollis every summer, runs away when she bumps into her at the grocery store, turns down every invitation to come to the house for dinner. Tatum is still angry at Dru-Ann because of the things that happened over the bachelorette weekend in Boston and also because of what Dru-Ann said to Tatum in the bathroom at the Wellesley Country Club during the wedding reception.

Tatum won't get into it. She's emotionally exhausted from the demands of this weekend, from hearing about Kyle and Jack's night out, and from trying to keep the biopsy results out of her mind, which is like holding back a wall of water. Tatum wants to go outside and have a cigarette, then go to her room, call Kyle, and take a nap.

She stands up. Chat over.

31. Heart-to-Heart

Brooke is so happy, she has to make sure her feet are touching the ground. Yes, yes, they are; her feet are in the wet sand at the water's edge. Dru-Ann has asked Brooke to go for a walk, just the two of them. Brooke wishes Caroline were filming them right now; she feels like a character in a movie. The afternoon sun has mellowed and the breeze off the water has picked up; the waves froth at their ankles, and the bottom of Dru-Ann's ivory caftan is getting damp but she doesn't seem to care, just like Brooke doesn't care that her stomach is pooching out because she showed so little restraint at lunch. Brooke and Dru-Ann are both facing forward, which somehow makes it easier to talk. Watching Dru-Ann dress down Charlie was beautiful, nearly arousing.

Now Dru-Ann is saying things like *You don't need to put up with a guy like that, someone who doesn't respect women, who has an inflated sense of entitlement just because he has a penis, he doesn't deserve you, Brooke, you are sweet and kind and pretty, there are lots of men out there who would treat you better.*

Brooke has doubts about this. She's fifty years old with no career and a poor self-image. If she leaves Charlie, he'll find someone else within minutes—men always do—but Brooke will be left to create a profile on a dating app where she'll meet men old enough to be her grandfather with plasticky-looking dentures and hair growing out of their ears. She'll give up quickly and either move down to Boca to live with her mother or stay put in the Poet's Corner house while Charlie shacks up in the Seaport with his new girlfriend (she'll be named Callie or Brianna and she'll be either a newscaster or one of the Patriots cheerleaders), and Brooke will have to find a way not to be a burden to Will and Whitney as they finish college and launch their own fabulous lives. Leaving Charlie has never been a realistic option because life without him has always seemed a touch less appealing than life with him.

Except now, on this walk, having what can only be described as a heart-to-heart with Dru-Ann, Brooke starts to see things differently. She's sorry when they turn around to go back.

"What about you?" Brooke asks. "Do you have a special someone?"

"Ah," Dru-Ann says. "That's complicated."

Everything is complicated; this Brooke has come to understand. But her emotions at this moment are delightfully simple and straightforward. She's happy! She's liberated! She pictures Charlie walking dejectedly down the hydrangea-lined driveway in his stupid FREE BRADY T-shirt and all she thinks is *Good riddance, don't let the door hit ya where the good Lord split ya, these boots were made for walking* and all the other sassy sentiments expressed by people who have finally had enough.

Brooke's good mood is dampened only a little when they get back to Hollis's property and see Caroline waiting for them.

"I'd love to borrow Dru-Ann for a minute," she says. "If that's okay?"

"Of course," Brooke says. Even her voice sounds different. Her tone is cool and casual.

There's plenty of time to relax before the next item on the itinerary, which is predinner cocktails. Brooke decides to lock herself in the Board Room, stretch out on the bed, and make some magic happen.

32. The Shot

"Did something else happen?" Dru-Ann asks Caroline as they walk toward the house. "Am I being called to testify before Congress?"

"No, no," Caroline says. "I just want to talk to you about your friendship with my mom and film it, if that's okay?" She leads Dru-Ann inside and down to a home theater in the basement.

"Nobody's going to see this but us, right?" Dru-Ann says. After watching the video of herself at Gypsy, the last thing she wants to do is sit in front of a camera. *Thanks a lot, SexyBexxx.* The video probably has a million views by now.

"In theory, this is for my mom's website," Caroline says. "But I'm starting to think it might turn into something else? I'm doing an internship with Isaac Opoku—"

"I know his work," Dru-Ann says. "He was interested in making a film about an Egyptian ultramarathoner I represented."

"Isaac is a genius," Caroline says. "He's the most intelligent, sensitive person I've ever met."

"Uh-oh," Dru-Ann says. "Sounds like somebody has a crush."

The word *crush* irks Caroline; she's not twelve years old. "I..." Is she really going to spill this? It's been agonizing keeping it to herself, and Dru-Ann is her godmother. Isn't this what godmothers are for?

"You...what?" Dru-Ann says, her eyebrows lifting. "You're getting with Isaac Opoku?"

Caroline deflates a little. She has to use the past tense. "I was," she says. "We were together for a couple of weeks while his girlfriend was on a modeling job in Sweden."

"By *girlfriend,* I assume you mean Sofia Desmione?" Dru-Ann says. "I do read *People* magazine, you know."

"Yes, Sofia. When she got back to New York, the affair ended, and I came here."

"So we're talking fresh heartbreak," Dru-Ann says. "You should have told me sooner, sugar."

"It seemed like you had a lot on your plate."

"Who, me?" Dru-Ann says and they both laugh.

"Isaac lent me his equipment, including his drone. At first I thought, *Whatever, I'll just get the requisite shots of you guys and the food and the camaraderie—*"

"Has there been camaraderie?" Dru-Ann asks, deadpan. She smiles. "I'm kidding."

"There's some tension too, I can feel it," Caroline says. "This weekend is revealing things about my mom that I never knew. So I just want to ask you some questions about your friendship."

Caroline's phone starts buzzing but she ignores it. "That I can handle," Dru-Ann says. She's feeling *calm* and *present.* She's in a soundproof home theater on Squam Road on the island of Nantucket where the internet can't find her. She isn't going to talk about golf or mental health or cancel culture. She's going to talk about Hollis.

Caroline says, "How did you and my mom become friends?"

There's a song that Dru-Ann's male colleagues listened to back in the mid-aughts called "I Love College" by Asher Roth. The song has a distinct white-frat-boy vibe—it's about drinking, idolizing the basketball stars of the day, and getting girls naked. But Dru-Ann secretly found the song catchy and she certainly agreed with its thesis statement: *I wanna go to college for the rest of my life.*

* * *

Dru-Ann is fresh out of Mother McAuley, an all-girls Catholic school in Chicago. The instant she sets foot on the UNC Chapel Hill campus, she feels like she's home. She was a basketball star in high school and is a sports geek in general thanks to her dad and three older brothers. She's knowledgeable on topics from the 1984–1985 Bears season to the depth of the Bulls bench. She's a Michael Jordan fan, and she doesn't care if that's a cliché; she is such a fan that it's been her dream to attend UNC so that she might walk on the same ground that MJ did.

Her freshman roommate is a white girl named Hollis Shaw from Nantucket, Massachusetts. All Dru-Ann knows of Nantucket is *Moby-Dick* and the lewd limerick. She has a vague idea that it's a summer playground for rich people, maybe not so different from Petoskey, Michigan, where Dru-Ann's parents have a second home on the lake. Hollis is a WASPy name, but instead of being put off by the idea of having some East Coast elite for a roommate, Dru-Ann is intrigued. Dru-Ann is something of a snob; her father is a bigwig at the Merc and her mother is the in-house counsel for Grant Thornton, and they live in an Oak Park home filled with Stickley furniture. Dru-Ann has known about Stickley furniture since she was eight years old.

Dru-Ann's first impression of Hollis is favorable and she can tell Hollis's impression of her is as well; there's a chemistry and an easy agreement about the particulars of the room. Both of Dru-Ann's parents help her move in, but only Hollis's father has come and he's not at all what Dru-Ann expects. In fact, when Dru-Ann first sees Tom Shaw in jeans and a T-shirt advertising a place called Steamboat Pizza, she thinks he's been sent by maintenance to fix something in the room. He has a thick Boston accent; he shakes hands with both of Dru-Ann's parents, but he seems *very* uncomfortable and he asks Hollis three separate times, "All set, then?" He has to hit the road, he says. He's driving through the night to catch the first ferry back the next day.

Hollis says she'll walk him back to the van to say goodbye, which makes Dru-Ann think there might be some crying. Dru-Ann's parting from her parents is unsentimental. The elder Joneses have gone through this three times before with her brothers at Bowling Green, Michigan, and Colgate, respectively. Dru-Ann loves her parents but she's been ready for college since seventh grade.

When Hollis returns to the room looking a little weepy, Dru-Ann asks her about her mother. "Are your parents divorced, or—"

"No!" Hollis says. She opens the packaging of a set of extra-long twin sheets that Dru-Ann can see came from a place called Ocean State Job Lot. "She's back at the hotel. My dad is going to pick her up."

"But she didn't want to come?" Dru-Ann says, and Hollis shakes her head.

To Caroline, Dru-Ann says, "Your mother and I became real friends at the final bid party for Beta Beta Beta." (This isn't the sorority's real name, but Dru-Ann isn't about to say the real name on camera; with the luck she's having, they'll probably file a lawsuit.)

It's safe to say that neither Dru-Ann from Chicago nor Hollis from Nantucket fully understands what rushing a sorority at a Southern university entails. But the siren call is too alluring to ignore. Junior and senior girls come through the dorms with flyers for rush events, all of which sound like fun. There are teas, luncheons, crab boils, picnics with real Carolina barbecue. Dru-Ann and Hollis decide they'll attend as many events as they can to figure out where they belong. They agree from the start that they might decide to pledge different houses. Dru-Ann, for example, is considering going Alpha Kappa Alpha, a historically Black sorority.

The intensity of the experience unnerves them both. Other girls in Old East wake up at three a.m. to set their hair in hot rollers and put on a "full face." Everyone—except Dru-Ann and Hollis—wears panty hose and heels. Dru-Ann wears designer pieces that she bought at Vintage Underground in Wicker Park, while Hollis wears one of her two skirts—a pinkish-red miniskirt or a khaki A-line skirt that she pairs with boat shoes—and either a white or navy alligator shirt. Neither girl wears makeup and they both pull their hair back into ponytails (it's a thousand degrees in Chapel Hill in September).

By chance, they both decide the only sorority they would consider is Beta Beta Beta. Beta strikes a balance between girls from the North and those from the South; it feels like the most laid-back sorority (they host a pajama-party event), and they have a robust philanthropic program that focuses on childhood hunger. Beta is popular with a lot of other girls as well. The sorority house is the most tasteful and has the best food, and a group of senior sisters throw Sunday-afternoon pool parties at their rental on Rosemary Street.

Dru-Ann is confident she'll get a bid—she receives a lot of attention from the upperclasswomen (the word *fawning* comes to mind)—but she has doubts about Hollis. The final bid party is a formal affair. Dru-Ann wears a 1960s pink Chanel suit, and Hollis wears her khaki skirt with a pink oxford button-down and a pair of black pumps that belong on a middle-aged civil servant. Dru-Ann offers to let Hollis wear anything in her closet—*Take the Pucci!*—but Hollis says she's fine as she is.

At the party, the sorority president, Stacia Starmack, pulls Dru-Ann aside and says, "We're definitely offering you a bid. The other girls aren't sure Hollis is polished enough to be a Beta, but I'm willing to go to bat for her on your behalf." She squeezes Dru-Ann's arm. "We *need* girls like you."

"When Stacia used the word *need,*" Dru-Ann tells the camera now, "a light came on. Beta wanted me because I was Black. Now, was I being racially sensitive? Could Stacia have meant that the sorority needed someone with my sophistication and sense of style? Maybe, but I also didn't love what she said about Hollis. Because what she meant by not 'polished enough' was that Hollis didn't have enough money. So I grabbed Hollis and we left the party without saying goodbye. She never asked me what happened, though maybe she suspected. But on that night, Hollis told me that her mother, Charlotte, who was a kindergarten teacher, always maintained that a child would be just fine as long as she had one good friend. So we decided to be a sorority of two." Dru-Ann feels her eyes mist up. "And from that moment on, we were."

There are things about this story that make Caroline cringe, but that's the beauty of it. *Find the chink in the armor.* Caroline tries to picture her mother—who Caroline thought had always been popular and well liked, even before she became internet-famous—wearing the wrong shoes and not getting into a sorority.

"So the two of you were best friends all through college?" Caroline says.

"We were," Dru-Ann says. "We lived together all four years. Senior year, there was no stopping us."

In their senior year, Dru-Ann and Hollis were both twenty-one—and this meant Franklin Street was theirs for the taking! Wednesday nights they went to Goodfellows; Thursdays meant the Cave because of the cute guitar player. Fridays and Saturdays they went to He's Not Here, which they referred to as "She's Not Here," and they drank Coors Light from blue cups. Sunday nights were pizza at IP3.

"We had traditions," Dru-Ann says to Caroline. "On our birthdays, we went to the Flying Burrito. And every night before we went out, we listened to Stephanie Mills singing 'Never Knew Love Like This Before.' "

Caroline's eyebrows shoot up. "So that was your song, then? Did you guys coordinate a dance to it, like my mom and Tatum?"

Dru-Ann scoffs. "No dance. That's strictly high-school stuff." Dru-Ann sighs. "Chapel Hill was a Carolina-blue bubble. We never wanted to leave."

"Did you two ever argue?" Caroline asks. "Were there any bumps in the road?"

"Well," Dru-Ann says. "That's an interesting question. For that, I have to back up."

Sophomore year, Hollis asks Dru-Ann if she can spend Christmas in Chicago with her.

"Won't your parents miss you?" Dru-Ann asks. Hollis seldom speaks about her family. All Dru-Ann knows is that Hollis's mother teaches kindergarten, her father is a plumber, and she has no siblings.

Hollis shrugs and says, "I'll call them." Hollis has made it clear that Nantucket is a place she wants to leave behind, and Dru-Ann can't blame her. The island is four miles wide, thirteen miles long, and thirty miles off the coast; it's overrun with tourists and billionaires in the summer and cold, windy, and desolate in the winter. It sounds like a nightmare.

So Hollis spends the holidays with the Joneses in Oak Park. Dru-Ann is able to appreciate her family and their traditions anew through Hollis's eyes—the twelve-foot Christmas tree, the cocoa Dru-Ann's mother makes with Ghirardelli chocolate, Christmas Eve dinner at the Phoenix in Chinatown. Hollis is as wide-eyed as a child; their days are gilded by her sense of wonder.

On Christmas morning, after present opening and eggs Benedict,

Hollis calls home. “I’ll be quick,” she tells Mrs. Jones. “I don’t want to run up your phone bill.” She uses the phone in Dru-Ann’s bedroom, and who knows what gut instinct drives Dru-Ann to pick up the extension in her parents’ room and listen in, but she does. She hears Hollis say, “I’m sorry you have to spend Christmas alone, Daddy.”

Tom Shaw says, “It’s not so bad. I’m going to put a wreath on your mother’s grave, then meet some of the guys at the Anglers Club.”

Ever so quietly, Dru-Ann presses down the button to disconnect, then lowers the handset into the cradle. *Your mother’s grave.* For a year and a half, Dru-Ann has believed that Charlotte Shaw is alive and well, teaching finger-painting and assuring kids that they need only one good friend.

Does Dru-Ann storm down the hall to confront Hollis? She does not. It’s Christmas; Mrs. Jones has roasted a goose, and the relatives are on their way over, among them Dru-Ann’s uncle Jimmy, who will play carols on the piano while the rest of them sing. So Dru-Ann keeps quiet, but she smolders with this new knowledge. It’s more than a secret Hollis kept; it’s a deception.

Dru-Ann says nothing the next few days. On New Year’s Eve, Dru-Ann’s parents go to a party and her brothers head downtown to the bars. Hollis and Dru-Ann stay home, order Italian beef sandwiches, and turn on Dick Clark. Dru-Ann has a “New Year’s tradition” she wants to share—a bottle of something called Jeppson’s Malört Liqueur. It’s the foulest-tasting liquid ever invented, but Dru-Ann assures Hollis that drinking it is a Chicago rite of passage. They each do one shot chased by a beer, then a second shot. After the inevitable grimace, Hollis visibly relaxes and Dru-Ann thinks, *Now—now, while it’s still 1988 and not yet 1989.* If Dru-Ann doesn’t ask now, the lie might fester right up until graduation, when Hollis will have to explain why her mother isn’t coming to the ceremony. It’s too awful for Dru-Ann to contemplate.

"Your mother is dead," Dru-Ann says.

Hollis claps a hand over her mouth and runs for the bathroom. Dru-Ann follows and holds her hair back.

In the final hour of the year, Hollis spills it all. "My mother died when I was a baby. I couldn't tell you the day we moved in, I was already too emotional, I had never been away from home and I'd never met anyone who didn't already know my mother was dead. I didn't have the words. And then once I lied about it, I wasn't sure how to tell the truth. I'm so sorry, Dru-Ann, the most fundamental fact about me is that I've never had a mother. I was raised by my dad and a bunch of other people who pitched in. But I never wanted you to see me as someone who was defective, by which I mean *I* didn't want to think of myself that way. College allowed me to start fresh, and I guess I thought I could just change the parts of me that I didn't like."

Dru-Ann considers her options. For days, she has been ready to be infuriated and indignant. *You lied to me for a year and a half! A major lie, Hollis!* This, she suspects, is what anyone else in her position would do. But the truth is, her time in Chapel Hill has been the happiest of her life for one reason only, and that's the sniffling girl who smells like Jeppson's sitting on the floor of the Joneses' downstairs powder room right now.

"It must have been hard for you," Dru-Ann says. "And I hope that you feel lighter now that you've told me the truth."

"I do," Hollis says.

"And I'm sorry you had to grow up without a mom. I'm sure that sucked."

Hollis shrugs. "It's the only way I knew. But there have been lots of times when I could have used a mom."

Yes, Dru-Ann thinks, remembering the outfits Hollis wore during rush. "Did your mother really say that a kid would be okay as long as she had one true friend?"

"That's what I was always told."

Dru-Ann helps Hollis to her feet. The girl needs a shower. "Well, then, it looks like we're going to be okay."

Caroline has to wipe away tears. "Wow," she says. "I don't mean to get all emo, but I never knew any of this."

"Yeah, well," Dru-Ann says. "We didn't talk about it much after that. We moved on." She takes a deep breath. "This has been a fun stumble down memory lane." She's being a smart-ass, but she means it. For the past forty minutes, she has been transported to the Chapel Hill of decades ago. What an unexpected gift. "But I should get back upstairs and get ready for dinner."

"Yes," Caroline says. "Thank you for this."

Dru-Ann heads upstairs and Caroline takes some time to compose herself. Is she having an aha moment about her mother? She has always known that Hollis's mother died when Hollis was a baby. But it's only now that Caroline realizes Hollis didn't have... a Hollis of her own. She had to borrow Tatum's mother—and once she left Nantucket, she had to figure things out by herself.

Caroline has romanticized the memories of her father because he's gone. But Hollis was the one who showed up with Caroline's forgotten flute case; Hollis was the one with a regular spot at Sprague Fields during Caroline's soccer games. Hollis took Caroline on her college visits and spent six hours at Copley Place helping Caroline shop for a cotillion dress. Hollis kept up with the friend drama, the boy drama, the academic drama. Hollis was her every day. Hollis was her unconditional. How had Hollis known how to be a mom? Thinking about it now, Caroline finds it sort of amazing.

Caroline is yanked from her feelings by the buzzing of her phone. She checks the screen. It's Isaac.

33. Intermezzo

Hollis garnishes the sour cream and roasted onion dip with a sprinkle of chives snipped from the herb pots on the back deck. She puts out two bowls of potato chips—one kettle, one truffled—and sets out cocktail napkins she bought specifically for this weekend: an image of two women, one whispering to the other, *Who is this Moderation we're supposed to be drinking with?* The kitchen smells divine. Hollis takes a few pictures of the chips and dip, then gets a close-up of the napkins. Her followers will go crazy.

Hollis doesn't care.

She pours herself a glass of Sancerre—just that morning she'd sworn she'd never drink again, but she needs something to improve her mood—and heads to her bedroom to get dressed for dinner. She puts Dru-Ann's playlist on the sound system and the first song is "Poison" by Bell Biv Devoe. Hollis tries to summon the energy of her twenty-one-year-old self dancing on the deck at He's Not Here, her T-shirt soaked with beer. It seems impossible she was ever that young and carefree. Her black linen Eileen Fisher dress hangs on the back of the bathroom door. It's a shapeless sack, and the black strikes her as funereal rather than elegant. She pulls out white jeans and a white silk halter top that she hasn't worn in years because she doesn't like the way her arms look. But who cares? No one cares. She'll look happier in white.

She takes another swallow of wine and pulls her hair out of its elastic. The song changes to "Suicide Blonde" by INXS and Hollis thinks about how these "getting ready" moments used to be some of the happiest of her life. The night ahead should be amazing—the reservation at Nautilus, dancing at the Chicken Box—but Hollis wants to tell everyone to go without her.

She sits on the bench at the end of her bed and drops her head into her hands.

Caroline is right. She *is* a phony, overly concerned with the appearance of things. Her dip is garnished, her cocktail napkins clever. *You've changed,* Matthew said. *And we've changed.*

Hollis wants to go back in time. (*Right,* she thinks. Her and everyone else who has ever lived.) She can see it so clearly now: She and Matthew could have been happier. They just needed another try.

Brooke wakes up from her nap to find she has four missed calls from Charlie as well as a string of profane texts from him.

"Hmmmpf," she says. She feels sorry for him. He'll be driving back to Wellesley with the start of a hangover while she takes a glorious outdoor shower. Hollis wasn't kidding when she said it was the best. It's located under an arbor draped in climbing roses; the water is hot, the pressure is as strong as a Swedish massage, and Hollis has stocked the shower caddy with luxury bath products that smell of lemongrass.

Brooke wraps herself in the soft white Turkish-cotton towel and squeezes the water from her hair. Tonight, she decides, she'll blow out her curls, something she does approximately twice a year. Her skin is tight from the sun; she might have gotten a bit of color. A little moisturizer will make her glow against the white eyelet of her dress. Brooke *loves* the idea of matching colors; the five of them will look like members of an exclusive club.

When she steps into the house, she sees Gigi in the hall, wrapped in a pink silk robe.

"The outdoor shower is *just gorgeous,*" Brooke says in her new faux-British accent. The words just pop out of her mouth. Why, she wonders, must she be so weird?

Gigi laughs. "I had such fun with you in town today. Sit next to me at dinner, will you?"

Brooke has to stop herself from gushing, *I will! I will! I had so much fun too!* Instead, she says, "I'd like that," and disappears into her room.

Tatum sits on her bed in a towel. She spends fifteen minutes on WebMD and other websites that offer "expert medical knowledge" studying the survival rates for breast cancer. Stage 0 means you have a noninvasive tumor. Stage 1—before the cancer spreads to the lymph nodes—is curable, though lots of stage 1 patients have mastectomies. Triple positive is good—this means the tumors respond to hormones—though triple-positive patients often go on a drug called tamoxifen, and everyone hates it because it makes you gain weight and zaps your sex drive. In stage 2, the cancer has spread to the lymph nodes; they sometimes feel swollen. Tatum checks under her arms again; she thought she felt some swelling the other night, but tonight, nothing. HER2-positive breast cancer is aggressive—treatment is effective but it nearly always includes chemotherapy. You can order a "cold cap" so your hair won't fall out, but it's expensive. What even *is* a cold cap? Tatum imagines an old lady's bathing cap made of ice. Does it put you in a prolonged state of brain freeze? Stage 3 has to do with the size of the tumor, and stage 4 is metastatic breast cancer, which means the cancer has spread to other parts of the body, such as the brain or the liver. Stage 4 can still be treated but the cancer will get you eventually unless you get hit by a bus or drown in a riptide first.

Or give yourself a heart attack by looking at all these websites, Tatum thinks.

She remembers the expression on her mother's face when she and Kyle took pictures in the living room before the senior banquet: part delight, part longing, part resignation. It would be the last time she ever saw Tatum dressed up. *You look beautiful, Tater.* Eyes shining.

Tatum moves on to what she thinks of as Mastectomy TikTok—cancer survivors, most of them even younger than Tatum, who have had their breasts removed and reconstructed. They're all preposterously upbeat. *I love my new boobs! I will never wear a bra again!*

Tatum sighs. She doesn't want new boobs; she likes the ones she has. Kyle likes the ones she has. She knows that what these women aren't mentioning is that they can't feel their new boobs. All sensation, all sexual arousal, is gone. Who cares about how they *look,* Tatum thinks, if you can't feel anything? Then again, she does care about the way they look. She reads about tattooed-on nipples; one woman got her breasts tattooed with middle fingers. That's what Tatum will do too, she decides, if it comes to that.

Will it come to that?

Tatum finally sets her phone down and gets dressed. She pulls on her white jeans and a black lace bustier that she bought at Forever 21; it shows a lot of cleavage. If you've got it, flaunt it, she thinks. And she's got it. For now, anyway.

She picks up her phone and texts Kyle. You and Jack should meet us in town after dinner. Then she sends him a picture of herself.

He responds immediately: If that's what you're wearing out, I'm meeting you before dinner.

Good boy, Tatum thinks, but her eyes burn with tears.

Dru-Ann is in such a fine mood once she's showered and dressed—she abandoned her usual blazer-and-jeans-look for an ivory Halston jumpsuit, a choice she might regret once she's in the ladies' room—that she decides it's time to face down her voice mail.

She sits at the Formica table in the kitchenette with the bottle of tequila and a silver-fade shot glass in front of her.

She'll get the worst out of the way first: JB.

"Hello, Dru-Ann, it's JB again. I'm not exactly thrilled to leave this in a voice mail but you've left me no choice. I want your resignation on my desk first thing Monday morning." Pause. "I had Jim from Legal reach out, we went to the trouble of drafting an apology statement, and you've summarily ignored us both, which we assume means you don't care about your image or the image of this company. If you don't resign, Dru-Ann, I will fire you." His tone becomes softer. "Why did you let it come to this? I thought we were friends. I gave you a way out." Clears throat. "Anyway, Monday, please."

Dru-Ann pours a shot and throws it back. Resignation, she thinks. Is he *serious?* Yes, she knows he is. She's losing the best job in the world.

Next, she listens to the voice mail from Zeke. She hears "Terminating your contract" . . . "permanently replacing you with Gabriella LeGrand" . . . "I'm sorry, fam."

Ha! Zeke is *not* her fam, he's a bro who pretends to be woke enough to produce a woman-forward show (when he's texting, he uses a Black thumbs-up even though he's as white as Wonder Bread; can *she* cancel *his* contract for that?). Zeke is going to hear it from Dru-Ann's fan base. Nobody can stand Crabby Gabby, especially not Marla. Maybe Marla will quit in solidarity, though why would she? She'll have seniority.

Dru-Ann pours another shot; the first one hasn't made a dent.

She listens to the voice mail from Dean Falzarano at *New York* magazine. She can guess what's coming, and she's right: He's not going to run the article about rampant eating disorders in the nation's most elite figure-skating academy. The article took Dru-Ann six months and four trips to the Twin Cities to research; she had to earn the trust of the girls and the parents and the school psychologist and the team doctor. Now their story won't be told—or maybe *USA Today* will send a stringer out to cover it.

Dru-Ann pours a third shot and throws it back.

Last one, she thinks, and she pushes Play on Rosemarie Filbert.

"Hi, hon, it's Rosemarie from down the street. Just checking to see how you're doing." Long exhale. Rosemarie is an old-school chain smoker; the filters of her Newports are stained Revlon Stop-light Red. "If you're thinking of listing your property, you know where to find me. I'll get you double what you paid for it." Inhale. "Take care, hon."

Dru-Ann closes her eyes; her disgrace is now complete. Rosemarie Filbert is circling like a buzzard over the roadkill that is Dru-Ann's life.

Dru-Ann pours a fourth shot. She has been fired from all three of her jobs, and Rosemarie is probably printing up a listing sheet for Dru-Ann's town house that very second. Dru-Ann stares at the fourth shot of excellent tequila but instead of drinking it, she rises from the table, throws the shot in the sink, grabs her clutch, walks out the door, and crunches through the white shells of the driveway to the main house, where she is, if not exactly adored by all, at least expected.

34. My Little Cabbage

Caroline isn't fool enough to answer Isaac's call—it's definitely Sofia, laying a trap! But after she declines, a text comes in: Pick up, mon petit chou.

Mon petit chou, a French endearment, one Caroline hopes he uses only with her. He calls Sofia *ma chérie.*

The phone rings again and Caroline is helpless to resist. She is his little cabbage. She picks up. "Hello?" She tries to make her voice as bright and sunny as a Nantucket afternoon.

"Caroline," he says, emphasis on the last syllable, which he always pronounces as "lean."

"Hey," she says. She has been strong up to this point, but hearing his voice is too much. "What's going on? Sofia texted, then called."

"She suspects something," he says. "Not you, just someone. Because she says I sounded too happy while she was away. She was calling you to see if there had been any women visiting or if I'd gone out."

There's a lot to unpack in those statements but Caroline is, initially, relieved. "So she doesn't suspect me?"

"No," Isaac says, and Caroline realizes that she would fall way beneath Sofia's consideration. Sofia is reaching out only to use Caroline as a spy. Ouch.

"Are you sure?" Caroline says. "Because when she met me, she said, 'Please, no trouble.' What did that mean?"

"*No trouble* meant don't be late, pay attention, don't check your phone all the time, don't use me as a network," Isaac says. "You were not that kind of trouble."

There's a moment of silence during which Caroline and, she assumes, Isaac think about what kind of trouble Caroline was.

"If she calls again, just assure her it was no one, there was no one, I was a good boy. Please, I need you to do this for me."

"Because you love her?"

"Yes," Isaac says. "But she is right, I was happy while she was away. I was happy because we were together."

Caroline would like to point out that if she is the one who makes Isaac happy, then maybe he should be with her and not Sofia! But she senses there's some elusive knowledge about love that she's not adult enough yet to understand. Something like *True love makes you miserable.*

"How's your little project coming?" he asks.

"Oh," Caroline says, perking up, though she's wary of saying too much lest she jinx herself. "It's turning out better than I expected."

"Hmm," Isaac says. "When you get back to New York, we'll take a look together at what you have. Okay, *mon petit chou?*"

He's patronizing her, but she likes imagining the two of them shoulder to shoulder in front of Isaac's computer. "Okay," Caroline whispers. She wants the conversation to end sweetly, she wants Isaac to say he misses her, but at that second, there's a beeping on her phone.

Sofia is calling.

"She's calling me now," Caroline says. "What should I do?"

"Decline, please," Isaac says. "She's been out to lunch with Mauricio and Gemma; I'm sure she's been drinking. Wait and call her back tomorrow, then put her mind at ease."

"Okay," Caroline says. The beeping ends; Caroline knows Sofia won't leave a message.

"You'll be back Monday?" Isaac asks.

"Tuesday," Caroline says.

Isaac sighs. (With longing?) "Until then, *mon petit chou,*" he says, which isn't exactly what Caroline is hoping for, but she'll take it.

She hangs up just as a text from Sofia comes in. Are you on the phone with Isaac?

A chill rolls up Caroline's spine. The loneliest place in the world, she realizes, is between two other people.

35. Happy Hour III

When Caroline walks into the kitchen, the mood is festive. The only grouch is Henny, who resumes her growling at Gigi.

"I can't keep blaming my cat," Gigi says. "I think Henrietta has something against me."

"Finish your pot!" Brooke says. "How could anyone have anything against you?"

Caroline has to admit, her mother's matching-colors idea *works.* Dru-Ann is in white, Gigi is in black, Brooke is in white, and Tatum is in black and white.

The music is so good—Tracy Chapman's "Fast Car"—that Caroline catches both Tatum and Dru-Ann singing along together. *We've gotta make a decision, leave tonight or live and die this way.* Everyone is glowing from the sun. Brooke shows Dru-Ann her sunburned shoulders, and Gigi looks at pictures of Orion on Tatum's phone.

Caroline gets some footage of the ladies singing and dancing to "Whatta Man." Still no music from this century; maybe that will happen tomorrow.

Brooke says, "Caroline, would you take a group picture with my phone? I'll text it to everybody."

Yes! Everyone loves this idea! But wait…the room comes to a standstill.

"Where's Hollis?" Gigi says.

"I'll get her," Tatum says.

"No, *I'll* get her," Dru-Ann says.

Caroline watches the two women stare at each other. "I'll get her," she says. And she heads down the hall.

Before knocking, Caroline presses her ear to the door. She hears nothing. There's a stripe of light at the bottom. Her mother is in there. But something must be wrong. Hollis is always the first person ready. There's no good reason why Hollis would miss even one minute of the cocktail hour. There are only bad reasons.

Caroline raps with one knuckle. "Mama?" she says. There's no answer.

Well, this is an interesting reversal. Caroline feels a sickening guilt. She has been awful to her mother. She has been narcissistic, sarcastic, mean. Caroline isn't the only one in the family who lost someone. Her mother lost her husband. And long ago, her mother lost *her* mother. Caroline's mind is fresh with the vision of nine-year-old Hollis reading a poem she wrote for a dead woman she never knew, eighteen-year-old Hollis keeping the death of her mother a secret from even her closest friend. Is it any wonder her mother has spent all these years creating a picture-perfect life?

Caroline opens the door.

Hollis is sitting on the bench in her mom undies and her mom bra, her elbows on her knees, her face in her hands.

"I'm sorry," Caroline says. "Mama, I'm sorry."

Slowly, Hollis turns her head. Caroline is holding out her arms. "I'm sorry. Mama, I'm sorry." Caroline takes a breath to say more, but Hollis doesn't need to hear more. She stands up and Caroline squeezes her around the middle, and Hollis thinks, *This is enough.* She has, finally, gotten her little girl back.

They stand in an embrace, rocking back and forth, until finally Caroline pulls away.

"Mom," she says. "You have to get ready. They're all waiting for you."

A splash of cold water, some concealer. Hollis brushes her hair out, puts on lipstick, spritzes herself with Grand Soir.

Caroline makes Hollis's entrance into the kitchen not awkward by gathering the ladies for a group photo. Where should they stand for optimal lighting and in what order? Hollis in the middle, Brooke says. Well, obviously. Should the onion dip be in the picture? No, Hollis took pictures of it earlier before it was ravaged; she'll post those on the website when the weekend is over. Wineglasses? Sure, why not, let's keep it real. Should they move over by the fireplace? Wait, why are they taking the picture inside when it's such a glorious evening? They should be out on the deck! Gigi leads the way, she's a long cool woman in a black dress that clings to her figure and pools by her feet. The sun is just setting; the light is golden syrup. Hollis plants her feet and extends her arms. She feels better, stronger.

Caroline thinks Tatum and Dru-Ann should be on one side, Brooke and Gigi on the other—that way it makes sense when other people are looking at it, the friends in chronological order. But Tatum and Dru-Ann gravitate to different sides of Hollis. Brooke goes with Dru-Ann, Gigi with Tatum.

"On the count of three," Caroline says. She's holding the camera over her head for the most flattering angle. Her mother is self-conscious about her chin. Gigi and Dru-Ann know to set one foot in front and pivot. Caroline takes a stream of pictures even before she says, "One... two... three!" and everyone smiles.

Cute, Caroline thinks. The song changes to "Good Vibrations" by Marky Mark and everyone swarms Caroline because they *want to see the pictures!*

Caroline pulls her mother aside. "I'm going to stay home and edit the footage I have. You ladies take pictures and videos at Nautilus and I'll meet you at the Chicken Box later, I promise. Just text me when you're leaving town."

Caroline expects her mother to protest and maybe mention the twenty-five hundred dollars she's being paid, but Hollis just smiles. "I will, sweetie."

Caroline follows the ladies to the driveway and films them as they pile into the Bronco. Tatum sits up front, and Brooke is sandwiched between Gigi and Dru-Ann in the back. Hollis turns the key in the ignition. The song on the radio is "Believe" by Cher. Oh, boy. Caroline knows the ladies will be shout-singing *Do you believe in life after love?* into the salt-tinged evening air.

Once they're all buckled in, they turn to wave goodbye to Caroline.

"Bye, ladies!" Caroline calls out. "Have so much fun!"

"We will!" they say.

And Caroline thinks, *Right. How could they not?*

36. Captain's Table

Only the luckiest among us witness Hollis Shaw and her stars walking into Nautilus; it is, after all, an impossible reservation. Or *nearly* impossible. Blond Sharon and her sister, Heather (who is brunette), are sitting at a two-top against the wall, and Sharon is, naturally, facing out so that she can see everyone who comes and goes plus keep tabs on all the action at the bar. When Sharon spies Hollis and her friends, she literally gasps—and this gets Heather's attention because, as the years pass, Sharon has become harder and harder to impress. Who could it be? Heather wonders. The Duchess of Cambridge, Sydney Sweeney, cute Jack Harlow?

"It's Hollis Shaw." Sharon is doing that thing where she talks without moving her lips. "And her four stars."

Even Heather, whose idea of "home cooking" is DoorDash sushi, knows who Hollis Shaw is. She discreetly pivots in her chair and sees five women of a certain age take seats at the Captain's Table—of course. It's a large, live-edge wood table snugged into the front corner of the restaurant; it's not only the best table at Nautilus, it's the most sought-after table on the island of Nantucket.

"We should book that table sometime," Heather says.

"Ha!" Sharon says. "You'd have to sneaky link with one of the owners."

Their server arrives with their cocktails—an Ack Nauti for Sharon (she drinks tequila) and the Nauti Dog for Heather (she prefers vodka).

"Here's to being Nauti," Heather says as she raises her glass for a toast.

But Sharon's attention is elsewhere.

Hollis and her friends are all wearing black, white, or both. Is this a coincidence? *It can't be,* Sharon thinks. They must have planned it—and Sharon approves. In town that morning there appeared to be some discord among the women, but they seem to have found harmony. Sharon rises from her seat and strides over to the Captain's Table.

"Okay, cheers," Heather says to Sharon's empty chair. She takes a long swallow of her drink before turning around to see what kind of trouble Sharon is getting into.

"Would you like me to take a group photo?" Sharon asks.

Hollis herself answers. "That would be amazing, thank you for offering." She hands over what Sharon can only assume is the very phone that Hollis uses to film her cooking videos. Sharon is so dazzled that she nearly fumbles it.

Get ahold of yourself, Shar, Heather thinks. It wouldn't be an exaggeration to say the entire restaurant is watching as Sharon directs Hollis and her friends to get closer—really close!—then snaps a zillion pictures from various angles. This goes on a bit longer than it needs to, but finally, Sharon relinquishes the phone.

"You're a stunning group," Sharon says, and she's not just fangirling, she means it. There's glamorous Dru-Ann Jones, whom Sharon recognizes from television; a gorgeous woman with a pixie cut; a brunette who, if Sharon isn't mistaken, works for Irina Services (Sharon uses Irina Services whenever she has houseguests coming, and hasn't she noticed this woman's perfect figure?); a curly-haired woman who is smiling so brightly, it looks like her face is going to break open in a burst of confetti; and, finally, the golden-butter-and-sugar glow of Hollis herself.

"Thank you," Hollis says. The other women slide back to their seats and pick up their menus. Sharon is about to introduce herself and maybe provide her Instagram handle in case Hollis wants to give her a photo credit when she feels a hand on her elbow. It's Heather, who gently guides Sharon back to their table; their blistered shishito peppers have arrived.

"Excuse my sister," Heather murmurs to Sharon once they are both seated again. "She has a stalking problem."

Sharon doesn't mind the teasing. "They all seem so happy," she says. "Leave it to Hollis Shaw to make that crazy idea work."

The Captain's Table is worth all the hype and more, Hollis thinks. It screams *special occasion.* Their server, Sean, leads them through the menu, globally inspired small plates meant to be shared and larger "feasts." Then he takes their order. The others call out the dishes they want to try: yellowfin tuna lettuce wraps, tempura oyster tacos, Japanese street corn. Hollis throws in an order of the Thai lobster curry, the chicken frites, and, her personal favorite, the blue crab fried rice with two crispy eggs.

Hollis is at the head of the table with Gigi and Brooke on one side and Tatum and Dru-Ann on the other. She can't believe Tatum and Dru-Ann are voluntarily sitting next to each other.

She raises her glass for a toast. "I just want you to know how much it means to me that you're all here." She feels her eyes misting up. "When I lost Matthew, I thought my world would collapse. But I have a strong foundation beneath me, and that is all of you."

"Love you, sis," Tatum says, and she clinks glasses with Hollis.

"You're the *best,* Hollis!" Brooke says, a bit too loudly.

Gigi says, "I'm sure the other women know the story, Hollis, but I don't. How did you and Matthew meet?"

"The old-fashioned way," Hollis says. "At a bar." She takes a sip of her wine. Can she tell the story? Earlier tonight, the answer might have been no; it was too painful to think about Matthew in that much detail. But right now, she feels okay. "This was in Boston in 1995."

Hollis is twenty-five years old and her life is exactly as she'd hoped it would be. She rents a studio apartment with wood floors and an exposed brick wall on Cedar Lane Way on Beacon Hill. She fills the apartment with plants and decorates it with pillar candles, throw pillows, and white fairy lights. She gets takeout Thai food from the King and I, listens to her Natalie Merchant CD, and marvels at her own happiness.

She has a dream job: assistant food editor at *Boston* magazine, a position that comes with the use of the corporate credit card.

In February of 1995, the real food editor comes down with mono and will be out of commission for three weeks. This gives Hollis a chance to pitch an article entitled "Are There Any Decent Restaurants on Beacon Hill?" Popular opinion in 1995 is "No, there aren't," but the editor in chief is willing to give Hollis a chance to prove everyone wrong.

Hollis goes to the Paramount for brunch (she waits in line for ninety minutes, but the caramel-banana French toast is worth it), to the *Cheers* pub where everybody knows her name (not really, nobody knows her and the places is filled with tourists, but she finds nice things to say about the potato skins and the chowder), and to the Sevens (it's a storied dive bar with a better-than-it-needs-to-be French dip). She goes to Figs for pizza, the Marliave for Welsh rarebit, and the neighborhood darling, Toscano (which, Hollis believes, has the best steak in the city). She intentionally stays away from the culinary wasteland of Cambridge Street, but then her friend Regency, who lives in the apartment upstairs from her, tells Hollis she can't write an article about Beacon Hill restaurants and not include Harvard Gardens.

Ugh, Hollis thinks. "Even the name of the place is a turnoff," she says. "The restaurant has nothing to do with Harvard, and there are no gardens."

"That may be so," Regency says. "But meeting a cute doctor there is as easy as shooting fish in a barrel."

"It turned out Regency was right," Hollis says now. "Because sitting at the bar that night was Matthew Madden."

"Was it love at first sight?" Gigi asks.

"I bet it was!" Brooke says. She's leaning forward, drinking her Lemon Krush way too quickly, but who cares? She's sitting next to Gigi and across from Dru-Ann; she feels pretty in her dress and she wants to hear this story. She has no idea how Hollis and Matthew met.

"Not even close," Hollis says. "He only noticed me because I had a notebook."

Hollis walks into Harvard Gardens prepared to be underwhelmed but immediately finds that the restaurant has what would in later years be called a "good vibe." The lighting is low, there's a lot of chat and laughter, and the air smells enticingly of French fries and bacon. Hollis goes to the bar, where the only free seat is next to a rumpled-looking guy in glasses and blue scrubs. He's reading a textbook and wolfing down a Reuben; Hollis watches a strand of sauerkraut fall onto the page of his book. When Hollis asks if the seat is free, the guy mumbles something that sounds affirmative.

"Are you a doctor?" Hollis asks.

He nods without even looking up, but Hollis isn't offended; she watches *E.R.* and understands that residents work long hours without eating or sleeping and conduct their love lives in empty exam rooms.

"How's the Reuben?" Hollis asks. She can tell just by the buttery grilled rye and the oozing melted Swiss that it's exceptional. Hollis orders one even though the guy hasn't deigned to answer her. She's just an unpleasant buzzing in his ear.

Hollis also orders a glass of chardonnay (she has not yet discovered sauvignon blanc) and the onion soup and the strawberry arugula salad (she has to sample the menu, after all), and when her food arrives, she whips out her notebook and starts writing: *Onion soup classically prepared with notes of bacon; salad is both sweet and peppery; Reuben well constructed, perfect meat-to-sauerkraut ratio, and the Russian dressing is made in-house.* Surprise, surprise: There *is* good food on Cambridge Street. This bar meal at Harvard Gardens proves it!

An even bigger surprise is when the guy next to her slams his textbook closed, turns to her, and says, "What's that you're writing?"

"A restaurant review," Hollis says. "I'm the food editor at *Boston* magazine." She leaves out the word *assistant* because she sees this guy's green eyes behind the lenses of his glasses and suddenly wants to seem impressive.

"That's neat," the guy says and Hollis giggles. Who in the year 1995 uses the word *neat?* "I'm Matthew Madden, a surgery resident across the street. Sorry if I was rude earlier, I just wanted to finish up reading on takotsubo cardiomyopathy, otherwise known as 'broken-heart syndrome.' I saw an unusual case in the cath lab earlier and I didn't know what it was."

"I'm Hollis Shaw," she says. She and the green-eyed surgery resident at Mass General shake hands. Hollis thinks, *It's neat that he knows how the human heart works and can fix it if it breaks.*

It's possible there's more conversation. She must mention that she lives a few blocks away; he must say that he still lives with his parents in Wellesley, which isn't as pathetic as it sounds because he's *always* at the hospital. She must say she grew up on Nantucket, and he must say that his family are summer-in-Maine people. But Hollis has lost most of this. What she does remember is that, after she pays the bill with her company card and after she tucks her notebook into her bag, Matthew says, "There's a hospital fundraiser next Friday night. I'm expected to attend and bring a date. Are you free, by any chance?"

Hollis knows she should be surprised—they've been acquainted for maybe thirty minutes, and he's asking her to a work function? Aren't there a hundred hot nurses across the street?—but she doesn't miss a beat. "I *am* free," she says. "I'd love to go."

"It's black-tie," he says. "At the Ritz. I'll come pick you up at six thirty?"

Hollis smiles. "Sounds great!" she says, and when she gets home, she slips a note under Regency's apartment door. *You were right,* the note says. *It was as easy as shooting fish in a barrel.*

* * *

Sean, the server, delivers their food and everyone digs in. Dru-Ann says, "If you think I'm sharing this chicken, you're wrong. Look at this beauty!"

Gigi helps herself to the blue crab fried rice. "So your first date was a black-tie work event. Was it happily ever after from there?" She feels a keen, almost manic, interest. Matthew never talked about his history with Hollis.

"Pretty much," Hollis says, though this is a wild oversimplification. Phrases like *love at first sight* and *happily ever after* aren't realistic. But Hollis has always been good at recognizing *quality,* in food, in service, in linens, in movies and books—and in people.

When Hollis sees Matthew Madden upright and groomed (his hair cut and combed, glasses polished) in his tuxedo (his own tuxedo, not a rental), she realizes that he is the rarest of finds. He's not only a superstar surgery resident; he has also been raised a gentleman. He owns a tuxedo, he knows about wine (it's Matthew who introduces Hollis to sauvignon blanc); he can handle elevated dinner conversation about topics as varied as the Sargent portraits at the Isabella Stewart Gardner Museum, the budgetary woes of the Big Dig, and Seiji Ozawa's expert conducting of the Boston Symphony Orchestra.

Hollis is dazzled by Matthew's moves on the dance floor and then by the make-out session when he takes her home.

The week following the fundraiser, Matthew invites Hollis to dinner at his parents' house. The brick mansion in Wellesley Hills is grand but warm; there's a fire lit in the library, where they have cocktails and talk about books. Matthew's father, Robert, is an attorney who loves Boston crime novels; he lends Hollis *The Friends of Eddie Coyle.* His mother, Judith, sits on the board at the Boston Public Library; she turns Hollis on to Barbara Kingsolver and, since Hollis likes to write about food, the collected works of M. F. K. Fisher. They eat dinner in the formal dining room, which sounds stuffy but Robert and Judith make it feel intimate and fun. The two of them are clearly madly in love, clinking wineglasses and kissing before they eat. Hollis is mesmerized, watching them. She makes a joke about how many forks there are and if she doesn't use the correct one, don't hold it against her, she grew up in a five-room cottage on an island thirty miles off the coast. Judith says, "You could eat with your hands and we'd still find you delightful."

When Hollis leaves, Judith gives her a squeeze and says, "I hope I'll be seeing a lot more of you."

Finding Matthew seems like an impossible stroke of luck, and yet it makes a certain kind of sense. Hollis hasn't dated anyone seriously since breaking up with Jack Finigan seven years earlier. She has been waiting for the right person—and her patience has finally paid off.

"Matthew and I built a beautiful life together," Hollis says. "I was blessed to have met him."

In general, nothing drives Tatum crazier than when someone uses the word *blessed,* though honestly, she could use a blessing herself. *If Gigi picks up her wineglass before I count to ten,* Tatum thinks, *then I don't have cancer.* Tatum counts really slowly, but Gigi's attention is fixed on Hollis.

Tatum feels a stab of dread. *HER2-positive cancer,* she thinks, *must have been the kind her mother had. Aggressive.*

Dru-Ann hands Tatum the platter of roasted chicken and crispy fries. "You'll like this."

You have no idea what I'll like or won't like! Tatum thinks, but she accepts the platter and takes some chicken. The fries look good too, actually. Tatum ended up sitting next to Dru-Ann because Brooke said, "Gigi asked to sit next to me," as though they were girls in the middle-school cafeteria. Tatum turns to look out the front windows for Jack and Kyle. They said they'd meet her and Hollis "later"—and "later" can't come fast enough.

Dru-Ann tries to be *calm* and *present.* She won't dwell on, or even fully acknowledge, the fact that she has been fired from all three of her jobs. It's actually funny (from, say, a nihilist's perspective) how with one sentence, Dru-Ann vaporized her entire life. So what now? Well, now she enjoys her cocktail and helps herself to the Thai curry lobster and wonders what Hollis will say when Dru-Ann asks if she can live in the Twist forever.

Gigi wants to know more, she wants to know it all, a full history of Hollis and Matthew, how they acted when they closed on their first house, which side of the bed each of them slept on, how they named their daughter and chose their dogs. And where did things go wrong? How did Matthew Madden turn into a man who would lie about being divorced to a woman he met at an airport lounge—and then sustain that lie for seven months afterward?

But Gigi knows better than to ask any more questions right now. She turns to Tatum. "What do you do, Tatum? I don't think I know."

Tatum says, "I clean houses and run errands for a company called Irina Services."

"That sounds so fun!" Brooke says. Brooke stopped working after she got married. Charlie is one of those men who want to be the sole provider. It's a self-esteem thing, but also a power thing; he has spent the past twenty-something years calling the shots because he *brings home the bacon.* "I'm jealous that you have a job. I basically do the same things—clean and run errands—only nobody pays me."

"It's honest work," Dru-Ann says.

"I would appreciate it if the two of you would stop patronizing me," Tatum says. "I'm not a fancy sports agent, I'm not an airline pilot, I'm not internet-famous. I'm a maid and a gofer. I work for people like you."

Dru-Ann is about to say she wasn't *patronizing* anyone, but she knows Tatum won't believe her.

Brooke says, "If I leave Charlie, I'll probably get a job like you have."

"At the rate I'm going," Dru-Ann says, "I might too."

"Please just stop," Tatum says. "You don't have to try to level the playing field. I'm a big girl. I can handle it."

An awkward silence falls over the table, and Gigi deeply regrets asking the question.

Hollis can feel their ship about to capsize. How can she right it? She starts to say, *My first job was opening scallops in sixth grade, down on Old North Wharf,* but at that moment, a woman wearing a sundress in dramatic black-and-white-zigzag stripes walks into the restaurant, and Hollis's first thought is that this woman somehow belongs to their group.

But their group is complete. This woman just happens to be wearing black and white—*And isn't that funny, we should buy her a drink*—but then Hollis wonders if it's a superfan who decided to crash (with all the people who subscribe to her blog's newsletter, there are bound to be a few with questionable judgment).

Then Hollis takes in the dark red hair and the snide one-arched-eyebrow-pursed-lips expression and thinks, *Lord have mercy.*

It's Electra Undergrove.

If a hungry Siberian tiger had walked in, Hollis would have been less alarmed.

Electra must be here on vacation. Hollis has heard through the Wellesley grapevine that Electra still comes to Nantucket, and what can Hollis do about that? She doesn't *own* the island. Hollis instinctively lowers her face. They've finished eating; all that remains on the plates are chicken bones, a smear of egg yolk, some garnishes. Hollis was going to suggest espresso martinis for dessert but never mind that now.

Hollis and Electra's friendship ended five years ago under very bad circumstances because of how Electra treated Brooke. Brooke! Hollis glances up to see if Brooke has noticed Electra. Yes, Brooke's eyes are as round as plates and she's shaking her head at Electra but Electra glides right over to the table and says, "Good evening, ladies."

Hollis rises from her chair. She feels like a queen in a chess game or like a character in *Game of Thrones* facing her rival. *Poor Brooke,* she thinks. *First Charlie, now Electra.* But Hollis will protect her. "What do you want, Electra?"

Electra tips her head back and laughs. Her hair is different (it used to be brown), and her posture has changed—she's leading with her chest. Yes, that's right, Hollis heard she had her boobs done. They look lovely, good for her, Simon must be thrilled, but Hollis doesn't care. For years, this woman was Hollis's closest confidante. They kept each other sane when the kids were growing up. Hollis loved Electra's sense of humor and her joie de vivre. She made every playdate a party and single-handedly created an enviable social life for all the Fiske Elementary School moms, then the middle-school moms, then the Wellesley High moms. Her rock and roll football parties became so legendary, there was an article about them in the *Globe.*

Then everything soured.

Electra says, "Brooke and I had drinks yesterday at Slip Fourteen and she shared the itinerary for your little weekend, so I thought I'd pop by to see how it was going."

"You..." Hollis isn't sure what she's hearing. Brooke and Electra had *drinks?* Yesterday afternoon...when? Before Brooke came to the house? Hollis remembers Brooke saying she'd already had a couple glasses of rosé, but she'd assumed she'd meant on the ferry. "You and Brooke had drinks?"

Electra turns her laser-blue glare on Brooke. "You mean to say you didn't tell Hollis I treated you to a bottle of rosé?"

"You didn't treat me," Brooke says. "I treated you. Or we split it."

"That bottle cost a hundred and fifty dollars, Brooke. You didn't give me even half," Electra says. "But it's fine because we were celebrating, weren't we?"

"Celebrating?" Brooke says.

"We were celebrating the rekindling of our friendship," Electra says. She smiles at Hollis. "Brooke is coming back to rock and roll football this year. Sunday, September tenth. Brooke wrote it in the calendar on her phone."

"I did not!" Brooke says. "I mean, yes, I did, but Charlie and I have no intention of coming."

"From what I hear, Charlie will be tied up in court," Electra says. "Liesl called this afternoon and told me he's looking at another lawsuit for groping a coworker."

Brooke wants to hide under the Captain's Table—but no, she won't cower. Not in front of Gigi and Dru-Ann. She raises her face and in the coldest voice she can muster, she says, "Leave me alone, Electra."

Good for you, Brooke, Hollis thinks, though she can't *believe* Brooke was gullible and, she'll just say it, *weak* enough to fall prey to Electra. Hollis pictures Electra promising to include Brooke in all the fun, and Brooke, in return, offering up the itinerary for the weekend, which Hollis had sent only to her blog's subscribers.

As Hollis is about to say, *Leave us all alone, Electra, you're not welcome here,* she notices Electra staring at Gigi, of all people. "Have we met before?" Electra asks.

An uneasy expression crosses Gigi's face, and Hollis thinks, *Good God, even Gigi is intimidated by Electra.*

"No, I don't think so," Gigi says. "I'm not from here."

"The British accent!" Electra says. "Yes, I'm certain we've met somewhere—"

"Definitely not." Gigi's voice is clipped.

Tatum finishes what's left of her wine. This is precisely what she thought Hollis's friends would be like—*Real Housewife*–type bitches. She supposes she should be glad that Brooke and Gigi are nice and normal. Even Dru-Ann is a peach compared to this hellcat.

Dru-Ann is dying to push back her chair and take this woman on—nobody talks to Hollis and Brooke that way, not while she's around—but out of the corner of her eye, Dru-Ann sees her old friends Gucci Bex and Laura Ingalls walk into the restaurant. *No,* she thinks, *not possible.* But of course possible, because she simply can't catch a break this weekend. Dru-Ann has lost everything, and you can't fall off the floor, as the saying goes, but even Dru-Ann isn't brave enough to create a scene while those two are in the building.

As it turns out, Dru-Ann isn't needed, because someone else takes hold of Electra's arm, pulls her away from the table, and whispers angrily in her ear—and that person is Blond Sharon. Sharon recognized Electra Undergrove the second she walked into Nautilus because earlier that day, Sharon had received a text from her old friend Fast Eddie, the well-known real estate agent. The text said: Meet the worst renter I've had in thirty years in this business. Wait until I tell you the stories! And underneath was a picture of this woman.

All Sharon has to say to Electra is "You will leave everyone at that table alone right now or I will see to it you are forever banned from this island. Trust me, I have that power."

For one moment, Electra looks like she might challenge Sharon, but then she waves a hand and laughs it off. "I just thought it was funny that we were all wearing the same colors. I thought maybe they would buy me a drink, but not to worry, ha-ha-ha, I'm going to LoLa!" And she disappears out the door.

37. Night Changes II

Brooke needs to talk to Hollis alone. She needs to *explain*. But Hollis is busy flagging their server and asking for the bill. Dru-Ann offers a credit card, and Gigi offers a credit card; Hollis says, "No, no, everything this weekend is my treat," though her cheerful tone sounds forced. All of the heat and light they brought with them into the restaurant has been sucked out. What can Brooke do to salvage the evening?

"We're going to the Chicken Box now, right?" she says. She's been looking forward to the Chicken Box all weekend. It's just a bar, there isn't one piece of chicken, but Brooke has the perfect buzz for dancing to live music on a beer-sticky floor and pretending she's single again.

Gigi says, "I'm absolutely knackered. I'll get a taxi home, but you all have fun, thanks for dinner, Hollis, good night!" She's out of her seat so quickly that by the time Hollis looks up from calculating the tip, she's disappearing through the door.

"To be honest, I'm not sure I'm up for the Box," Hollis says.

"Me either," Tatum says quickly. A text has just come into her phone from Kyle: Jack and I are having a drink at Queequeg's. Let me know when you're finished, we'll meet you out front.

"So nobody's going to the Box?" Brooke says. Why is she surprised? Everyone heard what Electra said: Charlie is being sued again for sexual misconduct, and Brooke is tainted by association. Nobody wants to hang out with her.

Dru-Ann sighs. "I'll go with you." She checks over her shoulder; Gucci Bex and Laura Ingalls are sitting at the sushi bar. "But let's leave right now."

"Thank you!" Brooke says. "I just have to use the ladies' room real quick—"

"Now," Dru-Ann says. "Before I change my mind." She winks at Hollis and mouths, *You owe me.* Then she takes Brooke's hand and yanks her out of the restaurant into the dark Nantucket night.

"Do you want a ride home?" Hollis asks Tatum.

"Are you crazy?" Tatum says. "The boys are at Queequeg's. They want us to meet them."

"What?" Hollis says. "No, I can't. I'm not doing that."

"Why not?" Tatum says.

"It's too soon for me to move on," Hollis says.

"Holly," Tatum says. "Real talk here, you and me." She squares Hollis's shoulders and looks her in the eye. "No one is asking you to move on. It's one drink. And it's not like I'm setting you up with a stranger. It's Jack Finigan. Don't overthink it."

"If I go anywhere, it should be to the Box," Hollis says. "Caroline is going to the Box."

"Trust me," Tatum says. "The last person Caroline wants to see at the Box is her mother. I'm making an executive decision. You're coming with me."

As Hollis follows Tatum out of the restaurant—with a wave to the nice blond woman who saved her from Electra—she thinks, *The night has already sort of fallen apart, everyone else has left. It's just one drink.* It's not like she and Jack are getting back together and planning a Viking River Cruise.

"Fine," she says.

* * *

When Hollis sees Jack standing on the sidewalk in front of Queequeg's, she nearly turns and runs. He's *so* handsome. He's wearing jeans, flip-flops, a white linen shirt turned back at the cuffs. He flashes his dimples as she approaches.

Jack says, "You can't get enough of me."

"This wasn't my idea," Hollis says, but she lets half a smile slip onto her face. "In fact, I actively resisted."

"Actively?" Jack says. "I wish I'd seen that."

"I have an idea," Tatum says. She looks a thousand times happier than she did at dinner, and for this reason alone, Hollis is glad they came. Kyle has his arm wrapped around Tatum's shoulders and she leans her head into his chest. "Let's go to the Brotherhood for a drink."

Ha! Hollis thinks. Thirty million years ago, the four of them ate dinner at the Brotherhood before their junior prom. The restaurant has been sold and renovated and sold and renovated again since then, but the downstairs still has the feel of a cozy, brick-walled pub with low lighting and a fireplace. However, when they arrive, Tatum leads them upstairs to the new Cisco Surf Bar.

There was no upstairs to the Brotherhood when they were growing up, but now one side is an upscale whiskey lounge and the other side is a cheerful, hip space where the walls are lined with surfboards and Lauren Marttila photographs. There are, miraculously, four seats at the bar, near where a guy is playing acoustic guitar. They take the seats; the boys get beers, and Hollis and Tatum order espresso martinis.

When Hollis clinks her martini glass against Jack's frosted Bud Light bottle, she says, "I can't believe I'm sitting here with you." She isn't sure what to call the feelings welling up inside of her. Nostalgia, maybe? She thinks back to May of 1986.

* * *

Hollis's junior prom dress is white; her father, Tom Shaw, is uncharacteristically mushy during the pictures. He kisses Hollis on the forehead and says, "Do me a favor and don't elope tonight."

"We'll wait until senior prom, sir," Jack says with a wink as he helps Hollis into his pickup, which he has washed and vacuumed for the occasion.

At dinner at the Brotherhood, at a table right downstairs from where they are now, Hollis and Tatum order the chicken piccata—they both want burgers, but they're worried about onion breath and spilling ketchup on their dresses—and the boys whisper about whether they'll be carded if they try to order beer.

"Yes, you'll get carded," Tatum says. "We're *high-school students going to our prom.* Terri's brother is the manager. Everyone here knows us."

There's an older couple sitting at the next table; they lean over and say, "Enjoy it, kids. It goes by so fast."

Yeah, yeah, Hollis thinks. *Hold on to sixteen as long as you can,* blah-blah-blah. All the four of them want, in that moment, is to be older.

When they finish eating, the server tells them that the couple picked up their entire check.

"Damn!" Kyle says. "I knew I should have gotten the lobster."

It goes by so fast, Hollis thinks now. What if she'd had a crystal ball that night and could see the four of them together thirty-seven years later at the new bar upstairs? What would she have thought? It's dizzying to consider.

Jack takes a sip of his beer. "You won't be sitting for long." He goes over to the guitar player, whispers something in his ear, slips him some money.

Does Hollis know what's coming?

Of course she does—but the first chords of the song give her the shivers nonetheless. The guitar player sounds just like a young Mick Jagger. *"I know living is easy to do…"*

Suddenly Jack is behind her, singing in her ear. *"The things you wanted, I bought them for you."* He reaches for her hand. "Dance with me, Holly."

Hollis looks at Tatum but she and Kyle are in their own world. Kyle is stroking Tatum's hair; Tatum's eyes are closed.

Hollis is shy—nobody else is dancing—but what does she care about anyone else? She and Jack slow-dance in the space between the guitar player and the bar. Hollis clings to Jack, inhales his scent, thinks about the boy who rode his bike seven miles out to Squam every Saturday morning and chopped wood with Tom Shaw just so he could spend an hour with Hollis on the beach alone. She thinks about her father saying, *Don't elope tonight,* and Jack responding, *We'll wait until senior prom, sir.* He'd been kidding but also serious. They had planned to get married. All the years they'd dated, that had been the plan.

Oh, Jack, she thinks. She can't imagine how badly she hurt him.

Wild horses, she thinks. *We'll ride them someday.*

But things had turned out the way they were supposed to. Hollis was meant to marry Matthew, that much she's sure of.

There's a tap on her shoulder. It's Tatum.

"We're leaving."

"But you're coming back to Squam tonight, aren't you?" Hollis says.

"I'll bring her out there," Kyle says with a wink. "But we're taking the long way 'round."

After they disappear down the stairs, Jack says, "Can I buy you another drink?"

"I've had enough, I think," Hollis says. "I parked my Bronco on India Street, but I should probably get a cab."

"I'll drive you home in the Bronco," Jack says, "and catch a ride home with Kyle." He tilts his head. "But we'd better take the long way 'round."

Hollis would have said there was no way she would recognize their spot—the place, deep in the moors, where she and Jack used to park in high school—but Jack drives there without even having to think about it. It's a quarter mile from Gibbs Pond, where the high-school parties are, a tiny enclave surrounded by fir trees: the Round Room. All these years later, it looks exactly the same—one reason, Hollis thinks, why she'll always support the Nantucket Conservation Foundation. Jack cuts the engine and snaps off the lights. There's a smattering of stars straight up but the crescent moon is obscured by the trees.

Hollis says, "How many couples do you think parked here after us?"

"And before us," Jack says.

"But it was ours for years," Hollis says. They came here nearly every weekend junior and senior years and the summer in between. The other kids knew to stay away.

"I want to talk," Jack says. "Tell me everything."

"You tell *me* everything," Hollis says. "What happened to Mindy?"

"We had a good run," Jack says. "Seven and a half years. She was a cool chick; she gave me space. She worked for a drug company selling Botox and whatnot. It was a little disturbing, all those women wanting to freeze their faces, but she enjoyed it. She was good at darts and made a mean chicken cacciatore."

"But?"

"She wanted to get married. I threw her a surprise fortieth birthday party at my bar and after everyone left, she sat me down and told me I needed to put a ring on it or she was leaving."

"Ultimatum 101," Hollis says.

"She married someone else; she's happier now. It all worked out."

"Except you're alone," Hollis says.

"You can be in a relationship and alone," Jack says. He clears his throat. "How are you doing, Holly? I imagine it's been rough."

Hollis exhales. "I'm not sure I have the words to describe what it's been like," she says. "Everything changed in an instant. My whole life *became* that car wreck. But I had to be strong—for Caroline, obviously, but also because I thought that's what people expected."

"Which people?"

"My friends, my community, my blog's subscribers. Everyone sees me as, I don't know, some kind of—"

"Domestic goddess?" Jack says. "Earth mother?"

He's probably not far off. "They see me as in control—steady, well adjusted. I'm the one who provides comfort. I didn't feel like I was allowed to fall apart." Tears drip down her face. It feels so good to cry that she just lets the sobs come. Jack reaches out and pulls her into his arms. He murmurs into her hair, "I'm here, Holly berry."

Hollis sits up and gropes at her feet for her bag, where she keeps a pack of lavender-scented tissues; she's on brand even when she's having a breakdown. "There's guilt too," she says, then blows her nose. "Matthew and I were having problems. It was a low-grade fever, nothing splashy or dramatic; we just drifted apart. He was always working, then my website took off and I put my energy there. Caroline was away at college. Both of us talked to the dog more than to each other." Hollis wipes under her eyes. "We had a conversation the morning he died...we were both trying to express how unhappy we were. He told me that I'd changed, that we'd changed, and he was right."

"Oh, Holly."

"When things were bad with Matthew, I would check up on you. I'd stalk your Facebook page. I did it when I was feeling low and I wanted to remember what it felt like to be really loved." The tears start up again. Whatever she thought might happen this weekend, it wasn't ending up in the Round Room confessing all her secrets to Jack Finigan. "I saw the picture of you and Mindy—"

"Three years ago?" Jack says. He's laughing and she can't blame him; it sounds so silly.

"I wanted to know if you were still with her," Hollis says. "I guess what I really wanted to know was if you ever thought about me."

"Of course I thought about you, Holly. You're a part of who I am."

"But you never come back here."

"I come back now and again," he says.

Without thinking, Hollis says, "I saw you once."

"That one Thanksgiving," he says.

Yes, she thinks. What year would it have been? Caroline was in middle school, so maybe almost ten years ago. It was the Friday after Thanksgiving, and Hollis, Matthew, and Caroline were downtown for the tree-lighting ceremony. It was a favorite evening of Hollis's—all of Nantucket coming together on Main Street, the ceremonial lighting of the Christmas trees in town. Hollis was wearing a chunky knit sweater and a down vest; she and Matthew and Caroline usually walked to Languedoc for lobster bisque and steak frites after the lighting. Hollis had been swaddled in a bubble of contentment.

But when the switch was flipped and Main Street came aglow, Hollis was arrested by the sight of one face through the crowd. She squinted. Was it him? Was it Jack? Yes—and he was looking at her. He smiled, flashing his dimples, and lifted a hand to wave.

Hollis felt a rush she hadn't at all expected. Jack! She was suddenly self-conscious. She looked around for Matthew, but he and Caroline were over on the sidewalk with their phones out, snapping pictures of the trees. Hollis knew she appeared to be alone, and she was glad. She locked eyes with Jack, thinking, *What do I do?* A normal response would have been to lead Matthew and Caroline over and introduce them. *This is Jack Finigan, a friend of mine from high school.* Matthew would have known that it was Jack, her old boyfriend, though he wouldn't have cared one bit; Matthew was the least jealous person Hollis had ever known. Why didn't she do that? The answer: She didn't want to introduce Jack to her family; she didn't want Jack to know she *had* a family. In that instant, she'd wanted to go over and hug Jack, kiss him, even. She'd had the urge to pull him down Quince Street, hide between two of the summer homes, and make out.

Instead, she lamely waved back, then looked away, and when she rejoined Matthew and Caroline, she claimed she had a headache and should probably go home. "I'll take a cab," she said. "You two go to dinner."

"That's ridiculous," Matthew said. "We'll all go home. There are a ton of leftovers."

This was true; Hollis cooked Thanksgiving for ten people, even though there were only three of them. "We had leftovers for lunch," she said. "You two go, keep our reservation, it would be rude not to. I'll get a cab and see you back at the house, love you, bye." Hollis then weaved her way through the crowd to where she'd seen Jack standing, but he was gone. She had wandered around searching for him, fully aware that she was acting like a crazy person—she was a happily married woman, a mother—though at the time she hadn't cared. She'd just wanted to see him. Had he been with someone? She knew this was possible, but if he was alone, they could have a moment. That was all she'd wanted: a moment with Jack, alone.

"I came looking for you," Hollis says now. "I ditched Matthew and Caroline and tried to find you."

"I know," he says. "I was watching you. I thought you might be looking for me."

"What?" Hollis says. "Why didn't you say something?"

He sighs. "Oh, Holly, because you weren't mine anymore." He reaches for her again. "Come here."

She leans into him and without even thinking about it, she raises her face to his and they kiss, despite her tears and her runny nose. Hollis's emotions are heightened, *operatic,* and tagging right along with her grief and confusion is her desire. How long has it been since she's been kissed like this? She and Matthew were a long-married couple; they didn't make out. Somewhere along the way, kissing like this—with hungry, nearly desperate lips and tongues—just stopped happening.

But now, with Jack, it's ecstasy. Hollis can't get enough. The years fall away from her, she's a kid again, seventeen years old, parked in this very same spot in late August of 1987. She's leaving in the morning for Chapel Hill. She wants—needs—this to be a kiss they both remember the rest of their lives.

Jack pulls away and Hollis thinks, *Right*—what are they *doing?* She isn't ready for this kind of thing (though she does, in the moment, feel very ready). She wonders if Jack just isn't into it. Mindy, after all, is ten years younger than they are. He might not want to be kissing a fifty-three-year-old woman.

"Headlights," he whispers. "Over there. Are they coming this way?"

Hollis follows Jack's finger—through the trees, she sees a car. She wills it to turn off onto another path—the moors are crosshatched with narrow sandy roads—but the lights are coming straight for them. Is it the next generation of young lovers hoping to park here? She waits for them to notice the spot is occupied (by a couple of old people) and move on. Then she says, "Do you think it's Kyle and Tatum?" *That* would be funny. It's possible they guessed where Hollis and Jack would end up, and at Tatum's insistence (she's the prankster), here they are.

The car gets closer and Hollis says, "Should we just go?" There's nothing more incriminating than getting caught in a parked car. But it's too late now; the car has pulled behind them, blocking their way out of the Round Room.

"Oh, shit," Jack says.

It's the Nantucket police.

Eeeeeee! Hollis thinks. *This is truly mortifying.* In all the times she and Jack parked here, they'd had only two snafus: the dead battery (it was how they learned not to play the radio unless the engine was running) and getting stuck (during a particularly muddy April). They'd never been caught by the police; the cruisers back in those days couldn't make it down these roads. The vehicle behind them now is an SUV.

The officer gets out of the car—Hollis hears his door slam, though she's too embarrassed to turn around—and a voice says, "Good evening, folks. How we doing?"

Jack opens the door and steps out and Hollis thinks, *Just let me disappear.*

Jack says, "Holy cow! *Kevin?*"

Officer Kevin Dixon can't believe his eyes. He swings by the Round Room on a routine check (rising seniors Zack Crispin and Abigail Montero have been parking here lately, and he told them next time he'd call their parents), but it's *not* Zack and Abby this time, it's a couple Dixon's own age. It's not only a couple his age, it's Jack Finigan and Hollis Shaw.

What? Dixon thinks. Has he stepped into a time machine? Is it 1987 all over again?

"Holy cow! Kevin?" Jack says. "It's Jack Finigan, man, how the hell are you?"

Dixon shakes Jack's hand, then brings him in for a bro-hug. Jack Finigan was a tight end and one hell of a blocker for Dixon at tailback. Dixon hasn't seen the guy in freaking eons; he never comes to any of the reunions. "Good to see you, man." He turns to Hollis. "Hey, Holly, how're you doing?"

"Hi, Kev," Hollis says. She gets out of the passenger side and comes over to give him a hug as well. Dixon has seen Hollis around, mostly driving—in this very Bronco, come to think of it; it's a beauty, hard to miss—but they haven't talked much. One year he saw her at the Pops, another summer he bumped into her at Wicked Island Bakery (she was after the morning buns; he wanted the egg sandwich with short ribs). Dixon's ex-wife is obsessed with Hollis's website and actually brags to her friends that Dixon and Hollis went to school together. And of course, Dixon read in the paper that Hollis's husband died. Was that this past winter or the winter before? Dixon is getting to the point where the years blend. He won't offer condolences on the husband because it's pretty clear that Hollis and Jack are here together. Like, *together*-together. That's very funny because isn't this the place where Hollis and Jack used to park in high school? They *owned* this spot back in the day; nobody dared challenge them for it.

Dixon wants to ask what they've been up to, maybe congratulate Hollis on all her success, but it's obvious he interrupted something out here. Hollis's hair is mussed and she has dark mascara tracks down her cheeks. The last thing these two probably want to do is chat.

Dixon raises a hand. "Didn't mean to interrupt. I'm just on the lookout for kids drinking or smoking. It's so dry this summer that one cigarette butt could set the moors on fire. Anyway, good to see you both." He laughs. "You were definitely *not* who I expected to find!" Dixon heads back to his car and as he backs up, he watches Jack and Hollis climb back into the car.

Good for them, he thinks, and he chuckles about it all the way back to Milestone Road.

38. What Happens at the Box

The first person Caroline sees when she walks into the Chicken Box is . . . Dylan McKenzie.

Wait—what? she thinks.

He's standing at the bar by himself, and when he sees Caroline, his face brightens and he holds out a cold Corona.

"I hope this is okay," he says. "They don't have Pol Roger."

"Um, hi?" Caroline says. "What are you doing here?"

"We had a buyout tonight, private party, so I finished early and I figured you'd be here."

Caroline takes a swig of the beer. Did she misread the cues from last night? Dylan has been *waiting* for her? This is so weird. "That was thoughtful. Thank you for this."

"You look great tonight."

It just so happens Caroline *does* look great. She finally shed her sweatpants and put on cute jeans and a yellow halter top the size of a handkerchief. She blew out her hair and put on makeup because she has a plan, which is to photograph herself having fun at the Chicken Box and post it on her Instagram and Snapchat. She's sure now that Isaac will see it and she wants him to know what he's missing.

It would be even better if she posted a picture of herself having fun at the Box with Dylan, she thinks.

"Let's take a selfie," she says. She checks with Dylan—does he want to be seen with her beyond the confines of this bar?—and he immediately wraps an arm tightly around her and cheeses (he is *so* hot, that can't be denied). She snaps a bunch of pics.

"Is my mother here?" she asks.

"She and my mom are MIA," Dylan says. "And I'm *not* unhappy about that."

The band, Maxxtone, is playing "The Middle" by Jimmy Eat World, and although Caroline is grateful for music that isn't off the Sirius XM oldies channels (her mother's playlists are *seriously* painful), she says, "I'm going to the ladies' room real quick."

"I'll wait here," Dylan says. "Then we can dance."

Caroline threads her way through the crowd of young, aggressively beautiful summer kids. Dylan could hook up with literally any girl he wants to, so Caroline isn't sure why he's paying attention to her, though it's nourishing to her wounded ego. When she's alone in the bathroom stall, she scrolls through the pictures, picks the one where she and Dylan look (a) the hottest and (b) the most "together," and for a caption she writes, What happens at the Box... Then she posts. Mission accomplished.

When she gets back to the bar, she sees Dylan waiting with fresh beers, but before she reaches him, someone calls her name.

Caroline's head swivels—she spies Dru-Ann and Brooke walking in the door. She waves them over to the bar and introduces them to Dylan.

"This is Tatum's son," she says. "Dylan, this is Dru-Ann, Mom's friend from college, and Brooke, her friend from Wellesley."

Dylan says, "Whoa, Ms. Jones, I watch you every week on *Throw Like a Girl*. This is so cool. You're part of the weekend thing with my mom? She didn't tell me."

Dru-Ann thinks, *Well, dude, there's a reason for that.* Then she thinks, *I've been fired by ESPN, as you'll find out when you tune in on Tuesday and find Crabby Gabby in my seat.* But she won't be a buzzkill tonight. "Yes, I am," she says, offering a hand. She assesses Dylan's stature and build. "Don't tell me—college lacrosse."

"Good guess," he says. "I played one year at Syracuse."

Syracuse? She's impressed. "Only one year?"

"Yeah," he says. "Then some things came up."

Well, as Dru-Ann has learned with young athletes, "some things" could be grades, drugs, or sex. This kid is obviously a lady-killer so Dru-Ann is going to guess it was sex.

"Can I treat you to a round of shots?" he says.

"Yes, please!" Brooke says. It's so warm in the bar that she gathers her hair in a bun on top of her head; she feels her cheeks flushing. She can't believe she's at the Box with Dru-Ann, who is so super-famous even Tatum's son recognized her! Who cares about Electra Undergrove? (As she thinks this, she scans the crowd for Electra because if she *is* here, Brooke will have to leave.) "Should we do Sex on the Beach?"

"There's only one acceptable shot," Dru-Ann says.

"Tequila," Caroline and Dylan say together, and Dru-Ann thinks, *Maybe there is hope for this generation.*

Dylan orders four shots of Patrón; they all clink glasses, and down the hatch it goes.

The band segues into "Kiss" by Prince. "I want to dance!" Brooke says. She looks to Dru-Ann.

"I'm not your babysitter, girlfriend," Dru-Ann says. "Go find some hot guy and hit the floor."

Brooke wants Dru-Ann to come with her. She isn't quite intoxicated enough to forget that she's a middle-aged suburban housewife. But she won't be needy. She was at a bar not unlike this when she met Charlie; she'll just channel her carefree twenty-five-year-old self and try to attract a person who is the polar opposite of Charlie. She heads into the pulsing crowd.

Dru-Ann says, "I could use another shot. You guys?"

"Bet," they say, and Dru-Ann brandishes her credit card like the girl-boss she used to be.

One hour and an undisclosed number of tequila shots later, Dru-Ann, Caroline, and Dylan head out to the dance floor as well. They find Brooke—okay, wow—in the center of a circle of Chads. (Dru-Ann can't remember what a group of Chads is called. It's either a *privilege* or an *inheritance.*) These boys are wearing white pants, pastel polos, belts needlepointed for them by their rich, idle mothers, and loafers without socks. They're sloshing their vodka sodas around, cheering on their new mascot, Brooke.

"MILF!" pink-shirt Chad cries out while lilac-shirt Chad twirls Brooke under his arm.

"I have to go save her," Dru-Ann says to Caroline and Dylan. She taps Brooke on the shoulder, and when Brooke sees her, she shrieks and throws an arm around Dru-Ann's neck.

"This! Is! My! Friend!"

"Hey, it's Dru-Ann from *Throw Like a Girl*!" peach-shirt Chad says. He holds up his phone for a selfie, but Dru-Ann swats the phone away.

"No pictures."

"Didn't you get *canceled?*" seafoam-green-shirt Chad says.

"I'm here, aren't I?" Dru-Ann says. She assesses the group and thinks: *They aren't tall enough for basketball, broad enough for football or hockey, lean enough for lacrosse or soccer. They probably play sucky golf and worse tennis.* "I'm going to borrow the MILF. See you boys." She leads Brooke to a spot over by the fire-exit doors where there's room to breathe.

"Those guys just started talking to me," Brooke says. The one in the peach, Archie, noticed Brooke during the band's break when the DJ played "Through the Storm" and Brooke belted out every word. (Both her kids listen to rap and hip-hop exclusively; Brooke has heard the song hundreds of times.) Archie seemed to think a mom who liked YoungBoy Never Broke Again was cool—or maybe just an oddity—and he introduced Brooke to his friends. That was fun, but she'd much rather have been dancing with Dru-Ann.

When the band plays "Watermelon Sugar," Dylan grinds up behind Caroline. She raises her arm with her phone and snaps some pictures. These will drive Isaac crazy. The band segues into "Champagne Supernova" and Dylan puts his hands on Caroline's hips and spins her around to face him. Then he leans down and kisses her. This time it goes much better—maybe because of the music or the crush of bodies around them or all the tequila. Caroline is making out with Dylan McKenzie and she's enjoying it!

But a second later, there's a shockingly cold, wet assault to the side of Caroline's head. Someone's drink runs down Caroline's face and neck—it smells like rum and Coke—and stains her yellow top brown. Caroline wipes her eyes and sees—surprise, surprise—horrible, awful mean girl Aubrey Collins holding an empty plastic cup.

"Get away from him!" Aubrey screams.

"Aubrey, what the hell?" Dylan says. "I'm so sorry, Caroline." He pulls a bar towel out of his back pocket and Caroline uses it to mop herself up.

"So the two of you are Instagram official, then?" Aubrey says, sneering at Caroline. "I saw your post. But I'm sorry to tell you, he's *my* baby daddy—so, girl, bye."

Oh my God, Caroline thinks. *Is this happening again?* The good thing is that now Caroline knows exactly what to do. She's been thinking about it for years.

Caroline smiles and presses the gross bar towel into Aubrey's hand. *What happens at the Box,* she thinks.

"He's all yours, psycho," Caroline says, and she heads out the side door—wet, sticky, and deeply satisfied.

39. Slice

The band plays one great song after another—the Violent Femmes, the Cure, Weezer—and the group of Chads keep Brooke's and Dru-Ann's drinks flowing. When the lights come up and the lead singer launches into "Closing Time," Dru-Ann steers Brooke around the couples who are about to hook up and out the side door—where they run smack into a ridiculously long line of people waiting for cabs.

No, Dru-Ann thinks. *This won't do.* She'll call an UberXL. Hell, she'll use Alto, the world's most expensive rideshare app. Do they have Alto on Nantucket? No, it turns out, they do not. UberXL, then—but the nearest one is thirty-seven minutes away. They should have left the bar earlier. It's past one now; at this rate, they won't make it back to Hollis's until two. Dru-Ann hits Confirm Ride because what else can she do, it's too far to walk—then she sees the pizza parlor across the street, Sophie T's, is open.

Yes! she thinks. She's *starving;* the chicken and frites at Nautilus were a lifetime ago. "Follow me," Dru-Ann says to Brooke. "We're getting a slice."

Soon Dru-Ann and Brooke are holding hot, delightfully floppy pieces of pepperoni pizza. They take their paper plates outside and sit on the curb with their legs stretched out into the parking lot.

It's come to this, Dru-Ann thinks. "So what's up with your hubby?" she says. "He's in trouble?"

"He groped someone at work. The new twenty-three-year-old brand manager, Irish Fahey."

"Cool name," Dru-Ann says.

"She's pressing charges for sexual misconduct. The sheriff came on Thursday to serve Charlie."

"Did he have anything to say for himself?"

"He claims he was kidding around. What Charlie thinks is 'funny' is gross, inappropriate, and offensive." Brooke takes a bite of pizza and executes an impressive cheese-pull.

"I'm well acquainted with a lot of Charlies," Dru-Ann says.

"It's not the first time this has happened," Brooke says. "He groped a server at the Oak Room in Boston a couple years ago. That one settled out of court."

"Jeez, Brooke."

"I know. He sucks. And this time, he got fired." Suddenly she starts to cry. "Fired! We have twins going into their senior years at Yale and Wesleyan—"

"You have *twins?* At *Yale* and *Wesleyan?*" How did Dru-Ann not know this? Brooke is proving to be a deep well.

"Will and Whitney are amazing but I don't talk about them because I'm pretty sure that's one of the reasons Electra kicked me out of the friend group."

"Electra is the woman who showed up at dinner?"

Brooke nods and cries harder. "Everything is such a *mess.* I did show her the itinerary and I *did* write down rock and roll football in my calendar and now Hollis hates me."

"Hollis doesn't hate you."

"But that's why she didn't come to the Box. She didn't want to be with me."

"Well, her loss," Dru-Ann says. She sets her paper plate down. "You were a lot of fun tonight."

Brooke turns to Dru-Ann; she has a smudge of orange pizza grease on her nose. "I was?"

"Yes," Dru-Ann says. She takes her napkin and wipes the smudge away. "Yes, you were a very fun date."

Brooke touches her nose and before Dru-Ann knows what's happening, Brooke leans in and kisses her. At first, Dru-Ann thinks this is just Brooke's usual over-the-top enthusiasm, but then she feels Brooke's tongue dart between her lips. *Oh, for Pete's sake!* Dru-Ann thinks. She gently puts her hands on Brooke's shoulders and eases her away. This isn't the first time a woman has tried to kiss Dru-Ann; apparently people hear *sports agent* and see Dru-Ann in her signature blazer and assume she's gay.

"Brooke," she says.

Brooke gazes at Dru-Ann with wide, dopey eyes and a trembling lip. "You're not attracted to me? You just said I was a fun date. And the way you were dancing with me made me think..."

Was Dru-Ann dancing suggestively with Brooke? Maybe a little, but it was in good fun, because she thought Brooke was straight. She certainly hadn't meant her dancing to be a come-on. She danced with Brooke the way women who are having fun dance with each other!

Dru-Ann's phone bleeps—the UberXL is a minute away. *Praise the Lord,* she thinks. She collects her trash and pulls Brooke to her feet. "Our ride is here."

In the dark back seat of the Uber, Brooke falls asleep with her head on Dru-Ann's shoulder. As they drive down the long and winding Polpis Road, Dru-Ann tries to imagine what Hollis will say when Dru-Ann says, *Brooke kissed me in the parking lot of Sophie T's. With tongue!* She chuckles as she pictures the expression on Hollis's face.

This weekend is just full of surprises.

40. Should I Stay or Should I Go?

When Gigi gets back to First Light, the dog, Henrietta, growls at her, and Gigi sighs. "I know you hate me and you have every right." She gets a glass of ice water and heads down the hall to Hibiscus Heaven. She changes out of her jersey dress and into a T-shirt and running shorts, and then she packs her bags.

She can't believe what happened at dinner. That woman, Electra. *I'm certain we've met somewhere.*

Gigi has to be ready to leave at a moment's notice.

She climbs into bed but she can't sleep. She lies there for over an hour before she hears voices in the kitchen. Hollis and... Tatum, it sounds like. They're giggling. Gigi hears the suck of the refrigerator door, the crinkle of a bag of chips. Drunken late-night snacking and gossip that Gigi would ruin if she interrupted, though Hollis would be kind enough to pretend otherwise.

Eventually the voices grow fainter and Gigi nods off—but she's awoken a little while later when she hears Brooke and Dru-Ann stumbling down the hall. It sounds like Dru-Ann is helping Brooke to bed.

"Here's water and a couple of Advil. Trust me, you're going to want them."

"But you're not mad at me. Not mad at me, right? I'm soooooo, so, so, so sorry."

"No, I'm not mad. Try to get some sleep. Tomorrow morning, you won't remember any of this."

Gigi hears Brooke's bedroom door click shut and Dru-Ann sigh. Gigi reaches for her phone. There's a text from her neighbor Tim. How is it going??? Does she know? Are you going to tell her? Give me tea!

Gigi types, Fine, no, I'm not sure—then deletes it. How dull.

She types, Well, I'm still here! And she hits Send, thinking, *But who knows what tomorrow will bring.*

41. All Rise

At eight o'clock the next morning, Henrietta the Serbian sheepdog is the only one awake. This is highly unusual: Hollis sleeps in only on New Year's Day or when it's pouring rain.

Henrietta needs to go out. She takes a quick trot through the kitchen—there's no breakfast, not even coffee brewing; what is going *on* here?—and considers her options. She can nudge open the back screen door with her nose—she's tall enough—but she'll have to bark to get back inside. It will be better to simply find Hollis.

Henrietta pads into Hollis's room and hears her soft snoring. Henrietta hates to wake her; for months after Matthew died, Hollis barely slept at all. But Henrietta has no choice. She pants in Hollis's face; her breath is so horrid (she's been told this repeatedly), it will wake Hollis up.

Except it doesn't, so Henrietta resorts to licking. This sometimes results in a swat across the nose, but this morning, Hollis just laughs, grabs Henrietta's face, and starts kissing her.

"Hello, beauty!" Hollis says, springing from bed. "Do you have to whiz?" She throws on a robe, and Henrietta follows her out to the back deck. The sun is fully up and the dew has already dried off the grass but there are still a lot of good morning smells. Before Henrietta goes to investigate, she turns back to look at Hollis, who is hugging herself with an inscrutable smile on her face.

What has gotten into her? Henrietta wonders.

Tatum wakes up in Fifty Shades of White to find half a bag of Doritos on the nightstand. Are there orange fingerprints on the duvet? Yes, a few—but a little baking soda and lemon juice will get them right out. (Irina Services has taught Tatum a hack for every domestic oops.) Tatum can't believe Hollis and Jack got caught in the Round Room by Kevin Dixon! Hollis said that at first, she thought it was Tatum and Kyle coming to prank them. Tatum is disappointed she didn't think of this because that would have been a good one. But Dixon showing up is better. What must he have thought?

Tatum allows herself a moment to imagine a future where Jack and Hollis get back together and live on Nantucket with Tatum and Kyle.

Then she touches her breast. The biopsy spot is no longer sore but Tatum knows the tumor is still there, like a rotten spot in an otherwise perfect apple.

She can't think about the future until Monday.

Brooke wakes up with a pounding headache. There's a glass of water and some Advil on her nightstand. She props herself up on an elbow and swallows the pills, then collapses back into the luscious pillows.

She kissed Dru-Ann last night. Although Dru-Ann didn't kiss her back, it wasn't a total loss. The secret Brooke has been keeping is out. She, Brooke Kirtley, is *out*.

It feels good in a way Brooke can't quite explain. For her entire adult life, Brooke has felt like a puzzle piece with gaps around the edges—off-kilter, a little wonky, not quite *right*.

But last night, finally, she snapped into place.

Hollis is just calling Henny in—she should get some coffee brewing and set out granola and the fruit salad—when she sees Gigi walking over the footbridge. Gigi gives Hollis a sheepish wave.

Predictably, Henny begins to growl. Hollis takes her by the collar and swats her rump. "Would you *stop* it, sister? Gigi is our *guest*. She's our *friend*."

Gigi shrugs. "She's entitled to her opinion."

"Did you get home okay last night?" Hollis asks. "I should apologize for what happened at the end of dinner. That woman used to be a friend of mine but something happened and we no longer speak."

"It's fine," Gigi says quickly. "And yes, I found a taxi straightaway and was home in a jiff, thanks." She steps past Hollis and dips her feet into the shallow bath before reaching for the screen door.

"Can I get you some coffee or fruit?" Hollis asks. "Granola?"

"All set, thanks," Gigi says. "I'm still a bit tired. I'll probably hang in my room this morning."

"Oh," Hollis says. "Okay." She's the first to admit she doesn't know Gigi that well, but she can tell something's off. Where is the sunny, cheerful Gigi who's ready for anything? She's probably exhausted by all the drama—and can Hollis blame her? "Is everything all right, Gigi?"

"Yes," Gigi says, though she barely turns around. "Why wouldn't it be?"

When Dru-Ann wakes up in bed under the bubble chandelier staring at the vintage George Nelson sunburst clock on the opposite wall, she thinks, *I'm never leaving the Twist.*

What, after all, does she have to go home to?

She'll ask Hollis if she can stay another week, maybe two weeks. Hollis will probably want to be rid of them by tomorrow, but once Dru-Ann tells Hollis she's been fired from her life, Hollis will have to say yes.

Dru-Ann makes an espresso and wonders how Brooke is feeling. That poor woman. She never has orgasms with her husband because she isn't into men!

Dru-Ann is just programming the Peloton—she always rides with Jenn Sherman on Sundays—when her phone dings with a text. *That,* she thinks, *will be Brooke, begging her not to tell anyone.* Dru-Ann has already realized she can't tell Hollis what happened in the pizza shop's parking lot. It isn't her news to share.

But the text is from Nick. *Well, well,* she thinks. *He lives.*

It says: Phineas tied for the lead.

Dru-Ann squawks and opens her laptop. Sure enough, Phineas Pine and Rory McIlroy are tied at eight under going into the back nine.

He had a dream he was going to win, Posey said.

Given all that has happened, does Dru-Ann *care* about any of this? Phineas playing the British Open is the whole reason Dru-Ann is where she is. In theory, she should want him to lose—and badly. But instead, she feels excited. Is Phineas mentally tough enough to beat McIlroy? Nine holes is a lot of golf. If he gets overconfident, he might bogey a hole or three. Dru-Ann sees that Hovland is at six under, and he's known for finishing strong. This is far from over. Coverage in the U.S. starts at noon, which is when they're going to lunch. Damn.

Should Dru-Ann respond to Nick? If he's letting her know about Phineas, then she's at least *on his mind.*

She'll take that as a win, she thinks—and she hops on the bike.

Caroline hears her phone buzzing on her nightstand but she's in that stage of sleep where she feels like she's underwater and can't move.

The buzzing stops and Caroline descends back into her slumber like a stone falling to the ocean floor.

Her phone buzzes again and for whatever reason, Caroline jolts awake. *Okay, okay, I'm here.* She grabs her phone.

Sofia.

"Hello?" Caroline says. She knows she's supposed to lie to Sofia—or maybe she's supposed to tell the truth; she can't remember.

"Caroline?" Like Isaac, Sofia pronounces her name "Caro-leen." From her, it's annoying.

"Yes, Sofia, hi, good morning."

"Caroline, you didn't call me back last night."

Caroline sits up, clears her throat. Can she take a tone with Sofia? She can, she decides. "I know, Sofia. I'm filming here on Nantucket. I've been too busy to call, I'm sorry. What's up?"

"We have to talk about Isaac."

"Is he okay?" Caroline asks with faux concern. "Did something happen?"

"He was unfaithful to me." Sofia's voice is so filled with conviction that fear leaps like a flame inside Caroline's chest. Was Isaac mistaken? Does Sofia suspect Caroline?

Caroline takes a breath. She can do this. "Don't be ridiculous, Sofia. He would never be unfaithful. He loves you."

"Love and sex," Sofia says, "are two different things."

Ouch, Caroline thinks. She says nothing. To speak, she thinks, is to reveal herself.

"Who was at the loft while I was in Sweden?" Sofia asks.

"Nobody," Caroline says.

"Nobody except you?"

"Right," Caroline says. "Nobody except me." Her mind races. The loft doesn't have a doorman and they don't have neighbors Sofia can check with who will tell her they saw Caroline leaving very late at night or sometimes not at all. Do they?

"And he gave you his camera?" Sofia says. "His tripod? His drone? Isaac doesn't give *anyone* his equipment, and certainly not a puny intern."

Puny? Caroline thinks. "He did. I needed to borrow them for the weekend."

"Yes, he told me. You're filming something for your mother, he said. A family reunion."

Caroline shakes her head. Whatever. She's not going to explain the Five-Star Weekend to Sofia, that's for damn sure. "There was nobody in the loft the whole time you were away," Caroline says. "I would tell you if there were."

Caroline hears Sofia exhale; she's smoking.

"I would suspect you and Isaac together, but..." She laughs. "That is so silly!"

Caroline bristles. *It was anything but silly, Sofia. Your boyfriend and I had—have—real feelings for each other. And the sex was incandescent.*

"Obviously very silly," Caroline says.

"Yes, because I saw your post last night with the other boy. Such a smoke-show. I show it to Isaac. He agreed the two of you look beautiful together."

Caroline and Dylan *do* look beautiful together in that picture on Instagram—but Instagram isn't real life. In real life, Dylan was using Caroline to make Aubrey jealous. Caroline received a spate of texts from him after she left the Box.

Are you okay?

Aubrey is just really jealous of you, she has been since high school.

I'm going to take her home, maybe talk with her in the morning about trying again. LOL, my parents won't like that. They hate her. But it will be better for O-Man.

It was fun hanging out this weekend. Ty!

Caroline composed several responses, which ranged from *Are you kidding me right now?* to *This tracks, you two totally deserve each other.* But in the end, the text she sent said: No prob. She doesn't care about Dylan McKenzie in any meaningful way. It probably *will* be better for O-Man to have his parents back together, and if Caroline helped facilitate that, good. It gives her enormous satisfaction that *she* is the person Aubrey Collins is jealous of.

Sofia says, "I'm going to do a better job loving Isaac. I'm going to travel less and no more clubbing." She inhales, exhales. "Maybe get married, have a—"

"That's great, Sofia," Caroline says. Sofia has speared Caroline's heart with her stiletto; she can't bear to hear another word. "I'll be back Tuesday, see you then!"

"Maybe we can go to dinner, the three of us," Sofia says. "You can tell us about your special weekend."

Absolutely not, Caroline thinks, but she says, "Okay, ciao!" and hangs up. A second later, she's tempted to call Sofia back and say, *It was me! It was me with Isaac!* But she won't. She will let Sofia and Isaac be happy. She will let Dylan and Aubrey be happy.

She's left with...her funny little project. And to that end, Caroline drags her ass out of bed. She wants to talk to Brooke.

42. The Drop II

Caroline finds Brooke in the kitchen making herself a cup of herbal tea. She's still wearing her dress from the night before, the white LoveShackFancy, which is, Caroline has to admit, very pretty, though now it's a bit rumpled and holds an odor that Caroline thinks of as classic Chicken Box—beer and sweat—and there's an orange drip stain (it looks like pizza grease) on the front.

"You had fun last night?" Caroline asks.

She expects Brooke to say, *So fun, best night of my life, those boys were so cute, can you believe they wanted to dance with me?*

But Brooke just smiles and hops her teabag around in her mug as the air fills with jasmine steam.

"Do you have a few minutes to come downstairs so we can have a little one-on-one chat about your friendship with my mom?"

"Of course," Brooke says. "Lead the way."

Caroline shows Brooke where to sit and sets up the ring light.

"It feels like I should know this," Caroline says once she gets the camera rolling. "But I don't. How did you and my mom meet?"

Brooke takes a breath. "I met Hollis at Dr. Lambert's office in Newton-Wellesley Hospital. She was pregnant with you, due three months sooner than I was, but we were the same size. There was some amazement about this on Hollis's part—I'm sure she thought I'd way overdone it on the Oreos—until I told her I was expecting twins."

Caroline laughs. She can't believe how smooth and poised Brooke is in front of the camera. She's a natural.

"Hollis introduced herself, said she and your dad had just moved to Wellesley from the city. We exchanged numbers and became friends. When you were born, I took her a platter of sandwiches from the Linden Store. When Will and Whit were born, Hollis brought over a roasted chicken with potatoes au gratin, a green salad with vinaigrette, freshly baked bread, a caramel and chocolate tart, a six-pack of Belgian ale that she'd found helped with her milk production, and two of the softest baby blankets I'd ever felt. I knew from the time and effort and *thought* that your mom put into dinner and the gifts that we would be friends until our children graduated from high school, and beyond." Brooke winks. "I was right."

"What are your fondest memories of your friendship with my mom?"

Brooke takes a moment to think.

"There was the golden age, the years our children were nine, ten, eleven. Fourth and fifth grade." Brooke pauses. "Of course you never realize it's the golden age until it's over."

It's 2011 in Wellesley. Brooke's twins and Hollis's daughter attend Fiske Elementary. Brooke and Hollis are part of a larger group of mothers that include Liesl, Bets, Rhonda—and Electra Undergrove, the unspoken leader. She organizes post-drop-off coffee at Maugus on Wednesdays and a monthly "Moms Night Out" in downtown Boston where they go to dinner at places like Mistral and the Bristol Lounge, then inevitably end up singing to the dueling pianos at Howl at the Moon. (The following morning, there's always a round-robin of texts, the moms complaining about their hangovers and how they can't handle soccer practice so the husbands will just have to do it for once. *But it felt so good to be wild and free for a night, to be a person again, not just a wife and mother.*)

When the kids enter middle school, Electra invents rock and roll football. The idea is a Sunday Funday at Electra's house, which has an open floor plan with a huge television and a basement tricked out for her kids, Carter and Layla. (Beanbag chairs, video games, pool table, and a refrigerator filled with soda.) Every Sunday of football season, parents and kids gather at the Undergroves. Electra makes the main dish—fish tacos, white chicken chili, a spiral-cut ham—and the rest of the friends bring appetizers, side dishes, dessert. Electra's husband, Simon, is the mixologist. He turns beers into Micheladas; he creates large-format cocktails that he serves out of an enormous glass jug with a stand and a tiny spigot; he blends up margaritas and daiquiris. The parents get . . . pleasantly buzzed while the kids are safely downstairs.

After the football games end, when the ticking clock of *60 Minutes* begins, when most normal people would pack up their kids and head home to prepare for the busy week ahead, the music starts. Simon deejays—he likes it loud—and the kids come running upstairs. Everyone dances.

It's the end of the world as we know it, and I feel fine.

Dancing lasts an hour, sometimes longer, depending on the mood in the room (and how strong the cocktail is). Liesl, Bets, and Rhonda can all walk their troops home; Hollis has to drive, but it's less than a mile away. Brooke and Charlie live the farthest and for this reason, Brooke has to stay somewhat sober, because Charlie certainly isn't going to.

Monday mornings at school drop-off, items of clothing, sunglasses, and serving dishes are returned and exchanged among the members of the group. The teachers and other parents notice this, along with the bloodshot eyes and sagging countenances of the football parents. A rumor goes around that there's an orgy at the Undergroves' every Sunday and that the parties involve switching sexual partners.

Electra loves these rumors. *Everyone is so jealous!*

Rock and roll football is the coolest thing going on in Wellesley. Brooke looks forward to it all week—studying up on the teams playing, planning her outfits, ordering the cheese platter from Wasik's (she can't cook so this is what she brings every week). What she loves most isn't the food or even the dancing—it's the camaraderie. Raising children is hard (and twins are *really* hard!) and it can be lonely—but for years, when they're in an insular, unified group in the trenches together, Brooke feels like part of the proverbial village.

* * *

Yes, Caroline remembers those parties. Things in the basement weren't quite as wholesome as the parents might have believed. One week, they watched *Ted* even though it was expressly forbidden. Once the kids hit eighth grade, Carter Undergrove would steal a couple of his father's beers and they would pass the cans around, each taking a sip or two. Then there were the hookups in the powder room—Will Kirtley and Layla Undergrove, for example. But Caroline won't tell Brooke any of this. Why ruin her burnished memories?

"Are there any not-so-fond memories?" Caroline says. This is a leading question. She knows the answer is yes, the whole thing with the Undergroves fell apart, but as a kid, Caroline was never quite clear on what, exactly, transpired.

"Well, yes," Brooke says. "Electra dropped me."

Everyone knows there's a hierarchy at rock and roll football, with Electra and Hollis at the top of the pyramid and Liesl, Bets, Rhonda, and Brooke down at the bottom. Brooke doesn't care much about Liesl, Bets, and Rhonda. They're perfectly nice women with perfectly nice husbands and kids the same age as her kids. If she were to nitpick, she might say Bets can be judgy, Liesl needs more cowbell, and Rhonda is always bragging about how hot her marriage is (which makes Brooke think maybe it's not so hot). Brooke prefers the company of Hollis and Electra, but really that means Electra.

Brooke always offers to clean up, following right behind Electra every time she leaves the room, complimenting Electra on her hair, her earrings, the new mirror in the powder room; she inserts herself into conversations between Electra and Hollis, she apologizes too much and generally emits a cringey "Will you please sign my yearbook" vibe. Electra has a tic of her own: She's fixated on the accomplishments of Brooke's children. Will is the captain of soccer, basketball, and lacrosse, he's also class president and started a chess club. Whitney is the lead in the school play and she scored in the ninety-ninth percentile on the MCAS. Brooke tries not to talk about them, because to talk about the twins is to brag, but Electra is always asking where Brooke gets them tutors, if she hires personal trainers, if she gives them vitamin supplements.

"No," Brooke says. "They're just good kids. I have no idea why." She belatedly (too belatedly?) adds, "They certainly don't get any of it from me or their father."

Who knows which reason it is—pick one or all—but one random Thursday, Brooke receives a text from Electra. This isn't unusual; Electra sends the whole football group a text every Thursday. But this one is sent only to Brooke.

It says: We're trying a different format with football this week. We'll miss you and Charlie. Thanks for understanding! XO, E.

It's only looking back now, today, that Brooke can admit to herself that she had a terrible crush on Electra, and sublimating it turned her into someone weak, vulnerable, and—she'll just say it—very annoying. Brooke regards the camera frankly. "I can be slow to pick up social cues," she says. "But even I got the message: Charlie and I were no longer invited."

Immediately Brooke calls Electra, but she's treated to her voice mail. Brooke calls back—voice mail. She tries a third, fourth, fifth time. Finally, she leaves a message so pathetic, she can't bear to think about it: "Electra, please, I'm not sure what I did wrong. Please, Electra, call me. Let's talk this through."

She considers calling Charlie or even Simon Undergrove—but they're bros and are therefore useless.

By the time Brooke calls Hollis, she's in full-blown hysterics. She can barely get a coherent word out, so finally she just cuts and pastes Electra's text and sends it to Hollis. What can Hollis say? "You're right, it sounds like maybe—"

"Did she text *you?*" Brooke asks.

In a meek voice, Hollis says, "Yes, she said she's making shrimp fried rice in the wok. I'm bringing potstickers."

"Who else was on the text?" Brooke says.

Hollis checks: Liesl, Bets, Rhonda. "I'm sorry," Hollis says. "I didn't realize you weren't on it too. You're always on it."

It makes no sense! Brooke has been racking her brain, trying to remember anything that was out of the ordinary the Sunday before. Electra's sister, Nadine, had been visiting from Manhattan. Nadine was a slicker, shinier version of Electra, all done up with hair, makeup, clothes, nails, perfume. She was like a woman fashioned from enamel. Brooke had exchanged only a few words with her before Nadine turned away to talk to Rhonda. Had Nadine asked Electra why someone as underwhelming as Brooke was included in the football group? Then Brooke gasps. Had Charlie been inappropriate with Nadine, maybe followed her to the powder room and made advances?

"Can you call her?" Brooke asks Hollis. "Can you ask what I did?"

"Oh, Brooke," Hollis says. "I don't want to get in the middle of this. You and Electra need to work it out between yourselves."

"I've called her six times," Brooke says. "I've left messages. She doesn't want to talk to me. She just…*kicked me out,* like we're kids in a clubhouse."

"I'm so sorry, Brooke," Hollis says. "It won't be the same without you."

"Your mother kept going to Electra's house. Not only *that* Sunday but every Sunday for the rest of the football season," Brooke says. "She went to Electra's knowing that Electra had dropped me from the group." Brooke holds up a hand. "I could see why Liesl and Bets and Rhonda didn't take action. They were followers. But your mom is a good person, a strong person, and I guess I assumed she would stand up for me."

"She did at some point," Caroline says. "She and Electra are no longer friends."

"She waited until after the Super Bowl," Brooke says. "Electra and the other girls were planning your senior spring break in Harbor Island, and Hollis told Electra she wasn't going. She called me up and we planned a trip to the Virgin Islands instead."

"Ah," Caroline says. This makes sense. She and Hollis did go to the Virgin Islands with Brooke and the Kirtley twins. Charlie stayed in Wellesley because it was tax season and Matthew had a paper to present somewhere. Caroline, for one, had been glad to be rid of Carter, Layla, and the other kids. She'd known there was some kind of drama going on with the adults, but what did she care? Because they were eighteen, she and Will and Whitney were legal to drink in St. John and they had spent the week inhaling rum punches and listening to live music at the Beach Bar.

Caroline shuts the camera off. "Wow, Electra is a real bitch. I'm sorry that happened to you."

Brooke shrugs. As she was telling the story, she felt a refreshing detachment, as though she were talking about someone else. "Electra is a small person who steps on others to make herself feel big," Brooke says. She worries she sounds like a pop-psychology cliché. "In her defense, I always felt insecure in the group, insecure in my *life*—and that affected how I acted. I tried too hard, I lacked confidence. I thought that to make people like me, I had to defer to them instead of acting natural." Brooke sighs. "It doesn't matter now. Your mom and I are friends and Electra is irrelevant."

Something is different about Brooke this morning, but Caroline can't put her finger on what. The first part of the weekend, she was *such* a meme—showing up in her overblown straw hat, oversharing about her sex life with Charlie, getting badly sunburned even though she'd wrapped herself up like King Tut—but now she exudes self-possession. It's as though she took a Brené Brown seminar in her sleep.

"I should go," Brooke says. "I want to read my new book by the pool before we leave for lunch."

Caroline checks her phone. It's ten forty-five already; how did that happen? She won't have time to talk with Gigi now, which means she'll have to do it after the sail. She feels bad that Gigi has to go last. Gigi has known her mother for only a short time, and virtually at that. There's no way Gigi will have a story that rivals the ones Caroline heard from Tatum, Dru-Ann, and Brooke. It's just not possible.

43. Table 20

The best table at Galley Beach is the round six-top in the corner closest to the sand, known as Table 20. To those of us eating lunch at the Galley at noon on Sunday, it comes as no surprise that this table is where Hollis Shaw and her stars are seated. The ladies are all wearing pink or orange or both, which brings a splash of summer color to the already stunning aesthetic of the restaurant.

The Galley is open-air with white tablecloths and rattan captain's chairs. There's a zinc bar and, on the beach, a lounging area with chaises and fireplace tables. To the left is the pleasing vista of the Cliffside Beach Club, with its iconic blue, green, and canary-yellow umbrellas in neat rows and five blue Adirondack chairs sheltered by a pavilion. The art in the Galley is eclectic, and so is the clientele. This is where the celebrities come (though we pretend not to notice them).

Ethan and Terri Falcone are enjoying a bottle of Domaines Ott rosé at a high-top out on the deck—both Ethan and Terri have indoor jobs, so they prefer to be in the sunshine any chance they can get—and Terri has a fine view of Hollis and her friends as they take their seats. She thinks the matching colors are a bit much, but that could be jealousy talking. She notices right away that Hollis has invited Tatum McKenzie. Terri knows both girls from high school—oh, does she! She subbed in as Tatum's best friend when Hollis left for UNC.

Ethan splits the last of the rosé between their glasses. (It pains Ethan to pay $140 for a bottle of wine when he orders it for his liquor store, Hatch's, for $28 a bottle, but he knows at the Galley, you're really paying for the view.) "Should we stay here and eat lunch?" he asks Terri. (He assumes she'll say no, that it's too expensive. Terri is the frugal one.) "Or should we swing by Something Natural for sandwiches and go to the beach?"

"Stay here," Terri says, eyeing Hollis and Tatum's table. "Definitely."

Ethan is pleasantly surprised; he's been dying to try the halibut tostada. He flags their server.

"This place is divine," Gigi says. "I feel like I'm in St. Tropez."

Tatum has always thought the Galley was as pretentious as South Beach, but now that she's here, she feels differently. She is, once again, sitting next to Dru-Ann, who is on her phone. Tatum can't help but peek at her screen, wondering what could be more intriguing than the views at the Galley. She sees some dude in a visor standing in the fog making a golf putt. Whatever.

"Shall we get champagne?" Hollis says. She calls over their server, Louis, and orders a magnum of Veuve Clicquot. She wants to celebrate—they're at the best table at the Galley, on the beach, on a glorious summer Sunday. They're all wearing their pink and orange. Although Dru-Ann looks smoking hot in a fuchsia bodycon dress, the fashion winner is probably Brooke, who's wearing an off-the-shoulder pink-and-orange paisley cover-up with a pom-pom fringe.

After Louis presents the magnum and pops the cork (Hollis senses the whole restaurant sneaking peeks at their table), Hollis lifts her flute. "Cheers, friends," she says. "Happy Sunday."

"Here's to the five-star-drinking weekend," Dru-Ann says with a wink-wink, though she's as eager as anyone for a little hair-of-the-dog. The U.S. coverage of the British Open is in full swing and the big story is Phineas Pine neck and neck with Rory McIlroy after fourteen. They have four holes to go.

Tatum takes a sip of her cold, crisp Veuve Clicquot as she gazes at the ferry crossing Nantucket Sound, and she finds herself wishing that the weekend would last a little longer. Turns out, she's grown accustomed to the lap of luxury, and it might be difficult to return to her regular life. Kyle and Jack drove to Great Point to surf-cast and for the first time, Tatum doesn't wish she was with them.

Off to the Galley for lunch, she texted Kyle earlier. Then sailing on the Endeavor!

Brooke turns to Tatum and says, "Dru-Ann and I met your son last night at the Chicken Box." She sips her champagne. "I'm holding him responsible for my hangover."

"Dylan was at the Box?" Tatum says.

"He was there with Caroline," Brooke says.

Tatum catches Hollis's eye; they exchange a look.

"Stop it, you two," Caroline says. "I'm sorry to tell you, Dylan's ex-girlfriend showed up, threw her drink *in my face,* and claimed Dylan for her own."

"Ugh," Tatum says. "Aubrey is such a pill."

"You said it, not me." Caroline pulls the camera out and starts filming the ladies around the table as Louis comes to take their orders. She zooms in on Gigi, who is wearing a hot-pink halter top and long, tangerine-hued tassel earrings. The colors pop against the sand and water behind her.

"She threw her drink at you and you didn't come get me?" Dru-Ann says.

"You were dancing with Brooke," Caroline says.

Brooke feels herself flush. Her cheeks are probably the same color as her cover-up.

Brooke should be hungry—she skipped breakfast because of the interview with Caroline—but she finds all she wants for lunch is today's omelet (Brie, sautéed zucchini, and thyme) and a green salad. Warm rolls make their way around the table and Brooke isn't tempted to take one. Next to Brooke, Gigi orders the Galley burger, which comes with a pile of thin, crispy fries, but Brooke turns down Gigi's offer to sample them. The omelet is enough; it pairs perfectly with her champagne, though unlike everyone else, Brooke is only on her first glass.

Gigi, however, is on glass number three, and the bubbles have gone straight to her head since she also skipped breakfast. It makes no sense that she's feeling so nervous now that the weekend is nearly over, does it? She supposes she's still spooked about the night before, that awful woman, and also by her own random impulses to tell Hollis the truth. *Gah!* Gigi can't imagine doing that now. She likes Hollis, likes her friends, and wants to enjoy the rest of the weekend in peace, then go back home and figure out how to forgive herself.

Dru-Ann inhales her lobster roll and then excuses herself and goes to the ladies' room, where, she's amused to find out, they pipe in a soundtrack of crashing waves and seagull cries. She sits on the toilet lid and checks her phone. McIlroy has just birdied fifteen, which probably means *Good night, Phineas.* Hovland is two strokes behind. The coverage switches to Phineas on the green at fifteen. He has an eighty-foot putt to make for birdie, and although Dru-Ann has now been in the bathroom too long to reasonably explain, she can't stop watching. Phineas lines up his shot, crouching down to eyeball the hole in a way that reminds Dru-Ann of Phil Mickelson, and then he stands up and hits the ball.

It's rolling, it's rolling, it breaks left, and Dru-Ann finds herself leaning right, whispering, *Come on, come on!* And sure enough, at the very last minute, the ball curves and drops into the cup.

Dru-Ann jumps up. He birdied fifteen! She can't freaking believe it! Is there any way she can get out of going on the sail? She needs to watch the end of this. Nick must be losing his mind! (Posey, too, but Dru-Ann doesn't care about Posey.)

When Dru-Ann takes her seat at the table, their plates have been cleared and dessert menus set down. Caroline is out on the beach, barefoot with her camera, taking atmospheric panoramas, then turning to film their table from a different vantage point. Everyone waves, Dru-Ann belatedly.

"Should we get dessert?" Hollis asks. "The brownie à la mode is not to be missed."

"I'm fine," Brooke says. "I may have coffee."

"I'd split a brownie," Gigi says.

"Get it, sis," Tatum says.

Ugh, Dru-Ann thinks. She wants to move this thing along. She was in the bathroom for so long that she can just tell Hollis her stomach is funky and she probably shouldn't get on a sailboat. She takes a breath. That's her out. She'll be in front of her TV in thirty minutes, forty tops—plenty of time to see how the tournament ends.

* * *

The fudge brownie topped with ice cream and whipped cream goes around the table once, then twice, then Tatum announces that she's finishing it. As she's bringing the final bite to her mouth, she sees a familiar-looking couple sitting at a high-top on the patio outside the bar. *Oh, boy,* she thinks. It's Terri and Ethan Falcone. (How can they afford to eat here? she wonders. The liquor store must be doing well.) Terri is staring down their table, saying something to Ethan. Tatum almost waves, but the last thing she wants is for Terri and Ethan to come over.

Tatum sits up a little straighter. *Yes, Terri, I am wearing an orange Lilly Pulitzer dress eating lunch at Table 20 with Hollis Shaw. Deal with it.*

Terri is definitely talking about them, Tatum can tell. But what is she saying?

"You know what I always think about when I see Hollis Shaw and Tatum Grover together?" Terri says to Ethan.

"What's that?" Ethan says, pushing his plate away and splitting the remains of their second bottle of Domaines Ott between their glasses. *This is the life,* he thinks. Sitting in the sun, drinking good wine, enjoying a leisurely lunch. Terri is pretty tipsy; Ethan is hoping there might be some afternoon delight in his future.

"I think about how we lost the state softball championship our senior year," Terri says. "Tatum dropped a ball in left field and the other team scored the winning run."

Ethan nods. He has heard this story countless times. He's tempted to sing Bruce Springsteen's "Glory Days," but Terri would not be amused.

"Tatum was always pranking people," Terri says. "And there was a split second when I thought she was only *pretending* to drop the ball to fake us all out, doing a sleight of hand, you know, that she would pull the ball from her glove in the end. Because it *looked* like she had it. But then the next second, it was in the grass."

"You think she dropped it on purpose?" Ethan says. This would be a new twist to the story.

"What reason would she have to do *that?*" Terri says. "Tatum is the most competitive person I have ever known. But even so, that drop has always bothered me." Terri's eyes are fastened on the other table. "Anyway, that's what I think about."

Ethan squeezes Terri's hand. This is one thing he has always loved about his wife: In her heart, she is eternally seventeen.

Hollis asks for the check, but it takes forever—or maybe it only seems that way to Dru-Ann. She peeks at her phone under the table. Hovland is on the green at sixteen. The check arrives; Hollis hands over her credit card. *Thank you, Hollis,* everyone says, Dru-Ann belatedly.

There's another lull, and Brooke, who has been unusually quiet throughout lunch, clears her throat and says, "I have something I'd like to share with you all, and it may come as a bit of a shock."

Dru-Ann's head snaps up. Is Brooke going to come out of the closet *now?*

But before Brooke can speak, there's an interruption. A woman in a flowing pink-and-orange caftan comes billowing toward them from the beach. She's wearing oversize sunglasses that Dru-Ann can only classify as "straight out of divorce court in the 1970s," so it takes Dru-Ann a minute to realize that this woman is the same cray-cray from the night before.

The woman sails right past Caroline with her camera and steps up to speak to the ladies through the open side of the restaurant.

"Hey there, girls!" she says.

Hollis whips around and comes face-to-face with Electra. She's wearing pink and orange. This is a joke, right?

Caroline zooms in as Electra Undergrove says hello, even though she and Hollis—and Brooke!—are no longer friends. They are, in fact, something like enemies. Electra is wearing a muumuu in the colors of the day. What the hell is going on?

Brooke scoffs. "You have *got* to be joking. You're making an ass of yourself, Electra. Nobody wants you here."

Hollis is impressed by Brooke's moxie but the last thing she wants is a scene here at the Galley after they've enjoyed such a lovely lunch.

"We were just leaving, Electra," Hollis says as she reaches for her purse. She catches Brooke's eye to indicate they should stand up. That's the solution: Walk away. Brooke pushes back from the table, but the other three women sit tight, staring at Electra.

"I just stopped by because late last night, I realized why you look so familiar." Electra moves her ginormous sunglasses to the top of her head; she's staring at Gigi. "I met you with Matthew in Atlanta. You two were coming out of the Optimist when my husband, son, and I were going in."

What? Hollis thinks. *Did she just say "with Matthew"?*

"Please stop, Electra," Hollis says. "Gigi never knew Matthew. Gigi and I became friends after Matthew died."

Electra's gaze is locked on Gigi. "It was you. You were with Matthew. I remember your face and I certainly remember your accent."

Hollis says, "What is *wrong* with you, Electra? Why are you harassing us like this?" She scans the restaurant to see if there's a manager who can intercede. But the restaurant is bustling, the staff is busy; Louis is across the room taking an order. No one is paying attention to them, and Hollis supposes she should be relieved.

"I just thought you should know," Electra says to Hollis.

"Know *what?* That you're a sociopath?"

"Know that this woman, your friend, your *star,* was with Matthew in Atlanta," Electra says. "They were *together.*"

Hollis shakes her head. It's absurd, impossible, and Electra is the consummate unreliable narrator. Hollis turns to look at Gigi, but Gigi's chair is empty. Hollis sees her weaving her way through the tables toward the door. She's leaving.

Gigi! Hollis thinks, but she doesn't call out because she is determined to maintain her composure.

"Thanks for the chat, ladies," Electra says. "Enjoy your time on the 'Tuck!"

The 'Tuck? Tatum thinks, rolling her eyes. Only the most irritating tourists call it that.

What has Electra *done?* Brooke thinks.

Is Gigi going home? Dru-Ann wonders. Can Dru-Ann go with her?

Caroline cuts the camera and lets it drop to her side. She sees Gigi climb into a taxi out in the parking lot. "Mom?" she says.

Hollis is up on her feet. "You four go straight to the *Endeavor,* please," she says. "Gigi and I will meet you there."

44. The Friendship Sloop

Their sail on the *Endeavor* is scheduled to go from two to four, but at two fifteen, neither Hollis nor Gigi has arrived, and Caroline can tell that Captain Jim is getting antsy. The first mate is Captain Jim's son, James, who asks Caroline how much longer she thinks it will be until they can get under way.

"They should be here any minute," Caroline says. "They're just parking."

But a few minutes later, Caroline receives a text from Hollis that says: Go without us.

Srsly? Caroline texts back. Where are u?

Go, Hollis texts. Just please go.

"Actually my mom isn't coming," Caroline tells James. "So I guess we're ready, then."

Caroline, Brooke, Dru-Ann, and Tatum choose seats in the cockpit and they listen as James gives a briefing—lifejackets, no toilet paper in the head, et cetera—and a quick history of the boat. The *Endeavor* is a thirty-one-foot Friendship sloop that Captain Jim built himself.

Very cool, Dru-Ann thinks, but as James is talking, Dru-Ann peeks at her phone. Hovland bogeyed seventeen; he's out. Phineas and McIlroy are tied headed into eighteen.

She should have gone with Gigi and Hollis, she thinks.

Tatum sends a quick text to Kyle: You will not believe what happened at lunch! Some woman is stalking us! Tatum is actually grateful for all the drama, it's keeping her mind off the other thing. She considers Electra's accusation. Gigi was *with* Matthew, as in his *lover?* Tatum doesn't blame Gigi for walking away; Tatum would have slapped the woman, *then* left.

Brooke is listening to James, but she's also still stunned by Electra's audacity. Who approaches a group of women at lunch and accuses one of the women of sleeping with another woman's dead husband? Being provocative is Electra's superpower—but something is niggling at Brooke. It's the thing Electra said at Slip 14 when she was telling Brooke about bumping into Matthew. *I think we caught him by surprise.* Maybe what Electra meant was that Matthew was with a woman? *Maybe,* Brooke thinks. *But it certainly wasn't Gigi!*

Caroline is worried about her mother. Are you okay? she texts.

Yes, darling, everything is fine. See you when you get back to the house.

She sounds normal; she's probably at home prepping the dough for the pizza party tonight. Gigi will help her with the toppings, and they'll laugh about what a fiend Electra is.

Caroline pulls out her camera and takes what has to be the most breathtaking footage of the weekend. As soon as the sloop leaves the Boat Basin, Captain Jim raises the sails; they rumble in the wind. He cuts the motor and the world quiets; they glide past the beach at Brant Point Light, where a gentleman is surf-casting and little kids are building a sandcastle. The kids wave and Caroline and Brooke wave back. Caroline films the stately summer homes that front the harbor. There's nothing like seeing Nantucket from the water to make you fall in love with the island all over again.

Dru-Ann moves up to the bow and enjoys the feel of the wind against her face. Okay, that was a nice moment where she was present and calm—but now she has to check in on St. Andrews. She gasps: McIlroy's drive at eighteen lands in the water. That's going to be…challenging to come back from. Phineas is next. He hits a beauty, straight up the fairway. *Holy cow,* she thinks. He has a chance. *He has a chance!*

He had a dream he was going to win.

"Hey."

Dru-Ann looks up from her phone. Tatum sits down next to her. "I know I've been a real bitch this weekend."

You? Dru-Ann thinks.

"I thought maybe we could talk," Tatum says.

"Now?" Dru-Ann says. She wanted to clear the air with Tatum all weekend and at this moment, when Dru-Ann's attention needs to be elsewhere, Tatum is finally ready. It figures.

"Yes, now."

Well, sure, why not make things as cinematic as possible? Dru-Ann thinks. They're sitting on the bow of a sailboat—a Friendship sloop!—with the sun on their faces and the wind in their hair. Although it pains her, Dru-Ann sets her phone down. "Okay, shoot."

"I'm sure you think it's juvenile or petty or whatever that I've held a grudge for so long."

Dru-Ann sighs. "We were young; I was territorial about my friendship with Hollis." She clears her throat. "But so were you, Tatum."

"You said that horrible thing to me at Hollis's wedding."

"It was meant to be a joke," Dru-Ann says. "But if you'd like me to formally apologize for it, I'll do so now. I'm sorry, Tatum. What I said was crass, thoughtless, and not at all funny."

"It was more than just that joke," Tatum tells her. "It was also the bachelorette weekend and the way you made unilateral decisions without considering other people's socioeconomic circumstances." Kyle would be amused that Tatum is using all her big words, but Tatum has been planning this speech for a long, long time. What was SAT prep *for* if not to teach you words that will intimidate your enemy?

It's the fall of 1998: Hollis's wedding is the following February, and Dru-Ann is the maid of honor. Hollis informs Dru-Ann that Tatum is "also" maid—well, matron—of honor and Tatum's one request is that she walk down the aisle last. This irks Dru-Ann, who says, "Why do you always give in to her? You've been doing it your whole life."

Hollis says, "I've known her my whole life. She's like a sister. Please, Dru, be the bigger person and roll with this."

Dru-Ann is (obviously) the bigger person, and fine, she'll roll with it. Her own "one request" is planning the bachelorette weekend in Boston.

It will be epic. They'll spend two nights at the Ritz-Carlton on Arlington Street; they'll hit the North End for Italian on Friday night, shop Newbury Street on Saturday, get massages at the hotel spa, and on Saturday night, they'll do a fancy dinner at Biba. Dru-Ann sends a letter to each of the girls on Hollis's list, outlining the activities and estimating the cost, depending on what kind of room they want at the Ritz. (Dru-Ann is booking a suite and inviting Hollis to share with her.)

Dru-Ann estimated the total cost of the weekend for each bridesmaid to be between six and seven hundred dollars, because in addition to their own expenses, they would split Hollis's costs.

I can't go, Tatum thinks. *It's too much money. The Ritz, Sorellina, a massage?* Tatum waits tables at the Lobster Trap, but by November they're closed for the season. Tatum is pulling a couple of shifts at the Anglers Club. She makes, maybe, three hundred bucks a week. She has a car payment, and she and Kyle are saving to buy a house.

She calls Hollis to tell her she can't swing the bachelorette weekend and Hollis, predictably, goes into problem-solving mode. Tatum can skip the massage, she can skip the Ritz altogether. Why doesn't she stay in Hollis's apartment, a ten-minute walk away? All she'll have to pay for then is the boat and bus to Boston and her meals.

"You can't miss the weekend, Tay. You're my matron of honor."

It's the first time Tatum and Dru-Ann have met in person. Dru-Ann hugs Tatum right away, saying, "I feel like I know everything about you. Seriously, *everything.* Hollis never stops talking about you."

This is such a nice thing to say! Tatum thinks. But it turns out to be window dressing. Dru-Ann spends the rest of the weekend making Tatum feel irrelevant—like a second-class citizen, the weak link. Tatum stays in Hollis's apartment instead of the hotel and she misses the best parts of the weekend—the room-service breakfasts, the champagne that Dru-Ann orders to the suite before they go out, the late-night chatting and gossiping. Tatum skips the massage; she follows mutely along as the other girls shop at Kate Spade and Pierre Deux on Newbury Street. She orders chicken at dinner while everyone else gets crab, lobster, foie freaking gras. She's constantly obsessing about how much money she's spending or might spend in the next hour. It's exhausting. On the way back to Hollis's apartment Saturday night, she buys a lottery ticket. If she wins ten million dollars, she'll book a suite at the hotel that second and cover everyone else's bills as well. There will be caviar for breakfast, and a stretch limo—not a Peter Pan bus—will take her back to the Cape.

She doesn't win; of course she doesn't. Back in Hollis's apartment, she calls Kyle and cries.

"You commandeered the bachelorette weekend," Tatum says. "I'm *still* paying it off."

"I know," Dru-Ann says. "I'm sorry. When I look back on it now, I see it was an obnoxious flex."

Tatum turns to study Dru-Ann's profile. Does she seem contrite behind her designer sunglasses?

"I was jealous of you," Dru-Ann says. "You had history with Hollis, years longer than me, all the growing-up stuff. You knew who she was at her essence, and I just knew who she wanted to be once she left home. And what can I say? I'm competitive. I wanted to be the best friend. I wanted to be the one who loved her the most, the one she loved the most."

"I felt the same way," Tatum says. "I thought of her love as a pie and I wanted the biggest piece. Hell, I wanted the whole pie."

"Because I couldn't make your importance to Hollis smaller, I tried to diminish you in other ways. What I said at the reception was inexcusable," Dru-Ann says. "Believe me, Tatum, I *am* sorry. I think about it and I just hate myself."

The ceremony at St. Andrew's Episcopal followed by the reception at the Wellesley Country Club are both lovely and fun. Tatum brings Kyle, and they notice that Hollis hasn't invited another soul from Nantucket other than her father. Nearly all the guests at the wedding are friends of Matthew's parents. Fine, great; Tatum still enjoys herself. The bridesmaids wear silk sheaths in a dusty-rose color, and Mrs. Madden has instructed them to accessorize with "a pearl choker, nothing opera-length or longer." (Tatum didn't own pearls of any length, so she had to go out and buy a pearl choker.)

Mrs. Madden pays for all the bridesmaids to get their hair and makeup done, and Tatum chooses a French-braid crown with pink roses woven in. She is, as she requested, the last one in the bridal party to walk out, and the program reads *Matron of honor: Mrs. Tatum McKenzie,* which makes her very happy.

Right before the reception, Dru-Ann tells Tatum that she'll be giving the toast. Tatum has written a rhyming poem, but in truth, she's terrified of public speaking, so she accepts Dru-Ann's announcement gracefully; she'll hand her poem to Hollis later. However, Mrs. Madden overhears the girls talking and tells Dru-Ann that the only people who will be giving toasts that evening are her husband and the best man.

Ha, Tatum thinks. She gives Dru-Ann a sorry-not-sorry smile and goes to find more champagne.

In the middle of the dancing, the bandleader pauses between songs and says, "This next one is a special dedication from our bride to the matron of honor, Tatum McKenzie." The band launches into "Take My Breath Away." Tatum meets Hollis out on the floor and they do their dance while the other guests—who are fairly inebriated by this point—cheer. It's the greatest honor Tatum could have imagined.

Near the end of the reception, Tatum goes to the ladies' room. She's had a lot to drink and her feet hurt from dancing in her dyed-to-match-the-dress silk pumps. Tatum stands in front of the mirror and unwinds her French-braid crown—it's giving her a headache—and her fingers catch on her choker. The strand snaps, and the pearls go raining all over the bathroom floor just as Dru-Ann steps out of a stall.

Dru-Ann gazes at Tatum in the mirror as she washes her hands. "That's what happens when you buy them at Kmart," she says—and walks out.

Thinking about it now makes Dru-Ann want to throw herself overboard. Who *says* something like that? She was every bit as thoughtless and idiotic then as certain young people she has the pleasure to know are now. "I apologize for making a classist joke," Dru-Ann says. "It was a crappy thing to do and I feel like a jerk." She rests a hand on Tatum's forearm and squeezes. "I'm sorry, Tatum."

Tatum is quiet for a moment and Dru-Ann hopes Tatum realizes her apology is authentic.

"I forgive you," Tatum finally says. "I have bigger things to worry about now than my Kmart pearls."

Dru-Ann laughs. "Yeah, me too."

Caroline creeps around the boat with her camera. She manages to film the moment between Dru-Ann and Tatum. Finally, they've made up.

Dru-Ann and Tatum are having a moment on the bow and Caroline is filming, so Brooke sits alone in the cockpit. Only yesterday, this would have bothered her, but today, Brooke is content to take in the scenery and think. The first mate, James, comes by and says, "How's it going?"

He looks like a nice kid and the way he asks makes it seem like he really wants to know: How *is* it going?

She smiles at him. "I came out of my walk-in closet this weekend," she says.

He tilts his head like he's heard her but doesn't understand.

"I'm gay," she says.

James breaks into a surprised grin. This is probably *not* what he expected to hear, Brooke thinks. "Good for you," he says. "Congratulations!"

Not everyone in her life might view her announcement as something to celebrate, but first mate James does. Brooke loves kids this age. The future, she decides, is bright.

45. Hiding in Plain Sight

Hollis drives the Bronco home as fast as she can without attracting the notice of Kevin Dixon or any other Nantucket police officer.

I met you with Matthew in Atlanta, Electra said.

The words Hollis has overlooked until just now are *in Atlanta.* How would Electra have known Gigi lived in Atlanta? It wasn't written anywhere on the itinerary.

They were together, Electra said.

Maybe Gigi left the restaurant, *fled* it, because she'd been caught.

Matthew and Gigi?

When had Gigi started posting on the Corkboard? Six months before Matthew died? Nine months? Had Gigi endeared herself to Hollis on *purpose?* Had she commented so often in order to get Hollis's attention?

Did *this* explain why she came to Nantucket?

Hollis replays the things Gigi said on the beach: *The man I was with… we weren't married and we didn't have children together. But in a way, that makes it harder. I don't have much to hold on to now that he's dead except my memories.* Had she been talking about *Matthew?* Hollis thinks about Gigi studying their family photos in the library. And then there are smaller, sillier things: Gigi asking who faked their orgasms; Gigi wanting to hear the story about how Hollis and Matthew met.

Hollis hits the gas. The wind lifts her hair like a cape, and her eyes water behind her sunglasses. She's going to spin out and wind up dead herself, but she can't get to Squam fast enough. Electra is a poison—but as the ponds and fields of Polpis Road rush by, Hollis becomes more and more convinced she was telling the truth.

Matthew and Gigi. It sickens her. Hollis *confided* in Gigi! Hollis described how she and Matthew had quarreled before he left for the airport and then how she'd had breakfast with Jack. Gigi had seemed like a safe spot for Hollis among all the dramas of the weekend.

The twist: *Gigi is the drama.*

Hollis wants to scream. She *does* scream, at the top of her lungs, into the bright Nantucket afternoon. She screams a profanity over and over again, stopping only when she sees two women riding their bikes on the Polpis Road path.

The two women are Blond Sharon and her sister, Heather. Sharon comes to a sudden stop, and Heather nearly runs her over.

"Whoa!" Heather says as she veers out of the way. Sharon laughs. They're like a female Abbott and Costello.

"Was that Hollis Shaw who just drove by screaming the F-bomb?" Sharon says.

"She was probably singing," Heather says. "And next time you stop like that, how about some warning?"

Hollis wants to believe there's a reasonable explanation for all this. Maybe Gigi's boyfriend had some rare heart problem that only Dr.

Matthew Madden at Mass General could fix, and despite Matthew's best efforts, the boyfriend died on the operating table, and Matthew remembered that Gigi lived in Atlanta and took her out to dinner to see how she was doing.

Maybe Matthew or Gigi took a DNA test and discovered they were cousins or even half siblings.

Hollis is, of course, fooling herself. She and Matthew had grown apart; he was away all the time, and when he was home, he was distracted. There had been countless moments when Matthew was looking right at Hollis, but she knew he wasn't seeing her.

He was seeing Gigi.

Hollis pulls into the hydrangea-lined driveway, and its beauty mocks her. She had been so comfortable, so *complacent,* that she hadn't seen what was right in front of her.

What's right in front of her now is Gigi, who's carrying her suitcase and her tote down the front steps of First Light. She's checking her phone, no doubt waiting for an Uber. When she sees the Bronco, a frightened expression crosses her face.

No, not frightened, Hollis thinks. *Guilty.*

Hollis gets out of the car and slams the door so hard, people can probably hear it in Quidnet. She points to the house.

"Inside," she says through clenched teeth.

"I'm leaving," Gigi says. "I won't cause you any more trouble."

"Inside!" Hollis says, walking up the front steps. She opens the door to find Henrietta, who starts growling at Gigi.

Of course, Hollis thinks. *Henny knew all along.*

46. The Hot Seat

Down in the home theater, two chairs are turned toward each other, interview-style. Next to one is a tripod and a ring light. Hollis sits there and points Gigi to the other chair.

"You were having an affair with Matthew?" she says.

Gigi nods. *The truth will set you free,* she thinks. A cliché, but one with legs. She feels nearly weightless. There are multiple ways to make this seem not nearly as bad as it was, but Gigi will tell the truth, all of it. She will give five-star testimony.

"For how long?" Hollis asks.

"We met the October before last," Gigi says. "So we were together for a little over a year before he died. The evening we met, I was supposed to fly to Argentina for vacation and Matthew was trying to get home to Boston. I met him in the Delta lounge. There was a hailstorm, all flights for the night were canceled."

The October before last. Hollis would have to go back and look at her calendar. What was going on in her life the October before last? She can only guess she was layering slices of potato into a gratin dish, perfecting caramel apples, picking up her cashmere sweaters from the dry cleaner.

"How many times were you together?" Hollis asks. Her champagne and lunch are churning in her stomach; she's light-headed, and her cheeks are burning. She's angry enough to tackle Gigi, choke her. Has she ever in her life been this angry? Has anyone ever betrayed her this way? Of course not. "Where did you go other than Atlanta?"

"We saw each other every few weeks. Either I flew where he was speaking—San Francisco, Baltimore—or he met me in Madrid or Rome."

"Madrid?" Hollis says. "Rome? You had an international love affair?"

"Those were my routes back then."

So Matthew lied to Hollis. He created fictional conferences, knowing Hollis would never check, and he must have lied to the hospital as well, maybe claiming he was whisking Hollis off for a romantic weekend.

Mr. Wonderful.

Hollis imagines Matthew and Gigi strolling around Madrid and Rome hand in hand. They probably had their favorite spots—little hole-in-the-wall wine bars, cafés, shops where Matthew would buy Gigi a scarf or a beautiful belt. They would stop to listen to street performers. Gigi would have wowed Matthew with her fluency in the languages. But thinking about Matthew and Gigi in those foreign cities is far preferable to thinking of them in cities where Matthew and Hollis traveled together.

"Where did you stay in San Francisco?" It's masochistic to ask, but she has to know.

"Oh," Gigi says. She seems to think for a moment. "The Four Seasons once..."

So Matthew had the decency to take Gigi someplace other than the Fairmont. But Hollis won't give him points for that; the Four Seasons sounds like an upgrade.

"And the St. Regis once, and then we stayed at Auberge du Soleil in Napa once."

"You met him in San Francisco *three times?*" Hollis says. She's so horrified by this, she can't even cry. Matthew took her to *Napa? The gall,* she thinks. *The hubris.* He could have run into any number of people who knew him or Hollis.

"I didn't find out he was married until last May," Gigi says. "The night we met, he told me he was divorced with one daughter—"

Hollis cries out.

"And I believed him. He didn't wear a ring. He wasn't on social media, and Google turned up only his professional accolades, his professional profile."

"But then he told you?"

"Yes. We were in Greece. Santorini."

"Greece!" Hollis says. Can this get any worse? She has to remind herself to breathe. Greece last May—yes, while Hollis was here, opening the house by herself.

"He said he wouldn't see me much over the summer because he'd be on Nantucket with his daughter...and wife." Gigi pauses. "I screamed, I cried, I threw things. But I was too in love with him by that point to end it." She looks straight at Hollis. "That is my crime."

Yes, Hollis thinks. Matthew had a wife, a family, two homes, a dog, friends, colleagues who respected him, a community, a life. To stay with him after learning this *was* a crime.

She's intrigued to hear Gigi say she was too in love with him to end it.

"Was he in love with you too?" Hollis says. "Did he tell you that?"

"He did not," Gigi says. "I think he felt things for me but I'm not sure he felt love." *Now is the time,* she thinks. "There's something else you should know."

Hollis holds a hand up. "Please just let me *finish!*" she says. She can't believe this is her speaking. She feels possessed. "When did you reach out to me on Hungry with Hollis?"

"Right after he told me who you were."

"And why? *Why?*"

Gigi puts her palms to her cheeks like she's in Edvard Munch's *The Scream* and exhales. "I think it's natural to want to know all you can about the wife of your lover."

Hollis laughs bitterly. "Oh, is it?" She almost adds, *I wouldn't know,* but then she thinks about the way she clicked on Mindy's Facebook page after seeing her in Jack's pictures. Mindy's profile showed a quilt. And hadn't Hollis then searched for quilting clubs in Western Mass., hoping to find other pictures of Mindy? She certainly had.

"Yes," Gigi says. "And you're a public figure, so it was all there."

"Why did you engage with me?" Hollis asks. "You weren't just watching from afar—you commented on all my posts, you said smart things, you wanted me to notice you. When you were *sleeping with my husband.*"

"Maybe it was a bit unhinged," Gigi says. "I wanted you to know me, even though you would never realize who I was. I wanted you to... *like* me."

"It worked!" Hollis says. "I *did* like you. When Matthew died, I waited to hear from you. It took you a week."

"Yes," Gigi says. "I wasn't sure what to do."

"Then you told me you were there to listen."

"I was."

"I *confided* in you. I told you things I didn't tell another soul. I thought it was safe because I didn't know you. You were like a... virtual therapist. I told you Matthew and I quarreled right before he left the house"—Hollis swallows—"and you *ghosted* me! You made me feel like I was to blame for his accident."

"Oh, Hollis," Gigi says. "Can I please speak now?"

"No," Hollis says. "Because I haven't gotten to the best part. Do you know what the best part is, Gigi Ling?"

Gigi grips the pale suede arms of the club chair. She doesn't have to stay. She can order another Uber, head to the airport, fly to Boston, New York, or DC and make her way home from there. Outwardly, her life will remain much the same. She'll cuddle with Mabel, go to Tim and Santi's for dinner, fly her routes—she might even ask for Europe back. She can leave Hollis and this drama behind.

Except she can't.

Gigi understands *best* to mean "worst." "The best part is that you invited me to your Five-Star Weekend on Nantucket and I accepted. And now here we are."

"You entered my house, you ate my food, drank my wine, slept in the finest of my guest suites—if I'm being honest, I wanted you to have it; you were the one I felt I had to impress—and relaxed on my beach. *I made a playlist for you!* The smart-woman playlist, because I thought you'd appreciate it." Hollis stops for a moment; she's frightening herself. "You met my friends, women I have known for decades. Women who have stood by me, supported me. Women who love me. You took a place among them, but you're a liar, a cheat, a *charlatan*."

"Yes," Gigi says.

"Why?" Hollis says. "Why did you come?"

That's the question, isn't it? Gigi could give many answers: *I came for the same reason you invited me—because we hit it off. I came because I wanted to feel closer to Matthew. I came to find out what I could about your marriage. I came because I was inexplicably drawn to the person I betrayed.* She could even say: *I came because I was lonely.*

Gigi did *not* come to Nantucket to reveal her secret—but now that it's out, there's something else Hollis needs to know. Something important.

47. Under the Influence II

The *Endeavor* delivers the ladies back to Straight Wharf at four o'clock. Caroline expects Hollis to be waiting at the dock with a tray of iced tea and perhaps some homemade gougères as an apology for missing the sail. But her mother is nowhere to be seen. She checks her phone—and there's an alert of a text from Isaac.

She feels a jolt of adrenaline at seeing his name. Has he realized he's not in love with Sofia after all, did the picture Caroline posted of herself and Dylan make him jealous, are his feelings for Caroline too strong to be denied?

As long as she doesn't read the text, the answers to these questions can still be yes.

She calls her mother but she's shunted straight to voice mail. *Fine,* she thinks. They'll take a cab.

Caroline watches the others disembark. All three women seem caught up in their own thoughts.

Tatum is thinking that, at this time tomorrow, she'll know the answer. She also thinks how excited she is to tell Hollis that Dru-Ann finally apologized. *It only took twenty-five years, but now we're good.* More than good. Against all odds, Tatum and Dru-Ann are going to be friends. Because the truth is, Tatum kind of *likes* Dru-Ann.

* * *

Dru-Ann is thinking about how miraculous it is that Phineas Pine, ranked number 127 in the world, has won the British Open. (She went to the head and checked her phone.) This is why Dru-Ann loves sports—competition is fun and exciting and unpredictable. Everyone loves an underdog.

Brooke is thinking how easy it was to tell James she was gay. She tried to tip him when she got off the boat, but he pressed the money back into her hand and said, "You already gave me a gratuity. Thank you for sharing your news with me."

Honestly, what a cutie.

As Caroline is walking by Provisions, she sees a guy sitting at the café table out front who looks, from behind, like Dylan. When she gets closer, she sees that the chick sitting across from the guy looks like Aubrey. Then she sees the little kid between them with a piece of bacon hanging from his mouth.

Dylan, Aubrey, and Orion are having lunch—or an early dinner before Dylan has to go to work—at Provisions.

Caroline feels a hand on her arm. It's Tatum, pulling her in the other direction.

"You don't want to end up with another drink on you," she says. "Let's just pretend we didn't see them."

A minivan from Roger's Taxi idles at the curb in front of the Club Car. Caroline climbs in, and Brooke and Tatum follow. Before Dru-Ann ducks in, she hears someone calling her name.

She looks across the street to see Gucci Bex and Laura Ingalls pop out of the Blue Beetle—and Gucci Bex is waving her arms. "Dru-Ann! Wait!"

You want me to wait so you can publicly ridicule me in front of my friends? Dru-Ann thinks. *No, thank you.*

"Dru-Ann, I'm sorry, we're sorry!" Gucci Bex says. She runs across the cobblestones in a pair of platform Mary Janes. "We were wrong, you were right."

Dru-Ann blinks.

"About Posey," Laura Ingalls says. (*Another day,* Dru-Ann notes, *another prairie dress.*)

"What about Posey?" Dru-Ann says. *Her boyfriend pulled off the biggest coup of the year,* Dru-Ann thinks. *He'll be on the cover of* Sports Illustrated *this week for sure. It's crazy.*

"Are we going to Squam or what?" the taxi driver says. "It's so far away, we need to leave now to get there by nightfall. And I hope you brought snacks."

"Get in, sis," Tatum says and Dru-Ann can't help but smile. *Sis!*

"Check Twitter," Gucci Bex says. "And again, our apologies."

"Whatever," Dru-Ann says. She climbs into the taxi and slides the door shut. The taxi bounces up the street.

"Were those fans?" Brooke asks.

Dru-Ann rolls her eyes. "Influencers."

"They're so stylish!" Brooke says. "What are their accounts? I'm going to follow them."

48. Accident Report II

Gigi says, "You know how Matthew was presenting a paper at the conference in Leipzig?"

The mention of Leipzig brings it all back: the December morning, snow falling outside, Matthew's shaving lotion, his reindeer cuff links, the beautiful wedge of quiche that ended up in Henny's dog bowl, the carols. The knock at the door. Hollis freezes as though Gigi is holding a gun.

"Yes?" she whispers.

"I was supposed to meet him on Friday evening in Paris for the weekend," Gigi says. "It was going to be *our* Christmas."

"*Your* Christmas? In Paris?" Hollis says. "That Saturday was our annual holiday party. Matthew was missing it. He told me he wanted to stay in Leipzig until the conference was over and then visit his professor in Berlin." Explaining the ways she was deceived makes Hollis feel like she's sitting in front of Gigi buck naked.

"Yes," Gigi says. "He told me about the holiday party."

He'd told Gigi about the party.

"Get out!" Hollis says, pointing at the stairs. "Get out of here right now and never contact me again. I'm going to block you from the website." Hollis feels a stabbing pain just below her breastbone. She thinks of Matthew the night she first met him at Harvard Gardens. *I just wanted to finish up reading on takotsubo cardiomyopathy, otherwise known as "broken-heart syndrome."*

Broken-heart syndrome.

"Please just let me finish," Gigi says. "Matthew called me the morning he died. He called me from the car."

What? Hollis thinks.

Gigi says, "We often talked while he was in the car—it was safest, no one would overhear. His call woke me up; my flight to Paris wasn't until much later that night."

"Please stop," Hollis says. "I don't want to hear any of this."

"You do, though," Gigi says.

Matthew tells Gigi that he's on his way to Logan; he's running late, and it's snowing like crazy. "I had a conversation with Hollis before I left the house." There's a long pause. "I'm conflicted about things."

"Conflicted?" Gigi says. She assumes Matthew is having a crisis of conscience—this happens from time to time. He must feel guilty about leaving Hollis at Christmastime and about missing their party.

"I'm not sure I can do Paris, Gigi," Matthew says.

This, Gigi thinks, *is what you get when you sleep with a married man.* She says, "Do you want me to meet you in Leipzig?" Even an overnight would be better than nothing.

"Hollis is calling," Matthew says.

"That's fine," Gigi says. "Do you want to call me back?"

"Gigi," he says. She doesn't like the tone of his voice. It sounds like he's maybe going to tell her...

"I want to work on my marriage," he says.

There's a moment when neither of them speaks, though Gigi can hear the quiet pulsing of another call coming in on his phone.

"Are you...breaking *up* with me?" Gigi asks.

He sighs. "It's not fair for you to be somebody's number two when you deserve to be somebody's number one."

"No," Gigi says. "You don't get to make it sound like you're ending our relationship out of concern for me." She hears the rub of his windshield wipers—back and forth, back and forth.

"You're right," he says finally, and there's a clicking noise. Turn signal? "I want to be at home for Hollis. I'm going to cancel Leipzig."

"You're kidding me." Matthew is canceling a conference where he's expected? Or is he just telling her that so she won't ambush him at the hotel?

"I love her, Gigi."

"She's your wife," Gigi says. "And I'm someone you met at an airport bar who can be broken up with over the phone ten days before Christmas."

"I'm sorry, Gigi. For all of it. Be well."

* * *

Gigi says, "He must have crashed not long after we hung up. I didn't learn he was dead until I saw the announcement on your website." Gigi stands up. "I'm sorry, Hollis. I know you won't see it this way, but I lost someone too. And I sought out the one person who knew how I felt."

Matthew had decided to cancel his trip? He'd told Gigi he wanted to work on his marriage? Hollis wants very badly to believe this—but Gigi could be making it all up in order to soften the blow of the affair. Hollis can't trust a word that comes out of Gigi's mouth.

Gigi rises from the chair. "You should also know that I've had a wonderful time. You're very lucky to have such an accomplished daughter..." Gigi's voice cracks; she clears her throat. "And to have friends like Tatum, Dru-Ann, and Brooke. So as twisted as this sounds, I want to thank you for including me. I'm not sorry I came." With that, Gigi heads up the stairs.

"Hold on," Hollis says. Maybe it's all the camera equipment around her, but she feels like an actress in a movie. But why is she stopping Gigi? *Let her go!* Hollis certainly can't *forgive* her. "Can you please just wait? I want to check one thing. Would you sit down here for a minute? I'll be right back."

Slowly, Gigi comes back down the stairs—though why, she isn't sure. She should leave before the others get home. There's no way Hollis is going to let her stay tonight.

Is there?

Hollis heads upstairs to the library, opens her laptop, clicks on the folder labeled MM, and among all the documents—the death certificate, life insurance, transfer of deeds—she finds the accident report.

What is she looking for? She's not sure.

Driver's name: Madden, Matthew

Hollis scrolls down to FATALITY OR INJURED. The FATALITY box and the DRIVER box are both checked. Hollis tries to steady her breathing. She scrolls down a little farther.

There's a diagram of the road, marked with lines. The legend tells her the solid line is before the crash, the broken line is after the crash, the two *x*'s indicate the deer—the mama and baby. Hollis traces the broken line: it swerves sharply before the vehicle veers off the road into the field and flips. Hollis's hands are clammy; she feels nauseated. There's a reason she's never looked at this.

She reads the description of what she's looking at: **Vehicle heading southeast on Dover Road.**

Southeast, Hollis thinks. To get to Logan, Matthew would have been traveling northwest on Dover. She looks at the diagram again, then double-checks it with the map on her phone.

Gigi must be telling the truth—Matthew had turned around.

He was on his way home.

Hollis bows her head, closes her eyes.

She grants herself one moment to rewrite the past.

It's December 15 and Matthew has left for the airport. Hollis wraps foil around his uneaten breakfast and sets it in the fridge next to the pastry dough. She sits down at her laptop, but instead of stalking Jack Finigan on Facebook, she goes to the Hungry with Hollis website and posts her recipe for cheddar tartlets; her fans have been clamoring for it. Over the sound system, "Carol of the Bells" is playing.

She hears the door open, then footsteps, then the jingling of Henny's collar. By the time Hollis reaches the kitchen, Matthew is there, his head and shoulders dusted with snow, his glasses fogged. Before she can ask, *What happened, is something wrong?* he has his trench coat and suit jacket off. He rapidly unfastens his reindeer cuff links and loosens his Santas-in-speedboats tie.

"Wait!" Hollis says. She's close enough now that she can smell his shaving lotion. "Are you not going?"

"I'm not going," Matthew says.

She's about to ask if he's hungry, if he wants her to warm up his breakfast... when he reaches for her hand and leads her upstairs.

Gigi is sitting, still as a statue, right where Hollis left her. Hollis is impressed. If it were her, she would have run while she had the chance.

"I just checked the accident report," Hollis says, sitting down. "Matthew had turned around. He was on his way home."

Gigi nods but doesn't speak.

Hollis isn't sure what to say or do now. Gigi has the countenance of a delinquent student waiting to be dismissed. Is that what Hollis should do? Tell Gigi she's free to go?

Suddenly Hollis hears a commotion upstairs: A happy bark from Henny, Brooke calling out that she's taking the first outdoor shower, Tatum asking if there's any onion dip left because she's *starving,* and Dru-Ann saying that she's heading back to the guest cottage to change but when she comes back they'd all better be prepared to woman up because she has half a bottle of tequila to finish before the weekend's over.

She hears Caroline say, "I actually think I have enough footage for a short *film.* What if I end up making you all *famous?*"

"As long as it's not infamous," Dru-Ann says. "I've had enough of that this weekend."

"The interviews with you three are the best part," Caroline says. "I learned a lot about my mom, so thank you for your honesty. I know some of those stories were difficult to tell."

Hollis doesn't need to watch the interviews to be reminded of all the ways she failed the women a floor above. She promised Tatum she was staying in Massachusetts, then she left for North Carolina;

she lied to Dru-Ann about her mother for a year and a half; she never stood up to Electra about ousting Brooke from the football group.

Tatum, Dru-Ann, and Brooke have forgiven her. This is, Hollis sees now, an example of their innate decency, generosity, nobility. Hollis could argue that Gigi's betrayal is somehow greater than any of hers. Gigi slept with Hollis's husband. Gigi used the Hungry with Hollis website to spy on her. Gigi wooed them all with her elegant style and her irresistible accent—under false pretenses.

Hollis takes one breath, then another, and considers the term *five-star.* What does it mean? In her mind, it means "remarkable, best in class, of a rarefied quality, a standout." It's one thing to place fresh flowers on a nightstand or create an Instagram-worthy charcuterie board. But what if the five-star experience went deeper? What if it extended to this moment? What if instead of casting Gigi out, Hollis said, *Please stay. I may not arrive at a place of grace right away—the pain of the betrayal is still new, shocking—but I will get there eventually, and until then, I'm willing to play through.*

Is there such a thing as five-star forgiveness? If not, can Hollis invent it now?

"Stay," she says to Gigi.

"What? Hollis—no, absolutely not."

Hollis rises from her chair and approaches Gigi. Her loveliness is newly agonizing when Hollis thinks about Matthew appreciating it—but that's in the past.

"Please," Hollis says. She can't bring herself to hug Gigi, but she does offer a hand to help her up from the chair. "It's just until tomorrow morning. If I can do it, you can do it."

"Are you planning to tell the others?" Gigi asks. She imagines the other women stoning her like she's a character in a Shirley Jackson story.

"Heavens, no," Hollis says. "It's nobody's business but ours. And anyway, they've all got other things to worry about."

49. The Twist

Dru-Ann has been meaning to try out the Bakelite record player in her guest cottage. She stands in the little niche and flips through the short stack of albums on the shelf underneath: The Turtles, Marvin Gaye, Joni Mitchell. All the album covers are worn; they've been lovingly handled, and Dru-Ann wonders if Hollis ordered them from some website for vintage records or if maybe these belonged to her mother and father.

She picks up the Marvin Gaye—this feels like the mood she's seeking—and then she peers at the framed 45 that's hanging on the wall above the turntable.

Chubby Checker, "The Twist." And it's signed!

Ahhhhhh! Dru-Ann thinks.

Does "the Twist" have another meaning for Dru-Ann? When she sees all the notifications on her phone—she heard it buzzing away in the car but ignored it—she wonders if it just might.

Check Twitter, Gucci Bex said.

Dru-Ann blinks. Is she *seeing* things or is #TeamDruAnn trending?

She can't help but sing along with Marvin Gaye. *"What's going on? What's going on?"*

Dru-Ann scrolls and clicks until she finds a very cute picture of Phineas Pine holding aloft the venerated Claret Jug (the silver jug isn't as well known in the States as the Masters' green jacket is, but who's to say the Masters isn't next for Phineas?). Standing beside Phineas, Posey Wofford is gazing up adoringly at her beloved.

Twitter has things to say about this photo. Didn't Posey Wofford quit her own tournament due to "mental-health issues"? Is it possible she used mental health as an excuse so that she could fly to Scotland to cheer on her boyfriend? That's certainly what it looks like, Twitter says. And if so, how appalling. Posey Wofford is not only antifeminist (prioritizing Phineas's career over her own) but also disrespectful of people who do suffer from anxiety and depression.

Posey Wofford was "depressed" until her beau @phinpinegolf started sinking putts, one tweet says. Then she perked right up! #supportmentalhealth #cancelPosey #TeamDruAnn.

This feels like the usual Twitter noise—surely these people realize that Posey could *look* happy on the outside but still be suffering. Then Dru-Ann finds a clip of Phineas's press conference. He's incandescent with joy, as well he should be. It's a big deal, winning the British Open at the Old Lady. His name will go down in history, and Dru-Ann is certain that every time he blinks, he sees dollar signs.

When asked about Posey's mental state, Phineas says, "I told her I had a dream I was going to win and that I wanted her here to see every bit of it."

"So she's not battling mental-health demons, then?" a reporter asks.

"Mental-health demons?" Phineas says. "Posey? No way." He sounds so incredulous that Dru-Ann wonders if he's *trying* to ruin Posey's reputation. Maybe now that he's golf's new sweetheart, he plans on trading up. Maybe next month he'll be dating Zendaya.

Ha! That *would be a twist,* Dru-Ann thinks.

A text comes in from Nick: I think Posey needs your help managing this mess.

Posey is fired, Dru-Ann writes back. But I'm willing to make Phineas my first male client. Have him call me.

Three dots rise. What about me? Nick says. Can you forgive an indulgent father?

Decision pending further review, Dru-Ann writes, and she hits Send.

She wades through her voice mails. Dean Falzarano from *New York* has called to apologize. The magazine will not only run Dru-Ann's piece about the ice skaters, they'd also like to commission five thousand words on "the Posey Wofford situation." Do you have anything to say on the subject? Dean wants to know. *Oh, do I,* Dru-Ann thinks.

Zeke from *Throw Like a Girl* has left a voice mail saying, "Expecting you in the studio on Tuesday. Sorry about the mix-up." Dru-Ann would like to tell Zeke to go pound sand but she loves that gig and she feels a duty to save Marla—and her viewers—from Crabby Gabby. Maybe now is the moment to ask for a better time slot. Monday evenings, right before *SportsCenter*?

Finally, there's a voice mail from JB walking back his request for Dru-Ann's resignation. Dru-Ann sighs. She's not sure if she should sue JB, orchestrate a hostile takeover of his company, or call Phineas's agent, Gannon, to see if he wants to partner up and launch a new agency.

She's going to think about it.

Caroline sits on the front steps of First Light, where she can see the rows of hydrangea bushes lining the driveway, and opens the text from Isaac.

It's a selfie of him and Sofia, their faces squished together. They're grinning like goofy kids; there's love in their eyes. Below the picture it says: Thank you.

Caroline clicks out of texts. It's unfair—first Dylan and Aubrey, now Isaac and Sofia. Caroline is left with no one.

She hears a door open and sees Dru-Ann step out of the guest cottage. "Looks like someone's in their feelings," Dru-Ann says. She takes a seat next to Caroline on the stairs. "Spill it, girl, what's going on?"

It's stupid, Caroline nearly says, but she knows Dru-Ann actually *wants* to hear about her problems. She tells her, in a very disjointed fashion, about all of it: The long-ago bonfire with Dylan where Aubrey kicked sand in her face, Isaac crying about his mother, who died when he was nine, Orion sucking on bacon, *Please, no trouble,* ain't it funny how the night changes, the Lyft of Shame, Isaac's golden tea and cashews from Kalustyan's, their kiss, their drone lesson in Central Park, Thomas the Tank Engine, Sofia's return, Dylan waiting for her at the Box, making out, Sofia's texts, Caroline's Instagram post, Aubrey throwing a drink in her face, her call with Sofia, seeing Dylan with Aubrey and Orion at Provisions, *mon petit chou.*

When Caroline finally stops to take a breath—did any of that make sense?—Dru-Ann says, "So you're telling me you made out with your longtime high-school crush *and* you had a brief, steamy love affair with your genius boss?"

Caroline nods.

"You do realize," Dru-Ann says, "that those are romantic achievements most of us only dream about."

"Also," Caroline says, "I really miss my dad."

"Oh, sugar," Dru-Ann says. She takes Caroline in her arms, where, finally, Caroline starts to cry. "That just means you're human."

Brooke is in the Board Room suite changing into her Nantucket Reds miniskirt and new boatneck sweater that she bought at Murray's. Before she heads to the kitchen, she pulls out her laptop and logs on to Facebook. She considers posting her news, because coming out to everyone individually seems daunting. She types, Hey, everyone, big news: I'm gay!

People will leave supportive messages like *I'm an ally!* And hopefully those who "don't get it" will keep scrolling. Her mother will call in tears, not because Brooke is gay but because she had to hear about it on Facebook.

No, Brooke can't post about it on Facebook, or at least not yet. She has to talk to Charlie, the twins, and her mother. She knows what Whitney will say: *One drunken kiss doesn't necessarily mean you're gay, Mom. Maybe take the time to figure that out.*

She sends a text to Will and Whitney: Can we have dinner tomorrow night at Juniper? I have something exciting to share!

Will says that he'll be at the gym until eight but could meet after that. Whitney asks, Is it exciting-exciting or just Mom-exciting?

Brooke thinks it's best to keep expectations low, so she says: Mom-exciting. But definitely worth postponing a Bumble date for.

After Brooke divorces Charlie, will she create a profile on Bumble—or is there some other dating app for women looking for women? Is there one for bi people and a different one for queer people? She has some research to do.

Brooke hears the faint strains of music playing in the kitchen. It's "Stacy's Mom," by Fountains of Wayne. Brooke loves this song! This must be, finally, the playlist that Hollis made for her. Brooke can't wait to pour a glass of rosé, help Hollis make the pizzas, and dance around the kitchen.

But first, Brooke goes back into Facebook and unfriends Electra.

Tatum hears the music start as she's shedding her Lilly dress. Tonight is pizza, ice cream truck, and fireworks, and Tatum wants to be comfortable. She reaches into her suitcase for her cutoffs—and screams!

The damn snake is curled up inside it.

Tatum laughs. Ha-ha-ha, Dru-Ann got her back, oh, did she—Tatum nearly peed herself. She throws the snake across the room as her phone dings. It's Kyle.

What would you say if Jack and I snuck over to watch the fireworks tonight?

Tatum can't believe it, but her first thought is *No.* This is their last night. It should be only girls.

Tatum has been completely brainwashed.

Just girls tonight, Tatum says. Tell Jack to stay an extra day and he can see Holly tomorrow after everyone leaves.

Kyle says, He's talking about coming back in the fall and staying an entire week! We'll never get rid of him.

Oh, baby, Tatum writes, adding the winking emoji, he might not be staying at our house.

"Since You've Been Gone" is playing when Caroline walks into the kitchen. Definitely Brooke's playlist (even Caroline remembers Brooke's obsession with *American Idol*).

Hollis is at the marble-topped pastry station rolling out perfect disks of pizza dough.

Caroline gives her a hug. "Was everything okay with Gigi?" she asks. "She didn't know Dad, did she?"

"Of course not," Hollis says. She pats Caroline on the back to seem extra-reassuring. She made the right decision with Gigi, she thinks, if only for her daughter's sake. Caroline doesn't need to lose her father a second time. "Electra was just doing what Electra does. Gigi is in her bedroom getting changed."

"Okay," Caroline says. She pulls away and studies her mother. Hollis doesn't meet her eye but that doesn't necessarily mean she's lying; she has pizzas to make. What if, Caroline thinks, Gigi had appeared out of the blue and befriended her mother through the website because she was sleeping with Matthew? Then after Matthew died, the two women became even closer and Hollis invited Gigi to her Five-Star Weekend as her "best friend from midlife," never knowing Gigi's true identity?

That, Caroline thinks, would be some *serious* podcast material.

* * *

As she films, Caroline feels a surprising melancholy. The weekend is drawing to a close. The ladies pour drinks and dive into the chips and guacamole. Dru-Ann regales them all with the tale of her reversal of fortune—the internet loves her again.

Gigi is the last to appear, and she's as captivating as ever in a pale yellow patio dress. Hollis ushers everyone out to the back deck. The sun is glazing the surface of the pond a fiery pink, and clouds glow on the horizon. There will be a cotton-candy sky tonight.

Brooke's playlist is Caroline's favorite; these are the songs she remembers her parents playing when she was growing up—"Umbrella" by Rihanna, "Need You Now" by Lady A, "Mr. Brightside" by the Killers.

Tatum tells Gigi about the sail. "I've lived on Nantucket my entire life, but being on the water on a day like today never gets old."

Dru-Ann tells Hollis, "You're lucky my fortune changed because I was ready to move into the Twist permanently."

Hollis slides the first pie, a classic Margherita, into her portable pizza oven. *You're doing fine,* Hollis tells herself, *just focus on the food.* But then the song "Fake Ass Friends" comes on and as everyone else dances, Hollis feels her temper coming to a slow boil. She pulls the pizza out and is horrified to see it's black, charred, smoking; the toppings all slide right off the peel onto the deck.

No, she's hallucinating. The pizza has turned out perfectly—melty and gooey with a thin, crispy crust.

Her entire body is tense with fury. She can't sit down at a table across from or next to Gigi—and so she decides they will all eat standing up.

Gigi feels like she has a slash of paint across her face or like she's been branded; she is Hester Prynne, an adulteress, a scarlet woman. She senses Hollis keeping her distance—every time Gigi gets near her, she feels a chill like she's walking past an open refrigerator—and it seems like the other women are keeping their distance as well. Caroline has her camera out—the guilt Gigi feels about Caroline is at another level altogether—and Gigi does her best to stay out of the frame. She knows the other women have had one-on-one chats with Caroline, and Gigi has been dreading her turn all weekend for obvious reasons. But now they're out of time, and unbeknownst to Caroline, Gigi has endured an interview of another kind.

Gigi doesn't know how she'll make herself eat. She takes a piece of pizza just to be polite, to seem normal. With the first bite, she discovers it's the best she's ever tasted, including pizza she's eaten in Italy. She considers telling Hollis this—*Your food is pure sorcery*—but Hollis will think Gigi is trying to flatter her, so Gigi simply loads her plate with a slice of the shrimp and lobster pizza and a slice of the Brie and pear one. She stands at the edge of the deck and looks at the pond and the footbridge.

Brooke appears at Gigi's elbow. She's wearing the skirt and navy-and-white-striped boatneck sweater that Gigi helped her pick out... was it only the day before? Gigi feels like she's been on Nantucket for weeks.

"You look so pretty," Gigi says. Brooke's face has some color, and she's smoothed her curly hair back into a bun; the sweater emphasizes Brooke's delicate collarbones, and the skirt shows off her slim calves.

"Did you know that Matthew had that bridge built for Hollis as a surprise one winter?" Brooke says. "Because Hollis loves the footbridge at Monet's home in Giverny. Isn't that romantic?"

"Very," Gigi says. It hurts to hear this, though it's helpful too. Gigi inserted herself between two people who had created a life together. Matthew built Hollis a bridge.

Gigi would like someone to build her a bridge someday—a metaphorical bridge, anyway. *You deserve to be somebody's number one,* Matthew said in their last conversation. It sounded patronizing at the time, but Gigi knows he was right. She does deserve that.

Brooke says, "I am so happy I met you. You've been such a good influence on me."

"Oh, Brooke, no, stop—"

"It's true," Brooke says. She turns around to face the others. "Hey, you guys, don't we all just love Gigi?"

Tatum raises her wineglass but says nothing because her mouth is full. Dru-Ann says, "We just love you, Gigi," in a way that is both teasing and sweet.

Caroline sets down her camera for a second so she can eat. "Only my mom could invite a complete stranger to this thing and have it turn out to be someone as chill as Gigi," she says.

There's a beat of silence. Are they all waiting for Hollis to speak? She looks up from the cutting board. "Who wants a slice of veggie supreme?"

50. The Grand Finale

The ice cream truck from Island Kitchen arrives at nine o'clock, and the ladies go out front to choose their flavors.

This isn't your average Good Humor man, Dru-Ann thinks. She orders Snickers cheesecake in a cup. Brooke picks cherries jubilee in a waffle cone. Tatum can't decide between French lemon custard and peach and biscuits. She wants peach and biscuits but her mind is back to doing that thing again: *If I get lemon custard, the tumor will be benign.* She gets a scoop of lemon custard in a sugar cone. Gigi gets banana cream pie. She just has to make it through the fireworks, then she can excuse herself and go to bed. She's booked the first flight off the island, which leaves at 6:45 a.m. She'll be gone before anyone else wakes up. The other women might feel sorry or slighted that they didn't get to say goodbye. Maybe Hollis will tell them then, and they can all trash her over their morning coffee.

Hollis materializes next to Gigi and says quietly, "Funny, the banana cream pie was Matthew's favorite too."

Hollis spreads blankets out on the beach and places ice buckets for the wine in the sand along with bowls of truffled popcorn. Hollis has curated every single detail of this weekend—and yet nothing turned out like she expected.

Caroline walks Malik, the fireworks guy, around the pool deck. "This place is *fire,*" he says. "I've lived on this island since sixth grade, but I've never been out this road."

"Welcome to Squam," Caroline says. She and Malik go over the dunes to the beach; he needs to set up a certain distance away from the women, the dunes, and the house, otherwise the place will be *literal* fire. "Do you mind if I take some video footage of you?"

"Is this my fifteen minutes of fame?" Malik says with a grin.

Malik is kind of cute, Caroline thinks. And a little while ago, James, the first mate from the *Endeavor,* requested her on Snapchat.

I'm still standing, she thinks, then she groans. She's becoming one of her mother's playlists.

Although Caroline is the only one who learned the names of the fireworks—silver pistil to red peony, coconut pistil to blue peony—their effect is appreciated by everyone on the beach. Dru-Ann notes that Brooke has returned to form; she claps and whoo-hoos for each display. She's especially enthusiastic about the "fireflies"—the strobe lights that pop all over the sky. Dru-Ann prefers the whistling rockets that shoot up super-high, then drip down like the branches of a weeping willow.

If the next one is blue, Tatum thinks, *I'll be okay.*

The next one is purple. Purple, she reasons, is practically blue.

Gigi has always loved watching fireworks shot off over the water—lights in the sky, lights reflected off the surface of the ocean. She pours herself some more wine, eats the buttery truffled popcorn. What would Matthew think if he could see her here, sitting three people away from his wife? Would he be angry with Gigi for stalking Hollis or angry at himself for creating a situation where Gigi would want to stalk Hollis? Would he be amazed that Gigi is still here? *Matthew,* Gigi would like to tell him, *you were married to a remarkable woman.*

Malik is proud of the grand finale. He heard that the lady who hired him was some kind of famous food blogger—Malik's mother follows her—so he threw in a couple of extra kits for free. He lights them with precision not only for safety but for perfect timing until there's one sustained blowout of light and color, spirals and blossoms, rings and crowns, whistles and bangs. *Pop-pop-pop-pop!* Malik loves the sounds, he loves the smell of cordite, but most of all, he loves hearing people ooh and aah—and seeing their briefly illuminated expressions of wonder.

That's it, Brooke thinks, Dru-Ann thinks, and Tatum thinks when the sky goes dark. *It's over.*

They head inside, carrying empty popcorn bowls and wineglasses.

Tatum shakes the blankets out and folds them. In less than twelve hours, she'll know.

On the deck, Gigi starts stacking dirty plates and tossing pizza crusts into the empty guacamole bowl.

"No!" Hollis shouts at her. "Stop it!"

Hollis's voice is so sharp, so *fierce,* that Gigi nearly drops what she's holding. Very gently, she sets the plates down.

"I'm sorry," she says.

The other women have frozen in place. Brooke takes in Hollis's livid expression; her eyes are clamped on Gigi.

"Holly?" Dru-Ann says. "Are you okay? Gigi was just trying to help."

Gigi's guts turn to liquid. *Here it comes,* she thinks. The big dramatic confrontation at the end of the weekend. The real fireworks. The grand freaking finale. *Don't defend Gigi!* Hollis will say. *She was screwing my husband! She was his mistress! They met in Atlanta! San Francisco! Madrid! Rome!*

Instead, Hollis seems to snap back to her senses; whatever force was holding her loosens its grip. "Forgive me," she says. Her eyes fill with tears. "I'm just not ready for this to be over."

"I don't know about everyone else," Brooke says. "But I'll remember this weekend for the rest of my life."

"You spoiled us, sis," Tatum says. "Thank you for letting me live like a summer person for a few days."

"It was exactly the escape that I needed," Dru-Ann says. "Thank you, Holly."

Gigi wants to offer her own tribute to Hollis, but she's too afraid to speak. When it's clear she's not going to say anything, Brooke jumps back in. *Thank God for Brooke,* Gigi thinks, *and her aversion to awkward silences.*

"You must be so proud of yourself, Hollis," Brooke says. "It all went so smoothly!"

The ladies drift off to their rooms in the opposite order that they came into Hollis's life. Gigi excuses herself first. (Hollis can't deny the relief she feels when Gigi says good night.) Brooke retires soon after. Then Dru-Ann hugs both Hollis and Tatum good night, and Hollis blinks. What kind of magic happened aboard the *Endeavor*? she wonders. Those two seem almost like...friends?

This leaves Hollis and Tatum alone.

We end where we started, Hollis thinks. She and Tatum dry the wineglasses and set them back in the cabinet; Hollis wipes down the countertops and sets up a fresh pot of coffee to brew in the morning.

She says, "Kyle told me about the biopsy, Tay. When you went to the bathroom during breakfast yesterday."

Tatum nods slowly. She isn't surprised, Kyle McKenzie hasn't managed to keep a secret once in his entire life. "Yeah," she whispers. "I just...I'm scared...I don't want to end up like my mom. The diagnosis, the chemo, and then...well, and then I'm dead." She looks at Hollis; she's frankly too terrified to cry. "I don't want to die, Holly."

Hollis gathers Tatum up in her arms. "You aren't going anywhere, Tatum McKenzie, do you hear me? I know you're scared, but you won't be alone. I'm staying on Nantucket through the fall this year. I'm thinking about selling the house in Wellesley and moving back permanently."

Should Tatum let herself get excited about this? She imagines calling Hollis to go see a movie at the Dreamland in the middle of February. She envisions Downyflake breakfasts and afternoons lying by Hollis's bougie-ass pool. Hell, Tatum will even take up yoga if she can have the greatest friend of her life returned to her.

"Really?" Tatum asks.

"Really," Hollis says. "Does Kyle have any room for me on the McKenzie Heating and Cooling softball team?"

"As a matter of fact," Tatum says, "we need a pitcher." She laughs and shakes her head. "I'm going to bed. I find out the biopsy results in the morning."

"Will you be able to sleep tonight?" Hollis asks.

"Hell yes," Tatum says. "I'm exhausted."

Hollis kisses Tatum on the forehead. "Sweet dreams, sis."

* * *

The person who has a hard time sleeping is Hollis. At midnight, Henny comes strolling into the kitchen—she can be a night owl—and plops at Hollis's feet as Hollis opens her laptop and goes to the Hungry with Hollis website. She has promised her subscribers a full accounting of the Five-Star Weekend, but how does she begin to describe what happened? A part of her, of course, would love to tell everyone the truth: Gigi Ling, the woman Hollis chose from the site's very ranks, turned out to be her husband's mistress. What would Molly Beardsley or Bailey Ruckert say to *that?* There would be outrage, indignation. Only a very few among Hollis's followers would even *understand* forgiveness; no one would expect it. They would expect Hollis to kick Gigi out on her perfect ass.

Hollis recalls Brooke's words. She types: It all went so smoothly!

As she's deleting this line—she can't lie like that; the weekend was so filled with drama someone could write a novel about it—her phone buzzes with a text. Henny raises her head.

"I know, right?" Hollis says. "Who's texting me at midnight?"

It's Jack: I just made it back home. I'm sorry I didn't get a chance to say goodbye. It was good to see you, Holly berry.

Hollis writes: It was good to see you too.

That kiss, she thinks. If Kevin Dixon hadn't come patrolling, she might have wished she'd read that "Sex and the Widow" article.

But what she had with Jack this weekend was just enough. She can now go back to stalking him online.

Guess what? he texts.

What? she thinks. A part of her wants him to say he's actually outside on their beach, waiting for her to grab a blanket and meet him.

She types: ????

I'll be back on Nantucket the first week in October. We could go scalloping together.

You just want me to show you my dad's secret spot, Hollis types.

I've waited a long time, Jack says. So is it a date?

Hollis smiles. Wild horses, she types.

Then she tells Henny good night and goes to bed.

51. Happily Ever After

Gigi wakes up with the first birdsong, though it's barely light out. She gets dressed, packs her final things, strips the sheets off the bed, and piles them with the towels. No one will say she wasn't a considerate houseguest.

She gets an alert that her Uber is five minutes away, and she decides she'll wait at the end of the driveway. More than anything, she wants to make a clean exit; she can't manage any kind of goodbye.

To that end, she very quietly leaves her room and tiptoes past Brooke's door to the kitchen. Gigi gets lucky; the dog is nowhere to be seen.

She smells coffee and notices that Hollis has left out to-go cups, along with almond milk and raw sugar. The woman thinks of everything. Just as Gigi is securing the top on her coffee she hears the whisper of bare feet on a wooden floor. Hollis appears from down the hall.

Gigi's heart free-falls. She was so close.

"Hey," Gigi says. Hollis is wearing a Harvard Medical School T-shirt. Her enormous diamond engagement ring sparkles in the light coming through the window.

"Are you leaving?" Hollis asks.

"Yes," Gigi says. "My Uber is nearly here." She pauses, wondering how to make this not-agony for both of them. "Thank you, Hollis. For everything."

Hollis stares at Gigi, then shakes her head. "I wish I didn't think you were so cool," she says. "That would make this a lot easier."

Gigi nods. "I feel the exact same way."

The Fifty Shades of White suite is closest to the kitchen, so Tatum hears Hollis, Brooke, and Dru-Ann as they chatter away: *The coffee is ready; Take a to-go cup; Does anyone want granola?; This is the fruit salad that refuses to die; Is Gigi gone already?*

Henny barks.

Dru-Ann says, "You know what was so funny? Henrietta *definitely* had beef with Gigi."

"I don't understand why, though," Brooke says. "Gigi was *just* so great. And you didn't even really know her, Hollis. She could have been some wacko."

This is met with a beat of silence.

Then Tatum hears Caroline join the fun. "I booked the earlier flight. I can't wait to get back to New York and edit the footage; I think it's going to be really good, and the interviews are the best part."

"Am I going to see these interviews at some point?" Hollis asks.

This, too, is met with silence.

"I'll send it to all of you once I finish," Caroline eventually says. "Is anyone headed to the airport?"

"Me," Dru-Ann says. "My driver is here. Get your things, sugar."

Tatum checks her phone; it's ten minutes to eight. She has a text from Kyle: Should I wait at home so I can be here when you call the doctor?

No, Tatum says. I'll call when I know. And I'll see you after work.

But you are calling, right?

Yes, babe.

I love you, Mrs. McKenzie, he texts.

Tatum hears footsteps and the thumping of luggage on the front porch. There's the sound of car doors closing, a trunk, the crunch of tires over the shells of Hollis's driveway. Goodbye to Caroline and Dru-Ann. Tatum closes her eyes and tries to achieve some kind of Zen, but her mental clock is ticking. In a few minutes she'll know.

Tatum hears Brooke say, "I never gave you your hostess gift. It's a scented candle from the Christmas Tree Shop. I think my gift is going to be not giving it to you."

Hollis laughs and Tatum thinks, *Good move.* Irina gave all her employees off-brand scented candles for the holidays last year, and Tatum's powder room still smells like coconut tanning oil.

Brooke says, "There's something else I want to tell you, Hollis."

"Please don't worry about what happened with Electra," Hollis says. "She was just seeking attention, as usual."

"It's not that," Brooke says. "I wanted you to know that I've realized..." She laughs, nervous. "I mean, this is going to come as a huge shock, but yeah, I've realized...that I'm gay."

Whoa! Tatum thinks. This weekend has had no shortage of zingers. Brooke is gay!

Hollis stammers for a second. "W-wow, okay, *not* what I was expecting...but Brooke, you know I have only ever wanted you to find happiness."

There's some more conversation. Brooke is a little weepy; she's going to tell her husband and kids when she gets home. Tatum is tempted to go out to the kitchen to give Brooke a hug herself; this is a major thing to come to terms with at their age, good for her, she should leave the jerky husband, find some hot new chick, and start over.

Brooke has a ferry to catch, her Lyft is pulling in; she and Hollis say goodbye and then the house is quiet. Tatum hears Hollis ask the dog if she wants to go for a walk.

Tatum gets out of bed, creeps to the window, and watches Hollis and Henrietta head down the hydrangea-lined driveway.

It's now three minutes past eight.

Tatum sits on the edge of the bed. Her stomach makes a squelching noise. Should she try to use the bathroom? *No, just call already,* she thinks.

The call is picked up on the first ring. "This is Dr. Constable."

"Good morning, this is Tatum McKenzie?" Tatum clears her throat. "You left a message on Thursday morning saying my biopsy results were in?"

"Oh, hello, Tatum, yes, sorry I missed you."

Tatum can't speak; she's holding her breath. She hears Dr. Constable shuffling papers. Files? She's looking for the results? She can't remember?

Dr. Constable breathes out in a long stream. "Well, the results weren't what we'd..."

Tatum's thoughts spiral. It's the bottom of the ninth, two outs, two runners on, Nantucket is up by one run. If she had it to do over, she would not have dropped the damn ball.

She would have taken lunch shifts at the Lobster Trap and spent every night with Dylan when he was growing up.

She would have come out to Squam Road the past however many years for dinner when Hollis invited her.

Kyle, she thinks. *Dylan. O-Man. And Holly.* Her best friend, whom she's just gotten back. Tatum has never let a lot of people get close to her, but she's had the best people.

And she's had the best place: Nantucket Island. Tatum's mind rolls over her favorite beaches—Steps and Ladies and Smith's Point.

It cruises over the moors; she loves the hike through the woods to Jewel Pond and the view from Altar Rock. Every Fourth of July weekend, Tatum makes Kyle drive around Sconset so she can get pictures of the cottage roses; the entire village blooms with them, it's like something from a storybook. Tatum thinks about sitting on a bench on Main Street in April when the town emerges from its winter hibernation—the trees are budding, storefronts are opening, but it's still just locals. Tatum knows every single person who passes by.

Nantucket, too, has been the love of her life.

"...feared," Dr. Constable says. "The biopsy was negative."

"What?" Tatum says. She's confused. *Negative* in this context is good, right?

"The biopsy was negative. It's just a cyst, nothing to worry about," Dr. Constable says. "Though due to your family history, we have to be vigilant. Keep an eye on things. But for today, good news."

Tatum hangs up the phone, and as she exhales, tears fall. Without thinking, she pulls on her cutoffs and her Tretorns and runs out to the front porch.

"Holly!" she calls out. "Holly!"

Hollis and Henrietta have only made it past the first few hydrangea bushes, and when Hollis hears Tatum call her name, she drops Henny's leash and runs back to the house.

Tatum comes charging down the steps. She's crying, but it's the right kind of crying, Hollis can tell. Hollis grabs her friend and they hug and jump up and down. Anyone who saw them might think they'd just won ten million dollars in the lottery.

But, oh, Tatum and Hollis think, *it's so much better than that.*

Epilogue: Nantucket

By midweek, chatter about Hollis Shaw's Five-Star Weekend has subsided, although those of us who follow the *Hungry with Hollis* blog are still patiently waiting for Hollis to post the recipes like she promised. The sour cream and roasted onion dip! The cilantro-and-lime-marinated swordfish! The Paloma sugar cookies!

Although Blond Sharon is very busy—finding a parking spot at Nobadeer Beach, shepherding her reluctant teens to the Maria Mitchell Observatory so they can witness the once-in-sixty-years viewing of Neptune, and trying to secure reservations at the back bar at Cru—she finds that thoughts of Hollis's Five-Star Weekend still linger in her mind.

"You're starting to frighten me," Sharon's sister, Heather, says. "You're completely obsessed."

Sharon isn't sure how to explain it. She has heard stories about many a girls' weekend (college reunions in Tulum, Moms do Coachella)—but somehow this one hit different. *Your life story in friends.* Sharon doesn't know Hollis well (or, truthfully, at all), but even so, a part of her wishes she'd been included.

"There's a solution to that," Heather says. "Host a Five-Star Weekend of your own!"

Of course! Sharon thinks. That's what she'll do. All she has to do now is figure out whom to invite.

* * *

Oh, what a difference a year makes.

Hollis Shaw sells her home in Wellesley and permanently moves to First Light out on Squam Road. We are overjoyed to have her back among us where she belongs. But is this enough of a happily ever after for Hollis?

No—we can do better.

Hollis Shaw and Jack Finigan have, slowly, started dating, though Jack still lives in Western Massachusetts. The distance is good for them both; they can each have their space and take their time, though they occasionally talk about Jack buying a small place on Nantucket.

Hollis's daughter, Caroline, graduates from NYU with honors and is offered a dream job—assistant producer at KeepItReal Films in Los Angeles. The glowing letter of recommendation from Isaac Opoku doesn't hurt, but the execs at KeepItReal are more impressed by Caroline's short-film submission, *The Five-Star Weekend*.

With Caroline successfully launched, Hollis and Jack decide they want to take a trip. They do the some might say predictable thing and book a Viking River Cruise in Italy. During the welcome cocktail hour, they're asked how long they've been together, and Jack tells everyone they're "high-school sweethearts." Neither of them feels the need to explain further. Let's say Tatum and Kyle McKenzie are on the cruise as well—after all, they have a lot to celebrate—and while we're at it, what about Dru-Ann Jones and her fiancé, Nick Wofford, and Brooke Kirtley and her new girlfriend, Trinh Nguyen? (Trinh is the Wellesley College professor who runs the book group that Brooke used to find so intimidating; now Brooke is an avid reader and offers the most insightful opinions during the discussions.)

It's a five-star reunion—or nearly.

On the flight home from Rome, they hear the usual announcement:

"Good afternoon, ladies and gentlemen, this is your captain speaking."

The voice is unmistakable.

Brooke grabs Hollis's forearm from across the aisle. "It's *Gigi,*" she says. "She's our pilot! I can't believe this. We need to go up and say hello!"

Is Hollis alarmed or even horrified that Gigi is flying their plane?

Not at all. Though Hollis and Gigi no longer text, Hollis does sometimes zoom in on the Kitchen Lights that are glowing in the Buckhead area of Atlanta. She imagines the light on in Gigi's kitchen, imagines that Gigi is, perhaps, trying her hand at Hollis's shatteringly crispy fried chicken recipe. Hollis hopes Gigi has someone new at her side—maybe a fellow pilot, maybe a guy she met at the gym, maybe Mabel's veterinarian. It doesn't matter who it is, as long as Gigi is his number one.

"We will," Hollis says. "But let's wait until we've landed safely." She leans her head on Jack's shoulder and closes her eyes.

She has already landed safely.

Acknowledgments

This novel is dedicated to two of the most important men in my life: Michael Carlisle and David Forrer, my agents at Inkwell Management. I met Michael while I was a student at the University of Iowa Writers' Workshop. There's a whole story that goes with this, but the short version is that we bonded over our mutual love for Nantucket, and when I told Michael I was writing a novel set on the island, called *The Beach Club,* he asked me to send it to him. That was in the spring of 1998; he has now been my agent for twenty-five years. (I always say that agent-author relationships are like marriages—half of them end in divorce. But happily, Michael and I are celebrating our silver anniversary!) David Forrer joined us in the summer of 2006, bringing his keen editorial eye, sense of humor, attention to detail, and deep well of kindness. Michael and David have created a safe space for me in the often chaotic world of publishing. I would not be here writing the acknowledgments of my twenty-ninth novel if it weren't for them. They are not only five-star agents, they are five-star human beings.

Thank you to my editor, Judy Clain, who has done it again! I stand in awe of Judy's sensibility; she consistently brings out my best writing and the most engaging story.

Huge thanks to the entire team at Little, Brown, including (but not limited to) Anna de la Rosa, Mariah Dwyer, Bryan Christian, Danielle Finnegan, Jayne Yaffe Kemp, Tracy Roe, Terry Adams, Craig Young, Karen Torres, Brandon Kelly, Lauren Hesse, Sabrina Callahan, Bruce Nichols, the legend that is Michael Pietsch, and my beloved publicist Katharine Myers.

Debbie Briggs's descriptions and details of life in Wellesley, Massachusetts, were invaluable. (Any inaccuracies, changes, or exaggerations are mine alone.) When I borrow a secondary location, I try to get it right, and I could never have come close if Debbie hadn't told me about the Linden Store, Fireball nips at the Wellesley–Needham Thanksgiving Day game, Poet's Corner, and all the other reasons why the town is known as "Swellesley."

Thank you to Grace Bartlett for helping me create a character who is an aspiring documentary filmmaker. (Caroline can only hope she is half as talented as Grace!)

My inspiration for Hollis's recipes came from several places. The bacon and rosemary pecans are courtesy of Lulu Powers. (She made these for me in the fall of 2021 and I think about them every day.) The sour cream and roasted onion dip is from one of my favorite food bloggers, @bevcooks. The peach cobbler with the hot sugar crust is by Chef Renee Erickson. And anyone who has been to Liz Georgantas's Nantucket home knows where I got the idea for the pizza party—as well as the chandelier made from Coke bottles.

To my work husband, Tim Ehrenberg of @timtalksbooks and Nantucket Book Partners, there aren't words for how much I love (and need) you. Santi is one lucky man.

Thank you to Timothy Field for saying and doing and being all the things I need on any given day.

Thank you to my sister, Heather, for always, always, always having my back—since the days of red knee socks and George Washington pageboys.

Thank you to my Nantucket people: Rebecca Bartlett, Wendy Hudson, Wendy Rouillard, Margie and Chuck Marino, Richard Congdon, Anne and Whit Gifford, Liz and Beau Almodobar, Evelyn and Matthew MacEachern, Helaina Jones, Heidi Holdgate, Shelly Weedon, West Riggs, Manda Riggs, David Rattner and Andrew Law, Sally Horchow, Sue Decoste, Linda Holliday, Jeannie

Esti, Melissa Long, Katie Norton, Deb Gfeller, the fabulous Jane Deery, Bill Emery, and Julie Lancia (French bobby pins forever!). I want to thank my ex-husband, Chip Cunningham, who is not only my co-president in running the Cunningham family but also my treasured friend.

This brings me to the kids: Maxx, Dawson, Shelby, and Alex. This past year, I watched you grow up, shine your lights, and make your beautiful ways in the world. I am lucky for so many reasons, but mostly because I have you.

About the Author

Elin Hilderbrand lives year-round on Nantucket, where she enjoys going to the beach, cooking for her young-adult children, and occasionally dancing in the front row at the Chicken Box. She is a grateful ten-year breast cancer survivor. *The Five-Star Weekend* is her twenty-ninth novel.

LOOK FOR THESE OTHER NOVELS BY
ELIN HILDERBRAND

The Castaways

"Hilderbrand provides the perfect summer read as she explores love, loss, and, ultimately, absolution."

—Patty Engelmann, *Booklist*

"A juicy novel...Hilderbrand captivates with a racy narrative and characters who are both familiar and memorable." —*People*

The Rumor

"Rich people behaving badly—perfect poolside...Hilderbrand is the queen of the summer." —Susannah Cahalan, *New York Post*

"Packed with details of the wonder that is summer on a small, chic island off the coast of Massachusetts."

—Catherine Mallette, *Fort Worth Star-Telegram*

"As sweetly satisfying as a glass of Sancerre."

—Kim Hubbard, *People*

LOOK FOR THESE OTHER NOVELS BY
ELIN HILDERBRAND

The Perfect Couple

"A fantastic and clever whodunit that keeps readers in suspense... Well thought-out and meticulously written... Hilderbrand's books keep getting better and better." —Bookreporter.com

"Hilderbrand throws enough curveballs to keep readers guessing, but not too many, maintaining the breezy pace... The mystery element is new, but *The Perfect Couple* is classic Hilderbrand."
—*Booklist*

The Hotel Nantucket

"One of Hilderbrand's best books ever... Packed with great surprises, fabulous writing, and an army of wonderful characters, *The Hotel Nantucket* will keep you pinned to your beach chair until the very last page." —Brad Thor, *Today*

LOOK FOR THE WINTER STREET SERIES BY ELIN HILDERBRAND

Winter Street

"Open this diverting tale of family dysfunction, and you'll find a holiday package filled with humor, romance, and realism."
—Jocelyn McClurg, *USA Today*

Winter Stroll

"Addictively readable...A slice of holiday life from a master of domestic fiction."
—Susan Maguire, *Booklist*

Winter Storms

"A perfect mix of love, tears, and joy."
—Kathleen Gerard, *Shelf Awareness*

Winter Solstice

"Hilderbrand is a quality storyteller who keeps the reader riveted, and her characters come alive on the page."
—*Publishers Weekly*

LOOK FOR AND LISTEN TO THE POPULAR NEW PODCAST

Books, Beach & Beyond
with Elin Hilderbrand & Tim Talks Books

BOOKS
BEACH & BEYOND
WITH ELIN HILDERBRAND & TIM TALKS BOOKS

Join Elin Hilderbrand and Tim Ehrenberg, creator of Tim Talks Books, as they talk shop and host spirited conversations with special guests, from bestselling and internationally recognized writers, to publishing industry insiders, to local Nantucket legends who feature prominently in Hilderbrand's novels. Discussing topics ranging from what it's like to bring a book to the screen, to the connection between a reader and a story's characters, to the intricacies and intimate details of an author's writing process, Hilderbrand and Ehrenberg take listeners on an exciting (and amusing) journey each episode, bringing books to life in a brand-new way in this podcast presented by *N Magazine.*

Scan to subscribe & listen